THE
ANDY McNAB
DOSSIER

CONFIDENTIAL

ANDY McNAB

⮞ In 1984 he was 'badged' as a member of 22 SAS Regiment.

⮞ Over the course of the next nine years he was at the centre of covert operations on five continents.

⮞ During the first Gulf War he commanded Bravo Two Zero, a patrol that, in the words of his commanding officer, 'will remain in regimental history for ever'.

⮞ Awarded both the Distinguished Conduct Medal (DCM) and Military Medal (MM) during his military career.

⮞ McNab was the British Army's most highly decorated serving soldier when he finally left the SAS in February 1993.

⮞ He is now the author of eleven bestselling thrillers.

BRAVO TWO ZERO

In January 1991, eight members of the SAS regiment, under the command of Sergeant Andy McNab, embarked upon a top secret mission in Iraq to infiltrate them deep behind enemy lines. Their call sign: 'Bravo Two Zero'.

IMMEDIATE ACTION

The no–holds–barred account of an extraordinary life, from the day McNab as a baby was found in a carrier bag on the steps of Guy's Hospital to the day he went to fight in the Gulf War. As a delinquent youth he kicked against society. As a young soldier he waged war against the IRA in the streets and fields of South Armagh.

SEVEN TROOP

Andy McNab's gripping account of the time he served in the company of a remarkable band of brothers. The things they saw and did during that time would take them all to breaking point – and some beyond – in the years that followed. He who dares doesn't always win . . .

Nick Stone, ex–SAS trooper, now gun–for–hire working on deniable ops for the British government, is the perfect man for the dirtiest of jobs, doing whatever it takes by whatever means necessary...

REMOTE CONTROL
✠ Dateline: Washington DC, USA

Stone is drawn into the bloody killing of an ex–SAS officer and his family and soon finds himself on the run with the one survivor who can identify the killer – a nine-year-old girl.

> 'Proceeds with a testosterone surge'
> *Daily Telegraph*

CRISIS FOUR
✠ Dateline: North Carolina, USA

In the backwoods of the American South, Stone has to keep alive the beautiful young woman who holds the key to unlock a chilling conspiracy that will threaten world peace.

> 'When it comes to thrills, he's Forsyth class'
> *Mail on Sunday*

FIREWALL
✠ Dateline: Finland

The kidnapping of a Russian Mafia warlord takes Stone into the heart of the global espionage world and into conflict with some of the most dangerous killers around.

> 'Other thriller writers do their research, but McNab has actually been there'
> *Sunday Times*

LAST LIGHT
⊕ Dateline: Panama

Stone finds himself at the centre of a lethal
conspiracy involving ruthless Colombian
mercenaries, the US government and Chinese
big business. It's an uncomfortable place to be ...

> 'A heart thumping read'
> *Mail on Sunday*

LIBERATION DAY
⊕ Dateline: Cannes, France

Behind its glamorous exterior, the city's seething
underworld is the battleground for a very dirty
drugs war and Stone must reach deep within
himself to fight it on their terms.

> 'McNab's great asset is that the heart of his
> fiction is non–fiction'
> *Sunday Times*

DARK WINTER
⊕ Dateline: Malaysia

A straightforward action on behalf of the War on
Terror turns into a race to escape his past for Stone
if he is to save himself and those closest to him.

> 'Addictive ... Packed with wild action and
> revealing tradecraft'
> *Daily Telegraph*

DEEP BLACK
⊕ Dateline: Bosnia

All too late Stone realizes that he is being used as
bait to lure into the open a man whom the darker
forces of the West will stop at nothing to destroy.

> 'One of the UK's top thriller writers'
> *Daily Express*

AGGRESSOR
⊕ Dateline: Georgia, former Soviet Union

A longstanding debt of friendship to an SAS
comrade takes Stone on a journey where he will
have to risk everything to repay what he owes,
even his life . . .

> 'A terrific novelist'
> *Mail on Sunday*

RECOIL
⊕ Dateline: The Congo, Africa

What starts out as a personal quest for a missing
woman quickly becomes a headlong rush from his
own past for Stone.

> 'Stunning . . . A first class action thriller'
> *The Sun*

CROSSFIRE
⌗ Dateline: Kabul

Nick Stone enters the modern day wild west that is Afghanistan in search of a kidnapped reporter.

> 'Authentic to the core . . . McNab at his electrifying best'
> *Daily Express*

ANDY McNAB
FIREWALL

CORGI BOOKS

FIREWALL
A CORGI BOOK : 9780552152372

Originally published in Great Britain by Bantam Press,
a division of Transworld Publishers

PRINTING HISTORY
Bantam Press edition published 2000
Corgi edition published 2001

17 19 20 18 16

Copyright © Andy McNab 2000

Set in 11/12pt Palatino by
Falcon Oast Graphic Art.

Corgi Books are published by Transworld Publishers,
61–63 Uxbridge Road, London W5 5SA,
a division of The Random House Group Ltd,

Addresses for Random House Group Ltd companies outside the
UK can be found at: www.randomhouse.co.uk
The Random House Group Ltd Reg. No. 954009

The Random House Group Limited supports The Forest
Stewardship Council (FSC), the leading international forest
certification organisation. All our titles that are printed on
Greenpeace approved FSC certified paper carry the FSC logo.
Our paper procurement policy can be found at
www.rbooks.co.uk/environment

Printed and bound in Great Britain by
CPI Cox & Wyman, Reading, Berkshire.

FIREWALL

1

HELSINKI, FINLAND
Monday, 6 December 1999

The Russians were serious players. If things didn't go as planned, Sergei said, I'd be lucky to be shot dead in the hotel lobby. If they captured me, I'd be taken to a remote bit of wasteland and have my stomach slit open. They'd pull my intestines out and leave me to watch them squirm around on my chest like a bucket of freshly caught eels for the thirty minutes it would take me to die. These things happen, he had explained, when you mess with the main men in ROC (Russian organized crime). But I didn't have a choice; I desperately needed the cash.

'What's it called again, Sergei?' I mimed the disembowelment.

Eyes staring straight ahead, he gave a brief, sombre smile and muttered, 'Viking's revenge.'

It was just before 7 p.m. and it had already been dark for three and a half hours. The air temperature had been well below freezing all day; it hadn't snowed for a while, but there was still a lot of the stuff about, ploughed to the sides of the roads.

The two of us had been sitting very still for the

best part of an hour. Until I'd just spoken, our breathing was the only sign of movement. We were parked two blocks away from the Intercontinental hotel, using the shadows between the street lights to conceal our presence in the dirty black Nissan 4x4. The rear seats were down flat to make it easier to bundle the target inside, complete with me wrapped round him like a wrestler to keep him there. The 4x4 was sterile: no prints and completely empty apart from the trauma pack lying on the folded seats. Our boy had to be delivered across the border alive, and a couple of litres of Ringer's Solution might come in handy if this job turned into a gangfuck. Right now, it certainly had all the ingredients of one. I found myself hoping it wouldn't be me needing the infusion.

It had been a while since I'd felt the need to pre-canulate, making it quicker for me to replace any fluid from gunshot wounds, but today had just that feel about it. I'd brought a catheter from the UK and it was already inserted into a vein under my left forearm, secured by tape and pro-tected by Tubigrip. Anti-coagulant was preloaded inside the catheter's needle and chamber to stop the blood that filled it from clotting. Ringer's Solution isn't as good as plasma to replace blood loss – it's only a saline mix – but I didn't want anything plasma-based. Russian quality control was a contradiction in terms, and money was what I wanted to return to the UK with, not HIV. I'd spent enough time in Africa not treating any-one's gunshot wounds because of the risk of infection, and I wasn't about to let it happen now.

We sat facing Mannerheimintie, 200 metres down the hill from our position. The boulevard was the main drag into the city centre, just fifteen minutes' walk away to the right. It carried a constant stream of slow, obedient traffic each side of the tram lines. Up here it was like a different world. Low-level apartment blocks hugged each side of the quiet street and an inverted 'V' of white Christmas lights sparkled in almost every window.

People walked past, straining under the weight of their shopping, crammed into large carrier bags with pictures of holly and Santa. They didn't notice us as they headed home to their smart apartments; they were too busy keeping their footing on the icy pavements and their heads down against the wind that howled and buffeted the 4x4.

The engine had been off all the time we'd been here, and it was like sitting in a fridge. Our breath billowed like low cloud as we waited.

I kept visualizing how, when and where I was going to do my stuff, and more importantly, what I was going to do if things got fucked up. Once the target has been selected the basic sequence of a kidnap is nearly always the same. First comes reconnaissance; second, abduction; third, detention; fourth, negotiation; fifth, ransom payment, and finally, release – though sometimes that doesn't happen. My job was to plan and implement the first three phases; the rest of the task was out of my hands.

Three members of the loud-tie-and-braces brigade from a private bank had approached me in London. They'd been given my name by an ex-Regiment mate who now worked for one of the big security companies, and who'd been nice enough to recommend me when this particular commission had been declined.

'Britain', they said to me as we sat at a window table in the roof bar of the Hilton, looking down on to the gardens of Buckingham Palace, 'is facing an explosion in Russian mafia-organized crime. London is a money-laundering haven. The ROC are moving as much as £20 billion through the City each year, and up to 200 of their senior players either live in Britain or visit regularly.'

The executives went on to say they'd discovered that millions had been channelled through Valentin Lebed's accounts at their bank in just three years. They didn't like that, and were none too keen on the thought of the boys with the blue flashing lights paying him a visit and seeing the name on all his paying-in slips. Their solution was to have Val lifted and taken to St Petersburg, where, I presumed, they had either made arrangements to persuade him to move his account to a different bank, or to channel even more through them to make the risk more acceptable. Whichever, I didn't give a fuck so long as I got paid.

I looked over at Sergei. His eyes glinted as he stared at the traffic below us and his Adam's apple moved as he swallowed. There wasn't anything left to say; we'd done enough talking during the two-week build-up. It was now time to do.

The conference of European Council members

was due to start in Helsinki in two days. Blue EU flags already lined the main roads, and large black convoys of Eurocrats drove around with motorcycle outriders, heading from pre-meeting to pre-meeting. The police had set up diversions to control the flow of traffic around the city, and orange reflective cones and barriers were springing up everywhere. I'd already had to change our escape route twice because of it.

Like all the high-class hotels, the Intercontinental was housing the exodus from Brussels. All the suits had been in the city since last week, wheeling and dealing so that when the heads of state hit town, all they'd have to do was politely refuse Tony Blair's invitation to eat British beef at some dinner for the media, then leave. All very good, but for me security around here was tighter than a duck's arse – everything from sealed manholes to prevent bombs being planted to a heavy police presence on the streets. They would certainly have contingency plans for every possible event, especially armed attack.

Sergei had a folding-stock AK – a Russian automatic, 7.62mm short assault rifle – under his feet. His cropped, thinning brown hair was covered by a dark-blue woollen hat, and the old Soviet Army body armour he wore under his duvet jacket made him look like the Michelin man. If Hollywood was looking for a Russian hard head, Sergei would win the screen test every time. Late forties, square jaw, high cheekbones and blue eyes that didn't just pierce, they chopped you into tiny pieces. The only reason he would never be a leading man was his badly pockmarked skin.

Either he'd steered away from the Clearasil in his youth or he'd been burned; I couldn't tell, and I didn't want to ask. He was a hard, reliable man, and one I felt it was OK to do business with, but he wasn't going to be on my Christmas-card list.

I had read about Sergei Lysenkov's freelance activities in Intelligence Service reports. He had been a member of Spetnaz's Alpha Group, an elite of special-forces officers within the KGB, who used to be deployed wherever Moscow's power was under threat or there were wars of expansion. When hardline heads of the KGB led the 1991 coup in Moscow, they ordered Alpha Group to kill Yeltsin as he held out in the Russian White House, but Sergei and his mates decided that enough was enough and that the politicos were all as bad as each other. They disobeyed the order, the coup failed, and when Yeltsin learned what had nearly happened he took them under his direct command, cutting their power by turning them into his own bodyguards. Sergei decided to quit and make his experience and knowledge available to the highest bidder, and today that was me. It had been easy enough to make contact: I just went to Moscow and asked a few security companies where I could find him.

I needed Russians on the team because I needed to know how Russians think, how Russians do. And when I discovered that Valentin Lebed would be in Helsinki for twenty-four hours of R and R, and not in his fortress in St Petersburg, Sergei was the only one who could organize vehicles, weapons and the bribing of border guards in the time available.

The people who'd briefed me on the job had done their homework well. Valentin Lebed, they were able to tell me, had been smart during the fall of communism. Unlike some of his gaucher colleagues, he didn't keep the designer labels on the sleeves of his new suit to show how much it had cost. His rise was brutal and meteoric; within two years he was one of the dozen heads of the 'mafiocracy' who had made ROC so powerful around the world. Lebed's firm employed only ex-KGB agents overseas, using their skills and experience to run international crime like a military operation.

Coming from dirt-poor beginnings as a farmer's son in Chechnya, he'd fought against the Russians in the mid-Nineties war. His fame was sealed after rallying his men by making them watch *Braveheart* time and time again as the Russians bombed them day after day. He even painted his face half blue when attacking. After the war he'd had other ideas, all of them involving US dollars, and the place he'd chosen to realize them was St Petersburg.

Much of his money came from arms dealing, extortion and a string of nightclubs he owned in Moscow and elsewhere, which served as fronts for prostitution rackets. Jewellery businesses he had 'acquired' in Eastern Europe were used as a front to fence icons stolen from churches and museums. He also had bases in the United States, and was said to have brokered a deal to dump hundreds of tons of American toxic waste on his motherland. In the Far East, he'd even bought an airline just so he could ship out heroin without administrative hassle. Within just a few years, according to the guys who'd briefed me, such activities were said to have netted him more than $200 million.

Three blocks the other side of the hotel, parked in a car that would be abandoned once this lift kicked off, were two more of the six-man team. Carpenter and Nightmare were armed with 9mm mini-Uzi machine guns, a very small version of the Uzi 9mm, on harnesses under their overcoats, the same as the BG (bodyguards) we were going up against. They were good, reliable weapons, if a little heavy for their size. It was ironic, but Sergei had obtained the team's Uzis and old Spanish, semi-automatic suppressed 7mm pistols from one of Valentin's own dealers.

Carpenter and Nightmare weren't their real names, of course; Sergei – the only one who spoke English – had told me that was how they translated, and that was how he referred to them – just as well, as I couldn't have pronounced them in Russian anyway.

Nightmare was living up to his name. He certainly wasn't the sharpest tool in Sergei's shed. Things needed to be demonstrated twenty or thirty times before he got the idea. There was a slight flatness to his face that, together with his constantly shifting eyes and the fact that he didn't seem too good at keeping food in his mouth, made him look a bit scary.

Carpenter had a heroin habit that Sergei assured me would not affect his performance, but it certainly had during the build-up. He had lips that were constantly at work, as though he'd swallowed something and was trying to re-capture the taste. Sergei told him that if he screwed up on the ground he would personally kill him.

Nightmare was like a big brother to Carpenter and protected him when Sergei gripped him for messing up, but it seemed to me that Nightmare would be lost without him, that they needed each other. Sergei told me they'd been friends since they were teenagers. Nightmare's family had looked after Carpenter when his mother went down for life for killing her husband. She'd discovered he'd raped his own seventeen-year-old daughter. As if that wasn't enough, Sergei was his uncle, his father's brother. It was *EastEnders*, Russian style, and the only thing I liked about it was that it made my own family seem normal. Carpenter and Nightmare would be in the hotel with me for the lift; perhaps I could keep some control over them if I had them with me.

The last two on the team I'd christened the Kray twins, and they were in a green Toyota 4x4. I wasn't so worried about them; unlike the other two, they didn't have to be told what to do more than twice. They had the trigger on the target's three black Mercedes, which were about two Ks away from the hotel. They also had folding-stock AKs and AP (armour-piercing) rounds in their mags, and, like Sergei, they wore enough body armour to cripple a small horse.

The target was well protected in the hotel and his vehicles were securely parked underground so that no device – explosive from his enemies or listening or surveillance from law enforcement –

could be placed. When they finally moved out to pick him up from the hotel with the rest of his BG, the Krays would follow. Carpenter and Nightmare would then take up their positions in the hotel, along with me. Sergei, Reggie and Ronnie would take on the vehicles.

The Krays were both ex-Alpha Group, too, but unlike Sergei they were far too good-looking to be straight. They'd been together since their time as young conscripts in Afghanistan, leaving after the previous Chechen war in the mid-Nineties, disillusioned with the leadership that had let them lose against the rebels. Both were in their mid-thirties, with dyed blond hair, very clean shaven and well groomed. If they'd wanted a change of career they could have become catalogue models. They had never been parted during their military career. As far as I could make out, all they wanted to do was kill Chechen rebels – and swap admiring glances.

I knew I could trust Sergei, but I still wondered about his selection procedure. He obviously wanted to keep most of the wad I'd promised him and had decided not to bring the A team.

It was the most unprofessional job I'd ever been on, and I'd been on a few. Things had got so bad that I'd even taken to sleeping with my door barred and my weapon ready. If the team weren't complaining to him about my planning, Sergei said, they were moaning about who was earning what and how they might get ripped off when it came to pay day. Carpenter was so homophobic he made Hitler look like a wet liberal, and it had taken as much effort keeping the two pairs away from each other as it had preparing for the job. I did my best to keep out of their way and concentrated on dealing exclusively with Sergei; he was the one I had to keep happy, because he was the only one who could help me get the target into Russia. But they'd got me flapping; people were going to die today, and I didn't want to be one of them.

I was with a scary crew, against a scary target, with the whole of Western Europe's leadership due in town, bringing along enough security to take on China. This wasn't a good day out but, fuck it, desperation makes people do desperate things.

I blew out another cloud of breath. The digital display on the dash told me another twenty minutes had passed – time for a radio check. Reaching into my inside jacket pocket, I felt for the send button of my very yellow Motorola handset, the sort that parents use to keep tabs on their kids on the ski slopes or in the shopping mall. All six of us had one, each connected to an earpiece which was hooked in place. With so many people using hands-free sets on their mobile phones, we wouldn't be conspicuous wandering around with them in.

I pressed twice, the squelch sounding off in my ear, then checked with Sergei. He nodded; I was sending. Reggie and Ronnie replied with two squelches, then Carpenter and Nightmare followed with three. If I'd hit the send button and there was nothing from the Krays, Carpenter and Nightmare would have waited thirty seconds and replied anyway. We would have no option then but to close in on the target and wait for the Mercs to arrive – not good, as it exposed us three in the hotel and messed up co-ordination. There was radio silence for two reasons. One, I couldn't speak the language, and two, EU land security would be listening in. With any luck, a few clicks here and there wouldn't mean a thing. There were many other standby comms I could have used, mobile phones for instance, but everything had to be kept pretty basic for Nightmare and Carpenter. Anything else to remember and they would have blown up. The old principle of planning – keep it simple, stupid – rang true yet again.

While Sergei had gone for the Michelin man look, I was very much the businessman: single-breasted suit, jacket one size up, dark-grey overcoat, black woollen scarf and thin leather gloves, and the stress to match. Nightmare and Carpenter were dressed in the same style. All three of us were clean shaven, hair washed and well groomed. Detail counts; we had to move about the hotel without anyone giving us a second glance, looking as if we were part of the all-expenses-paid, outrageous-salary Brussels gravy train. Across my lap I even had today's edition of the *Herald Tribune*.

My overcoat was doing a good job of concealing the body armour under my shirt. Sergei's might be as thick as the paving slabs outside the Kremlin, but mine consisted of just twelve paper-thin sheets of Kevlar – not enough to stop one of Sergei's AP rounds, but enough to see off the mini-Uzis that might soon be trying to hose me down. There was a pocket in the body armour for a ceramic plate to cover my chest area, but unlike Sergei I couldn't wear one as it was far too bulky. Carpenter had refused to wear any at all because it wasn't manly, and Nightmare had followed suit. Fucking mad; if I could have, I'd have covered myself from head to toe in the stuff. My feet were in all sorts of shit; with nothing on but thin socks and a pair of lace-up shoes, they were as cold as bags of frozen peas. I could no longer feel anything below my ankles, and had given up moving them around to generate heat.

I was carrying a South African Z88, which looked like a 9mm Berreta, the sort of pistol Mel Gibson uses in the *Lethal Weapon* films. When the world banned weapons exports to South Africa during apartheid, the boys just set about making their own gear and were now exporting more assault weapons and helicopters than the UK.

I had three twenty-round extended mags, which meant an extra two inches hanging out of the pistol grip, looking as if it had partially fallen out. The two spares went into my left-hand over-coat pocket. If things went to plan I wouldn't even be drawing down. The lift should be – would be – silent and take less than a minute.

The body armour was the lightest I dared wear, but even so it made it impossible to draw or sit down with a pistol placed where I would normally have had it: centre front, tucked down the front of my jeans or trousers in an internal holster. I wasn't feeling happy about my new weapon position. Now it had to be on the right-hand side on my trouser belt. I'd had to spend the

21

last two weeks practising and consciously reminding myself that the position had changed, otherwise I might go to draw down on someone and find my hand hitting Kevlar instead of a pistol grip. That was if I could get to it through all the layers of clothing. To be able to flick back the top layers quickly, I'd taped together some sockets from the set in the car and carried them in the right-hand pockets of both my coat and jacket. It was just one more thing making me feel uneasy. My only consolation was that this time tomorrow it would all be over: I'd get my money and never see these lunatics again.

There was rustling as Sergei unwrapped a chocolate bar and started to throw it down his neck without offering me any. Not that I wanted it; I wasn't hungry, just worried. I sat there waiting, with the sound of Sergei's teeth mashing and jaws clicking as the wind whistled around the wagon.

I sat and thought as he sucked his teeth clean. So far, Valentin had evaded the authorities, mainly because he had learned early on that it was good to have friends in powerful places and officials on the payroll. Key witnesses were routinely murdered before they could testify against him. Just a few months earlier, Sergei said, an American journalist who'd delved a bit too deeply into Val's business affairs was forced into hiding, with his family, after a phone call was intercepted in which Val was heard putting out a contract of $100,000, not just on the reporter's life, but also on those of his wife and child.

It was for those who betrayed his trust,

however, that the worst fate was reserved. Two senior managers who oversaw his prostitution empire had been caught skimming a bit off the top at his Moscow brothels. Even though they'd fought alongside him in the *Braveheart* days and had been faithful lieutenants ever since, Val had had them taken out and staked to the earth on wasteground not far from Red Square, where he'd personally slit their bellies, pulled out their intestines, and waited patiently for them to die. The 'Viking's revenge' appeared to have done the trick: ever since then, not a single rouble had gone astray from any of his tills.

I heard six quick squelches in my earpiece. The three pick-up Mercs were mobile towards the hotel.

I replied with two squelches, then heard another two from Nightmare and Carpenter, who should now be getting out of their car and heading for the hotel. All six of us knew it was time to start performing.

Sergei didn't say a word, just nodded. He might speak English, but it had to be squeezed out of him. I nodded back, checking my weapon was still in position.

I got out of the 4x4 and left Sergei staring downhill. Pulling up my coat collar to protect me from the wind, I headed in the opposite direction, away from the main. My route took me up the hill for thirty metres, then a right turn to the next T-junction. That put me on the road adjacent to the hotel and down to the main drag again.

I could see the large grey concrete hotel in front of me on the left-hand side of the road. Just short of it were roadworks surrounded by steel fencing; the cobblestones were up and the pipes were being repaired. I didn't envy the poor bastards who had to finish the job in this weather.

The noise from the main grew louder as I walked downhill. The Kray twins would be on it now, following the Mercs. Nightmare and Carpenter should be walking into the hotel from the opposite side and Sergei would be positioning himself so that he'd be able to move in on the Mercs at the front of the hotel.

I crossed the road, passing the hotel's rear service and car park entrance. Two white Hilux delivery vans were parked up on the red asphalt. There was a glass door giving access to the hotel beyond the delivery bays, but you could only get through it by buzzing reception, and I didn't want to make myself any more conspicuous than I had to. Neither of the two loading bays was open; it was far too cold. I continued downhill, the hotel now obscured by a line of high conifers.

Valentin Lebed's weakest point would be tonight, in Finland, in this hotel, before he left for the theatre. He was on his way to see *Romeo and Juliet*. The theatre was only across the road, a few hundred metres away to the left, but it was cold, he had always been a target for attack and he was incredibly rich, so why walk?

About thirty metres short of the main road I hit the driveway from the Intercontinental's front entrance. It was a semi-circle and one way. I turned left; in front of me, halfway down the concrete and glass building, was a large blue canopy to protect guests from the elements as

24

they got in and out of their cars. The ground-floor walls were glass, through which I could see the warm and cosy-looking interior. Small trees lined the driveway; they had lost their leaves and were now covered in white Christmas lights. The snow made them look as if they'd been sprinkled with icing sugar. I carried on past the illuminated reindeer that stood on the lawn between the driveway and main drag, which was about thirty metres down a gentle slope.

The plan was simple. Nightmare and Carpenter were to kill the close BG that were protecting the target as he came from the lift, then cover me as I took the target towards the main doors. While this was happening, the Kray twins would have blocked off the rear of the Mercs with their 4x4, Sergei would block the front with the Nissan and all three would be controlling the other BG and drivers with their AKs.

Once outside, I'd head for the back of the Nissan, dragging the target with me. We'd both lie under a blanket, with my pistol rammed in his gob, while Sergei drove to the DOP (vehicle drop-off point), where the target would be switched to the boot of a change-over vehicle *en route* to the border. Meanwhile, Ronnie and Reggie would be giving the area the good news with CS gas before leaving in the Toyota, along with the other two, to their DOP and changing vehicles. We'd all RV near the border and get into a truck that was rigged up with hidden compartments while Sergei drove us into Mother Russia. Then it was just a few hours to St Petersburg and payday. Nice work if you can get it.

I walked under the canopy and through the first set of automatic tinted-glass and brass-effect doors. Once past the second set I was in, my face flushed from the downward blast of the heaters above the doorway.

I knew the foyer area well. It had the air of an expensive, comfortable club. I hadn't seen any of the rooms, but they must have been stunning.

In front of me, about thirty metres away and behind a group of very noisy and confused Japanese tourists surrounding a mountain of matching suitcases, was the reception desk. In the far right-hand corner was a corridor that led to the restaurant, toilets and the all-important lifts.

By now Nightmare and Carpenter should be at the far end of the corridor, sitting by the restaurant entrance. From there they could keep trigger on the three lift doors.

Immediately to my right, behind a dark wood-panelled wall, was the Baltic Bar. To my left, efficient-looking bellboys were buzzing around a sprinkling of sofas, chairs and coffee tables. The lighting was subdued. I wished I'd just dropped in for a drink.

I headed for one of the sofas, sitting down so that I was facing the Japanese confusion at reception to my half right, with the corridor to the right of that, and the brass-effect lift doors in view. Like me, Nightmare and Carpenter had placed themselves out of sight of the video cameras that were covering the reception desk. I sat, spread out the *Trib* on the coffee table, un-buttoned my overcoat and waited for the convoy of Mercs to arrive.

It was pointless worrying about anything now. There is only so much training and planning that can be done. I used to get worried when this feeling came over me, but now I understood it. Basically, I accepted that I was going to die, and anything beyond that was a bonus.

2

The Japanese weren't at all happy, and they didn't care who knew it. There must have been about twenty of them, all with video cameras round their necks.

Three minutes later the headlights of the three Mercs raked the ground-floor windows. Reggie and Ronnie should have pulled up just short of the semicircular driveway where they'd be standing by. Sergei would be waiting to block their front.

I waited for the inside set of sliding doors to open, keeping my head down, concentrating hard on my newspaper.

In came the BG. Two pairs of shiny Italian shoes and expensive black cashmere overcoats over black trousers.

You always avoid eye contact, because they'll be looking for it. If your eyes lock you're fucked; they'll know you aren't there to talk about the beef ban.

I watched the two sets of heels make their way over to the far right of the foyer. They paused by the brass lift doors, now and again shielded by the Japanese as they went in pursuit of one very hassled hotel rep.

The middle door slid open with a gentle *ping*. The shoes went in, and two more sets of shoes were refused entry. The doors closed and the indicator light stopped at the Ambassador Suite. They were going to meet up with the other two BG who were already with Valentin, their principal, my target. My money.

I got up, folding the *Trib* into my coat pocket, and started to walk towards the main doors. As I moved past them, towards the leather-boothed, dark-wood Baltic Bar, I could see three very clean black Mercs on the other side of the glass, exhaust fumes condensing in the cold air, each with a driver waiting patiently at the wheel.

The bar was half full and not very smoky, considering the number of cigarettes I could see on the go. There were quite a few laptops open, and there was a general hubbub as suits talked shop over a beer or into their mobiles.

Unbuttoning my suit jacket as I walked, but keeping my overcoat on to conceal the body armour, I made my way around tables and leather chesterfields towards the far door.

I seated myself where I could see down the corridor to the three lift doors, set back slightly in the right-hand wall. Beyond them, and just out of sight, were the reception and foyer. At the other end of the corridor, Carpenter and Nightmare should be in position in the coffee area of the restaurant, with a clear view all the way down to the foyer. Under the table I pulled at my right glove and eased my index finger through the cut in the leather.

Five long minutes went by as lifts came and went, but Val still hadn't made an appearance. Two middle-aged couples emerged from the centre lift, dressed in furs and dinner jackets, looking as if they, too, were going to the theatre. It was now that I started to worry. The calm was over and the storm was about to begin. My heart was pumping big time. My body armour was wet with sweat and my shirt collar was soaking it up from the back of my neck. Any minute now someone was going to ask me if I was ill, I was sure of it. Mentally I was still the same, but my body was telling me something different.

About twenty seconds later there was another *ping*. The two pairs of expensive Italian shoes emerged from the right-hand lift and stopped in the corridor for a second or two, each pair facing in a different direction. The overcoat of the BG facing towards me swirled open as he turned, then both moved towards the foyer, disappearing from view as quickly as they'd arrived. I knew their jackets and overcoats would be like mine, open to access their weapons.

I moved my hand into my inside jacket pocket and gave the Motorola six clicks on the send button, hearing the squelch in my earpiece each time. Val would be down any minute now.

Sergei, Reggie and Ronnie would now know that the target and BG were heading towards them. The two pairs of shoes were going to secure the foyer, probably by the main doors. It wouldn't be long now before everything kicked off and the

Japanese would really have something to complain about.

Whatever these two BG did, we had them covered. If they stayed inside, it was Nightmare's and Carpenter's job to take them on once they'd sorted out the BG immediately around Val. Outside, it was down to the other three.

We all waited, and I sweated as people around me laughed, hit keypads and talked between mouthfuls of alcohol.

There was a *ping* from the far-right lift. Another two pairs of black patent-leather shoes, dress-suit trousers complete with silk stripe under black overcoats. They stepped out on either side of a light-grey cashmere coat and the smartest trousers of all, followed by a pair of very long, slim, well-toned, black-stockinged calves, topped off with the world's most luxuriant mink. Val's slapper, keeping him warm on those long lonely nights away from his family.

I had to be careful. There was always the possibility of someone you overlook during surveillance – the one who looks like the brother-in-law or secretary. Then, when you hit the target, they can prove very dangerous indeed. But not this one; she was definitely not part of the BG set-up.

They had turned right out of the lift without hesitating. I stood up slowly, waiting for my cue.

I caught Carpenter's scary, dancing eye as he and Nightmare crossed the doorway, moving right to left, matching the purposeful strides of the BG.

We'd rehearsed what was supposed to happen

next so many times. It had to work; there was no
stopping this now.

I turned left out of the door and fell in behind
them as they drew their suppressed weapons.

About five metres ahead of us, the backs and
very wide shoulders of the BG pair flanked Val
and the slapper as they moved towards the
Japanese-filled foyer. We needed to close in on
them fast, while they were still in the confines of
the corridor. Once out in the foyer the rest of Val's
team would be able to see what was about to
happen before the 4x4s could get into position.

Three more metres before we were on top of
them. There was another *ping*, then a bright light
from a lift interior as the doors opened and a
middle-aged couple began to step out between us
and the target.

I moved to push them back. This was a contingency I had rehearsed with them many times.
As I did so, Carpenter's right hand came up.
Without taking his eyes off Val, he fired three or
four suppressed rounds into the couple as he
passed. I could hear the top slide on his weapon
working back and forth inches from my face and
the dull thud of the rounds exiting the barrel.
Shit, her scream had turned the job noisy and we
hadn't even taken out the BG.

The couple fell back into the lift, the woman
taking all the rounds, her white silk blouse red
with blood. Fuck this guy; slotting players was
one thing, but real people meant big trouble.

The two BG turned and started to draw down
their weapons, but Carpenter and Nightmare had
closed the gap and gave them both two rounds in

the head from less than a foot away. They dropped without a sound.

Nobody in the vicinity had noticed anything yet – they were too busy doing their own stuff – but they soon would.

As the BG dropped, Carpenter should have moved on, but he continued firing down at the bodies. The BG were dead. He was wasting time.

Behind me, the man in the lift cried out as he cradled his dying wife.

I saw Carpenter's glazed eyes. He was high on whatever it was that he used to get through the long winters. Sergei would be busy tonight if we stayed alive and he stuck to his promise. Fuck it, I'd kill this maniac myself before this got out of control.

Keeping my eyes fixed on Carpenter's head as he fired yet another round into the BG, I shoved my right hand between my jacket and shirt, towards my 88, my left palm pointing towards him, arm bent and ready to receive the weapon that would soon be in my grip.

The screams from the lift were now muffled. I wasn't aware of anything else as I concentrated solely on Carpenter's head as he turned to fire into the other body on the floor.

My fingers scraped against the body armour as I leaned forwards slightly from the hip and pushed my coat and jacket back as aggressively as I could. The weight of the metal sockets helped me to expose my weapon for the second I needed. Pushing the web of my right hand firmly down into the 88's pistol grip, I closed my lower three fingers and thumb around it as firmly as possible.

Drawing the weapon, I started to insert my glove-free index finger into the trigger guard, making sure I could feel the steel of the trigger on the first pad. I pulled down on the safety catch with my thumb just before Carpenter fired his next round.

There was the glint of brass as the working parts ejected the spent casing between us. As he tried to fire again, I could see the top slide being held back by the locking lever. He had run out of rounds.

Jamming the 88 into my left hand, I punched forward and raised the weapon up, in between my focus on his head, waiting for that nano-second before the 88 came into view and I acquired the sight picture.

Real life burst into my eardrums once again. It was Nightmare, shouting into his Motorola at the 4x4s to move in on the Mercs as he gripped Carpenter's arm, dragging him towards the foyer.

I was now no more than two steps from Val. He was still looking at the bodies on the floor, taking in what he had just seen over the last ten seconds.

He went into survival mode, spinning round and looking back towards the restaurant, thinking that he could make his escape. We had eye-to-eye. He knew I was coming for him, and he knew it was too late to do much about it.

Everything went into slow motion as I focused completely on his neck. It was pointless paying attention to anything else around me. There was fuck all I could do about it.

I was now only one step away. He was expecting to get shot and stood there waiting, accepting.

There was nothing he could do. He must have known this would happen one day. I put the crook of my left arm around his neck, still moving forward so it jammed tight against his throat. He staggered backwards as I took another step, forcing his face upwards. I heard him gag. He was only five foot seven, so quite easy to get a grip of. If it had been his companion, I might have had to get on the balls of my feet. The slapper in the mink didn't react at all. I expected her to scream, but she just stood off to one side, back to the wall, and watched.

With the pistol in my right hand and still moving, I pushed my right arm behind his neck to complete the head lock, like a wrestler trying to get a better hold of his opponent. At once he started fighting for oxygen; there was no way he wasn't coming with me. There was no need to check him for weapons. He didn't need one tonight; he was a businessman on his way to the theatre.

I continued on towards the foyer. Val didn't like what I was doing to him, his back arched to try to take the weight of his body off his neck.

I was in a semi-crouched position, so I could carry his weight. I could feel the body armour he was wearing, disguised as a waistcoat. I concentrated on looking where we were going, towards the Russians shouting in the foyer and the suddenly silent Japanese. Nothing else mattered.

Four or five more seconds had elapsed and the people inside the hotel could not only see what had happened, but had had time for it to sink in. It takes a while for a brain not used to processing this sort of information to say, Yep, that's right, there are two dead men on the floor and others with sub-machine guns shouting and running around the foyer. Then, once one person starts becoming hysterical, they all do.

I turned into the foyer, heading for the exit. Nightmare came into view by the main doors, doing his stuff to one of the BG, shouting and screaming in Russian and kicking his hands away from his body.

I was twenty odd metres away from them.

The Japanese followed everyone else's example, running for cover and hiding behind the sofas, dragging their loved ones with them. That was great: the more they flapped the less they saw.

A two-tone alarm started to drown out the screams and I moved as fast as I could.

Nightmare was there, checking my back as he covered the BG. Gripping tight, I pulled Val along. He snorted like a horse, fighting for breath.

Through the windows, the blaze of headlights from the three Mercs lit Sergei's 4x4, which had the tailgate open, waiting for me and Val. Beyond the Mercs' roofs, I could see Reggie and Ronnie, AK butts unfolded and in the shoulder, muzzles pointing at the ground. Val's three drivers had already been dragged out of their seats and were face down on the tarmac.

Carpenter was to the left of the convoy. He, too, had his weapon pointing down. He must have been covering the other BG. All three were blowing out steam like kettles.

Sergei would be in the wagon, waiting for me to get out of this lunatic asylum.

With ten metres to go, World War Three broke out. I heard a series of short bursts from a 9mm, the muzzle flashes bouncing off the windows like flash bulbs.

It was Carpenter, giving the BG the best part of a mag. Then the shots were drowned out by the screaming in the foyer. It was like the sinking of the *Titanic*.

I couldn't believe it. More muzzle flashes lit up the darkness outside, the heavier 7.62 reports from Reggie and Ronnie echoing through the building. The drivers must have gone for their weapons, thinking they were next. Nightmare was frozen to the spot, shaking with fear as he stood over the last BG. He stared at me, waiting for direction.

I flicked a look at the BG. His eyes were switched on and waiting for a chance to get away from this gangfuck. There was nothing I could do for Nightmare, who was starting to flap big time. He would have to sort it out himself.

There was no way I was going out the front door with a firefight in progress, especially as I didn't know the result. Turning back towards the corridor, I moved Val as quickly as I could, nearly falling over the concierge and a bell boy, who were down on the floor in the open, too paralysed with fear to move.

I got back to the corner of the corridor. The man was still sobbing over his wife in the lift. Her legs, in flesh-coloured tights and sensible shoes, protruded into the corridor as the doors opened and closed against them.

The slapper was still there, well in control of

herself. She just stood, watching, not even bothering to wipe the dropped BG's blood and membrane off her face.

There was more hysteria as rounds starred the safety glass around the entrance. The BG had obviously seized his chance and got to his feet, firing as he went for freedom. Nightmare took the burst into his unprotected trunk and crumpled on top of two Japanese tourists, who stayed where they were, too shocked to move.

The BG started towards me, mini-Uzi in his right hand, its strap over his shoulder.

What was he going to do? He couldn't open up on me without hitting his boss.

Turning Val round to face his BG and protect me, I lifted my 88. I wasn't going to do much against his body armour, even if I could hit a moving target at fifteen metres one-handed with a pistol. I had to wait until he was nearer.

I fired at him from about ten metres, and kept on firing, aiming below centre mass. It was pointless aiming at his head at that range.

I'd emptied at least half of the twenty-round mag, not knowing whether it was going to drop him or not, when I heard him scream and he went down, his legs buckling. I didn't care where I'd hit him, just that I had.

Dragging Val, I passed the reception, trying to avoid the video camera, and headed towards the shop. I was going it alone now, leaving the contact outside to sort itself out.

The Money was wrapped in my arms and I wasn't about to give it up. I turned right down a wide corridor, heading for the rear car-park door.

I knew where I needed to go; time in re-connaissance is seldom wasted.

Passing the conference rooms and business centre, I pulled Val along the thick pile carpet, both of us finding it difficult to breathe. Me from fear and physical exertion, him from strangulation.

It was pointless checking behind me. I'd soon know if there was a drama: I'd get shot at.

People cowered in doorways as they saw us coming. That suited me fine.

Reaching the bottom of the corridor, I climbed four steps, then turned left and climbed ten more. The inner car-park door was held open by a fire extinguisher. I hit the crossbar of the second and burst out onto the red asphalt at the rear of the building. The cold took my breath away.

I could hear the odd shout from one or two locals crazy enough to come out of their apartments to see what all the fuss was about.

My breath was like a racehorse's on a winter gallop. I could hear Val moan. His nostrils were working overtime.

There was a stretch of twenty metres or so to the road. All around me steam escaped from pipes and ventilation shafts, and generators hummed like ship's engines. If I got one of the service vehicles, I'd turn left, downhill to the main, where the drone of traffic was coming from.

After about ten metres I could see the car park and loading bays. The only vehicle in sight was a small Hilux van. Fuck it, that would have to do.

With the security lights exposing me to the spectators at their windows in the apartments across the street, I tried the door. It was locked.

There were no passing vehicles to lift; the road-works just up the hill had seen to that. There was no choice but to drag Val up the concrete stairs and onto the loading bay.

Inside was what looked like a minicab office, with a desk, phone, and paperwork in piles. A woman in her mid-twenties was standing talking hysterically in Finnish on the phone, her left hand waving in the air as if beating off a swarm of wasps. At first she didn't recognize what was in front of her, until I shouted and pointed the 88.

'The keys! Give me the vehicle keys. Now!'

She knew what I was saying. She dropped the phone, the other end still talking, and pointed at the desk. I grabbed them and ran back down the stairs to the van, Val clenching his teeth as he took the pain in his neck.

It still wasn't worth checking around me. I knew I was being watched, and worrying about it wasn't going to make it stop. By now the woman in the minicab office would be back on the phone telling the world anyway.

I ripped off the cardboard that was keeping the windscreen ice-free and opened the passenger door using my left hand. My right was on the weapon, and I needed to keep the exposed trigger finger from making any contact. I might need to move my arse, but not at the expense of leaving prints.

'Get in, get in!'

He might not speak English, but with my pistol stuck into his neck, Val got the drift.

Once I'd finished kicking him in, I climbed

over on top of him, keeping the barrel of the pistol into his neck as I moved into the driver's seat and put the key in the ignition. Firing the engine, I threw it into gear.

The tyres pounded the cobblestones as I drove downhill to the main, the demister on full.

I could see the street lights ahead, with the traffic cutting across from both directions. I got level with the hotel drive. The Nissan was missing. Maybe Sergei had got away. All the other vehicles were still there.

Christmas lights had fallen off the trees and lay across the tarmac, amongst the scattering of empty brass cases. Bodies were strewn all over the ground. I couldn't tell who was who from this distance, though one of them had to be Reggie or Ronnie because the whole area was covered by a thin blanket of mist: one of their CS canisters must have got hit and was still spewing its contents into the wind.

One of the drivers had nearly got away. His suited body was slumped by one of the small decorative trees just before the exit. Steam rose from the blood oozing from his gunshot wounds. It looked as if their armour wasn't designed to take AP rounds either.

I passed by, suddenly thinking about the couple in the lift. Then, stopping at the junction with the main drag, I focused on what to do next. I turned right and merged with the traffic.

3

Flashing blue lights raced towards me as I headed in the direction of the city centre, nearly blinding me as they screamed past.

At the second option I turned right, up the road where Sergei and I had waited in the Nissan. The 88 was in my right hand, still rammed into Val's neck, forcing me to change gear with my left and hold the wheel in position with my knees.

The target was amazingly compliant; in fact, unless I was reading it wrong, his body language seemed to be saying, No sweat, I'll just wait and see what happens next.

The DOP was about ten minutes away and should have marked the end of Phase One and the beginning of Phase Two – the change of vehicles and move to the truck service station, from where we would all RV before moving over the border into Russia.

Plan B was in action now. In the event of a gangfuck we'd each make our own way back to the lakeside house where we'd been based for the last two weeks, and wait for twenty-four hours.

I was feeling very vulnerable and exposed

without Sergei. I might have the Money curled up in the footwell, but without help there was no way I was going to get it over the border. Sergei was the only one squared away with the world's most corrupt border guards, and he had been too switched on to tell anyone else how it was organized. I just knew that we were going in a truck adapted to conceal us all under the floor like IIs (illegal immigrants), which Sergei would drive. That was his insurance policy, and the reason I'd given him the least dangerous job on the operation.

The road started to bend right, heading out of the city. I had travelled this route to the DOP, both physically and in my head, tens of times. It went through residential areas with snow piled neatly at the sides of the wet roads, street lighting and Christmas decorations reflecting off the gleaming cobblestones. From all around me came the sound of sirens, jolting me out of my pissed-off-with-all-Russians mode. Blue lights flashed across a junction ahead of me. I took the next right; anything to get off the road and out of sight.

I'd turned into a driveway leading to the rear of an apartment block. There was no lighting back there as I drove over to the far side and stopped under a covered parking space. Keeping the engine running, I sat with the weapon stuck in Val's neck as sirens screamed from all sides. Now what? No way was I going on foot. If spotted, the only way to escape would be to leave him. That wasn't an option; the Money stayed with me.

Fuck it, there was nothing I could do but brass

43

it out. The longer I stayed there the more police would be in the area looking for the van. What was more, they'd have time to throw cordons around the city before we got out.

I needed to get to the DOP as soon as possible and detach myself from the hotel roadshow. Back on the road I put my foot down. It was dodgy, but sometimes it's best not to think too much.

Four more minutes and I was level with the chain-link fence of the car park. Over to my right, towards the hotel, a low-flying helicopter lit up the sky with its Nightsun. The beam bounced around, searching the park and frozen lake on the other side of the main drag from the Intercontinental. Their reaction time had been excellent, which pissed me off even more. If it wasn't for them being on heightened alert because of the EU conference, they'd have taken a lot longer to get their act together.

I moved towards the car-park entrance. The street lights illuminated the edge of the compound, so I could peer through the fence into the semi-darkness beyond, looking for anything unusual. Car parks are always the best place to lose a car; the downsides are that they're often monitored by video cameras and there's a strong chance of finding some jobsworth on the gate to take your cash. This one was free – no cameras, no staff and not lit up – which was why Sergei and I had decided to use it. The other four were using a park and ride about seven minutes away. At the moment, however, the slightest suspicious sign, like cars with no lights but engines running, would be enough to keep me driving past.

Carrying on to the junction, I turned left, crossing tram lines, and drove towards the entrance. People had stopped on the street and shop owners were standing in their doorways, looking up at the heli with its light and noise, talking excitedly to each other.

I kept my eyes on the car park. It looked less than half full; shoppers would have binned it for the day, any vehicles that were left were probably there to stay.

I indicated left, relieving Val's neck of my 88 as I needed both hands to manoeuvre the Hilux across the road and into a parking space. I felt exposed, waiting for a gap in the traffic, yet resisted the temptation to jump across and risk hitting an oncoming car.

A gap appeared, not before time, and as I drove under a height bar it was as if I'd entered a new world, dark and safe.

Driving a circuit to check the area, I ensured that the passenger side of the Hilux would face the row of vehicles where the Volvo saloon was parked. Valentin had all but disappeared into the shadow of the footwell.

The heli was quartering the night sky, raking the ground with its Nightsun.

The dark-blue Volvo saloon was nosey-parked, the boot sticking out. I stopped, making a T of the car and the Hilux. The only sounds were the van's engine ticking over and the heater on full blast. Val's shoes scraped across the ribbing of the rubber matting as he shifted position. It was almost peaceful until more sirens erupted.

Way over on the other side of the car park, an

interior light came on as somebody got into his car. The engine didn't start up; he was probably sitting in the driver's seat, watching the heli. I waited.

Now that my ears had adjusted to the new, safer environment, I could make out the metallic rumble of a tram fading towards the city centre. Police sirens wailed in the distance as the Nightsun continued to scour the lake and park.

The sirens got nearer. I sat, waited and watched, trying to work out where they were. Three or four police cars were following the tram lines along the fence, their flashing lights throwing bursts of colour across the roofs of the parked cars.

Seconds later, two more appeared.

I looked down at Val. I could make out his face in the glow of the dashboard. His eyes showed no fear. He was switched on enough to accept that overreaction at this stage could result in him being killed, or perhaps worse, seriously injured. He couldn't take that chance. From the moment he'd realized he wasn't going to die and that capture was inevitable, he hadn't panicked. He had to assume that I would be flapping, and that any unexpected move on his part might provoke a reaction from me, and the chances were it would be a bad one. The less he resisted, the less punishment he was going to get, and the more time he'd have to watch and wait for an opportunity to escape.

I pressed the release catch on the pistol grip with my right thumb and caught the magazine in my left hand as it slid from the grip. Inserting a full twenty-round mag in its place, I heard the click as it locked home, and pulled on the bottom to check it was going to stay put. I put the half-empty mag in my right pocket, along with the taped sockets. I didn't want to risk slapping a half-empty one back in if I was in the shit and had to change mags in a hurry.

Another three or four police cars crossed the entrance, lights flashing and sirens blasting. The Nightsun was now roaming around in quick, jerky movements. The heli-watcher in the car park had seen enough and drove out towards the main.

The warning buzzer sounded as I took the keys out of the ignition. My lights were still on. I looked down at Val. 'Stay.' I sounded as if I was talking to a dog.

I got out of the Hilux and could hear the *thud thud thud* of the heli's rotor blades as it hovered in the distance. All their attention was still in the immediate vicinity of the hotel, but I knew it wouldn't last.

The cold air scoured my face as I walked around the front of the wagon, cutting through the headlights, keeping my eyes on the cab, the weapon down by my side.

More flashing lights and sirens headed up the main. This time some of the squad cars started to peel off. One came down the road I'd made my approach on, brilliant blue strobes bouncing off me and the vehicles around me for a few seconds as it passed.

My attention was focused on the main entrance. Would the next set of lights come into

47

the car park? I knew there was nothing I could do about it but watch and wait, but that didn't stop my heart rate shifting up a gear or two.

Seconds later the darkness returned. Only the sirens were left, dying in the distance. The heli noise throbbed back into earshot.

I felt under the rear right-hand wheel arch of the Volvo with my fingers and retrieved the magnetic box that held the key. I hit the fob and there was a comforting *whoop* as the doors unlocked. I inserted the key in the boot lock and pulled it open.

Reggie and Ronnie had glued thick sponge all round the framework of the luggage area, mainly so the target didn't injure himself, but also to subdue any noise if he felt like having a kick and scream while we were in transit. As an extra precaution, the light units had been taped down on the inside. The last thing we needed was for Val to pull one off, stick his hand through as we waited at a set of lights and wave to a family on their way to give granny her Christmas presents.

They'd also lined the floor with a thick four-seasons duvet, with another on top, ready to stop him dying of hypothermia. Sitting on top was an orange plastic ball about the size of an egg, a roll of black gaffa tape and several sets of plasticuffs.

I opened the passenger door and Val looked up at me, then across at the boot and its contents. I didn't have a clue what would happen to him once we hit St Petersburg, and I didn't care. All I was concerned about was the $500,000 on offer, or what was left of it after Sergei got his $200,000.

Scanning the area once more, I brought the 88 up, angled my wrist at ninety degrees and rammed the weapon into the space above his bullet-proof waistcoat, then yanked it back into its normal position so the muzzle was twisted in his shirt. I didn't need to force his head downwards: he wanted to see what was happening as I placed my right index finger back on the trigger. Tilting the weapon up so the grip was near his face, I made sure he saw me remove the safety catch with my thumb and heard the click.

I didn't need to explain the facts of life to him. After all, he hadn't got where he was today by helping old ladies across the road. As far as Val was concerned, this was just another day in paradise. He wasn't about to fuck about now.

With my free hand I reached under his waistcoat. 'Up, up, up.'

There was no argument. His knees came out of the footwell and he staggered onto the tarmac.

I turned him round so the backs of his thighs were against the boot of the Volvo and leaned forward onto him as more sirens wailed in the distance and the heli fought to keep position against the wind. He got the idea and manoeuvred himself in, keeping his eyes fixed on mine. Still no fear in them, though; the look was more analytical now, as if he was conducting some sort of character assessment, trying to figure me out. He was in total control of himself. It was not the reaction you'd expect from the victim of a lift, and I found it unnerving.

He ended up on his back in the boot, knees up and hands across his stomach. Swapping over

49

hands on the 88, I got hold of the orange plastic ball and stuffed it into his mouth. Still there was no resistance, just some snorting through his nose as I rammed the ball home.

Reggie and Ronnie had folded over the last four inches of the roll on the gaffa tape so I could do the next bit with just one hand. I taped round his mouth and chin, then carried on up around his ears and eyes, leaving just his nose uncovered.

More sirens and lights, this time moving along the side road, the same way I had come. It wouldn't be long now before they started to check the car parks.

I heard the heli's engine change pitch. It was moving again, its Nightsun now at forty-five degrees, illuminating everything in its path, working its way towards me.

Slamming the boot shut on Val, I jumped back into the Hilux as the noise increased and the beam got brighter. There is no hiding place from those beams once they ping you. If they did, I'd change my mind about the $500,000 and just make a run for it on foot. I had my escape route worked out: straight over the fence and into the maze of apartment blocks opposite.

I sat and waited; there was nothing else I could do. The car and van took a direct hit and it felt like a scene from *Close Encounters* as both vehicles were flooded with light. A second or two later the engine note changed and the heli lurched in the direction of the main route out of town. The shadows returned as it moved away across the sky.

I drove the van into an empty space, got out

and went to check on Val. He was breathing heavily. I watched him and waited. He might have sinus problems, a blocked nose, the flu. I didn't want him to die; I only got paid for meat on the hoof. He snorted loudly to clear his nose.

Headlights veered towards me, but I hadn't heard a car door slam. It wasn't somebody from the car park. I leaned over Val to make it look as if I was sorting out my packages. Our faces were close to one another and I felt his breathing against my cheek. It was the first time I'd actually smelled him. After my little stay with Carpenter and Nightmare, I was expecting a combination of strong cigarettes, homemade alcohol and armpit. What I got was gaffa tape with a hint of cologne.

The problem had gone. Either the vehicle had found a parking space or left the area, I didn't give a shit which. I stood up slowly and had a look around, then rammed the pistol into his neck. With my other hand I got hold of his shoulder and started to pull.

He got the drift. I wanted him on his front. The car rocked slightly with his exertions, but it didn't matter, there was nobody around to notice.

Once he was on his stomach, I got hold of one of the plasticuffs, looped it round his wrists and pulled it tight.

Then I wrapped the second duvet around him, still making sure he had room to breathe.

The Volvo started first time. I headed left, out onto the main, away from the hotel. I only hoped that Sergei was doing the same.

* * *

I headed east out of Helsinki, towards the motor-way. The RV was at Vaalimaa, about 180Ks away.

I hit the seek button on the radio and turned up the volume to drown out the noise of the heater. I drove, thinking about everything and nothing. Twice I saw the flashing lights of a heli.

Eventually I passed the Vaalimaa service station area. This was trucker's heaven, the final stop before Russia. They used it as a meeting point so that they could move on in convoy. Hijacking was rife in the Motherland. In amongst them, somewhere, was our vehicle, with welded compartments for us all to play IIs.

Vaalimaa was just a few Ks from Sergei's tame checkpoint. Ten Ks north of the town was the lakeside house.

I turned off the radio and reached into the glove compartment for the digital scanner, which Sergei had tuned into the police channel. It was about the size of a mobile phone. The plan had been to use it from the time we exited Helsinki. That was another reason I needed Sergei: he spoke Finnish.

I tried to make sense of the squelchy radio traffic, but didn't have a clue what I was listening to. What I was hoping not to hear was, 'Volvo, Volvo, Volvo,' because then it would be odds on that I had a one-way ticket to havoc.

I checked every lay-by and minor gravel road for any hint of activity. There was nothing.

My lights hit the marker I was looking for, mailbox 183, a red plastic pedal bin on a white pole. I turned right, onto a deeply rutted track that led into the forest.

It was only a few hours since we'd last driven up it. About ten metres in, a white-painted chain, suspended between two poles, barred the way. Attached to it was a wooden sign saying Fuck Off, Private Property, in Finnish.

I left the engine running and got out of the car, checking in the headlights for recent sign of another vehicle. The compacted ice was giving very little away.

I looked carefully at the point where the last link of the chain was looped over a hook screwed into the right-hand pole, but could see nothing in the shadow cast by the Volvo's headlights. I took the weight of the chain so the first links came loose and pulled gently. I could feel the pressure of the cotton that still fastened it to the hook, and then the sudden pressure release as it broke. No-one had been through here who shouldn't have.

I drove over the chain, then jumped out and replaced it. To the side, under a pile of stones, the reel of cotton thread was just where I'd left it. I tied the first link to the hook again, replaced the reel and got back in the car.

The pines were so tall and close to the track it was like driving through a tunnel. After 250 metres the trees retreated, leaving a stretch of open ground about the size of four football pitches. I knew that in the summer it was all grass and tree stumps because there were framed pictures of it in the house, but now everything was covered by a metre-deep blanket of snow.

The track dipped slightly and the two-storey house was caught in the beam of my headlights. There were no lights on inside, no vehicles outside.

The track led to a wooden lean-to with enough room for three cars. Both buildings were made of timber and painted dark red with white window frames, and wouldn't have looked out of place in the Yukon during the Gold Rush.

I drove into the lean-to. A huge stack of firewood filled the whole of the back wall. A door on the far left led to the other side of the house and the lake.

I killed the engine, and for the first time in hours there was almost total silence. No gunfire, shouts, sirens, helis or car heaters, just low-volume hiss and mush as Finnish police talked Finnish police stuff on the scanner. I didn't really want to move.

The entrance was in the gable end of the main building, and the key was hidden in the log pile – very original. I went inside and was hit by wonderful warmth. The heaters worked off the mains and we'd left them all on. The labour-intensive wood fire was for holiday makers; besides, chimney smoke would have advertised our presence. I threw the light switch and went back to the car for Valentin.

4

The duvet had kept him alive, but only just. After two hours in the boot he was shaking with the cold.

'Right, come on, up, up.' I moved his legs over the sill and pulled him out by his body armour. He couldn't do much with his hands behind his back, but he seemed to be concentrating most on not having the ball fall to the back of his mouth and choke him. Fair one; that was why I'd used it.

I guided him inside as his legs started to come back to life and sat him on an old green velour settee next to a radiator. The decor was functional, just bare wooden floors and walls, and the downstairs was one very large open space. A stone fireplace stood opposite the door, and three wooden pillars, each about a foot in diameter and evenly spaced, helped to support the floor above. Most of the furniture, apart from the settee, was chunky pine, and the place smelled like a timber yard.

I pulled hard on the gaffa tape around Valentin's face. He winced as the adhesive took neck and eyebrow hair with it. His skin was cold, the colour of a dead cod.

He spat out the ball, coughing and spluttering. I was the typical Brit abroad: when in doubt, just keep to your own language and shout. 'Stay there.' I pointed at the radiator, not that he would be going anywhere plasticuffed up. 'You'll be warm in a minute.'

He looked up and nodded. A gust of wind whistled under the eaves. I expected Vincent Price to turn up any minute.

I went back to the car and retrieved the scanner, putting it on the kitchen table. Every fifteen seconds or so there was some traffic on the net, but no detectable note of urgency, as there would be if they were sending in the helicopters. There wasn't any slow, deliberate whispering, either, so hopefully they weren't trying to sneak up on me. Maybe, who knew?

Next priority was to get a brew on. The kitchen worktop stretched along the wall behind me. I went over and checked the kettle for water. Standing waiting for it to boil, I watched Val shivering. He was sitting close enough to the heater to make it pregnant. He'd had a hard life, judging by the lines on his face. But he still had his Slavic good looks: wide cheekbones, green eyes and dark-brown hair, the grey at the temples making him look pretty dignified for a hood.

I had to take my hat off to him, the boy had done good: Mercs, BG, the best hotels and a great line in slappers. I was jealous: my future was looking the same as my past.

The water boiled as I opened a packet of

crispbreads that was on the worktop. I munched on one and emptied the kettle onto ground beans in a cafetière.

Val had his knees up and was trying to use his body to flick his overcoat around him. His face was starting to regain its colour and his eyes followed my every move.

The team's kit had been piled into bags to the left of the main door. Sergei and I had planned to return here after delivering the Money to St Petersburg – me to drive to Sweden and then, via ferry, to Germany; him to clean up this place. I picked up a canvas kit bag and threw it on the table. Holstering the pistol, I fished inside for more plasticuffs, putting three interlocking strips together to make one long one. Moving around the table, I gripped Val's shoulders, then dragged him over towards the central pillar and pushed him down on his arse against it. I plasticuffed his upper right arm to the support, then, with the Leatherman, I cut the original plasticuffs so that his left arm was free. He wasn't going anywhere unless he did a Samson and took the pillar with him.

Returning to the other side of the table, I pushed the plunger down on the cafetière and filled two big mugs with steaming coffee. I threw a handful of sugar lumps into each and gave them a stir with my knife. I didn't know how he took his, but I doubted he was going to complain. I didn't normally take sugar myself, but today was an exception.

I walked over to him and put his mug on the floor. He gave me a brisk nod of thanks. I couldn't tell him, but I knew what it felt like to entertain all three of Mr and Mrs Death's little boys – wet, cold and hunger – and wouldn't wish them on any-one. Anyway, it was my job to keep him alive, not add to his misery.

The scanner was still giving the odd burst as I settled down at the table facing Val. I took a couple of sips and then it was time to get out of my costume. I felt uncomfortable in it, and if I had to start performing, the last thing I wanted to be wearing was a suit and a pair of lace-up shoes. Lugging my diving bag over to the table, I dug out jeans, Timberland boots, T-shirt, sweatshirt and a green Helly Hansen fleece.

The Chechen watched me intently as he drank coffee and I got changed. I got the sense he was enjoying my failure to interpret the scanner traffic.

I felt much more my old self as I tucked my weapon into the front of my jeans.

I went back to my coffee. Valentin had finished his and the empty mug was at his feet. I took him the cafetière and packet of crispbreads. He nodded as I poured new brews for both of us.

I sat at the table and ate the last of the bananas Reggie and Ronnie had left behind. The scanner continued to crackle away, and in the silences between bursts from the operating stations, all I could hear was the crunching of crispbread.

I couldn't stop thinking about Sergei. What if he didn't turn up? I hadn't worked that one out yet. I hadn't even wanted him to come on the lift. It would have been better if he'd just stayed with the truck; we'd all have RV'd with him, then been chauffeured across the border, but he insisted on being there in case there was any dodgy dealing. I would probably have done the same myself. But now what?

I had another thought. What would happen if one of Sergei's boys was still alive? It probably wouldn't take too long for the police to get him to talk. I stopped munching and put down my mug. Shit, we had to get out of here.

Getting to my feet, I grabbed Carpenter's and Nightmare's bags and took a red ski jacket and bottoms from mine. I put the 88 and the mags in the front pockets and threw Carpenter's cold-weather gear to Val. Carpenter was a big boy, so the fit wasn't going to be a problem.

Leaving him to figure out how he was going to put it on with his arm still secured, I ran upstairs to get two double duvets. Once back downstairs I pulled my weapon, cut him free and stepped back. 'Get dressed!' I shouted, miming putting on a jacket.

He got the hint and started removing his over-coat and tuxedo. I watched him, ready to react to any wrong move. Everything he was wearing stank of money. His shoes were so smart I looked at the label. English, Patrick Cox. A few pairs of those would have paid for my roof repair.

I let him keep his wallet, having checked through it and seen old pictures of children dressed in romper suits. I'd always avoided getting lumbered with stuff like that myself, but understood that these things were important to people.

Val was soon dressed in a pair of yellow

salopettes, a green ski jacket, an orange bobble hat with big dangling pom-poms, gloves, a scarf and a pair of cold-weather boots – all of which must have been at least three sizes too big. He looked ready for a stint as a children's entertainer.

I pointed the pistol up and back towards the pillar. He went over obediently. I showed him that I wanted him to hug it, an arm either side. Then it was just a matter of making up another set of extra-long plasticuffs, doing up two ratchets so it was like a lasso, looping it over his wrists and pulling tight.

I left him to adjust himself as I took my torch and went outside into the lean-to for a couple of shovels, one a big trough-type one, used for clearing pathways of snow, the other a normal building-site job. I dumped them on the table and the torch went into my salopette pocket.

Val was trying to work out what I was up to. He was looking at me in the same way as his slapper had done in the hotel, as if there was no danger and nothing was happening that might affect him. He appeared to think he was just a neutral observer.

I started ransacking the cupboards, looking for thermos flasks and food. I was out of luck. It looked as if we'd both had our last hot drink and crispbread for a while.

I picked up my mug and downed the last of the coffee as I walked over to him. I put his mug in his hand and indicated that he should do the same. He was soon busy manoeuvring his head around the post to meet his hands while I took candles and matches from the cupboard under the sink and threw them into one of the bags. Once I'd stuffed the duvets on top and done up the zip, I cut him free, motioning him to put the bag on his back. He knew what I meant and used the two handles as if they were straps on a bergen.

I put on my black woollen hat and ski gloves, then picked up the shovels from the table and used them to guide him out of the door. I walked behind, hitting the light switch. I left the scanner on the table. It would give our position away to use it out there.

I held him as I got the keys from the Volvo. It was my only transport out of here and I wanted to make sure it stayed that way. Once through the lean-to door we followed the well-worn track in the snow towards the lake shore. It was pitch-black out here and bitterly cold. The wind was much stronger now, swirling snow stung my cheeks as we moved forwards. The helis wouldn't be up around here in this wind.

5

A small wooden hut housing the wood-burning sauna stood about thirty metres away along the frozen lake shore. Beyond it was a wooden jetty, which stood about a metre above the ice.

The Chechen was still ahead of me, leaning into the wind and half turning from the waist to protect his face from the driving snow. He stopped when he got to the sauna, perhaps expecting me to motion him inside. Instead, I sent him round to the right. He obediently stepped out a metre or so along the jetty.

'Whoa. Stop there,' I shouted. 'Stop, stop, stop.'

He turned round, and I pointed with my pistol down at the frozen lake. He looked at me quizzically.

'Down there. On the ice, on the ice.'

Very slowly, he got down and sat in the snow, then rolled over, tentatively prodding the ice to make sure it would take his weight. I knew it would. I'd been messing about on it for the last two weeks.

Once he was standing I got him to move out of reach while I clambered down, in case he decided he'd had enough of this game and wanted to play stealing cars and driving home.

Prodding him along the ice with the shovels I paralleled the lake shore. By taking this route we wouldn't leave any sign from the house, but it meant we were more exposed to the wind. It was just a matter of leaning into it until we'd covered the 150 metres to the treeline. Once there, we carried on for a bit before I gave him another shout.

He turned again, awaiting new instructions, his head tilted against the wind screaming across the lake. I could hear his laboured breathing and just make out the shape of his face as I pointed at the trees to our right. He turned towards them and started to move as the wind buffeted the backs of our jackets.

The snow was no problem at first, no more than about two feet deep, but soon it was up to our waists. He did all the work ploughing through it; I just followed in his wake as his boots crunched down until they met compacted surface, lifted up and did the same thing all over again.

We moved another fifty metres – about ten metres inside the treeline – and that was enough. We were in direct line of sight of the house.

Having spent my childhood in South London housing estates, to me the countryside had always been just a green place full of animals that hadn't yet been frozen or cooked. I hadn't been into all the trapping stuff I was taught while in the Regiment. In fact, I'd forgotten most of it. I'd never felt the need to run around in a hat made out of freshly skinned rabbit. Building shelters, however, was a skill I did keep tucked away somewhere in the back of my head. I vaguely remembered that there would be spaces beneath the spreading boughs of the conifers at snow level.

Finding what seemed the biggest tree in the forest, I rammed the large shovel into the snow just short of where the lowest branches disappeared. Moving back out of the way so he couldn't hit me with it, I motioned for Val to take off the bag. No problem from him on that one. Then I gave him the other spade.

Val didn't need any further encouragement. The wind was blowing hard, flattening my jacket against my body, and if we were to stay alive out here we had to get out of it soon. The ambient temperature was low enough as it was, but the effect of wind-chill took it well below freezing. He might have been wearing a dinner jacket earlier on and heading for a night at the theatre, but he was obviously no stranger to physical graft. You can always tell whether someone's used to a shovel.

He worked efficiently, not tearing the arse out of it, obviously knowing better than to let himself break out in a sweat and have it freeze on him later. After a while he stopped digging, got on his knees and started to scoop out snow with his gloved hands; then he disappeared into the cave. A few minutes later, he turned and stuck his head out. I thought I could just about make out the hint of a proud smile from under his hat.

I waved him back inside, throwing the bag in

with him. Before I joined him I pulled back the index finger of my right-hand glove, pushing my trigger finger through the slit. I'd prepared this one just like the leather pair for the build-up.

I followed him head first, with the 88 up, hitting the torch button once in cover. The shelter could have taken three people kneeling; once in, I slid round and landed up on my arse with the pistol in the aim. I put the torch in my mouth.

For him, it was bondage time again. Pulling a set of plasticuffs from my pocket, I stuck the pistol into his neck, twisting it into his skin this time.

I plasticuffed his left hand to the branch above him. Snow fell on us as I ratcheted the plastic tight. We both shook our heads, trying to get it off our faces. With his arm now strapped above his head, Val sat there looking like a gibbon as I got out a candle and matches. The candle provided more light than it would normally have, thanks to the reflection from the brilliant white walls. I crawled back to the entry point, pulled in the shovels and used one to pile snow across the gap. It would keep out the wind.

It was time to get everything else sorted. I emptied the contents of the bag and started to spread out the duvets on the ground. Contact with the snow would conduct heat away from our bodies about twenty times faster than if we sat on the bedding.

Next, I smoothed out the sides of our hole with a gloved hand so that, as heat rose, the melting snow didn't form drip points and fall on us like rain. That done, I dug a small channel around the edge so that whatever did start to melt would run down the sides and refreeze there. In situations like this, 5 per cent extra effort always leads to 50 per cent more comfort.

The wind was no longer the prominent noise. The rustling of nylon clothing and both of us sniffing or coughing had taken over.

The cave was beginning to look like a steam room as our breath hung in clouds in the confined space. Using the grip end of a shovel, I dug a small tunnel. I needed to be able to see out towards the house, and we needed ventilation. The candle light wouldn't be seen directly from the house as it was low down and in an alcove; I just had to hope the ambient glow wasn't bright enough to be seen either, because there was no way we could do without it. Even the small amount of heat from a candle flame can help bring the temperature up to freezing point.

On my knees, I looked towards the house – well, it was out there in the darkness somewhere. Even with this amount of clothing on and some in-sulation beneath me my body was still cold because we weren't moving. I readjusted my position so that I was comfortable and could still see outside. Val continued to study me.

At least two very cold, boring hours must have passed with me listening to the wind and Val con-stantly fidgeting to get feeling back into his arm, when all of a sudden he said, 'The Maliskia must have offered you quite a sizeable amount of money to keep me alive. I am obviously more of a threat to them than I thought.'

I spun round in amazement.

It was a very confident, clear voice. He was smiling. He obviously liked my reaction. 'Now that you are alone, I should imagine it will be quite difficult to get me out of the country, to wherever it is the Maliskia want you to take me.' He paused. 'St Petersburg, perhaps?'

I stayed silent. He was right: I was in the shit.

'You have a name, I presume?'

I shrugged. 'It's Nick.'

'Ah, Nicholas. You're British?'

'Yeah, that's right.' I turned back to the house.

'Tell me, Nicholas, what did the Maliskia offer you? One million US? Let me tell you, I am worth considerably more than that to them. What is one million? It wouldn't even buy a decent apartment in London. I know, I have three.'

I carried on looking out of the hole. 'I don't know who or what the Maliskia are; they sound Russian, but I was employed in London.'

He laughed. 'London, New York, it doesn't matter. It was them. They would very much like to have a meeting with me.'

'Who are they?'

'The same as me, but infinitely more dangerous, I can assure you.' He got up onto his knees and a small shower of ice fell as the branch moved.

I couldn't imagine anyone being more dangerous. Russian *Organizatsiya* (ROC) were spreading their operations around the world, growing faster than any crime organization in the history of mankind. From prostitution to blackmail, bombing hotels to buying Russian Navy submarines to smuggle drugs, all the different gangs and splinter groups were infiltrating nearly every country to the tune of billions of dollars. These people were making so much money it made Gates and Branson look like welfare cases. With that much money and power at stake, I was sure there would be the odd disagreement between different groups.

There was silence for a while as I kept a trigger on the house, then Val spoke again. 'Nick, I have a proposition that I think will appeal to you.'

6

I didn't respond, just kept my eyes on the house.

'It's a very simple proposition: release me, and I will reward you handsomely. I have no idea what your plan is now. Mine, however, is to stay alive and at liberty. I am willing to pay you for that.'

I turned to look at him. 'How? There's nothing in your wallet but photographs.'

He tutted, a father addressing a wayward son. 'Nick, correct me if I'm wrong, but now that your plan has failed, I imagine you would like to get away from this country as quickly as you can. Release me, return to London and then I will get you the money. One of my apartments is in the name of Mr P. P. Smith.' He smiled; the name seemed to amuse him. 'The address is 3a Palace Gardens, Kensington. Would you like me to repeat that?'

'No, I've got it.'

I knew the area. It fitted the bill. It was full of Russians and Arabs, people with so much money they owned apartments worth millions and only used them once in a blue moon.

'Let's say that in two days' time, and for the next seven days after that, from noon till four p.m., there will be somebody at that address. Go there and you will receive one hundred thousand dollars US.'

A drop of melted ice hit me on the cheek. I took a handful of snow from the tunnel and ran it over the drip point, my mood as black as the night I was staring into. What the fuck was I doing freezing in this snow hole? I had half a million dollars sitting here with me, from doing something the Firm would have paid me a couple of hundred a day for. But I couldn't get at it. My only hope of ever seeing it was Sergei, and fuck knew where he was.

Val knew when to talk and when to shut up and let people think. I went back to watching the house for another hour or so, getting even more cold and miserable.

I was slowly convincing myself that, if Sergei didn't make an appearance, I should take my chances with Val in London. Why not? It wasn't as if I had anything to lose, and I was desperate for the pay cheque.

I could only hear the faint noise of the engine at first. It was tucked into the trees somewhere on the track and fighting to be heard above the wind. Then headlights appeared out of the treeline, heading towards the house. The noise got louder as it moved along the track. It was a 4x4 in low ratio. Sergei? It was impossible to tell if it was the Nissan from this distance.

Val had also heard it, and was keeping still so

his jacket didn't rustle and drown out the noise.

I watched the headlights briefly illuminate the front of the house before turning into the lean-to and cutting out.

I heard just one door slam and my eyes moved to the windows. I saw nothing.

I slid over to Val. Passively, he let me check his plasticuffs. They were secure; he wasn't going anywhere unless he happened to have a chain-saw hidden inside his coat. All the same, I wished I'd brought some tape to cover his mouth in case he decided to shout for help. It wasn't until I blew out the candle so he couldn't use it to burn the cuffs off, and started to push my way out of the snow, that he sparked up. 'Nick?'

I stopped but didn't turn. 'What?'

'Think about what I have said as you go to meet your friends. My offer is infinitely more profitable for you, and, may I say, safer.'

'We'll see.' I pushed myself out into the wind and was very much thinking about it, glad that Val wasn't going to scream and shout out. He knew what was happening. If it was Sergei at the house, Val could shove his offer. By the morning we would be in St Petersburg and I'd have my money and be on my way back to London.

As I retraced my route the wind was blowing head on, making my eyes stream. I could feel my tears turn to ice. I listened to the trees creak in the gale. Snow, whipped into a frenzy, attacked the exposed skin around my neck and face as I tried to focus on the house and surrounding area.

Kicking on about twenty metres, I checked the house again. The upstairs lights were on now, but there was still no movement inside. Moving off once more, I tried not to get too euphoric about the prospect of Sergei being there, but the feeling that this job could soon be over made the wind seem marginally less powerful.

Once below the sauna, on the lake, I pulled my trigger finger from its glove and pulled out the 88. It was far too dark to see with the naked eye, so I checked chamber with my exposed finger and ensured the mag was on tight, then climbed up onto the bank and moved forward in a semi-crouch until I got to the lean-to entrance.

I was eager to make contact with Sergei, but had to take things slowly. Only when I actually saw him would I feel safe.

I stood and listened at the lean-to door, not hearing anything apart from the sound of the wind bouncing it backwards against the lock.

Keeping to the right of the frame, I pulled the metal handle down and the wind did the rest, forcing it inwards. Fortunately, the bottom scraped along the ground, preventing it from crashing into the woodpile.

On my hands and knees in the snow, I eased my head round the bottom of the door frame.

The Nissan was parked the other side of the Volvo, the light from the ground-floor window reflecting off its roof. Things were looking up, but I'd have to wait a while before jumping with joy.

I moved into the lean-to and checked no-one was still in the Nissan. Then I pushed the door to, feeling warmer out of the wind.

The entrance to the house was closed, but the

warm glow from the window was enough for me to be seen if anyone came out of it.

I moved to the right of the frame, pushing my ear against the door. I couldn't hear a thing. I moved to the other side of the Nissan and looked in through the window. There was no need to get right up to the glass to see in; it's always best to stay back and use the available cover.

My heart sank. Carpenter. Still dressed in his suit, but now without a tie or overcoat, he was taking pills from a small tin and swallowing them, shaking his head violently to force them down. His mini-Uzi was exposed, rigged up over his jacket and dangling under his right arm, with the harness strap bunching up the material where it crossed his back.

He moved about the room with no apparent purpose, sometimes out of view. Then I saw he had Val's masking tape and ball gag wrapped in his massive hand. He brought them up to his face for a moment, and, realizing their significance, hurled them to the ground. Then he started lifting chairs and smashing them against the walls, kicking our overcoats about the room like a two-year-old in a tantrum.

It wasn't hard to work out what was going through his mind. He'd decided that I had left with Val for the border, leaving him in the lurch. Fair one; I'd think the same. No wonder he was chucking his toys out of the pram.

The table followed the chairs as the combination of narcotics and rage started to fuck with his head. There was no reason to consider my options; he had just made up my mind for me.

Moving back to the outer door, I left him to it.

Checking back every ten metres as I crossed the frozen lake, after several minutes I saw headlights in the darkness, heading away from the house and back towards the treeline. What the fuck was Carpenter up to? He probably didn't even know himself.

With legs apart and slightly bent to keep myself stable in the gusts, I stood and watched until the lights disappeared into the night. It was very tempting to go back and wait in the house, but Carpenter might return and complicate matters, and anyway, there was still the police to worry about.

Turning parallel to the shore, I carried on towards the snow hole.

Once in the treeline I could see the whole of the side of the house. Carpenter had left the lights on, but through the downstairs windows things didn't look right. It took me a second or two to realize what was happening.

Not bothering about leaving sign, I moved as fast as I could in a direct line towards the building, stumbling over in snow that sometimes came up to my chest. I was trying so hard to get there quickly that it didn't feel as if I was making any progress. It felt like one of the recurring dreams I'd had as a kid – running to someone, but never as fast as I needed to.

As I got closer I could see flames flickering in the room and smoke spewing out through a broken pane. A thick layer was gathering two or three feet deep on the ceiling and looking for more places to escape from. Fuck the house, it was the Volvo I was worried about.

By the time I reached the lean-to I could already hear the crackling of badly seasoned wood and the screams from the smoke alarms going apeshit. The door to the house was open. Smoke was pouring out from the top of the frame. Either Carpenter had been switched-on enough to know that he had to feed the fire with oxygen, or he just didn't give a shit. It didn't matter which, the fact was that it had taken hold big time.

I reached the car, the heat searing my back even through my ski jacket. The inside of the house was a furnace.

As I put the key in the lock there was a sound like shotgun rounds being fired. Spray-cans of something were exploding in the heat.

I reversed slowly out of the lean-to. It would have been pointless screaming out like a loony, only to get stuck in the snow. I just wanted to get clear enough so the Volvo wasn't incinerated. After a three-point turn I drove fifty metres up the track and killed the engine. Jumping out with the keys, I stumbled back into the cover of the treeline, feeling as if I was back in that dream again.

By the time I neared the hide I could make out my shadow quite clearly against the snow. The flames were well and truly taking over from the smoke.

Sliding into the snow hole, I pulled out my Leatherman, felt for the plasticuffs and started to cut Val free, letting him sort himself out as I scrambled out again into the wind. He soon followed and we both stared at the burning building. Bizarrely, he started to try and comfort me. 'It's all right, I knew you weren't abandoning me. I am worth too much to you, no? Particularly now. May I suggest that we leave here, and as soon as possible. Like you, I do not want to encounter the authorities. It would be most inconvenient.' What was it with this guy? Did his pulse rate ever go above ten beats per minute?

He knew that whatever had happened out here it had stopped me from meeting up with any of the team; he didn't have to convince me any more to let him go. He knew it was my only sensible option now.

The Volvo could easily be seen in the flames. They hadn't penetrated the walls yet, but they were licking out hungrily from the windows.

I stopped him short of the car, handed him my Leatherman and carried on to open the boot, shouting at him to cut the cord in his jacket. Even at this distance, I felt the heat on my face.

He looked about him, found the nylon cord that could be adjusted to tighten around his waist, and began cutting. There were loud cracks as the frame of the house was attacked by the flames.

Val looked at the fire as he heard the boot open. 'Please, Nick, this time inside the car. It's very cold in there.' It was a request rather than a demand. 'And, of course, I'd prefer your company to that of the spare tyre.'

Responding to my nod, he settled in the Volvo's rear footwell, giving me back the

Leatherman and offering his hands. I tied them around the base of the handbrake with the cord, where I could see them.

We drove out, leaving the fire to do what it had to do. Maybe it wasn't such a bad thing; at least there wouldn't be any evidence of me ever having been there.

There was no sign of Carpenter or anyone else as we bumped our way up to the chain gate. I left it on the ground where I found it, as a warning to Sergei. There was still a chance that he'd got away. There'd been two Hiluxes in the hotel car park; maybe he'd nicked the other one. It was too late now to hope that he might get us over the border, but I still didn't want him to get caught. He was a good guy, but fuck it, I was on a new phase now, and one that had nothing to do with any of them.

I had lost, I had to accept it. Now I had to take my chances with Val.

'I'll drop you off at a train station,' I said as we headed towards Vaalimaa. 'You sort yourself out from there.'

'Of course. My people will extricate me quite swiftly.' There was no emotion in his voice. He sounded like a Russian version of Jeeves. 'May I give you some advice?'

'Why not?'

My eyes were fixed on the road, heading for the motorway past the town, seeing nothing but piled-up snow on either side of me. The wind buffeted the side of the car enough for me to have to keep adjusting the steering. It was like having a heavy artic drive past on a motorway.

'You will obviously want to leave the country quickly, Nick. May I suggest Estonia? From there you can get a flight to Europe fairly easily, or even a ferry to Germany. After what has happened at the hotel, only a fool would try to leave Helsinki by air, or cross into Sweden.'

I didn't reply, just stared at the snow in the headlights.

Just over two hours later we were approaching Puistola, one of the Helsinki suburbs. Not that I could see any of it: first light wasn't for another four hours. People would soon be waking up to their cheese and meatballs and listening to the radio accounts of last night's gunfight at the OK Corral.

I looked for signs to the train station. The morning rush hour, if there was one, would start in an hour or two.

Pulling into the car park, I cut him free of the handbrake. He knew to stay still and wait for me to tell him when to move. He was so close to freedom, why jeopardize things now?

I got out and stood away from the car, my pistol in the pocket of my puffer jacket. He crawled out and we both stood in a line of frozen-over cars, in the dark, as he sorted himself out, tucking in his clothes and running his hands through his hair. Still looking ridiculous in Carpenter's salopettes and ski jacket, he clapped his gloved hands together to get some circulation going, eventually extending one of them to me. The only shaking I did was with my head; he understood why and nodded. 'Nick, thank you.

You will receive your reward for releasing me. P. P. Smith. Remember the rest?'

Of course I did. My eyes were fixed on his. I considered telling him that if he was lying to me, I'd find him and kill him, but it would have been a bit like telling Genghis Khan to watch himself.

He smiled. He'd read my mind again. 'Don't worry, you will see that I am a man of my word.' He turned and walked towards the station.

I watched him crunch along in the snow, breath trailing behind him. After about a dozen or so paces he stopped and turned. 'Nick, a request. Please do not bring a cell phone or pager with you to Kensington, or any other electronic device. It's not the way we conduct business. Again, I thank you. I promise that you won't regret any of this.'

I made sure that he was out of the way, then got back into the car.

7

NORFOLK, ENGLAND
Friday, 10 December 1999

The bedside clock burst into wake-up mode dead on seven, sounding more like a burglar alarm. As I rolled over it took me three attempts before I managed to hit the off button with my hand still inside the sleeping bag.

The instant I poked my head out I could tell the boiler had stopped working again. My house was a bit warmer than a Finnish snow hole, but not much. It was yet another thing I needed to sort out, along with some bedding and a bed frame to go with the mattress I was lying on.

I slept in a pair of Ron Hill running bottoms and sweatshirt. This wasn't the first time the boiler had packed in. I wrapped the unzipped bag around me and pushed my feet into my trainers with the heels squashed down.

I headed downstairs, the bag dragging along the floor. I'd spent most of my life being wet, cold and hungry for a living, so I hated doing it on my own time. This was the first place I'd ever owned, and in winter the mornings felt much the same to me as waking up in a hedgerow in South Armagh. It wasn't supposed to work like that.

The place was in the same state as I'd left it before I went away just over two weeks ago, to RV with Sergei at the lake house, except that the tarpaulin had blown off the hole in the roof, and the 'For Sale' sign had been flattened by the wind. If it had stayed there any longer it would have taken root anyway. There wasn't enough time to sort any of that out today. I had three vitally important meetings in London in a few hours' time, and they wouldn't wait for the boiler man.

The trip back to the UK had taken three days. I'd decided to find my own way rather than take Val's advice to get out of Finland via Estonia. It wasn't as if we were sharing toothbrushes or anything, so I wasn't in the mood to trust everything he had to say. I drove to Kristiansand in southern Norway, and from there I took the ferry to Newcastle. It was full of Norwegian students. While they got pissed I watched Sky News on the snowy screens. There was footage of the Intercontinental, with police apparently doing a search for forensic evidence, then came pictures of the dead, amongst them Sergei. A Finnish government spokeswoman gave a news conference, declaring that it was the worst incident their country had witnessed since the 1950s, but declining to confirm whether it was an ROC shooting, and stressing there was no connection with, or risk to, the EU conference. As far as they were concerned, this was an unrelated matter.

I made my way down the bare wooden staircase, trying not to snag the sleeping bag on the gripper rod that had been left behind when I'd ripped up the carpet.

The house was a DIY disaster zone. It had been ever since I'd bought it after bringing Kelly back from the States in '97. In theory it was idyllic, up on the Norfolk coast in the middle of nowhere. There was a small Co-op, and three fishing boats worked out of the tiny harbour. The highlight of the day was when the local pensioners took the free bus to the superstore eight miles away to do their big shop.

The estate agent must have rubbed his hands when he saw me coming. A 1930s, three-bedroomed, detached mess of pebble-dash, just 200 metres from the windy beach, it had been empty for several years after the previous owners had died, probably of hypothermia. The details said, 'Some renovation required, but with magnificent potential.' In other words, a shit load of work was needed. My plan was to gut the place and rebuild it. The ripping out was OK; in fact, I'd enjoyed it. But after a succession of builders had sucked through their teeth when giving me their quotes, and I'd got pissed off with them and decided to do it myself, I'd lost interest. So now the house was all bare boards, studwork and entrails of wiring that I didn't understand sticking out of the walls.

Now that I was responsible for Kelly, it had seemed the right time to fulfil the fantasy of having a real home. But no sooner had I exchanged contracts than it had started to make me feel confined.

I'd called the place in Hampstead, where she was being looked after, as soon as I'd got back last night. They said she was much the same as when

I'd last seen her. I was glad she was sleeping; it meant I didn't have to speak to her. I did want to, but just never knew what the fuck to say. I'd gone to see her the day before leaving for Finland. She'd seemed all right, not crying or anything, just quiet and strangely helpless.

The kitchen was in just as bad a state as the rest of the place. I'd kept the old, yellow Formica units, circa 1962. They'd do for now. I put the kettle on the gas ring, readjusting the sleeping bag around my shoulders, and went out into the porch to check for mail. It hadn't been stacked up on the kitchen unit as I'd expected. I also wondered why the tarpaulin hadn't been replaced in my absence.

I hadn't got a postbox yet, but a blue pedal bin did just as well. Very Finnish, I thought. There were four envelopes – three bills and a card. The handwriting told me who the card was from, and I knew before I read it that I was about to get fucked off.

Caroline had started coming here to look in on things now and again, to collect the mail and check the walls hadn't collapsed while I was away working as a travelling salesman. She was in her thirties and lived in the village. Her husband no longer lived with her – it seemed he took too much whisky with his soda. Things were going great between us; she was kind and attractive, and whenever I was here we would link up for an afternoon or two. But a couple of months earlier she had started to want more of a relationship than I felt able to offer.

I opened the card. I was right: no more visits or

mail collection. It was a shame; I liked her a lot, but it was probably for the best. Things were getting quite complicated. A gunshot wound in the stomach, a reconstructed ear lobe and dog-tooth scars along a forearm are hard to explain, whatever you're trying to sell.

Making a lumpy brew with powdered milk, I went upstairs to Kelly's room. I hesitated before I opened the door, and it wasn't because of the hole in the roof tiles. There were things in there that I'd done for her – not as much as I'd have liked, but they had a habit of reminding me how our lives should have been.

I turned the handle. There had probably been more wind than rain in my absence, as the stain on the ceiling wasn't wet. The blue two-man tent in the middle of the floor was still holding out. I'd put nails in the floorboards instead of tent pegs and they were rusty now, but I still couldn't bring myself to take it down.

On the mantelpiece were two photos in cheap wooden picture frames, which I'd promised to bring down to her on my next visit. One was of her with her family – Kev, Marsha and her sister Aida – all smiles round a smoking barbecue. It was taken about a month before I'd found them hosed down in their home in the spring of '97. I bet she missed this picture; it was the only decent one she had.

The other was of Josh and his kids. This was a recent one, as Josh was carrying a face scar that any neo-Nazi would be proud of. It was of the family standing outside the Special Operations Training Section of the American Secret Service at

Laurel, Maryland. Josh's dark-pink gunshot wound ran all the way up the right-hand side of his cheek to his ear, like a clown's smile. I hadn't had any contact with him since my stupidity got his face rearranged in June '98.

He and I still administered what was left of Kelly's trust fund, though as her legal guardian, I'd found myself shouldering more and more of the financial responsibility. Josh was aware of her problem, but it was just done via letters now. He was the last real friend I had, and I hoped that maybe one day he would forgive me for nearly getting him and his kids killed. It was too early to go in and apologize – at least that was what I told myself. But I had woken up late at night more than once, knowing the real reason: I just couldn't face all that sorrow and guilt stuff at the same time. I wanted to, I just wasn't any good at it.

As I picked up Kelly's photos, I realized why I didn't have any myself. They just made me think about the people in them.

I cut away from all that, promising myself that re-establishing contact with Josh would be one of the first things I got done next year.

I went into the bathroom opposite, and ran the buttercup-coloured bath. I had a bit of a soft spot for the foam tiles, now light brown with age, that lined the ceiling. I remembered my stepdad putting some up when I was a kid. 'These'll keep the heat in,' he'd said, then his hand slipped and his thumb left a dent. Every Sunday night, when I had a bath, I threw the soap at the ceiling to add to the pattern.

Returning to my bedroom, I put Kelly's photos

on the mattress to make sure I didn't forget them. I finished my brew, then dug into one of the cardboard boxes, looking for my bike leathers.

I checked the bath and it was time to jump in, after hitting the small radio on the floor, which was permanently tuned to Radio 4. The shooting was still high on the agenda. An 'expert' on ROC declared to listeners of the *Today* programme that it had all the hallmarks of an interfaction shooting. He went on to say that he had known this was going to happen and, of course, he knew the group responsible. He could not, however, name them. He had their trust. Sue MacGregor sounded as unimpressed as I was.

I lay in the bath and glanced at Baby G. Another ten minutes and I had to get moving.

The order of the day was first, the doctor's office at 11.30 to talk about Kelly's progress, then lie to the clinic's accounts department about why I couldn't pay the new invoice just yet. I didn't think they would completely understand if I told them everything would have been fine if a mad Russian called Carpenter hadn't fucked up my cash flow.

My next visit would be to Colonel Lynn at the Firm. I wasn't looking forward to that conversation, either. I hated having to plead.

The third stop on my agenda was Flat 3a Palace Gardens in Kensington. What the hell, I was desperate. I didn't see the Maliskia solving my financial problems.

My foray into the freelance market had only reinforced my reluctant dependence on the Firm. I had been weapons free from the Firm since the fuck-up in Washington with Josh eighteen months before. Lynn was right, of course, when he'd said I should feel lucky that I wasn't banged up in some American gaol. As for the Brits, I reckoned they were still trying to decide what to do with me – give me a knighthood or make me disappear. At least I was getting paid two grand a month in cash while they scratched their heads. It was enough to cover Kelly's treatment for about seventy-two hours.

Lynn made it clear that in no way did the retainer mean any change in my status; he didn't say it in so many words, but I knew from the look in his eyes that I was still lowlife, a K, a deniable operator carrying out shit jobs that no-one else wanted to do. Nothing would change unless I could get Lynn to put my name forward for permanent cadre, and time was running out. He was taking early retirement to his mushroom farm in Wales when he finished running the desk in February. I didn't have a clue who was taking over. Contacting the message service last night, I'd heard Lynn would see me at 13.30.

If I ever got back into the good lads' club, pay would be increased to £290 a day for ops, £190 for training, but in the meantime I was in the shit. The chances of selling this house were zero; it was in a worse state than when I'd moved in. I'd bought it for cash, but I couldn't raise a loan on it because I couldn't prove my income. Since leaving the army it had been cash in envelopes, rather than PAYE.

Getting out of the warm bath into the cold bathroom, I dried myself quickly and got into my leathers.

From inside the panelling that contained the cistern I retrieved my 9mm HK USP (Heckler & Koch universal service pistol), a chunky, square-edged semi-automatic 9mm, and two thirteen-round mags. Its holster was my usual one, which could be shoved down the front of my jeans or leathers.

Sitting on the toilet lid, I bit open the plastic bag protecting it and loaded the loose rounds. I always eased the mag's springs when the weapon wasn't needed. Most stoppages occur because of a misfeed from the magazine, either because the mag's not fully home in the pistol grip or because the mag spring has been under tension for so long that it doesn't do its job when required. When the first round is fired it might not push the next up into the breech.

I loaded the weapon, inserting a mag into the pistol grip and ensuring it was fully home. To make the weapon ready, I pulled back on the top slide with my forefinger and thumb and let go. The working parts moved forwards under their own steam and rammed the top round of the mag into the chamber. I had three USPs in the house, two hidden downstairs when I was here, and one under my bed – a little trick I'd learned from Kelly's dad years ago.

I checked chamber by pushing back slightly on the top slide and put the weapon and spare mag in my pocket, slung the daysack over my shoulder and locked up the house.

Waiting for me outside was the bike of my dreams, a red Ducati 966 that I'd treated myself to at the same time as the house. It lived in the garage, another pebble-dashed marvel of 1930s architecture, and there were times when I reckoned the sound of its engine bursting into life was the only thing that kept me from total despair.

8

The London traffic was chaos. There were plenty of shopping days left till Christmas, but you wouldn't have thought so from the number of cars.

As I rode down from Norfolk it had been cold, overcast and dull, but at least it was dry. Compared with Finland it was almost tropical. I'd got to Marble Arch in just under three hours, but progress was going to be slow going from now on. Weaving my way around stationary vehicles, I looked down Oxford Street, where the decorations blazed and twinkled. The season of goodwill was everywhere, it seemed, except behind the steering wheels of gridlocked vehicles and inside my head.

I was dreading this. The house I called in Hampstead last night was staffed by two nurses who, under the psychiatrist's supervision, were looking after Kelly twenty-four hours a day. They took her to a clinic in Chelsea several times a week, where Dr Hughes had her consulting rooms. Kelly's round-the-clock attention was costing me just over four grand a week. Most of the £300,000 I'd stolen from the drug cartels in '97, together with her trust fund, had been spent on her education, the house and now her treatment. There was nothing left.

It had all started about nine months ago. Her grades since coming to England had been poor; she was an intelligent girl, but she was like a big bucket with holes in it – everything was going in, but then it just dripped out again. Apart from that, she'd shown no visible after-effects from the trauma. She was slightly nervous around adults, but OK with her own age group. Then, at boarding school, she'd started to complain about pains, but could never be more specific or explain exactly where they were. After several false alarms, including the school nurse wondering if she was starting her periods early, her teachers concluded that she was just attention seeking. Then it slowly got worse; Kelly gradually withdrew from her friends, her teachers, her grandparents and me. She wouldn't talk or play any more; she just watched TV, sat in a sulk or sobbed. I didn't pay that much attention at first; I was worried about the future and was too busy feeling pissed off at not having worked since the previous summer while I waited for Lynn to make up his mind.

My usual response to her sobbing bouts had been to go and get ice cream. I knew this wasn't the answer, but I didn't know what was. It got to the point where I even started to get pissed off with her for not appreciating my efforts. What an arsehole I felt now.

About five months ago she'd been with me in

Norfolk for the weekend. She was distant and detached, and nothing I did seemed to engage her. I felt like a school kid jumping around a fight in the playground, not really knowing what to do: join in, stop it or just run away. I tried playing at camping with her, putting up the tent in her bedroom. That night she woke with terrible nightmares. Her screaming lasted all night. I tried to calm her, but she just lashed out at me as if she was having a fit. The next morning, I made a few phone calls and found out there was a six-month waiting list for an NHS appointment, and even then I'd be lucky if it helped. I made more calls and later the same day took her to see Dr Hughes, a London psychiatrist who specialized in child trauma and who accepted private patients.

Kelly was admitted to the clinic at once for a temporary assessment, and I'd had to leave her there to go on my first St Petersburg recce, and to recruit Sergei. I wanted to believe that everything would be fine soon, but knew deep down that it wouldn't, not for a long time. My worst fears were confirmed when the doctor told me that besides regular treatment at the clinic as an out-patient, she'd need the sort of constant care that only the unit in Hampstead could provide.

I'd been to visit her there a total of four times now. We usually just sat together and watched TV for the afternoon. I wanted to cuddle her, but didn't know how. All my attempts at displaying affection seemed awkward and forced, and in the end I left feeling more fucked up than she was.

I swung right into Hyde Park. The squaddies of the Blues and Royals were out exercising their horses before perching on them for hours outside some building or other for the tourists. I rode past the memorial stone to the ones who were blown up by PIRA in 1982 while doing the same thing.

I had some understanding of Kelly's condition, but only some. I'd known men who'd suffered with PTSD (post-traumatic stress disorder) but they were big boys who'd been to war. I wanted to know more about its effects on children. Hughes told me it was natural for a child to go through a grieving process after a loss; but sometimes, after a sudden traumatic event, the feelings can surface weeks, months or even years later. This delayed reaction is PTSD, and the symptoms are similar to those associated with depression and anxiety: emotional numbness; feelings of helplessness, hopelessness and despair, and re-living the traumatic experience in nightmares. It rang so true; I couldn't remember the last time I'd seen Kelly smile, let alone heard her laugh.

'The symptoms vary in intensity from case to case,' Hughes had explained, 'but can last for years if untreated. They certainly won't just go away on their own.'

I'd felt almost physically sick when I realized that if only I'd acted sooner, Kelly might have been on the mend by now. It must be how real fathers feel, and it was probably the first time in my life that I'd experienced such emotions.

The road through the park ended and I was forced back onto the main drag. Traffic was virtually at a standstill. Delivery vans were stopping exactly where they wanted and hitting their four-way flashers. Motorbike couriers screamed through impossible gaps, taking bigger chances than I was prepared to. I slowly worked my way in and out of it all, heading down towards Chelsea.

Things were just as bad on the pavement. Shoppers loaded with carrier bags collided with each other and caused logjams at store entrances. And as if things weren't bad enough, I didn't have a clue what I was going to get Kelly for Christmas. I passed a phone shop and thought of getting her a mobile, but fuck it, I wasn't even any good at talking to her face to face. At a clothes shop I thought of getting her a couple of new outfits, but maybe she'd think I didn't think she was capable of choosing her own. In the end I gave up. Whatever she said she wanted, she could have. That was if the clinic left me any money to pay for it with.

I eventually got to where I wanted to be and parked up. 'The Moorings' was a large town house in a leafy square, with clean bricks, recent repointing and lots of gleaming fresh paint. Everything about it said it specialized in the disorders of the rich.

The receptionist pointed me to the waiting room, a place I was very familiar with by now, and I settled down with a magazine about the sort of wonderful country houses that mine would never be. I was reading about the pros and cons of conventional compared with underfloor heating, and thinking that it must be rather nice to have any sort at all, when the receptionist appeared and ushered me into the consulting room.

Dr Hughes looked as striking as ever. She was in her mid to late fifties, and looked like she and her consulting rooms could have featured in *OK!* magazine. She had the kind of big grey hair that made her look more like an American newsreader than a shrink. My overriding impression was that she appeared incredibly pleased with herself most of the time, especially when explaining to me, over the top of her gold-rimmed, half-moon glasses that no, sorry, Mr Stone, it was impossible to be more definite about timetables.

I declined the coffee she offered. There was always too much time lost fannying about while waiting for it, and in this place time was money.

Sitting down on the chair facing her desk, I placed the daysack at my feet. 'She hasn't got worse, has she?'

The doctor shook her unusually large head, but didn't answer immediately.

'If it's about the money, I—'

She lifted her hand and gave me a patient, patronizing look. 'Not my department, Mr Stone. I'm sure the people downstairs have everything under control.'

They certainly did. And my problem was that supermodels and Premier League footballers might be able to afford four grand a week, but soon I wouldn't be able to.

The doctor looked at me over the top of her glasses. 'I wanted to see you, Mr Stone, because I need to discuss Kelly's prognosis. She is still really quite subdued, and we aren't achieving any sort of progress towards her cure. You will remember I spoke to you a while ago about a spectrum of behaviour, with complete inertia at one extreme and manic activity at the other?'

'You said that both ends of the spectrum were equally bad, because either way the person is unreachable. The good ground is anywhere in the middle.'

The doctor gave a brief smile, pleased and perhaps surprised that I'd been paying attention all those weeks ago. 'It was our aim, you will also remember, to achieve at least some movement away from the inertial state. Our best hope was to get her into the central area of the spectrum, not too low or too high, able to interact and make relationships, adapt and change.' She picked up a pen and scribbled a note to herself on a yellow Post-it pad. 'I'm afraid to say, however, that Kelly is still very passive and preoccupied. Stuck, if you like, or cocooned; either unable or unwilling to relate.'

She peered over her glasses again, as if to underline the seriousness of what she was saying. 'Young children are deeply affected by witnessing violence, Mr Stone, particularly when the victims of that violence are family members. Kelly's grandmother has been describing to me her previous cheerfulness and energy.'

'She used to be such fun to be with,' I said. 'She never laughs at my jokes now.' I paused. 'Maybe they're just not very good.'

The doctor looked a little disappointed at my remark. 'I'm afraid her current behaviour is such a contrast to how she was previously that it indicates to me that the road to recovery is going to be even longer than I at first thought.'

Which meant even more expensive. I was ashamed at even having the thought, but there was no getting away from it.

'What sort of time scale are we looking at?'

She pursed her lips and shook her head slowly. 'It's still impossible to answer that question, Mr Stone. What we're trying to repair here is not something as simple as a fractured limb. I appreciate that you would like me to give you some sort of schedule, but I can't. The course of the disorder is quite variable. With adequate treatment, about a third of people with PTSD will recover within a few months. Some of these have no further problems. Many take longer, sometimes a year or more. Others, despite treatment, continue to have mild to moderate symptoms for a more prolonged period of time. I'm afraid that you really must prepare yourself for a long haul.'

'Is there nothing I can do to help?'

For the second time, Dr Hughes smiled briefly. It was fleetingly triumphant rather than warm, and I got the feeling I'd fallen into some kind of trap.

'Well,' she said, 'I did ask you here today for a specific reason. Kelly is here, in one of the rooms.'

I started getting up. 'Can I see her?'

She, too, stood up. 'Yes, of course. That is the object. But I have to say, Mr Stone, that I'd rather she didn't see you.'

'I'm sorry? I—'

The doctor cut in. 'There's something I'd like you to see first.' She opened a drawer in her desk, pulled out several sheets of paper and pushed them across the desk. I wasn't prepared for the shock they gave me. The pictures Kelly had drawn of her dead family looked very different from the happy smiling photograph I had in my daysack.

The one of her mother showed her kneeling by the bed, her top half spreadeagled on the mattress, the bedcover coloured in red.

In another, her five-year-old sister, Aida, was lying on the floor between the bath and the toilet, her head nearly severed from her shoulders. The nice blue dress she'd been wearing that day was spattered chaotically with red crayon.

Kev, her father and my best friend, was lying on his side on the floor of the lounge, his head pulped by the baseball bat that lay next to him.

I looked at the doctor. 'They're the positions I found them in that day – exactly ... I hadn't realized ...'

I'd found her in her hidey-hole, the place where Kev wanted the kids to run to if there was ever a drama. She'd never said a word to me about it, and I'd never thought that she might have witnessed the carnage. It was as though the events were recorded in her memory with the clarity of a camera.

Hughes looked over her glasses. 'Kelly has even remembered the colour of the duvet on her bed that day, and what was playing on the radio as she helped lay the table in the kitchen. She has talked to me about how the sun was shining through the window and reflecting on the cutlery. She recalls that Aida had lost a hair band just before the men came. She's now just replaying the events immediately preceding the killings, in an effort, I suggest, to achieve another outcome.'

I was relieved that her flashbacks didn't go any further, but if the treatment worked she would surely begin to recount what had occurred afterwards. When it did, I would have to involve the Firm to sort out any 'security implications' that might arise; but for now, they didn't need to know that she was ill.

The psychiatrist interrupted my thoughts. 'Come with me, if you will, Mr Stone. I'd like you to see her and explain a little more about what I hope we can achieve.'

She led me a short way down the corridor. I couldn't make sense of any of this. Why wasn't Kelly allowed to see me? We turned left and walked on a while, stopping outside a door that had a curtain across a small pane of glass. She poked it very slightly aside with a finger and looked through, then moved back and motioned for me to do the same.

I looked through the glass and wished I hadn't. The images of Kelly I kept in my memory were carefully selected shots from before she got sick, of a little girl quivering with excitement at her birthday party on the replica of the *Golden Hinde*, or shrieking with delight when I finally kept my promise to take her to the Tower of London and she got to see the Crown Jewels. The real life Kelly, however, was sitting on a chair next to a nurse. The nurse seemed to be chatting away, all smiles. Kelly, however, wasn't replying, wasn't moving. Hands folded politely in her lap, she was staring at the window opposite her, her head cocked to one side, as if she was trying to work something out. There was something deeply scary about how still she was. The nurse wasn't moving much, either, but Kelly's was an unnatural kind of stillness. It was like looking at a frozen image, an oil painting of a young girl in an armchair, next to a film of a nurse who happened to be sitting still, but who would move again in a second or two.

I'd seen it before. It was four years ago, but it could have been four minutes.

I was on my hands and knees in her family's garage, talking gently as I moved boxes and squeezed through the gap, inching towards the back wall, trying to push the images of the carnage next door behind me.

Then there she was, facing me, eyes wide with terror, sitting curled up in a foetal position, rocking her body backwards and forwards, holding her hands over her ears.

'Hello, Kelly,' I'd said very softly.

She must have recognized me – she'd known me for years – but she hadn't replied. She'd just carried on rocking, staring at me with wide, scared, dark eyes. I'd crawled right into the cave until I was curled up beside her. Her eyes were red and swollen. She'd been crying and strands of light brown hair were stuck to her face. I tried to move it away from her mouth.

I got hold of her rigid hand and guided her gently out into the garage. Then I picked her up in my arms and held her tight as I carried her into the kitchen. She was trembling so much I couldn't tell if her head was nodding or shaking. A few minutes later, when we drove away from the house, she was almost rigid with shock. And that was it, that was the stillness I saw now.

The doctor's mouth came up close to my ear. 'Kelly has been forced to learn early lessons about loss and death, Mr Stone. How does a seven-year-old, as she was then, understand murder? A child who witnesses violence has been shown that the world is a dangerous and unpredictable place. She has told me that she doesn't think she'll ever feel safe outside again. It's nobody's fault, but her experience has made her think the adults in her life are unable to protect her. She believes she must take on the responsibility herself – a prospect that causes her great anxiety.'

I looked at the frozen girl once more. 'Is there nothing I can do?'

The doctor nodded slowly as she replaced the curtain and turned to head back up the corridor. As we walked she said, 'In time, we need to help her gently examine and review the traumatic events that happened to her, and learn to conquer her feelings of anxiety. Her treatment will eventually involve what are best described as "talking therapies", by herself or in groups, but she's not really ready for that yet. I will need to keep her on antidepressant medication and mild tranquillizers for a while yet, to help lessen some of the more painful symptoms.

'The aim eventually will be to help Kelly remember the traumatic events safely, and to address her family life, peer relationships and school performance. Generally we need to help her deal with all the emotions she's having trouble making sense of at the moment: grief, guilt, anger, depression, anxiety. You notice, Mr Stone, I'm saying "we".'

We had reached her room and went back inside. I sat down again and she went to the other side of her desk.

'Parents are usually the most important emotional protectors for their children, Mr Stone. They can do a much better job of psychologically reassuring their children than professionals can. They can help them talk about their fears, re-assure them that Mummy and Daddy will do whatever is possible to protect them, and stay close. Sadly that's not a possibility for Kelly, of course, but she still needs a responsible adult whom she can depend upon.'

I was beginning to understand. 'Her grand-mother, you mean?'

I could have sworn I saw her shudder.

'Not quite what I had in mind. You see, a major factor in any child's recovery from PTSD is that the prime care giver must communicate a willing-ness to talk about the violence and be a non-judgemental listener. Children need to know that it's permissible to talk about violence. Kelly needs permission, if you like, to talk about what happened to her. Sometimes care givers may subtly discourage children from talking about violence in their lives for whatever reason, and this, I sense, is the case with Kelly's grandparents.

'I think her grandmother feels hurt and dis-couraged that Kelly has lost interest in family activities and is easily angered and so detached. She finds it very upsetting to hear the details –

maybe because she believes it will be less upsetting for Kelly if she doesn't talk about it. On the contrary, children often feel relieved and unburdened by sharing information with trusted adults. It also may be useful therapeutically for children to review events and air their fears by retelling the story. I don't mean that we should coerce Kelly into talking about what happened, but reassurance and validation once she has volunteered it will be immensely helpful to her recovery.'

She was beginning to lose me in all her psycho-babble. I couldn't see what I had to do with all this.

As if she'd read my mind, Dr Hughes pursed her lips again and did her trick with the half-moon glasses. 'What it all boils down to, Mr Stone, is that Kelly is going to need a trusted adult alongside her during the recovery process, and in my view the ideal person to do that is you.'

She paused to let the implications of what she was saying sink in.

'You see, she trusts you; she speaks of you with the utmost affection, seeing you as the nearest thing she has now to a father. What she needs, far more than just the attention and therapy we professionals can provide, is your acceptance of, and commitment to, that fact.' She added pointedly, 'Would you have difficulties with that, Mr Stone?'

'My employers might. I need—'

She held up her hand. 'You have seen the cocoon in which Kelly has placed herself. There is no formula that guarantees breaking through when someone is out of reach. But whatever the cause is, a form of loving has to be there in the solution. What Kelly needs is a prince on a white charger to come and free her from the dragon. It is my view that she's decided not to come out until you are an integral part of her life again. I'm sorry to burden you with this responsibility, Mr Stone, but Kelly is my patient, and it's her best interests that I must have at heart. For that reason, I didn't want her to see you today; I don't want her to build up hopes only to have them dashed. Please go away and think about it, but believe me, the sooner you are able to commit, the sooner Kelly's condition will start to improve. Until then, any sort of cure is on hold.'

I reached into my daysack and pulled out the framed photographs. It was the only thing I could think of. 'I brought these for her. They're pictures of her family. Maybe they'll be some help.'

The doctor took them from me, still waiting for an answer. When she saw she wasn't going to get one – not today, anyway – she nodded quietly to herself and ushered me gently, but firmly, towards the door. 'I'll be seeing her this afternoon. I'll telephone you later; I have the number. And now, I believe, you have an appointment with the people downstairs?'

9

I was feeling pretty depressed as I headed east along the northern side of the Thames, towards the city centre. Not just for Kelly, but for me. I forced myself to admit it: I hated the responsibility. And yet I had those promises to Kevin to live up to.

I had enough problems looking after myself, without doctors telling me what I should be doing for other people. Being in charge of others in the field was fine. Having a man down in a contact was straightforward compared to this. You just got in there, dragged him out of the shit and plugged up his holes. Sometimes he lived, sometimes not. It was something I didn't have to think about. The man down always knew that someone would be coming for him; it helped him stay alive. But this was different. Kelly was my man down, but it wasn't just a question of plugging up holes; she didn't know whether help was on the way or not. Nor did I.

I knew there was one thing I could do: make money to pay for her treatment. I'd be there for her, but later. Right now, I needed to keep busy and produce money. It had always been 'later' for Kelly, whether it was a phone call or a birthday treat, but that was going to change. It had to.

Working my way through the traffic, I eventually got onto the approach road to Vauxhall Bridge. As I crossed to the southern side, I looked up at Vauxhall Cross, home of SIS (Secret Intelligence Service). A beige-and-black pyramid with the top cut off, flanked by large towers on either side, it needed just a few swirls of neon to look totally at home in Las Vegas.

Directly opposite Vauxhall Cross, over the road and about 100 metres away, was an elevated section of railway that led off to Waterloo station. Most of the arches beneath had been converted into shops or warehouses. Passing the SIS building, I negotiated the five-way road junction and bumped the pavement, parking up by two arches which had been knocked through to make a massive motorbike shop – the one I'd bought my Ducati from. I wasn't going in today; it was just an easy place to park. Checking my saddle was secure so that no-one could nick my USP, I put my helmet in the daysack, crossed a couple of feeder roads and took the metal footbridge over the junction, eventually entering the building via a single metal door that funnelled me towards reception.

The interior of the Firm looked much the same as any high-tech office block, clean, sleek and with an efficient corporate feel about it, with people swiping their identity cards through electronic readers to get access. I headed for the main reception desk, where two women sat behind thick bulletproof glass.

'I'm here to see Mr Lynn.'

'Can you fill this in please?' The older one passed a ledger through a slot under the glass.

As I signed my name in two boxes she picked up a telephone. 'Who shall I say is here?'

'My name is Nick.' I hadn't even had any cover documentation from them since my fuck-up in Washington, just my own cover which I hoped they'd never know about. I'd organized it in case it was time to disappear, a feeling I had at least once a month.

The ledger held tear-off labels. One half was torn away and put in a plastic sleeve, which I would have to pin on. Mine was blue and said, 'Escorted Everywhere'.

The woman came off the phone and pointed to a row of soft chairs. 'Someone will be with you soon.'

I sat and waited with my nice new badge on, watching suited men and women come and go. Dress-down Friday hadn't reached this far upriver yet. It wasn't often that people like me got to come here; my last visit had been in '97. I'd hated it that time, too. They managed to make you feel that, as a K, you weren't very welcome, turning up and spoiling the smart plc image of the place.

After about ten minutes of feeling as if I was waiting outside the headmaster's study, an old Asian guy in a natty blue pinstripe suit pushed his way through the barrier.

'Nick?'

I nodded and got to my feet.

He half smiled. 'If you'd like to follow me.' A

swipe of the card that hung round his neck got him back through the barrier; I had to pass the metal detector before we met on the other side and walked to the lifts.

'We're going to the fifth floor.'

I nodded and let the silence hang as we rode the lift, not wanting to let him know that I knew. It saved on small talk.

Once on the fifth I followed him. There was little noise coming from any of the offices along the corridor, just the hum of air-conditioning and the creak of my leathers.

At the far end we turned left, passing Lynn's old office. Someone called Turnbull had it now. Two doors down I saw Lynn's name on the door plate. My escort knocked and was met by the characteristically crisp and immediate call of 'Come!' He ushered me past and I heard the door close gently behind me. Lynn's bald crown faced me as he wrote at his desk.

He might have a new office, but it was quite clear he was a creature of habit. The interior was exactly the same as his last; exactly the same furniture and plain, functional, impersonal ambience. The only thing that showed he wasn't a mannequin planted here for decoration was the framed photograph of a group, which I presumed were his much younger wife and two children, sitting on a stretch of grass with the family labrador. Two rolls of Christmas wrapping paper leaning against the wall behind him showed that he did have a life.

Mounted on a wall bracket above me to the right was a TV, the screen scrolling through

Ceefax world news headlines. The only thing I couldn't see was the obligatory officer's squash racket and winter coat on a stand. They were probably behind me.

I stood and waited for him to finish. Normally I would just have sat down and made myself at home, but today was different. There was what people like him tend to call an atmosphere, and I didn't want to annoy him any more than I needed to. We'd parted on less than good terms the last time we'd met.

His fountain pen sounded unnaturally loud on the paper. My eyes moved to the window behind him, and I gazed over the Thames at the new apartment building being finished off on the north side of the bridge.

'Take a seat. I'll be with you very soon.'

I did, on the same wooden chair I'd sat on three years ago, my leathers drowning the scratch of his writing as I bent down and placed my day-sack on the floor. It was becoming increasingly obvious that this was going to be a short meeting, an interview without coffee, otherwise the Asian guy would have asked me if I took milk or cream before I'd gone in.

I hadn't seen Lynn since the debrief after Washington in '98. Like his furniture, he hadn't changed. Nor had his clothes: the same mustard-coloured corduroy trousers, sports jacket with well-worn leather elbows and Viyella shirt. With his shiny dome still facing me, I could see that he hadn't lost any more hair, which I was sure Mrs Lynn was very happy about. He really didn't have the ears to be a complete baldilocks.

He finished writing and put aside what I could now see was a typed page of A4 that looked as if a teacher had marked it. Looking up with a half-amused smile at my outfit, he brought his hands together, thumbs touching as he rested them on top of the desk. Since Washington, he'd treated me as if he was a bank manager and I was asking for a bigger overdraft, trying hard to be nice, but at the same time looking down on me with disdain. That, I didn't mind, as long as he didn't expect me to look up to him with reverence.

'Wot can I do fer yer, Nick?' He was taking the piss out of my accent, but in a sarcastic, not jovial way. He really didn't like me. My Washington fuck-up had put the seal on that.

I bit my lip. I had to be nice to him. He was the ticket to the money Kelly needed, and even though I had the sinking feeling that my be-nice expedition wasn't going to work, I had to give it my best shot.

'I really would like to know if I am ever going to get PC,' I said.

He settled back into his leather swivel chair and produced the other half of his smile. 'You know, you are very lucky still to be at liberty, Nick. You already have a lot to be thankful for, and do bear in mind, your freedom is still not guaranteed.'

He was right, of course. I owed the Firm for the fact that I wasn't in some US state penitentiary with a cell mate called Big Bubba who wanted to be my special friend. Even if it was more to do with saving themselves even more embarrassment than protecting me.

110

'I do understand that, and I'm really grateful for all that you've done for me, Mr Lynn. But I really need to know.'

Leaning forward, he studied the expression on my face. It must have been the 'Mr Lynn' bit that made him suspicious. He could smell my desperation.

'After your total lack of judgement, do you really think you'd ever be considered for permanent cadre?' His face flushed. He was angry. 'Think yourself lucky you're still on a retainer. Do you really think that you would be considered for work after you' – his right index finger started to endorse the facts as he poked it at me, his voice getting louder – 'one, disobey my direct order to kill that damned woman; two, actually believe her preposterous story and assist her assassination attempt in the White House. God, man, your judgement was no better than a lovestruck schoolboy's. Do you really think a woman like that would be interested in you?' He couldn't contain himself. It was as if I'd touched a raw nerve. 'And to put the tin lid on it, you used a member of the American Secret Service to get you in there . . . who then gets shot! Do you realize the havoc you've caused, not only in the US but here? Careers have been ruined because of you. The answer is no. Not now, not ever.'

Then I realized. This wasn't just about me, and it wasn't early retirement at the end of his tour next year to spend more time with his mushrooms; he had been given the sack. He'd been running the Ks at the time of the Sarah débâcle, and someone had had to pay. People like Lynn

111

could be replaced; people like me were more difficult to blow out, if only for financial reasons. The government had invested several million in my training as a Special Air Service soldier. They wanted to get their money's worth out of me. It must have killed him to know that I was the one who'd fucked up, but he was the one to carry the can – probably as part of the deal to appease the Americans. He sat back into his chair, realizing he had lost his usual control.

'If not PC, when will I work?'

He had gained a little more composure. 'Nothing is going to happen until the new department head takes over. He will decide what to do with you.'

It was time for me to lose all pride. 'Look, Mr Lynn, I really need the money. Any shit job will do. Send me anywhere. Anything you've got.'

'That child you look after. Is she still in care?'

Shit, I hated it when they knew these things. It was pointless lying; he probably even knew down to the last penny how much money I needed.

I nodded. 'It's the clinic costs. She'll be there for a long time.'

I looked at his family portrait, then back at him. He had kids; he'd understand.

He didn't even pause. 'No. Now go. Remember, you are still being paid and you will conduct yourself accordingly.'

He pressed his buzzer and the Asian guy came to collect me so fast he must have been listening through the keyhole. At least I got to see the squash racket on the way out. It was leaning against the wall by the door.

Taking a breath, I nearly turned back to tell him to ram his patronizing, hate-filled words up his arse. I had nothing to lose; what could he do to me now? Then I thought better of letting my mouth react to what I was thinking. This would be the last time I ever saw him, and I was sure it was the last time he ever wanted to see me. Once he'd gone it would be a new department head and maybe a new chance. Why burn my bridges? I'd get my own back later. I'd jump all over his mushrooms.

10

I was still feeling philosophical about the meeting at 3a. If Val had been feeding me a crock of shit, well, there you go, at least I was on my turf rather than his. That was the way I wanted it to stay, so I'd tucked my USP into my leathers before I left the bike shop, just in case.

All the same, I knew I'd be really pissed off if no-one was at the flat with a little something for me, as long as it was wrapped in a big envelope and not a full metal jacket. I'd soon be finding out.

The traffic in Kensington was at a standstill. At one set of lights the bike got wedged between a black cab and a woman in a Merc with very dyed, long blond hair, held off her face by Chanel sunglasses, even though it was the middle of winter. She tried to look casual as she chatted on her mobile.The cabbie looked over at me and couldn't help himself from laughing.

Palace Gardens stretches the whole length of Hyde Park's west side, from Kensington in the south to Notting Hill Gate in the north. I rode up to the iron gates and the wooden gatehouse positioned between them. Sitting inside was a bald man in his fifties, wearing a white shirt, black tie and blue nylon jacket.

Beyond him lay a wide tree-lined road and pavements of clean beige gravel. The large mansion houses were mostly embassies and their residences. Flags fluttered and brass plates gleamed. The sale price of even one of the staff apartments would probably clear my debts at the clinic, pay Kelly's education right through to doctorate level and still leave enough to put a new roof over most of Norfolk.

The gateman looked me up and down as if I was something one of the posh embassy dogs had left coiled on the kerb. He didn't get up, just stuck his head out of the window. 'Yes?'

'Number 3a, mate. Pick up.' I pointed to the now empty daysack on my back. I really hadn't planned to be a courier today, but it seemed the easiest thing to do. At least I looked the part, with the leathers and my south London accent turned up a notch or two.

He pointed up the road. 'Hundred yards up on the left. Don't park in front of the building. Put your machine over there.' He indicated to the opposite side of the road.

I let in the clutch and waited for the steel bollards blocking my way to disappear into the road. The Israeli embassy loomed up on my left. A dark-skinned guard in plain clothes stood outside on the pavement. He must have been feeling quite cold, as his coat and suit jacket were unbuttoned. If anyone attacked the place he had to be able to reach his weapon and gun them down before the uniformed British policeman on the opposite side of the road got a chance to step in and make a simple arrest instead.

About seventy metres past them both I parked in the line of cars opposite the apartment building. Walking across the road towards its grand gates, I started removing my gloves and unbuckling my helmet, then I hit the bell and explained to a voice where I wanted to go. The side gate opened with a whirr and a click and I walked through and down the drive.

The building was bigger than most of those around it and set back from the road. It was made of red brick and concrete and was decades younger than its neighbours, with manicured gardens on each side of the drive that led downhill to a turning circle with an ornate fountain at its centre.

Pulling off the ski mask that kept the cold off my face, I walked through the main doors into a glittering dark marble and glass reception area. The concierge, another king sitting on his throne, seemed to view me the same way as his mate down the road. 'Delivery, is it?'

Nobody calls you sir when you're in bike leathers.

It was time to play courier boy again. 'Nah, pick-up P. P. Smith, mate.'

He picked up the internal telephone and dialled, his voice changing into Mr Nice Guy the moment he got a reply. 'Hello, reception here, you have a courier for a collection. Do you want me to send him up? Certainly. Goodbye.' The phone went down and he turned surly again as he

116

pointed to the lift. 'Third floor, fourth door on the left.'

As the lift doors closed behind me I had a quick check round for closed-circuit cameras, then pulled out my USP. Checking chamber, I hit the button for the third floor. I never knew why I checked chamber so much. Maybe it just made me feel more in control.

As the lift kicked in with a slight jerk and took me upwards, I folded the ski mask over the USP and placed it, and my right hand, in the helmet. If there was a drama, I could just drop the helmet and react.

The lift slowed. Placing my thumb on the safety catch, I was ready.

The door slid open with an upmarket *ding*, but I stood my ground for a few seconds, listening, helmet still in my left hand so I could draw with my right.

The temperature changed as I stepped into the corridor and the doors closed behind me. It was hot, but the decor was cold: white walls, cream carpet and very brightly lit.

I followed the carpet, looking for the fourth door on the left. It was so quiet that all I could hear as I moved was the creaking of my leathers.

The door didn't have a bell, knocker or even a number. Using my knuckles against the heavy wood, I stood off to the side, my right hand back on the pistol grip, thumb easing off the safety catch.

I hated this bit. It wasn't as if I was expecting trouble; it was highly unlikely to happen here, given all the security I'd had to pass. But still, I hated knocking on doors and not knowing who or what was on the other side.

Footsteps echoed on a hard floor and locks were undone. The door started to open, only to be stopped by a security chain. A face, or rather half a face, moved into the three- or four-inch gap. It was enough for me to recognize its owner at once. I was pleasantly surprised. It would be much friendlier dealing with her than some square head.

Looking almost innocent, Val's slapper from Helsinki was showing me just one very light-blue eye and some dark-blond hair. It probably got lighter in the summer, when the sun got to work on it. The only other thing I could see through the gap was her dark-blue woollen polo neck.

She looked at me without any expression, waiting for me to speak.

'My name is Nick. You have something for me.'

'Yes, I've been expecting you.' She didn't bat an eyelid. 'Have you a cell phone or pager with you?'

I nodded. 'Yeah, I've got a phone.' Fuck what Valentin had said. I needed one with me for when the clinic called later.

'Could I ask you to turn it off, please?'

'It is.' It was pointless wasting the battery while sitting on a bike.

Tilting the helmet slightly so the pistol wouldn't fall out, I reached into my right-hand pocket and pulled out the phone, showing her the display.

She gave a very courteous 'Thank you', then the door closed and I heard the chain being undone. The door reopened fully, but instead of standing there and ushering me in, she turned and started to walk back into the flat. 'Close the door behind you, would you please, Nick?'

As I stepped over the threshold I smelled floor wax. I followed her down the corridor, taking in the apartment's layout. A couple of doors led off either side, and one at the far end was partly open. The floor was plain, light wood, the walls and doors gleaming white. There was no furniture or pictures, not even a coat hook.

I switched my attention to Val's slapper. I'd thought it was her high heels that had made her look so tall in Finland, but I could see now that her legs did that all on their own. She was maybe just over six feet tall in her square-toed cowboy boots, which made a slow rhythmic clack as her heels hit the floor. She walked like a supermodel on a catwalk. Her legs were sheathed in a pair of Armani jeans, the logo on the back pocket moving up and down in time with her heels. I couldn't keep my eyes off it.

Slipping the pistol into my right-hand pocket, I moved the phone into my left, all the time looking at her and thinking that Armani should be paying her for this. I was almost tempted to buy myself a pair.

One door to the right was partly open, and I glanced through. The kitchen was just as sterile as the corridor: stark white stools at a breakfast bar, no kettle, no letters on the side. Nobody lived here.

I walked into the living room where she now stood, a large white space with three unmatching dining-room chairs at its centre. Muslin curtains

119

covered the windows, making the light dull and hazy.

The only other objects in the room were four very large Harvey Nichols bags, which looked as if they were about to split at the seams, and a black Waterstone's bag, the tell-tale shapes of books pushing at its sides.

I moved to the far corner of the room and leaned against the wall. Through the double glazing of the large picture windows I could hear the faint murmur of traffic.

She bent over one of the shopping bags and pulled out a buff A2-sized envelope.

'My name is Liv. Valentin sends his regards,' she said as she brought it over to me. 'And, of course, his gratitude. This is for you. One hundred thousand US dollars.'

Wonderful. That was the slate clean at the clinic, and another four months' treatment in the bank.

She extended a perfectly manicured hand that showed she was no longer a teenager. The skin on her face was crystal clear and had no need of make-up. I reckoned she was in her early thirties. Her hair was shoulder length, parted over her left eye and tucked back behind her ear.

If she was wearing nail polish today, it was clear. She wore no rings, no bracelets, earrings or necklaces. The only jewellery I could see was a discreet gold tank watch with a black leather strap. But then, she needed adorning like the Venus de Milo needed a velvet choker and diamond tiara. I was beginning to see why Val might prefer Finland to Russia.

I wasn't going to open the envelope there and then. I didn't want to look desperate and untrusting. I was both, but I didn't want her to know that.

I hadn't had the time to take much notice of her before. The first time I was aware of her was the day that Val arrived in Finland, three days before the lift. Recces are about planning, not admiring the view. But I did now. I'd never seen a woman with such a perfectly symmetrical face – a strong jaw, full lips and eyes that felt as if they knew everything but revealed nothing. Her statuesque body looked like it had been shaped by canoeing or rock climbing rather than jumping up and down to music in a gym.

The feel of the bundles in the envelope, even through the bubble wrap lining, brought me back to the real world. I put my helmet at my feet, unzipped my jacket and slipped the envelope inside.

She turned and went to sit on one of the chairs beside her purchases. I took up my position against the wall. She invited me to take one of the seats with a wave of her hand, but I declined, preferring to stand and be able to react if Liv had a few of her square-headed friends around and this encounter turned out to be not entirely friendly.

I was starting to get jealous of Val. Money and power always attract beautiful women. My pedal bin full of red reminders never had quite the same effect.

Liv sat there looking at me in the way that Mr Spock did on the bridge of the *USS Enterprise* when he thought things were illogical. It was the same look she'd given me at the hotel, penetrating and searching, as if she was staring right into my head, but somehow managing to give nothing back. It made me uncomfortable and I stooped to pick up my helmet before leaving.

She sat back and crossed her long legs.

'Nick, I have a proposition for you, from Valentin.'

I left the helmet where it was, but said nothing. I'd learned the hard way that it's worth remembering we have two ears and just one mouth.

Her gaze remained cool. 'Are you interested?'

I certainly was. 'In principle.' I didn't want to spend all day beating about the bush, and she didn't look or sound like the sort of person who'd do that anyway. So let's just get on with it. 'What does he want from me?'

'It's a simple task, but one that needs to be handled delicately. He needs someone – and he wants it to be you – to assist another person to enter a house in Finland. The other person is a cryptographer – a highly skilled hacker, if you like. Inside the house are computers which this other person will use his skills to access and then download the contents onto a laptop for removal. The contents, before you ask, are merely some competitive intelligence which Valentin is keen to have in his possession.'

She uncrossed her legs and pulled open one of her bags.

'You mean industrial espionage?'

'That's not entirely correct, Nick. More commercial than industrial. Valentin is asking you to assist in the procurement of this data, but without the house owners knowing that you have done so. We want them to think they are the only ones with this information.'

'It's as straightforward as that?'

'There are some minor complications which we will discuss if you are interested.'

I was, but minor complications don't exist. They always turn out to be major. 'How much?'

I had to wait for an answer while she fished a cream-coloured cashmere cardigan out of the Harvey Nichols bag with a rustle of tissue paper. Sitting back in the chair, she laid it across her thighs, tucked her hair behind her ear again and looked directly at me.

'Valentin is offering you one point seven million dollars – if you are successful, of course.' She put up a hand. 'Non-negotiable. That is his offer, more than a million pounds. He wanted you to have a round figure in your own currency. You're a lucky man, Nick; he likes you.'

So far it sounded like a dream come true. That alone made me feel suspicious, but fuck it, we were just at the talking stage. 'Valentin is power-ful enough just to take what he wants by force. Why does he need me?'

She expertly removed the tags from the cardigan, dropping them back into the bag. 'This is a job that requires finesse, not muscle. As I said, no-one must know that Valentin has this material. In any event, he would prefer this was accom-plished outside his normal channels. It's a delicate matter, and it was obvious in Helsinki that you have a certain skill in this area.'

That was all very nice, but it was question time.

'What exactly is it I'm trying to lay my hands on?'

She put on the cardigan, her eyes not leaving mine, still measuring me up, I was sure of it. 'That, Nick, you don't need to know. We just need to be there before the Maliskia.'

I had to cut in. 'You mean *steal* it before the Maliskia?'

She smiled. 'Not "steal", copy. Download it. Your task is to get our man in and out without anyone knowing it has happened. Those are the terms, if you wish me to continue.'

'I get it,' I said. 'Maliskia must be Russian for "minor complications".'

She smiled again, her lips parting slightly to show perfect white teeth. 'The West call us the Russian Mafia, or simply ROC, as if we were one big group. We're not. We are many groups. The Maliskia are one faction, and Valentin's only real competitor. Whatever you may think about him, he is a man with vision. The Maliskia are not; they are just gangsters. It is very important that they never have access to this information. It would be a disaster for all of us, West as well as East. That is all I am prepared to say on the matter. Now, do you wish me to continue?'

Of course I did. It's always good to know something about who you're racing against. Not that she'd told me anything Val hadn't. I listened intently as she explained that the target house was still in the process of being prepared to use the 'competitive intelligence' Val wanted. It wouldn't be online for another six or seven days, and only then would I be able to get their man in to copy whatever it was. The problem was that once it was online the Maliskia were likely to trace its location very quickly.

'That's the race, Nick. I emphasize again, we must get it first and no-one must know that we've got it.'

It sounded OK to me. I'd spent years doing this kind of thing for far less than $1.7 million. Maybe this was my chance to sort out my life – and Kelly's – once and for all. One big fuck-off finger to everyone, especially Lynn. The meeting with him had really pissed me off. He knew the reason I'd been spared and he hadn't was that I was more useful to the Firm as an operator on the ground, whereas Lynn was just another pen-pusher. And ever since Washington, the Firm knew they had me by the bollocks, and I hated it when people had me by the bollocks.

'I'm concerned about going back to Finland,' I said. 'I don't think I'm very popular there.'

She smiled patiently. 'They aren't looking for you, Nick. As far as the Finnish police are concerned it was a purely Russian event. Valentin has already made a statement to that effect to the authorities. Don't worry, it's not an issue. If it was, Valentin wouldn't have risked offering you this task.'

She gave me time to consider what she had said as she picked fluff off her new cardigan. 'They weren't your friends, I hope?' She looked up. 'Perhaps the choice of team was not one of your best decisions?'

I smiled and shrugged. I had no defence.

'I thought not.' She twisted her forefinger and thumb to release the fluff onto the floor.

For the next few minutes I asked questions and she failed to give adequate answers. The objective, she said, was simple enough, but it didn't sound low risk to me. There were far too many questions left unanswered: How many people were in the house? What defences did they have? Where the fuck was it? I wasn't even allowed to know who I was taking in. I would find out only when I signed on the dotted line. On the other hand, $1.7 million versus £290 a day wasn't the kind of discrepancy I could afford to live with.

She held out a piece of folded paper. I walked the five paces and took it.

'These are the contact details of the man you will be taking with you, assuming you can persuade him. If you can, the fee goes up to two million dollars, to cover his cut. Now, one other minor complication: neither Valentin nor I can risk being associated with this task, so you will be the contact point. It's up to you to convince him to do it.'

I turned back to my helmet, reading an address and phone number in Notting Hill.

Liv said, 'His name is Tom Mancini. I believe you know him.'

I turned to face her. The name did ring a bell, but that didn't concern me. What did was that she knew about me, that she knew things about my past.

My concern must have been plain to see. She smiled again and shook her head very slightly. 'Naturally Valentin has gone to the trouble of learning a lot about you these last few days. Do you think he would employ someone for such a task otherwise?'

'What does he know?'

'Enough, I'm sure. Also enough about Tom. Valentin is sure you are both the right people for this. Now, Nick, as you will appreciate, there is little time. You need to be in Helsinki by Sunday. All I will require are your travel details. Everything else will be looked after.'

She gave me the contact details. They were very basic, if not a bit over the top, but easy to understand, which was good, because my head was spinning around with 1.7 million other things at the time.

She stood up. Our meeting was obviously over. 'Thank you for coming, Nick.'

I shook her hand, which felt warm and firm. I looked her in the eye, probably for a fraction of a second too long, then bent to pick up my helmet.

She followed me to the front door. As I reached for the handle she said, 'One last thing, Nick.'

I turned to face her; she was so close I could smell her perfume.

'Please do not turn your cell phone on until you are far away from here. Goodbye, Nick.'

I nodded and the door closed. I heard the locks and chain being put back into position.

Going down in the lift I resisted the urge to dance a jig or jump up and click my heels. I had never been one to embrace good fortune blindly – I'd never had that much of it to embrace, really – but Valentin's proposition sounded rather good, and what few doubts I had were dispelled by the

A2 envelope inside my jacket – as long as it didn't go bang on the way home.

The lift slowed and the doors opened on the ground floor. The concierge was frowning at me as he tried to work out why I'd been up there so long. I pulled the ski mask from under my helmet and nodded to him. 'She was wonderful,' I said. By the time the sliding doors opened and I was facing the security cameras, the mask was over my head again.

11

Walking up the driveway I started to pull out the chinstrap on both sides of the helmet with my thumbs and forefingers. I'd just got past the gate and onto the pavement when I heard the noise of an approaching car. As I played with the straps I looked up and to the left to check it was OK to cross.

A Peugeot 206 was screaming towards me at the speed of sound. It was dark maroon, and dirty from the last couple of weeks of slush and road salt. Behind the wheel was a white-knuckled woman in her early thirties, with a chin-length bob. I waited for her to pass, but as soon as she was about ten metres away she slowed to a more controlled pace.

I checked to my right. The Israeli security guy about seventy metres away wasn't fussed about it, nor the uniformed officer, who was looking very bored and cold on the opposite side of road.

I watched her get down to the barrier, indicating left, then join the stream of traffic. I pinged the number plate. It was an R reg, but there was something else that was much more interesting – no sticker on the back window, telling me how wonderful the dealership was. I suddenly felt I knew what she was about. Just as quickly, I threw the idea aside. Shit, I was getting as paranoid about surveillance as Val and Liv were about mobile phones.

Pulling my helmet on, I put the key into the Ducati's ignition and was just starting to put my gloves on when I pinged another vehicle about forty or fifty metres further up the road – a midnight-blue Golf GTi in a line of vehicles, two up, both sitting back in their seats with no conversation or movement. The side windows were steamed up but the windscreen had a direct view of the gates to the flats. I took a mental note of their reg. Not that it mattered. Well, that was what I tried to tell myself, anyway. P116 something, that was all I needed to know.

I decided that if I didn't stop being paranoid I'd end up in the clinic with Kelly and began to give myself a mental slapping. Then I remembered: paranoia keeps people like me alive.

I had one more look around, my helmet down as if I was checking over the machine. I couldn't see anything else that made me feel uneasy, so I straddled the bike and pushed it off its stand.

Turning the engine over, I pushed down the gear selector with my left foot, got into first, revved it up a little, turned left and made my way down towards the main gates. If the Golf was a trigger, the team that was about to follow me would have just received a point-by-point, stage-by-stage description of exactly what I was doing over the net. They needed a visual picture of what

I looked like, what the bike looked like, its registration and what I was doing. 'That's helmet on, that's gloves on . . . not aware . . . now complete (on the bike). Keys turned, engine on, stand by, stand by. Mobile towards Kensington exit . . . approaching. No intention (no indicators on to show which way the vehicle is going) . . .'

Everybody had to know exactly what I was doing and where I was to the nearest ten metres so they could put good covert surveillance on me. It's not like *Miami Vice*, where the good guys are sitting there with hand mikes at their mouths and a big antenna stuck on the roof. All the antennas on E4 vehicles are internal, and you never see any mikes. All you've got to do is hit a pressel, a little switch placed wherever you want. My preference had always been to have it fixed internally in the gear shift. That way you can just talk, making it look as if you're having fun, or having a row. It doesn't really matter as long as you're giving the details. Which, if I was getting triggered away from here, these two would now be doing.

What made me still feel edgy was that the two cars were ideal for city surveillance. Both were very common models in dark, nondescript colours and they were compact, so they could zip in and out of traffic and were easy to park up, or even abandon, if the target went foxtrot (on foot). Not all cars have the retailer's sticker in the back window; it's just that surveillance cars would tend not to have them because they could become a VDM (visual distinguishing mark).

If they were a surveillance team they would have to be E4, the government's surveillance group that keeps tabs on every-body from terrorists to dodgy politicians in the UK. No-one else would be able to stake out anything along this road. There was more security here than at Wormwood Scrubs. But why me? It didn't make sense. All I'd done was go into an apartment block.

I got to the barrier and the guard looked out of his shed and into the cold, trying to work out if I was that bloke who said he was the courier half an hour ago.

I turned right and merged with the traffic, which was still a nightmare. I headed the opposite way from the Peugeot, and tried to be as casual as possible. I wasn't going to scoot away like a scalded cat and show that I was aware, but check to see if I was a target.

It was starting to get dark now as I checked my mirror, expecting a surveillance bike to be up my arse in no time at all.

Either the Peugeot driver was a loony and couldn't drive the thing, or she was a new or very useless member of E4. Val would have fitted very nicely into their portfolio, as would quite a few of the residents in this area. I could just be a new face that needed a picture for the sur-veillance log and general build-up of intelligence on the building.

If I was right, she was trying to make a photo-or video-run on me and had fucked up the timing. It's very hard to make these runs as you only have one chance and the pressure is always on, but this one was especially incompetent.

The car could be rigged with both video and

stills cameras, hidden behind the radiator grille or part of the headlight set up, or little bits of the bodywork cut out in the rear so there was just enough light for the lens. The cameras are activated electronically by the driver as they pass the target. The camera takes the whole reel of film at a very fast shutter speed. That's why the timing's so important: hit the button too soon and the film could be finished by the time you're on top of the target, or the target might have walked behind a parked car as you begin your run, producing nothing more for your efforts than a nice picture of a Ford Fiesta, and a hard time from your bosses at the debriefing.

The video camera is a much safer option, but all it takes on the move is a few bumpy seconds of the target walking. This time around, all they would have was a visual of a biker with a ski mask on. That made me feel a lot better. I had no idea where those pictures would turn up, but I knew Lynn wouldn't be in the best of moods if they found their way to him.

I looked down at my mirror. Right on cue I saw the reflection of a bike's headlight. It wasn't necessarily a surveillance operator, but I had ways of checking.

I was riding like one of those forty-something sad bastards. The family are all grown up, the house is virtually paid for, so now they want the motorbike their mum would never let them have. It tends to be the biggest, fattest touring bike their platinum Amex card can handle, and they ride to and from work without ever getting within spitting distance of a speed limit. Except I wasn't scared to open up the throttle. I wanted to see if the single light behind me would do the same.

It didn't.

He shot past me at speed on an eight-year-old greasy Honda 500 with a battered old blue plastic box on the back held down by bungees. He was wearing well-used leathers and wellington boots, and turned to look at me through his visor, all beard and disgust. I knew just how he felt.

There were other bikes behind me, weaving in and out of the traffic. I moved into the middle of the road and twisted the throttle to jump a couple of cars, then swung back into the stream, crawling along behind a rusting Transit van. I let a few more bikes and mopeds pass me, and even a push-bike, and after a couple more sets of lights it was obvious I had another weekend rider behind me, about two cars back.

I turned left at the next junction, and he followed me.

Looking for a natural stop, I pulled in at a newsagent's. Resting the bike on its side stand, I went through the charade of undoing my helmet and gloves, as an M-reg Yamaha VFR came past, probably waffling on the net, telling everybody where I was. 'Stop! Stop! Stop! Charlie one (the bike) static on the left. At the newsagent's, Bravo one (me) still complete (on the bike).'

I took the helmet off but kept the mask on once he'd gone, then got off the bike and walked into the shop. I couldn't just ride straight off again, because that would show I was aware.

The young woman behind the counter looked

alarmed because I hadn't taken my mask off. There was a sign politely asking me to do just that. If she'd asked I would have told her no – in my tear-the-arse-out-of-it cockney accent – and to fuck off because I was cold. I didn't want the team to come and requisition the security video tape with yours truly on it. She wasn't going to argue; why should she care if I was there to steal the money? It could be dangerous for her.

I went back to the bike clutching a copy of the *Evening Standard*. If I was right, there'd probably be a bike at either end of the road by now. The net would be in chaos as cars hit their horns at the dickhead drivers who had suddenly decided to throw up (turn 180) in the traffic, all out of sight to me, trying to get in position for the stake-out.

A static short-term target is always a dangerous time for a surveillance team. Everyone has to get in position, so that next time the target goes mobile they've covered every possible option. That way, the target moves to the team, instead of the team crowding the target. But where was the trigger? I couldn't be bothered to look; I'd find out soon enough.

I pushed the Ducati down into first gear and carried on in the same direction I'd been heading before, towards South Kensington tube station, about half a mile away. Parking up in the bike row on the north side, I walked into the packed station, looking as though I was unbuckling my helmet, though I didn't. Instead, I walked straight through and crossed the road, still with my helmet on. The south side of the station had a large, busy and very confusing junction, with

135

a big triangular island housing a flower stall. Their propane gas heaters not only blasted out heat as I went by, but also a very comforting bright red light in the gathering darkness.

I moved with a crowd of pedestrians to the far side of the junction, past a row of shops along the Old Brompton Road.

About fifty metres further along, I went into the pub on the corner, took off my helmet and mask, and settled on a bar stool just back from the window.

The pub was packed with shoppers wanting to get out of the cold and office workers having a drink with friends.

I saw the Golf within minutes, but without the passenger. He or she was probably foxtrot, scurrying around in the tube station looking for me.

Then I saw the VFR and its black-leather-clad rider. They would have found the Ducati now, and the whole team – maybe four cars and two bikes – would be bomb-bursting about, fighting the traffic, calling in the areas they'd covered so their control could try and direct them elsewhere in some kind of coherent pattern. I almost felt sorry for them. They'd lost their target and they were in the shit. I'd been there a thousand times.

12

I sat and watched as the Golf, with a dark-haired male at the wheel, came back round the one-way circuit and pulled in to pick up a short, brown-haired woman. They were off again before her door was even closed. They'd done all they could; now it was a question of waiting to see if the target returned to his bike.

It wouldn't have been a big deal to them when I became temporarily unsighted. This always happens for short periods. But the fact that it had happened at the tube station was a big problem for them. Once they'd failed to pick me up again, their next move would be to stake out the bike. Then some of the team would have checked out known target locations. There were only two: one was the apartment block, and they would be checking with the porter which apartment I'd gone to, for sure. The other was the address where the bike was registered – a PO box just a few shops down from where it was parked. It was an office suppliers, and instead of having a box number I had a suite number, because I wanted to make it sound like an expensive apartment block. No doubt that was what the woman was checking out.

Nick Davidson was the registered owner of the bike and Suite 26 was where he supposedly lived. The real Davidson was going to be incredibly pissed off if he ever came back from Australia, because I'd taken over his life in the UK. He was going to get a hard time from customs, immigration and Special Branch if he ever stepped off a plane now that this had happened. He'd be listed.

It also meant that having Nick Davidson as my safety-blanket cover ID was now history, and that pissed me off. It had taken painstaking months to get a National Insurance number, passport, bank account, all the things that bring a character to life, and now I had to bin him. Worse still, I'd have to bin the bike. There'd certainly be a trigger on it for the next few hours, depending on how important they thought I was. An electronic device might even be attached to it. The only thing that cheered me up was the thought of what would happen to the person who'd eventually steal it after seeing it standing there for a few days. They wouldn't know what had hit them when the E4 team closed in.

I'd nursed a Coke while keeping dog through the large Victorian windows. My glass was nearly empty, and if I didn't want to look out of place I'd need to get a refill. Fighting my way to the bar, I ordered a pint of orange and lemonade, and went and sat in the corner. No need to look outside now. I knew a team were on me. I just had to sit it out, keeping my eyes on the doors in case they started to check out the pubs. In an hour's time it would be the end of the working day. I'd wait until then and lose myself in the darkness and commuter traffic.

As I sipped my drink, I thought about Tom Mancini. His name was certainly familiar. One of my first jobs as a K in '93 had been to drive him from North Yorkshire, where he worked, down to a Royal Navy facility near Gosport, Hampshire. I was told to grip him so much that he'd beg to be handed over to the Firm's people, who I was delivering him to. It didn't take that much, just a few slaps, a scary face and me telling him that if he fucked me about the only thing left ticking on his body would be his watch.

Once we'd got him down in one of the 'forts' built along the coast, he wasn't even given time to clean himself up before the Firm's interrogation team explained the facts of life.

A technician at Menwith Hill listening station, he'd been detected trying to obtain classified information. I wasn't allowed in on the interrogation, but I knew they told him Special Branch would be arresting him the next day for offences against the Official Secrets Act. They couldn't stop that. However, if he didn't get smart, that would be just the start of his problems.

He *would* shut up in court about what he'd really been tampering with. Whatever that was, it seemed the Firm didn't want anyone to know about it, even Special Branch, for the charge would be for a lesser offence. He *would* tell them who he was getting the information for, and, of course, he'd have no recollection of this 'meeting' ever taking place. He'd serve a short sentence and that would be the end of it. If he ever uttered a word to anyone about the deal, however, someone like me would come and pay him a visit.

Tom had been fucking about with the big boys. I knew that RAF Menwith Hill, on the moors near Harrogate in Yorkshire, was one of the largest intelligence-gathering stations on earth. Its massive golfball-shaped 'radomes' monitored Europe's and Russia's airwaves. It might be a British base, but in reality it was a little piece of the USA on British soil, run by their all-powerful NSA (National Security Agency). It was manned by about 1,400 American engineers, physicists, mathematicians, linguists and computer scientists. The staff was complemented by 300 Brits, which meant that there were as many people working at Menwith Hill as there were for the Firm.

Menwith Hill operated in close tandem with GCHQ (Government Communications Headquarters) at Cheltenham, gathering electronic information from as far afield as Eastern Russia. GCHQ did not, however, have automatic access to the intelligence gathered at Menwith Hill. All information went directly to the NSA at Fort Meade in Maryland. From there, information collected on terrorism that might, for example, affect the UK, was redistributed to the security service, Special Branch or Scotland Yard. Britain's contract with the US is that we can only buy American nuclear weapons on the condition that bases like Menwith are allowed to operate on British soil, and that the US has access to all

British intelligence operations. Sad but true: they *are* big brother. Britain is just one of the little runt siblings.

From what I could remember, Tom was all mouth and trousers. He came on like a Jack the Lad cockney trader, which was rather strange, because he came from Milton Keynes and was about as boring as his post code. By the end of the drive south, however, he had been like a small child, curled up on the back seat.

It worried me that Val knew I had met Tom, that he had access to details about a twenty-four-hour period of my life that I'd all but forgotten about, but I was in it for the money, nothing else, and so I cut that thought away, just in case it made me change my mind.

I finished my drink, picked up my helmet and headed for the toilets. Placing the helmet on the cistern in a cubicle, I sat down on the lid, unzipped my jacket and pulled out the envelope.

After an afternoon of people missing the pan and flicking dog ends in the urinals, the place stank. I inspected the nylon-fibre type, bubble-wrap envelope. Then, resting it on my knees and using both hands, I pressed down and started to run my palms over it, fingertips moving up and down the contours of the contents. I turned it over and checked the other side.

I couldn't feel any sort of wiring, or anything more solid than what I hoped were the notes, but then again, that didn't mean a thing. A wafer-thin battery from a Polaroid film tucked between the bundles would kick out enough power to initiate a letter bomb. It might be Val's special little way of saying thank you.

I picked it up and put the fold to my nose. If it was a device, and they'd used any exotic or older-style explosives, I might be able to smell them. Sometimes it's marzipan, sometimes linseed oil. I was expecting something more sophisticated, but these things have to be tested for.

All I could smell was the urinals. The bar noise rose and fell as the outer door opened and closed. I carried on inspecting the envelope.

I decided to go ahead and open it. It felt like money, weighed like money. If I was wrong, the whole pub would know about it soon and a pissed-off insurance company would be shelling out for a refit.

I opened the knife blade of my Leatherman and gently cut down the centre of the envelope, checking inside every centimetre or so for wires. It was looking promising. I started to see green US banknotes. Each bundle of used hundred-dollar bills that I carefully pulled out was banded and told me the bundle contained $10,000; there were ten of them. I was a very happy teddy indeed. Val had put his money where his mouth was. I didn't just respect him now, I liked the man. Not enough to introduce him to my sister yet, but then again, I didn't have a sister.

Someone else entered and tried the toilet door. I grunted, making it sound like I was having a big-boy dump. He checked the next one, and I heard the sound of jeans coming down and him getting on with the business.

I smiled as I started to stuff the money into my

leathers, feeling quite pleased with myself as my next-door neighbour farted for England.

Staying in the pub for another half-hour, drinking more orange and lemonade and reading the *Standard* for the third time, I wondered if the team had been called off yet. Nine out of ten times it boils down to money. They were probably hoping to earn a little Christmas bonus out of me. E4 operators get treated as badly as nurses; they work their bollocks off and are expected to carry on regardless.

By now they'd know the address was a PO box arrangement, and that would have set their alarm bells ringing. They'd probably plan to go into the office tomorrow, open up my box and see what was in there. They'd even put me on their own special mailing list; as post addressed to Suite 26 came through the Royal Mail's sorting system, it would be sidetracked for a while so that prying eyes could have a little look-see. All they would find was my Access bill. Well, Davidson's bill. Perhaps they'd be nice enough to pay it. I certainly wouldn't bother any more.

By tomorrow, if they decided to dig deeper, they'd also know that Mr Davidson had been to Norway recently, returning by the same route he'd travelled all those weeks ago. What would they make of that? I doubted that their conclusion would be a skiing trip after Davidson had been seen coming out of the targeted apartment block where one of the owners was a Russian who'd got hit just days ago, in a country a mere day trip away from where Davidson had disembarked. Fuck it, it was too late to worry about all that now.

As long as they didn't have a photograph of me, I'd be OK.

I sat there with another Coke and a packet of ready-salted. Thirty-five minutes on, I finally decided to make a move. The rush-hour traffic on all sides of the triangle was moving at about a metre a minute, a confusion of headlights and exhaust fumes. Every fourth car had its indicator lights flashing, thinking the other lane was quicker. The pedestrian traffic, too, was much heavier, and moved quicker than the vehicles. Everybody was huddled over, fighting the cold and just wanting to get home.

Leaving the helmet under the table, I exited through a door that led out onto a different road. The motorbike helmet was a VDM. So were my leathers, but I could hardly discard them. All I could do was cut down on the things that would trigger me.

The priority was to get a hotel for the night, before I contacted Tom in the morning. I also needed clothing: without a bike, there was no way I could walk around looking like Judge Dredd.

If you want late-night shops, it has to be the West End. I grabbed a taxi to Piccadilly Circus, and changed $1,000 at various bureaux de changes, throwing in a couple of hundred at a time.

The shopping frenzy was another short cab ride away, in Selfridges, where I bought clothes, washing and shaving kit, and a nice little holdall for my new-found wealth.

Then I booked myself into the Selfridges Hotel

using my Nick Stone credit card. To have used Davidson's would have invited a knock on the door within hours.

After a bath and a change of clothes – all very predictable, jeans, Timberland boots, blue sweatshirt and a dark-blue nylon puffer jacket – I called room service for a club sandwich and coffee.

13

Saturday, 11 December 1999

I woke up and looked at Baby G. It was just after eight, time for a quick couple of laps round the bath before getting dressed.

Looking like a kid in his shiny new Christmas Day clothes, I left the jacket with my leathers and went down to breakfast, taking the money bag with me. There was $25,000 left after a very grateful clinic had received not only what was owing to them, but also a wedge on account. It's strange how finance directors will come in of an evening to collect a payment, even brew coffee and pour it.

The newspapers were full of doom and gloom, and as I downed my full English, listening to the Americans or Israelis talking about the shopping they were going to be doing before they went back home, I felt good about fulfilling my responsibilities to Kelly, even though I knew I should be doing a lot more than just paying out money.

Back in my room, I settled on the bed and called the number on the paper that Liv had given me.

A young woman answered. Her 'hello' sounded as friendly as if I was the fourth wrong number in a row.

'Oh, hi. Is Tom there?'

'No, he's not,' she snapped. 'He'll be in Coins. Who are you?'

It sounded as if all was not well in the Mancini household.

'Just a friend. Coins, did you say?'

'Yes.'

'What is that, a shop or—'

'It's the caff, off Ledbury Road.'

I was obviously stupid for not knowing. 'Thanks a—'

The phone slammed down.

Talking Pages told me that Coins was in Talbot Road, Notting Hill. I put my squeakily clean blue duvet jacket on, picked up my swag bag and jumped into a taxi to join Tom for a brew, borrowing a read of the cabbie's *A to Z* on the way to work out exactly where he lived. The sky might be full of dark clouds, but I was still feeling good.

I didn't know Notting Hill at all, just that it had a carnival each year and that there'd been a bit of a frenzy about Julia Roberts coming to stay. During the film's hype, I'd read all this stuff in the papers about the village atmosphere and how wonderful it was to live there. I didn't see much evidence of a village, just expensive clothes shops, the sort with one pair of shoes in the window surrounded by spotlights, a few antique shops and an Oxfam store.

We turned corners and drove past stucco-fronted houses, mostly cut up into flats and very run down, with chunks of plaster falling off the brickwork.

The cab stopped at a crossroads and the dividing window opened. 'It's a one way, mate. I'll drop you off here if that's all right. It's just down there on the left.'

I could see the large awning sticking out over the pavement, with plastic side panels keeping the elements off the brave ones who wanted to sip their cappuccinos outside.

I paid him and took a walk. Coins turned out to be double-fronted, with a few empty tables outside. The large windows on each side of the door were steamed up from cooking and people. As I went in, it was obvious from the rough wooden floors and plain laminated plywood that the café was trying to look down-to-earth and no-nonsense. The kitchen was open plan and the smells were very tempting, even with half a kilo of bacon and egg still weighing me down.

There was no sign of Tom, so I took a seat in the far corner. There were magazines lying around on the table tops, designer pictures on the walls and fliers for a shitload of artistic events. The menu was a sheet of A4 paper in a plastic folder, offering everything from neat cholesterol to vegetarian sausages and salads. The prices certainly didn't match the decor; someone was making a down-to-earth, no-nonsense fortune.

The clientele seemed to average late twenties, early thirties, trying so hard to look individual that they all looked like clones. Everyone was in baggy cargo trousers and sleeveless puffers, and must have taken ages to get their hair looking like they'd just got out of bed. Quite a few were wearing thick-framed rectangular glasses, more to be seen in than to see through.

'Hi, sweetie, what can I get you?' An American female voice floated down to me as I studied the menu.

Glancing up, I asked for a latté and toast.

'Sure, sweetie.' She turned and presented the world's second most perfect rear, covered in tight black nylon flares. As she walked away I couldn't help staring at it, and was pleased to catch others doing the same. She must bring in a lot of custom; no wonder Tom came here.

There was nothing else to do but sit and listen to other people's conversations. It seemed that everybody was either *just about* to get a movie or *just about* to be in a play, but it *just* hadn't quite happened yet and everybody had a fantastic script that was being read by a marvellous man who used to share a flat with Antony Minghella. The only time people stopped talking was when their mobiles rang, only to talk even louder than before. 'Jambo, dude! How's it going, man?'

Rear of the Year came back. 'Here you are, sweetie.' She gave me my glass of latté, which burned my fingers as I watched her walk back to the kitchen.

I picked up a copy of the *Guardian*, which a girl sitting on the table next to mine handed over as she left. We smiled at each other, knowing we were both thinking the same thing about our American friend.

Looking down at the front page, I waited for my toast, and Tom.

Half an hour later the toast was finished and I was on my second latté. Clones came and went, air-kissing as they met and being very important with each other. Then, at last, Tom entered. At least I thought he was Tom. His greasy hair was now ponytailed just past his shoulders, making him look like a member of a Los Angeles garage band. His cheeks were more hamster-like than I remembered; maybe the extra pounds he'd put on had changed the contours of his face.

The clothes looked as if they'd come from the same shop as everyone else's here – canvas daps, brown cargos and a faded green sweatshirt with a T-shirt that had started off white, then gone a few rounds with something blue. He must have been freezing.

Settling his chubby arse on a tall stool along the breakfast bar facing the window, he pulled a magazine out from under his arm – some kind of palm-top computer and games monthly. At least he looked the part.

A small Puerto Rican-looking woman took his order. I decided to wait until he'd finished eating, then do my, 'Hello, Tom. Well well, fancy seeing you here' bit, but my plan got cut short as he suddenly stood up and turned towards the door. Along with a very pissed-off waitress, I watched him cross the road and run up a side street, losing him in the moisture on the windows and the shadow of the awning.

He must have seen me.

I got up and paid my money to Rear of the Year, getting an extra-big and friendly, 'Bye, sweetie,' when she saw the size of tip I'd left on my saucer.

Tom had run towards home, so I headed in the direction of All Saints Road, past reggae-music stores and plumbers' shops. His address was a flat in a yellow-painted, stucco-fronted building just off All Saints. Going by the array of bell-pushes at the front door, it looked like there were eight flats in the building, which meant each one must have been the size of a broom cupboard. Most houses in the street had been converted into flats and were painted black, green or yellow, with grimy windows covered by dirty old netting, which drooped in the middle. I bet this road wasn't in the film.

I went to press the button for his flat – number four – but the wiring hanging out of the intercom was rusted and frayed. Some names were slotted into the recesses on torn pieces of paper, but half of them, like flat four, didn't even have that.

As I rang the bell, I could hear the slight buzz of an electric current. Chances were the thing did work. I waited, stamping my feet and digging my hands into my jacket, but there was no answer. I wasn't expecting one from the intercom, but thought there might have been a shout, or a face at a window. Eventually a curtain twitched on the third floor.

I rang again. Nothing.

It was turning out to be more amusing than frustrating. Tom just wasn't cut out for this sort of thing. If you want to do a runner, you don't head straight home. E4 would have had no trouble pinning him down. I found myself smiling as I thought of him up there, hoping I'd just go away and that everything would be all right.

Looking up again at the dirty window, I made sure that whoever was watching would hear me clunking down the steps, really tearing the arse out of it so they'd know I'd given up.

Walking back the way I'd come, I hung around at the junction with All Saints, knowing that he'd leave sooner or later. It was the wrong thing to do, so he was bound to do it. He might have the skill to hack into and download whatever it was in this Finnish house, but when it came to common sense, he had trouble inserting the disk, let alone playing the game.

Loitering in the doorway of a derelict shop, I was facing a massive pop art mural that covered the whole gable end of a building. Reggae music blared from a shop as two teenagers came out and danced their way along the road, sharing a cigarette. My own breath was doing a good imitation of smoke in the cold air.

I wasn't too sure that I'd be able to see Tom if he tried to do a bunk over the back of the house, but he was on the third floor, so it would be quite difficult for him. From what I'd seen of him, even if he'd been on the ground floor it would have been a bit of a challenge.

I must have looked like the local loony to the kids, grinning broadly as I thought about him trying to get himself over a six-foot wall. I wouldn't want Mancini as a wing man.

Sure enough, twenty cold, boring minutes later, out he came. Still with no coat on, hands tucked under his armpits, not exactly running but moving quickly. I didn't even have to follow him. He was coming towards me, probably on his way to screw up even more by going straight back to the café.

I stepped out in front of him and his look of horror said it all.

'Hello, Tom.'

At first he didn't move, he just stood there, rooted to the spot, then he half turned away, screwing up his face and looking down at the pavement, like a dog that thinks it's going to get hit. 'Please don't hurt me. I didn't say nothing to no-one. On my life. Promise.'

'It's all right, Tom,' I said. 'I have nothing to do with those people now. That's not why I'm here.'

14

'Tell you what,' I said, 'let's go back to your flat, get the kettle on and have a chat.' I was trying to sound nice, but he knew I wasn't offering him a choice.

I put an arm around his shoulder and he stiffened. 'Come on, mate, let's have a brew and I'll tell you what this is all about. It's too cold out here.'

Being only about five foot five, he was easy to get my arm around. I could feel the softness of his body. He hadn't shaved for a few days and the result wasn't bristle but the sort of thing you could fill a duvet with.

I started to make small talk as we walked, trying to make him feel at ease. Also, this meeting needed to look a bit more normal to any third party nosing out of their window. 'How long have you been living round here then, Tom?'

He kept his head down, studying the paving slabs. As we passed the multicoloured houses, I noticed he was shaking.

'About a year, I suppose.'

'Hey, I called your flat earlier on, and a woman answered. She your girlfriend?'

'Janice? Yeah.' There was a gap of a second or two before he stopped walking and looked up at me. 'Look, mate, I have never, ever said nothing to no-one about any of that stuff. Not a word, I swear on my mother's life. I haven't even told J—'

'Tom, all I want to do is talk. I've got a proposition for you. Let's just sit down, have a brew and a chat.'

He nodded as I got us both walking again.

'I think you'll like what you hear. Come on, get the kettle on.'

We got to the house and walked up the four or five stone steps to the door. Tom fumbled for his key which was tied to an old bit of nylon string, his hand shaking as he tried to get it into the keyhole. He still thought he was going to get hammered. I decided to let him think it; maybe it would lighten him up when he finally realized I wasn't here to put him in hospital.

It was just as cold in the hallway as it was outside. The threadbare, dirty carpet matched the damp, peeling walls. An old-fashioned pram blocked the hall, and I could hear what sounded like its passenger screaming in the flat to the left, trying to make more noise than the TV talk show sharing his room. Breathing in to pass the pram and get to the stairs, I felt quite cheerful. Even my house smelled better than this.

Heat rises, but not in this place. Number four had its own small landing, with paint peeling off the door and banisters. He managed to get the key straight in the lock and the door opened into what I supposed was the living room. Dirty-grey

155

net curtains made the dirty-grey light from outside even gloomier.

MFI's flatpack division had done well out of Tom. Shiny waxed pine shone everywhere in the small room; even the two-seater settee had wooden arms. The rest of the place was in a bad way – more damp walls, worn carpet and cold. The fireplace was boarded up and a mains gas fire was stuck in its place, just gagging to be turned on. I could still see my breath.

A ten-year-old wood-veneer TV stood on a waxed pine stand in the corner, with a video machine underneath, the LEDs flashing all the zeroes, and a dozen or so videos stacked next to it on the floor. To the right of that was a Sony PlayStation, with a stack of games scattered around it, and the world's oldest PC. The buff-coloured plastic was dark and dirty and the vents at the back were so black it looked like it ran on diesel. Its keyboard was really worn; I could only just make out the instructions on the keys. Not the best of equipment for such a high tech-guy, but very good news for me. It would have been harder to get him to come along if he was making a fortune and living in a penthouse. The need for money makes people do things they would never normally dream of. I was a bit of an expert on that front.

We both stood there and I could feel his embarrassment. I broke the silence. 'Put the kettle on, mate, and I'll get the fire going, eh?'

He walked into a tiny kitchen off the main room and I heard coins getting fed into a meter and the knob turning to give us some gas. I heard the tap filling up the kettle as I threw my money on the settee and tried to light the fire, clicking the pilot light several times before the gas ignited with a *whoomph*.

Opposite was another door that was open about six inches. MFI hadn't got round to the bedroom. A mattress lay on the floor, the duvet pulled aside, dangerously close to a portable Calor-gas heater. The only other furniture seemed to be a digital alarm clock lying on the floor. It felt just like home.

There was no telling where the bathroom was, but I reckoned it would be on the other side of the kitchen somewhere; in fact, it was probably part of the kitchen. I stayed down with the fire for a while to warm up.

'So what are you doing with yourself now, Tom? Still in the computer business?'

At last there was a spark of life from him. He hadn't been filled in, and I was taking an interest in his subject. He stuck his chubby head into the living room; I'd forgotten how it jutted backwards and forwards like a cockerel's when he larged it.

'Yeah, I've got a few irons in the fire, know what I mean? Games, that's where the money is, mate. I've got a few movers and shakers in the business gagging for my ideas. Know what I mean, gagging.'

I was still kneeling down, rubbing my hands by the flames. 'That's really good to hear, Tom.'

'Yeah, things are sweet. This is just temporary, while I decide who to sell my idea to. Then it's gravy time. Look for a house to buy – cash, of course – then start my own show. Know what I mean?'

I nodded, knowing exactly what he meant. He had no money, no job and was still full of bullshit. He was going to like what I was about to tell him.

His head disappeared back into the kitchen and things started to be washed up. Standing up to go over to the settee, I saw a pile of plain white cards on the mantelpiece. The top two had lipstick kisses and a handwritten message on: 'I hope you like my dirty panties. Love, Juicy Lucy xx'. I picked one up. At least the lipstick was genuine.

I raised my voice as I walked over to the settee. 'How long have you been with Janice?'

'She sort of moved in a couple of months ago.'

'What does she do?'

'Just part-time at Tesco's; bits and pieces, you know.' He stuck his head around the door again. 'Sugar?'

'No, just some milk will be fine.'

He came in with two mugs and put them on the not-so-new carpet. Sitting on the floor by the fire, facing towards me on the settee, he passed mine over. His, I noticed, was without milk.

I saw him clock the open bedroom door and worry whether I'd seen what lay beyond it. We both picked up our tea at the same time.

'Don't worry about it, mate. I spent my child-hood living in places like this. Maybe I can help you find somewhere better. Until the game thing kicks in.'

He tried to sip his tea as his eyes flicked towards the Mickey Mouse alarm on top of the fire.

Time to get down to business. 'By the looks of it, things ain't that good, are they? You on the social?'

Jack the Lad came back with a grin. 'Yeah, who ain't? I mean, free money, madness not to. Am I right or what?'

He went back to concentrating on his tea.

'Tom, I think I can help. I've been offered a job that would earn you enough to buy a flat and pay any debts outright.'

He didn't trust me: a fair one, it wasn't as if he knew me as Mr Nice Guy. His eyes were still checking Mickey Mouse now and again.

'How much?' He tried to make it sound casual, but didn't quite pull it off.

I avoided burning my lips on my tea and took a sip. It was horrible. It should have been in a scent bottle, not a mug. 'I don't exactly know yet, but I reckon your share would be at least one hundred and thirty thousand – cash. That's the minimum. All I need is a week of your time; two weeks at the most.'

I didn't have a clue how long the job was going to take, but once I got him to Finland, what could he do if it took longer? Getting him there was priority number one at the moment.

'Is it legal? I ain't doing anything dodgy, mate. I don't want any more trouble. I'm not getting banged up again, know what I mean?'

My brew went back on the carpet. It was shit anyway. 'Look, first of all, my name is Nick. And no, it's not illegal. I don't want to go to prison, either. It's just that I've been given this opportunity and I need someone brilliant with computers. I thought of you. Why not? I'd rather you had the money than anyone else. You even get a free trip to Finland out of it.'

'Finland?' Jack the Lad was returning once again, head jutting. 'Hey, everyone is online up there. It's the cold, know what I mean, Nick. Too cold, like. Nothing else to do.' He laughed.

I laughed along with him as his eyes moved over to Mickey again. 'Tom, do you need to be somewhere else?'

'Nah, you're all right, it's just that Janice is home soon and the fact is, well, she don't know nothing – you know, my old work, getting banged up, all that stuff. I haven't really got round to telling her. I'm just a bit worried that, you know, if she came in and you said something . . .'

'Hey, no problems. I'll keep quiet. Tell you what, when she comes in I'll just say that I've got a small computer firm and I'm offering you a couple of weeks' work up in Scotland, testing systems. How's that sound?'

'Nice one, but what's the form, you know, what are you after in Finland?'

'It's very, very simple. All we need is to access a system and then download some stuff. Until we get there I don't know what, how and when.'

He immediately looked worried. I had to get in there straight away. I needed some lies. 'It's not what you're thinking. It is legitimate. All we're going to do is find out about some new photo-copier technology. And we've got to do it in a totally legal way, otherwise the money men don't want to know.' I couldn't think of anything more boring and non-threatening than a photocopier and I waited for a bolt of something to come at me through the window.

God must have been asleep or had all his lightning still in the freezer. I carried on before Tom had a chance to think about it and ask questions.

'I can get us into the place,' I went on, 'but I need someone who knows what the fuck they're looking at once we're in front of one of those things.' I pointed at the heap of crap in the corner that was trying to look like a computer. He didn't say anything but looked at his greasy monitor screen, maybe thinking of the boiled-sweet-coloured Power Mac and matching iMac laptop he could buy with his cut.

'Everything will be laid on when we get there, Tom. They know where the place is, all you've got to do is access and download it. Not steal, mind, just copy. Easy money.'

I braced myself in case God had stirred in time to hear that last bit. Tom fidgeted on the carpet, so I kept going for it before God woke up or Janice got home. 'You know as much as me now, mate. I am going half on the money with you. One hundred and thirty grand, maybe more if we get the job done quickly. That's a shitload of cash, Tom.' I paused to let him visualize a wheelbarrow full of tenners.

Fifteen seconds was enough. 'Chance of a life-time, Tom.' I sounded like a double-glazing salesman. 'If you don't take it, someone else will.'

I settled back on the settee to signal that the pitch was over. The next stage would be a shedful of intimidation to make him come with me if the soft-soaping failed.

'You absolutely sure it's safe, Nick? I mean, banged up. I don't want that again. Things are sweet here, know what I mean? I'm gonna be earning big bucks soon.'

Explaining to him that I knew he was bull-shitting would have to wait until I read him his horoscope. 'Look, mate, even if it was illegal, there's no such thing as prison when it comes to these jobs. Think about it, if they discover that you've found out about their poxy photocopier, are they really going to go to the police? Are they fuck. Think about the shareholders, think about the bad publicity. It doesn't work like that, mate. Trust me. What happened to you before was different. That was government business.' I couldn't help my curiosity. 'By the way, what was it they caught you doing up at Menwith?'

He started to get edgy. 'No, mate, I ain't saying nothing. I've done my time and don't say nothing to nobody. I never want to go back.' He was start-ing to sound like an old record.

He was in a state. I knew he wanted the money, but he was struggling to make a decision. Time for a new tack. 'I tell you what, why don't you just come with me anyway, have a look, and if you don't like it, you can come back. I'm not try-ing to fuck up your life, mate. I'm just trying to do us both a favour.'

He was shifting from one buttock to another. 'I dunno. Janice wouldn't like it.'

I moved forward once again on the settee so my arse was on the edge, and went conspiratorial.

'Janice doesn't need to know. Just say you're going to Scotland. Easy.' The hiss of the gas fire could be heard clearly above my whisper. I decided I'd give him a bit more incentive. 'Where's your toilet, Tom?'

'Through the kitchen; you'll see the door.'

I stood up and took my bag with me. 'Nothing personal,' I said. 'Work stuff, you know.'

He nodded and I didn't really know if he understood or not, because I didn't.

I went into the toilet. I'd been right, the bathroom was part of the kitchen, partitioned off by a bit of plasterboard so the landlord could claim more rooms and charge the DHSS a fortune for people to live here. I sat on the pan and counted out six grand from the dollars. I was about to shove it in my pocket when I decided to calm down a bit and put two grand back in the bag. Pulling the flush, I came out talking.

'All I know is that it's an easy job. But I need you, Tom, and if you're honest, you need the money as much as I do. Look, this is what I want to do for you.'

Reaching into my pocket, I pulled out the four grand, making sure I rolled it with my other hand to make it look and sound extra attractive.

He tried hard to stop himself looking at it. Even this amount could probably change his life.

'This is how I'm getting paid, US dollars. Here's four grand. Take it; it's a gift. Pay your bills, whatever you want. What more can I say? I'm going to go and do the job anyway. If you're coming with me, though, I need to know today. I can't fuck about.'

163

If he didn't give me a yes by this evening it would be horoscope time. He'd still get paid; he just wouldn't enjoy the work so much.

He fingered the money and had to split it in half to get it into his jean pockets. He tried to put a serious business expression on his face. It wasn't working. 'Nice one. Thanks, Nick, thanks a lot.'

Whatever happened he could have the money. It made me feel good, and with everything else going down the tubes in my life, I needed that. But I needed to make sure he didn't fuck up with it and let it be traced back to me. 'Don't go to the bank to change it or make a deposit, they'll think you're a drug dealer. Especially with an address round here.'

His smile broadened.

'Take it to a few bureaux de change. The rates will be shit, but there you go. Have a nice day out. Hire a taxi; you can afford it. Just don't change any more than three hundred dollars at a time. Oh, and for fuck's sake buy yourself a warm coat.'

He looked up and the grin turned into a laugh as he did his cockerel impression. It stopped just as quickly at the sound of a key going into the door lock.

'Shit, it's Janice. Don't say jack. Promise me, Nick.'

He stood up and made sure his sweatshirt was covering the two bulges in his cargos. I joined him and we waited in front of the fire as if the Queen was about to visit.

She opened the door, felt the heat and looked

straight at Tom, ignoring me completely. 'Have you picked up the laundry?' Heading towards the kitchen, she started throwing off her brown greatcoat.

Tom grimaced an apology at me as he replied, 'Oh, er nah, it wasn't ready, the driers were broken. I'm going to pick it up in a minute. This is Nick. He's the one that called, you know, this morning.'

She threw her coat onto the arm of the settee, looking at me. I gave a smile and said, 'Hello, nice to meet you.'

'Hello,' she grunted, 'you found him then?' and disappeared into the kitchen.

Janice was mid-twenties, not unattractive, not attractive, just sort of ordinary. Her hair was pulled back in a ponytail, slightly longer than Tom's. It wasn't exactly greasy, but had that not-washed-today look. She was also wearing just a bit too much make-up, and there was a line around her chin where it stopped.

I sat back down, but Tom stayed standing by the fire, not really knowing what to say to me about his obnoxious girfriend. In the kitchen, cupboard doors were banged as she made her presence felt.

She came back into the living room with a bar of Fruit & Nut and a can of Coke. Pushing the coat onto the floor she plonked herself on the settee next to me, pulled the foil off the chocolate, opened the can and started attacking both. The noise of her drinking would have made a thirsty bricklayer proud. Between gulps she pointed at the mantelpiece. 'Tom, pass me the cards.'

He did as he was told. We both watched as she pulled out a lipstick from her coat pocket and threw it on her lips. Then, while she slurped and munched, she kissed the remaining blank cards.

She looked up, and stared at me for a few moments, then turned to Tom. 'Pass me the rest.'

He picked up an A4 envelope near the fire and passed it over, red with embarrassment.

Pouring the white cards onto the floor she started to reapply the red stuff and kiss away. The signing was obviously done later, during a gentler moment.

We weren't going to get any more talking done. It was time for me to leave.

'Thanks for the tea, Tom, I think I'll be off now. Nice to meet you, Janice.'

She nodded, not bothering to look up.

Tom looked nervously at me, then at Janice's head. As I got to my feet and picked up the bag, he blurted, 'Tell you what, I'll walk down with you, I've got to collect the laundry anyway.'

We didn't speak as we walked down the stairs. I knew what I wanted to say, but what was the point? Someone calling your girlfriend an obnoxious dog wouldn't exactly induce you to go away with him.

As we walked back towards All Saints Road, he stammered, 'It's not her, you know, Juicy Lucy. She gets a tenner for every two hundred. This week it's Lucy, I think next week it's Gina again. I help her out.' He rubbed his chin. 'I have to shave though, otherwise I leave stubble marks in the lipstick. 'We have piles of dirty knickers in the bedroom. A bloke drops them off on a Thursday.'

I couldn't help but laugh at the picture of him in front of the fire, kissing cards and packing knickers for the country's crotch sniffers.

His head went back into cockerel mode. 'Yeah, well, like I said, it's only until the money comes in. They're really keen – Activision, the *Tomb Raider* lot, all the big boys – I'm just about to hit it big time, know what I mean?'

'Yes I do, Tom.' I knew exactly.

I gave it one more try once we'd turned the corner into All Saints and Janice couldn't see us if she looked out. I stopped and faced him outside a window full of taps, waste pipes and assorted plumber's shit.

'Tom, think about this seriously. I'm not going to do anything that's wriggly. I'm too old for that sort of stuff. All I want to do is make some money, the same as you. I need you with me, but I must know by tonight if you're up for it.'

He was looking at the pavement, shoulders slumped. 'Yeah. But you know . . .' The cold was starting to get to him. I didn't know whether he didn't have a coat because they hadn't kissed enough cards or if he was just too stupid to remember to put one on.

We got to Westbourne Park Road, a main drag. I wanted a taxi so I stood on the corner. He stood next to me, shifting from one foot to the other. I put a hand on his shoulder. 'Listen, mate, go and change some money and think about it, and we'll meet up tonight, all right?'

I started looking for cabs as he nodded at the

pavement again. 'I'll call you about sevenish and we'll have a drink, OK?'

A yellow light appeared in the gloom and I stuck out my hand. The cab stopped and the diesel engine chugged away, but not as fast as the meter.

Tom was still stooped, hands dug deep in his pockets, shivering. I talked to the top of his head. 'Tom, this is a once-in-a-lifetime chance. Think hard about it.'

The top of his head moved in what I took to be another nod.

I couldn't stand his shivering any more and unzipped my jacket. 'For fuck's sake, put this thing on, will you?' He protested feebly, then returned my grin as he took the coat. At least I could see his face now.

'Once-in-a-lifetime, mate.' I got into the taxi, asked for Marble Arch and turned to close the door and pull down the window.

Tom was just finishing zipping up. 'Hey, Nick, bollocks to it. Why not, I'm up for it.' The cockerel had returned.

I didn't want to show how pleased I was. 'That's good. I'll call you tonight with the details. We have to leave tomorrow. Is that OK? You got a passport?'

'No probs.'

'Excellent. Remember,' I pointed to his cargos, 'there's plenty more where that came from. One week, maybe two, who knows?'

I put my thumb to my ear and little finger to my mouth to mime a call. 'Tonight at seven.'

He did the same. 'Nice one.'

'Tom, one last thing. You have a credit card?'

'Er, yeah. Why's that?'

'I haven't got mine. You might have to pay for the tickets, but don't worry, I'll give you the cash before we go.'

I didn't give him time to think too much about that one. As the taxi pulled away I was feeling pretty pleased with myself, and I had a sneaking suspicion that Tom wouldn't be sharing his new-found wealth with Janice. I knew I wouldn't if I was him.

After giving the cab driver a new drop-off point, I bought myself a blue ski jacket in Oxford Street, and went to a chemist's for some bits and pieces I'd need for the DLB (dead letter box), so I could leave our details with Liv. Before E4 pinged me at the flat, I'd thought Liv wanting to use a DLB just to hand over some flight details was a bit paranoid. But now I knew it was essential. If E4 were on to her, I didn't want any more contact with her in the UK. The last thing I needed was for Lynn to have a picture of that on his desk. The shit would be so high I'd never be able to dig myself out.

I booked the flights from a phone box, and they held them in Tom's name. I'd get him to pay for them with his credit card at the airport tomorrow; now that Davidson was history, I had no choice. No-one needed to know that Nick Stone was leaving the country. I wondered if Tom was still being monitored, now that he was a known sub-versive, but decided I'd have to take that risk. There wasn't time to do anything about it.

169

With my new coat to keep me warm I decided I'd walk it to the DLB she'd given me. It wasn't that far away.

Fighting my way through the Saturday shopping frenzy I eventually made the 200 metres or so to Oxford Circus. The BBC studios in Portland Place were in front of me on the right. I stayed on the opposite pavement and headed for the Langham Hilton.

About fifty metres short of the hotel I walked under some scaffolding. Beneath it were two old-style red telephone boxes. In the windows of each were maybe twenty calling cards, held in position by lumps of Blu-Tack. The council would be around at some point today to clean them out, but they'd be restocked an hour later.

I went into the left-hand box and saw Susie Gee's card three quarters of the way up, facing Oxford Circus. She looked very sultry, on all fours and kissing the air. At the same time as I peeled her off the glass I got out a large black marker pen and scored a line down the window.

Folding Susie into my pocket I moved on towards the hotel. It was a bit premature to leave the DLB loaded sign, but I wasn't expecting any problems.

With my bag in hand I walked through the hotel's revolving doors, which had been started for me by a guy dressed in a green three-quarter length tunic and something that looked like a cross between a turban and a beret on his head. He looked a right nugget.

The interior of the Langham was very plush, and very full of businessmen and wealthy looking tourists. It was Indian themed, with the Chukka Bar to my left as I walked into the marble reception area.

Liv's instructions were perfect. To the right and up a few steps was the reception desk, and ahead of me was a restaurant-cum-tea room. My destination, however, was the basement.

Down below was every bit as plush as above. Air-conditioned and soft-carpeted, it housed the conference rooms and business centre. Standing on an easel outside the George Room, a black felt board with white press-on letters announced, 'Management 2000 welcomes our conference guests.' Passing it and two wall phones that I would be coming back to, I headed for the toilets.

Opposite the toilet doors were more phones, a cloakroom and a table rigged up with tea, coffee and biscuits. Sitting ready to serve were a black guy and a white woman talking in that shifty tone that you just know means they're honking about the management. As soon as they saw me, they gave me their corporate smiles; I smiled back and headed for the gents.

Sitting down in one of the cubicles, I took out a little plastic pill box from my Boots bag, the sort that people use to hold their day's supply of vitamins, along with a pack of adhesive-backed Velcro patches. I stuck both a female and a male patch onto the pill box just in case she'd fucked up on what side to use; it would be embarrassing if it didn't stick.

Inside the pill box went a small scrap of paper with my message: 'Arriving 1515 12th.' That was all that she needed to know.

Putting the Boots bag back in my pocket and checking that the two little squares of Velcro were secure, I came out of the toilet, smiled again at the two people in the cloakroom, turned right and went back to the first two telephones I'd passed.

They were positioned quite low down the wall, for the convenience of users in wheelchairs. I put the bag between my legs and shuffled a chair up closer to the phone. Liv had chosen well: not too busy, no video cameras about and a reason to be there.

As I sat down, I got out a pound coin and Susie's card, picked up the phone and dialled, wondering if Janice and Tom had done any lipstick cards for her lately. I wanted the display to show money being used up; otherwise it would look suspicious if anyone passed and saw that I'd been there a few minutes and was only pretending to make a call. It was a small detail, but they count.

I used my right hand to keep the phone to my ear, waiting for Susie, and felt under the wooden veneer shelf below it with my left. In the far corner, there should be a large patch of Velcro that Liv had put there.

As I fumbled about, the doors to the George Room opened behind me and out surged a stream of Management 2000 delegates.

As I listened to the ringing tone, I watched the herd move to their grazing area by the cloakroom. A young woman in her twenties sat on the chair next to me and put a coin in the box.

An aggressive Chinese woman answered me. 'Hello?'

I could hear my fellow caller tap out her number as I replied.

'Susie?'

'No, you wait.'

I waited. The woman next to me started talking about her child, who needed picking up from nursery as she was going to be late. The person at the other end was obviously annoyed. 'That's not fair, Mum, it's not always the same excuse and yes, of course she remembers what her own mother looks like. Kirk is home early tonight. He'll pick her up.'

A man came from behind and placed his hand on her shoulder. She kissed it. His Management 2000 badge said David. Not quite the conference making her late home, then.

The noise level doubled as people talked management over coffee.

I found what I was looking for as I heard foot-steps approaching the receiver at the other end: it was female Velcro, the soft bit, just as Liv had said.

A very husky, middle-aged voice picked up the phone. 'Hello, can I help you, my love? Would you like me to run through the services?'

I ummed and aahed as the maid named the tariff for spending half an hour in France, Greece and various other countries of the world with Susie. To spin out the call I asked where Susie was based, and then for directions to the address near Paddington.

'That's great,' I said. 'I'll think about it.'

I put the phone down, picked up the bag, moved the chair back, stood up and headed back the way I'd come, leaving the woman telling her mother it absolutely would be the last time she'd have to do this.

I turned before going through the doors, checked the box couldn't be seen from that level and went upstairs. Gunga Din did his trick with the revolving doors and I was back on the street. Turning right, I headed back the way I'd come. Last light was soon; by four thirty it would be dark.

All I had to do now was call Tom at seven and tell him the timings for tomorrow morning's flight, then go and dump my leathers in a bin and my weapon in London's biggest armoury, the River Thames.

15

Sunday, 12 December 1999

Tom stood in a different queue for immigration. I'd told him in the nicest way that he must keep away from me until we were in the arrivals lounge – security and all that. He talked too much and too loudly to sit next to in an aircraft. We'd even checked in separately. He'd agreed with his usual, 'No drama, mate. Gotcha.'

On the tube to Heathrow, he'd told me that Janice was fine about him going away. 'I told her I had some work with my old mate Nick in Scotland,' he said. 'I told her straight.'

That version was about as straight as Elton John. Janice was probably severely pissed off that he was enjoying himself north of the border for two weeks while she slaved away kissing cards for Lucy. I wondered if he'd said anything to her about the money, but didn't ask. I didn't want him sounding off about his plans for world domination in the world of IT.

At least he hadn't wanted to drown himself in free alcohol on the way over. It seemed he didn't drink – a by-product, maybe, of serving a gaol sentence. Just as well, because there would be none of that until we were back in the UK.

He'd made an effort and smartened himself up a bit for the journey, which was good. I wanted him to resemble an average citizen, not look like food for customs to pull to one side for a slow once-over. He was still wearing my jacket, but had swapped the flared jeans for a new, normal pair, and he was also wearing a new red sweat-shirt. However, he still had the same canvas daps on, and though he'd finished off by washing and combing his hair, he hadn't shaved.

I watched him slap his jacket as if he was doing some sort of dance. This was the third time since leaving London that I'd seen him think he'd mis-laid his passport.

We got through immigration and customs and there was no need to wait for suitcases. I'd told him that all he needed was a bit of soap and a toothbrush, and he could wash his underwear in the bath with him at night.

The sliding doors opened to admit us separately into the arrivals hall. Tom didn't know it, but no-one would be there to meet us yet. We weren't on the flight that arrived at 15.15, as I'd told Liv; we were on the 13.45. I always liked to be early in order to watch who might be waiting for me. Walking into an arrivals lounge to meet people I didn't know gave me the same feeling as knocking on a strange door, not knowing who or what was on the other side.

We met up in the hall. Tom seemed to be feeling very laddish today, eyeing the women as they moved around the terminal.

'What now, mate? Where we going?'

'We're a bit early for our pick-up. Let's get a brew.'

We followed the signs to the coffee shop. The glass-and-steel terminal building wasn't packed, but busy enough for a Sunday, more with tourists than business traffic. I could see a dull, grey sky beyond the glass walls, with snow piled up at the roadside and ice hanging from parked vehicles.

As we neared the café, Tom bouncing along at my shoulder like some younger brother, we passed two tall, blonde and beautiful women at a phone booth. 'Cor, check out the arse on that. I love these Nordic birds.'

The two of them caught his drift and laughed to each other as they looked at us. I just walked on, embarrassed. They would have had him for breakfast.

Tom seemed not to notice. 'Hey, Nick, do you know there's more people up here who are on the Internet and have mobiles than anywhere else. You know, per capita.'

'That's interesting, Tom.' For once he had said something that was.

He liked that. 'That's right, mate. Must be all that darkness up here. Fuck all else to do, I s'pose.'

I looked at him and smiled, even though the joke had been better first time round.

His face beamed and his hamster cheeks nearly covered his eyes. 'These people are at the cutting edge, know what I mean?' He caught up the step that separated us and whispered in my ear, his head jutting in time. 'That's why the photocopier know-how is here. I'm right, aren't I?'

I was bored but managed a reply. 'It's probably the long hours of darkness. There's nothing else to do but Xerox, I suppose. Coffee, Tom?'

'Nah, tea. Herbal or fruit if they have it.'

We were soon at a table, me with coffee, Tom with a pot of hot water and an apple-flavoured tea bag wrapped in foil. Opposite was a bank of screens, obviously Internet stations. It was only a matter of time before Tom saw them, too, and I would be sitting alone, which wouldn't be a bad thing.

His eyes lit up and sure enough he was getting to his feet. 'I'm gonna have to go and check that out. You coming?'

He did, taking his tea with him. I didn't.

He was back very quickly, before I'd even tasted my coffee. 'You haven't got any coins, have you, mate? I've got no money, well, Finnish money. Only dollars, know what I mean?'

I hoiked out the change from the drinks as he grinned at his own joke.

I decided to have a walk around to see if I could spot anything threatening. I'd shaken off E4, but Val obviously had enemies, and while I was working for him that made them my enemies, too.

My documents always stayed with me, but there was something else I wanted from my holdall before I wandered off. Digging around for the leather zip-up organizer, I dropped both our bags at Tom's feet and headed for the departures lounge upstairs. There was nothing out of the ordinary, nobody waffling into their lapels or facing into the crowd while pretending to read a newspaper.

I took a walk outside, but not for long, the cold biting into my face and hands. I hadn't seen anything that looked as if it was bad and intended for me.

Back inside Arrivals and in the warm, there were a couple of boys in suits with A4 clear plastic folders showing the names of people they were there to collect.

Tom was still in Internet heaven. 'Look at this, Nick. Fucking cool or what? Look, virtual Helsinki.'

I was looking at a screen that displayed everything you needed to know about Helsinki, from street maps to images of hotels and booking facilities for travel or theatre tickets. There was even a route plan where you actually walked down a road as if you were in a game. Still leaving the bags with him, I went and got myself another coffee, sat at the same table and watched and waited, thinking how lucky I'd been not to have had a kid brother that I'd had to drag around with me when I was growing up.

Fifteen minutes later he was back with the bags. He must have run out of money. 'I just emailed Janice and told her I definitely can't get in touch for a while – up in the hills testing kit and all that.'

I put the organizer back in my bag and finished my brew. 'We might as well make a move. They should be here by now.'

Our lift was easy to spot, smartly dressed in a grey suit and overcoat, with spiky light-brown hair and a red complexion, presenting himself to the people pushing their trolleys through the automatic doors of the customs hall. He was holding up an A4 card with felt-tipped lettering on: 'Nick and another.'

We went up and introduced ourselves. As we shook hands he virtually stood to attention and clicked his heels together, then he offered to take both our bags. Tom refused after I did.

The short-term car park was opposite Arrivals. An aircraft roared overhead as we approached a silver Merc. Tom was impressed. 'Nice one.'

We put the bags into the boot and got in the back. Spike turned the engine on and the radio blared. I assumed the two presenters were gobbing off in Finnish, but Tom looked at me. 'They're speaking Latin. They're mad for it up here, mate. Dunno why, just are.'

Spike turned it off.

I said, 'How come you know so much about Finland?'

The Merc started moving.

'Got on the net last night and had a look, didn't I?'

'Are you going to bore for England the whole week?'

He looked at me, not knowing if it was an insult, then made up his mind and smiled. 'Nah, mate, just thought you'd like to know.'

He sat back into his seat. He was wrong, I wasn't joking.

We followed the road signs. They were in Swedish as well as Finnish, the Swedes having ruled here in the past as well as the Russians. The motorway tarmac was immaculately clear of snow and ice.

The airport was quite close to Helsinki and we were soon on the city ring road. On both sides of us were low-level industrial units and large piles of cleared snow. I had to smile as I thought of the UK, where a couple of snowflakes bring the entire nation to a halt; here they had snow for months and the country didn't miss a beat.

I saw a sign that said, 'St Petersburg 381km'. Within three or four hours we could be out of one of the wealthiest and most advanced places on earth and entering a city of chaos and anarchy. But I didn't have to worry; we followed the slip road and moved onto another motorway, the E75, and started to head away from the built-up area, such as it was.

The small floating ball compass that was stuck on the dash told me we were generally heading north. Every vehicle on the motorway had its lights on; it was the law.

We cruised comfortably along the motorway, passing through pine forests, snow and impressive cuts into massive granite outcrops. I looked over at Tom, who was resting his head on the seat, his eyes closed and his Walkman earphones in. I decided to take his cue and sit back and relax, though I kept my eyes on the road signs. Lahti and Mikkeli seemed to be likely targets, and after just under an hour it was quite clear where we were heading. We took the Lahti exit.

The town was dominated by two very tall Eiffel Tower-like structures, both painted red and white, their spires obscured by the cloud cover, and with aircraft warning lights flashing away on

181

all sides. The place was heaving with both traffic and people. It was a winter sports town; a ski jump towered over the houses, and as we started to rumble down the cobblestones of the main shopping area, I saw that even pensioners were using cross-country poles instead of walking sticks.

The inhabitants of Lahti were obviously in love with concrete and steel. Instead of traditional wooden dwellings with maybe a reindeer or two parked up outside, they went for new model Saabs, 4x4s and a blaze of Christmas decorations. We turned left by the town square and passed a brightly lit market, steam rising above the mass of canvas and nylon stall covers. Kitted out to stand in the cold all day, the traders looked more like astronauts.

We slowed down almost immediately at a sign telling us we were at the Alexi Hotel. Cutting left, over the pavement, we stopped by a garage door that instantly started to open. A group of mothers with tricycle buggies walked around the back of the Merc before bumping back up onto the walkway.

We drove quite fast down a steep concrete ramp into a large, badly lit underground parking area. Puddles of water covered the floor where snow and ice had melted off the vehicles already here, and just about every car had skis strapped to its roof rack.

We cruised about looking for a space. Tom was sitting up now, earphones out and eyes wide. 'It's like one of them spy films, Nick, know what I mean?' His tone changed as he thought about what he'd just said. 'It's all right, innit? I mean, you know what's happening, don't yer?'

I nodded, not really feeling too sure.

Nosey parking in a vacant space, Spike turned off the engine and swivelled round in his seat. 'Please, your phones, your pagers and your email devices,' he said in heavily accented English. 'You must leave them here. No worry, you get them back.' He smiled, showing a not-so-good set of teeth.

I explained that, as instructed, neither of us had brought any.

He smiled again. 'Good. Thank you, thank you.'

The boot clicked open behind us as Spike pulled on the lever next to his seat. I got out of the car, and Tom followed just as a black 4x4 Mercedes, the old square shape, moved slowly towards us. The glare of its headlights prevented me seeing who was inside.

I looked at Spike, who didn't seem remotely concerned. The 4x4 stopped, its engine running. It had blacked-out rear windows and the only occupant I could see was the driver.

She looked very different from the last time I'd seen her. Then, she'd resembled an off-duty Italian; now she was wearing a chunky grey Norwegian-style polo neck which came right up to her chin, decorated with weird and wonderful patterns. A Tibetan hat with ear flaps covered most of the rest of her face, but I could just make out some wisps of blond hair.

As the front window slid down, I was treated to a very pleasant but businesslike smile. 'Get in the back of the vehicle quickly, please.' She added something in Finnish to Spike, and he shook his head back to her as we climbed into the rear seats with our bags. The vehicle was cold; she must have been waiting for us without the engine running or the heater on.

'Please sit well down in your seats and keep away from the windows.'

Tom looked at me for an explanation. I shrugged. 'Later, mate.'

I turned back to face the windscreen and saw Liv watching me in the rear-view mirror. She smiled. 'Welcome to Finland.'

She then tilted her head to look at Tom. 'My name is Liv. I'm very pleased to meet you.'

Tom nodded, looking almost shy. She clearly had the same effect on him as she did on me. He turned to glance at his reflection in the blacked-out window, probably wishing he'd combed his hair.

We drove back out onto the road, turning left. The lights burned even brighter in the market place; it was getting quite dark.

'We don't have a lot of time,' Liv said. 'Events have moved on from our last conversation. You must carry out the task this Tuesday.'

Another of their minor complications. I didn't believe her; I bet that this had always been the timing Val wanted, but instead of telling me in case it put me off, she'd just bullshitted.

'I need to see the target,' I said. 'Two nights isn't a lot of time for preparation. You'll have to tell me all you know tonight, and I'll recce the place tomorrow.'

184

'Yes, of course. I am also concerned that Tom should have enough time to break through the firewall so he can access the system.'

Tom sat up, like a well-behaved child trying to please an adult. 'It'll be OK. Just show me what you've got.'

'I will, Tom. Very soon.'

There was a long pause as Tom sank back into the seat.

I looked at the road. 'Where are we going now?'

'It's not far, by the lakes.'

That wasn't much of a clue. The whole country was covered with the things.

The black and yellow fluorescent sign of a town's silhouette with a red line through it told me I was now out of Lahti. We hit a good-quality single-carriage road, lined at first with houses, their Christmas decorations glowing in the darkness, then giving way to trees and cuts through granite once again. Another sign told me that Mikkeli was now 106km away. We must still be heading north.

I kept my eyes on the odometer as we passed a succession of plastic pedal-bin mailboxes on posts, all neatly aligned by the roadside, the only sign that, somewhere deep in these forests, lay habitation.

The cloud cover and closeness of the trees made darkness fall on us completely, the reflection from the clean white snow almost doubling the effectiveness of the headlights.

The 4x4 Merc soon warmed up and Tom had his earpieces in and eyes closed. I found myself trying to think of things to say to Liv, but small talk wasn't on her agenda.

There was far more checking of mirrors than was required for normal driving; she was carrying out anti-surveillance. That was why we'd met in the car park and come straight out before any connection could be made between the two vehicles. If anybody had been following us from the airport, they would naturally have assumed we were going into the hotel.

I could see her face illuminated by the dash as I sat up. 'Liv? Why all the fuss about telephones and pagers? And why the dead letter box?'

'The old ways are the best.' She smiled. 'A Sicilian once told me that to be sure there's a future, you must learn the lessons of the past. For centuries his organization had used couriers who would exchange information person to person. That way there was control of anything sensitive. But then they started operating in America and they got lazy. In the late Fifties they started to use the telephone, and it was their downfall. If information is important and you want to keep it safe, you must communicate in person. That way you keep control.'

I started to see signs for the E75 and Mikkeli, then the treeline disappeared and the motorway came into view about 400 metres below me on the right. Lines of headlights moved in both directions, but we stayed on the old road and the trees returned to cut out the view. It would be easier to see if anyone was behind us.

Liv continued. 'As to the rest of your question, we take all necessary precautions. Not only with

186

our information, but with our people. That's the reason why all contact from now on will be exclusively with me.'

I decided not to tell her what had happened after leaving the flat. She and Val knew far too much about me already.

Street lights sprang up at the roadside and signs told me we were approaching a place called Heinola.

Tom sparked up, taking out his earpieces. A low-toned, tinny dance beat filled the air. 'Are we there yet?'

Liv helped out. 'Another thirty minutes, Tom.'

He became a bashful schoolboy again. 'Oh . . . thanks.'

Liv turned the heating down a notch and pulled off her hat. Her hair bounced around her shoulders.

Tom was looking out at the town and day-dreaming as he pulled a tissue from his pocket and blew his nose, then examined his effort in the street light, as if it held some sort of prophecy.

We finished moving around the town, another anti-surveillance manoeuvre, and left on a much smaller road. The houses and lights quickly dwindled and trees and darkness soon took over, with just the occasional track leading into the woods.

Liv was still checking behind us for lights, and Tom, having found the meaning of life in his Kleenex, went back to listening to his music.

Eventually we turned onto a tarmac road, tree-lined and cleared of snow, then carried on for another two to three Ks, down a slight hill, until the trees gave way to a house that was suddenly illuminated by ground lights as the vehicle approached. We must have passed a sensor.

The place looked like something out of a James Bond film. Blofeld was probably looking down on us from inside, stroking his cat.

It was maybe sixty or seventy metres long and looked just as if someone had taken an enormous slice out of an apartment block and perched it twenty feet off the ground on two massive concrete supports. Val certainly did things in style.

The driveway took us under the house, where glass panels sealed the area around the pillars to make an internal car park. Two large patio-type doors opened automatically as we approached, then closed behind us.

It was surprisingly warm as I stepped out of the Merc. The lights shining through the windows and the reflection of the snow made me screw up my face until my eyes adjusted.

Liv hit a key fob and a brown door opened in the left-hand pillar. Tom and I grabbed our bags and followed her into a hot stairwell. I noticed that light-brown walking boots had replaced the cowboy look.

We entered a vast high-ceilinged space, maybe thirty metres long and twenty wide, and, just like the London flat, it was clinically white and sparsely furnished. There was a door to my immediate right which led into the kitchen, through which I could see white veneer cup-boards and steel worktops.

The living area, where we were standing, was

straight out of a Sunday supplement. Two white leather settees faced each other across a glass-and-chrome coffee table, and that was it. No TV, music centre, magazines, flowers, pictures on the wall, nothing. White vertical blinds stretched from floor to ceiling where I expected windows to be. The lighting was low and supplied by wall lamps – white of course. There were no fittings on the ceiling.

Tom and I stood with our bags in our hands, taking it all in.

'I'll show you your rooms.' Liv was already walking towards the far right-hand door. I wondered if she ever waited for anyone, or if Armani insisted she always went in front.

We followed into a corridor, our shoes squeaking on the polished wooden floor.

My room was through the first door on the left. Again, it was a world of white, with a low, Japanese-style bed, en-suite shower, white marble tiling and stacks of brand-new white towels. There was no wardrobe, just small canvas storage spaces suspended from a chrome rail. Surprisingly, because the view must have been fantastic, there were no windows.

Liv said, 'No need. It's always too dark.'

I put my bag on the floor; there was nowhere else to put it.

She turned away. 'Tom, your room is next door.'

They disappeared, but I could hear the mumble of voices through the wall as I took my jacket off and listened to the constant hum of the air-conditioning. Her rubber-soled boots soon came squeaking past and she paused in the doorway. 'Would you like some coffee, Nick, and maybe something to eat? Then we must get to work. We don't have much time.'

'Yeah, thanks.'

She nodded and made her way back towards the living area.

I repositioned my bag in the corner of the room – it seemed out of place anywhere else – as Tom stuck his head round the door. 'Nice one, mate. She worth a few bob or what? You coming for a brew?'

A couple of minutes later, Tom and I sat facing each other on the white leather. The settee made creaking sounds as we got comfortable, and the clink of china came from the kitchen. It seemed I wouldn't get anything out of him while Liv was about, which wasn't a bad thing really. At least it shut him up. We sat and waited with only the low hum of the heating for company.

She reappeared with a full percolator, milk and mugs on a tray, and a plate of crispbreads and sliced cheese. Placing it on the glass table, she sat down next to Tom. I wasn't sure whether he was wriggling with pleasure or embarrassment.

'Let me explain the set-up,' she said. 'I will be staying here with you both. My room is over on the other side.' She pointed to the opposite door.

'The room across from your bedrooms is where the laptop is, for you, Tom, to decrypt the fire-wall. I'll tell you more about that in a moment.' She turned to me. 'Nick, also in there are maps of the house you'll be visiting.'

She started to pour. 'By Tuesday morning you

must have discovered the access sequence, entered the house and copied the files. If not, my instructions are that the deal is off.'

I sat and listened, knowing that even if I had to make a pact with the devil it would all be completed in time. I wanted this money. I *needed* this money.

Liv and I took a sip of black coffee. Tom didn't touch his, obviously not wanting to be a nuisance and ask for anything herbal. We lapsed back into a strained silence.

She sat and watched our discomfort, almost enjoying it. It made me feel as if she knew more about Tom and me than we did about her.

At length I said, 'It will happen.'

Tom nodded. 'No drama.'

'I'm sure it will. We will discuss the minor details of money, information exchange and so on later.' She stood up. 'Come, bring your drinks. Let's start work.'

We followed her down the corridor. The room on the right was just as white as the rest of the house, and very large and rectangular. There were two pine desks and chairs. One had an aluminium briefcase on it, the other, a small, black, sleek-looking IBM laptop a bit smaller than an A4 sheet of paper, together with the box it had come in, with spare leads draped over the top and a thin black nylon carry bag with a shoulder strap.

Liv pointed at the briefcase. 'Tom, that ThinkPad is for you. Nick, come.' She continued to the other desk.

As she and Tom started to talk firewall stuff, I

unclipped the case and lifted the lid. I found several marked maps, all of different scales. It looked as if we were aiming for a town called Lappeenranta, about 120Ks to the east of us and close to the Russian border.

The largest scale map showed that the whole area was a massive system of lakes, maybe more than a hundred Ks square, with hundreds of small islands and inlets dotted with villages and small towns. The target was just over 20K north of Lappeenranta, along a road linking some of the islands to an area called Kuhala. The house wasn't lakeside, but set back about a kilometre from the water and surrounded by forest.

Liv left us to it, and I watched her go. She was unbelievably cool. I realized that I was beginning to like her a lot.

'Hey, Tom?' I turned to face him. He was hunched over the small screen, his back to me.

He turned in his chair and looked up. 'What's the matter, mate?'

'I think it would be better if you didn't mention anything to Liv about the money. It's just that she may be getting less than us and will get a bit pissed off. If she asks, just say you don't know, OK?'

'Isn't this her place, then?'

'I doubt it. She's just working on the job, like us. I think it would be best if we kept our cards close to our chests, OK?'

He turned back to the desk. 'If you say so, mate. Whatever.' The keys started to clink away once more under his dancing fingers. 'Means jack to me.'

I returned to the material spread out in front of me. Maps are useful things, but they only go so far. I needed to get my arse on target and do a proper recce. I listened to Tom mincing around behind me as I sat and memorized the maps.

The best way I had learned to do this was by visualizing the route I'd take. It was far easier than trying to remember place names and road numbers. I sat there, staring at the blank wall, making my way from Heinola to the target house, when I noticed a piece of plasterboard missing around a two-pin plug.

I got on my knees and had a look, pulling back the edge of the board to reveal lead sheeting behind, covered with a plastic, cling film-type lining. I glanced back at Tom. He was still hammering on the keyboard like a man possessed.

I pushed the plasterboard back in place and walked around the room, looking for any more holes. Then I realized there weren't any phone jacks. Even in a modern house that was taking minimalism a bit far. Was it to make this place impossible to communicate with electronically? If so, Val took his work very seriously indeed, and it unnerved me a bit. I didn't like discovering things that I should know already.

I walked across to Tom's desk and stood over him, looking at a screen full of numbers and letters. Some of the vertical lines would change every time he hit a key.

'Do you understand what you've got there?'

'No problem; it's all about algorithms and protocols, hardened proxies, stuff like that. What it boils down to is that I need to find the access sequence among a million or so different sets of characters. That's the firewall between me and the rest of the system.' He pointed at the screen, never letting his eyes wander from it. 'This is quite a sophisticated crypto, as it has a learning program that detects unusual events, like me trying to hack in, and interprets them as an attack. If we were trying to do this on site I wouldn't be able to do it in time. But this set-up is perfect: I have time to play.'

His attention was drawn away from talking to me as he leaned forward slightly and studied the screen. We were both silent for a few seconds as he mumbled crypto stuff to himself, then he came back to planet earth. 'Anyway, once I've hacked into it here, all I have to do is configure the ThinkPad, bring it with me and then I can download all the files she wants. Easy life.'

I watched him as he did his stuff. He'd turned into the master of his universe, hands gliding over the keys, quick, confident and in command. Even his tone had changed as he explained what he was up to.

'Tom, will you be able to get past this thing?' The screen full of moving numbers, letters and symbols looked like total confusion to me.

'No drama, mate. No drama.'

I looked over at the broken plasterboard. 'One more question.'

His eyes still didn't leave the screen. 'What's that?'

I changed my mind. 'I'm going for a brew. You coming?'

'Nah, mate, I'm gonna stay here. Things to do, know what I mean?'

I left him to it. I wanted to know why the lead was there, and maybe he could help, but why risk him flapping? The less he knew the better.

16

I walked into the living area after having no luck finding a phone point in my bedroom. The light was still on, but the room was empty and the coffee things had been cleared away. There was only a thick paperback book on the glass table. I wandered around the room, checking for points, but didn't find any. There were none in the kitchen, either.

I couldn't see any gaps in the wall covering to check for lead, so I decided to go a different route. Walking over to the ceiling-to-floor blinds I gave one of them a poke. It didn't move, and was extremely hard and heavy.

There was a switch on the wall near by, and you didn't need to be a brain surgeon to work out what it did. When I flicked it, a motor whirred above me in the ceiling. I watched as they began to open from the centre. It was dark outside, but the living-room lights exposed a long narrow balcony beyond triple-glazed sliding doors. Virgin snow lay a metre deep all along it, resting against the glass. A little further out, the tops of a few snow-covered pine trees were also visible, but beyond that was inky blackness.

I turned, hearing bare feet moving towards me. Liv was six or seven steps away, wearing a blue silk dressing gown which finished just above her knees, exposing each thigh in turn as she moved.

Two more steps and she reached past me and hit the switch. She smelled as if she'd just stepped out of the shower.

The motor whirred and the blinds began to close again. She took a step back. 'Nick, the blinds must remain closed at all times when Tom is working on the computer.' She waved a palm in the direction of the settees. 'Shall we sit?'

As she crossed the room, I followed. She saw my eyes flick to the blinds and guessed what I was about to say. 'Yes, Nick, before you ask, they are lined with lead. The whole house is. Valentin doesn't like his competitors learning what he's doing. Millions of dollars are spent accessing information about rivals in this business. He ensures that it's money wasted as far as spying on him is concerned. Valentin knows the true value of information – not money, but power.'

'So that's why no phones?'

The blinds finished closing as we sat facing each other on the settees. As she tucked her legs underneath her, the silk followed the contours of her body.

'Please, Nick, will you tell Tom? House rule.'

'No problem. But will you do me a favour in return? It would make things a lot easier for us if you didn't tell Tom anything about the Maliskia, or about the deal we have. He's a worrier and I want him to concentrate on the job.' The last thing

I needed was her telling him how much money was really involved.

'Of course,' she smiled. 'I never have a problem with keeping information to a minimum. On the other hand, I also find it better to tell the truth about important matters. Maybe Tom would be better off knowing about the Maliskia, and the money, rather than possibly finding out at a later date? Lies can be so confusing and counter-productive; but then, I'm sure you don't need me to tell you that, do you?'

I wasn't too sure if it was a rhetorical question; whatever, I wasn't going to give her a full answer. I shrugged.

She leaned forward to pick up the book on the coffee table, and as she settled back, her silk dressing gown fell down on either side of her legs. I tried not to look, but couldn't help myself. Liv was one of the most beautiful, attractive and intelligent women I'd ever seen. It was a pity I had champagne tastes and a lemonade budget. I would never have what it took to attract somebody like her, and, sadly, she didn't strike me as the sort to dispense charity shags to the poor.

She pulled the gown together as she caught my eye. 'Does this bother you? You English are so strange; you're so repressed.'

'What about you lot?' I grinned. 'You seem to be so reserved with strangers, yet think nothing of sitting naked with them in saunas, chatting about the weather. Then you charge out and roll naked in the snow, beating yourselves with birch twigs. So who's running on a full tank?'

She smiled. 'We're all prisoners of our past, and maybe we Finns more than most.'

That one got me knitting my brow. It was a bit too deep for me.

'I don't expect you to understand this, Nick, but Nordic myth is more deeply ingrained in our psyche than in any of the other Scandinavian cultures. Probably a legacy of all those centuries of Swedish and Russian domination.' She tapped the book. 'A collection of Finnish folklore. See, we're captivated.'

'I'm more of a Harry Potter man myself,' I said. I didn't know what the fuck she was talking about.

It was her turn to look puzzled. She probably thought he wrote spy thrillers, or whatever crap I read.

'Nick, I need to finalize some drop-off' – she corrected herself – 'dead letter box details with you for the information and money exchange. We shall all go to Helsinki in the morning, even if Tom hasn't got through the firewall by then. It's important that he isn't kept in the dark.'

I opened my mouth to speak, but she seemed to have accessed my own firewall. I wasn't sure whether to be flattered or alarmed by the fact that she seemed to know exactly what I was thinking.

'Nick, I've already told you there is nothing to be concerned about. No-one is looking for you there. Otherwise it would be pointless going, wouldn't it? We all want you to be successful, so why would we be taking such a risk?'

That made sense, but it was less than a week since Carpenter had turned Helsinki into Dodge

City, and I didn't want to find myself next door to anyone who mistook me for one of his close personal friends.

'Once you and Tom have left tomorrow night, you must never return here, whatever happens. That way this place remains secure. In any event, no-one will be here, as I am leaving soon after you. I will take anything you want to leave behind, and return it at the exchange. You are to make your way to the DLB on Wednesday morning and leave details for a meeting between just the two of us.

'The details of the exchange are totally your concern. Valentin wants to give you control of the arrangements, as a gesture of good faith and to give you confidence that nothing uncomfortable will occur during the transaction. To help ensure this, you will still be in contact exclusively with me.' She gave me the full benefit of those wonderful eyes. 'Do not worry, Nick, this business is not being conducted in a way that jeopardizes any of us.'

I tried not to laugh. Maybe she hadn't noticed how people like Val conducted business. If he didn't have control of an apartment block he'd blow it up, no matter who was still inside. I wasn't quite ready to assume he was my new best friend. In the meantime, I would pick the time and place, and they would come to me. It made sense.

I nodded. 'What if I don't make the dead letter box?'

'If you don't, Tom will. That is why he needs to be with us tomorrow. If there's no message for me by Wednesday evening, I'll know that something is seriously wrong and the deal is off. Sometimes you win, other times . . .' She shrugged.

There was silence for a moment or two. 'How did you come to meet Valentin?'

'Like you, he asked me to work for him.' She smiled, crossing her legs. 'And no, Nick, I'm not his mistress.'

She'd read my mind again. Three hundred years ago she would have been burned at the stake.

'The only thing he wants from me is my doctorate in Russian political science. You see, Nick, this is where the money is – for now. And the fact is, I enjoy that money. I work hard and I'm well rewarded.'

She sat back, and when she spoke again her voice was low. 'My parents were Swedish. They are both dead now. I was born here, in Finland. I am a Finn. There, that is all you need to know about me. But what about you, Nick? Why did you become a kidnapper? Did you not work for the British government?'

I coughed, trying unsuccessfully to hide my embarrassment. It made sense that she would know: if she knew about the connection between Tom and me, then there was a whole lot more she probably knew, too. So much for being a deniable operator. I suddenly wasn't enjoying this as much as I thought I was going to. 'Money,' I said. 'Just like you. Maybe we're the same.'

She gave me her most inscrutable Mr Spock look. 'Of course. That is why you are here.' Her face broke into a smile. 'Are you married?'

'Divorced.'

'What happened, Nick? Did she not like to live with lies and half truths?'

'I think she just didn't like living with me.' I paused. 'I used to be in the military and—'

'Yes, Valentin knows about your military past, Nick. That is one of the reasons you are here.'

What else did he know? I didn't like the postman knowing what I looked like, let alone the head of a major organized crime group. It made me feel very uncomfortable.

I said, 'What about you? Are you married?'

'I'm not so sure it would be a good idea. And being a mother? It does not interest me. Do you have children?'

'No.' I made light of it. 'I can just about manage to look after myself. It would be such a responsibility. What would I do if they became ill?'

She gave me a level look. 'I think we have both done the right thing, Nick, don't you?'

I tried to read her expression and failed again. I didn't reply for a while, and when I did I answered one question with another. 'Are you staying with us all the time, Liv?'

'I'll come and go. But essentially I'm here to make sure things run smoothly.' She adjusted herself on the settee. I got another glimpse of thigh as she tapped the book by her side. 'There is a story in here about Väinämöinen, the creator of the Universe. One day he has an encounter with Joukahainen, a much younger god. The two meet riding on a narrow path and neither wants to give way. Joukahainen challenges Väinämöinen, with all the eagerness of youth and limitless self-confidence. The battle is waged by chanting magical songs, and ends with Joukahainen finding himself in a bog. You see, Nick, he simply didn't know who he was dealing with.'

I took the point. Knowing who you're dealing with had always been a big thing with me. And right now the message seemed to be, they did and I didn't.

'What time are we leaving in the morning?'

'Eight. Will you tell Tom?' She yawned. 'Time for bed, I think. Good night, Nick.'

I watched her walk towards the door. 'Night, Liv.'

She disappeared into the other half of the house. I couldn't help a smile of regret when I realized that her leaning across me to flick a wall switch was the closest we were ever likely to get. Will of the gods and all that.

17

Monday, 13 December 1999

We headed south along the motorway towards Helsinki, all dressed exactly the same as yesterday. Tom had headed straight for the back seat and crashed out, which left me with the option of joining him or sitting next to Liv in the front. I knew what I wanted to do, but I felt I should give her some space.

It was nearly eight forty-five, and after thirty minutes of staring at headlights it had begun to get light. It was going to be a sunny day; there wasn't a cloud in the sky, and the unfolding view of pine trees and glittering snow was straight out of a ski brochure.

I looked across at Tom, earpieces in and eyes closed. The scenery was lost on him. He was fast asleep, his head bouncing gently in time with the 4x4's movement. He'd been up late at his screen.

I'd got him to bring all his documents, even on this shopping trip. I told him it was just in case we needed to leave in a hurry – 'be prepared, Tom, know what I mean?'

He hadn't been too keen on coming, because after working much of the night, he was close to breaking the firewall. But I agreed with Liv; he needed to be aware of the game plan. We were both acting for our own selfish reasons. If there was a problem on target and Tom was the only one to get away, she had to know there was still a chance she could get the data to Val. And I wanted him along because, if I broke a leg, or wasn't able to make the DLB to collect my money for any other reason, I wanted Tom to be able to do it for me.

Another forty minutes and we hit Helsinki city limits. Liv gave me a guided tour as we came in, pointing out some landmarks and proudly telling about how her tiny nation had routed the Red Army in the 1940 winter war. All the while, Tom's head bounced about beside me.

It was quite strange seeing the place during the day. I'd never come in until last light during the recces for Val's lift; there was no reason to expose myself and the team to CCTV and the security set-up for the EU conference. No matter what the environment, it's always better to recce in the dark, and in this place there was plenty of it.

The city looked older than I'd been expecting; the airport and Intercontinental were both modern buildings, and Tom's ranting about how cutting edge the place was had led me to expect a city full of buildings like Vauxhall Cross.

As we weaved towards the centre, the heavy morning traffic jockeyed with the trams to gain ground, but was generally well behaved.

'I think it's time for Tom to pay attention now, Nick.'

I gave him a shake.

'What? What?' His eyes opened and he stretched as if he was coming out of hibernation.

I pointed at my mouth, indicating to him that he'd do well to wipe the dribble from his chin.

'Cheers, mate.' He looked outside at the traffic. 'This Helsinki, then? Looks just like the virtual tour.'

Liv smiled. 'I think you will find the real thing a bit chillier.'

We turned a corner, passing a large illuminated sign telling us that this department store was called Stockmann. She pointed at the large window displays as we drove past. 'We'll meet in the coffee shop on the sixth floor. The station is just a couple of minutes' walk away.'

We drove on a couple of blocks before stopping. As I got out, I felt the bitter cold for the first time that day. With the garage being a sealed, air-conditioned part of the house, the open air hadn't had a chance to get at us. She looked back at me through the rear doors as I put my hat and gloves on. 'I'll see you both in Stockmann in two hours. You'll need about half an hour to check out the station.'

I nodded and turned to Tom. 'We'll use the rest of the time to get our kit.'

I closed the door of the 4x4 and she drove off. Our breath hung in clouds in front of our faces and every inch of exposed skin prickled with the cold. Tom didn't like it one bit. 'Arctic or what, Nick? For fuck's sake, can we get inside sharpish?'

The station was in front of us. It looked like an

206

East German prison, very square and imposing, faced with what looked like dirty-brown concrete. It could have been used as a backdrop for *1984*. I checked the clock tower with Baby G and they agreed to the minute: 10.22.

As we joined the rest of the pedestrian traffic waiting obediently for the little green man, Tom frowned and said, 'Nick?'

'What?' I was concentrating more on looking for a gap between the trams that I could dash through. I had no intention of freezing to death, waiting for little green men.

'Do you trust her – you know, Liv? You sure everything's sweet?'

Liv's advice about being truthful flashed through my head, thankfully not powerfully enough for me to take it. I tried never to trust anyone, and after what had happened in Washington, I certainly wasn't going to now. There might not be too much time to do this job correctly, and I might be desperate for the cash, but I wouldn't be doing anything until I'd put my own and Tom's safety net in place today.

The lights changed and we started walking. 'Don't worry, mate, everything is fine. In fact, having a meeting point like this is one of the things that makes me feel better about her. It means these people are switched on and want the job done with no hassle. Don't worry about it.'

He shrugged. 'Yeah, but what can you do to guarantee we ain't getting stitched up like a kipper, know what I mean? Are you going to do what she wants? You know, come back here and give her the ThinkPad with the download and take the money? Or are you gonna ask for more? I bet it's worth a bomb.'

Even if the thought had crossed my mind, I wasn't going to admit it to him. 'No, mate, I just want to do this right. Just exchange that little machine of yours for the money and get back to the UK. That way everything stays safe and easy. Whichever way you look at it, it's still good money.' All the time I had my smiley face on. I felt like I was trying to encourage a small child to eat his sprouts.

I was expecting more questions, but he just shrugged his shoulders again. 'Only asking, mate. If it's good enough for you, it's good enough for me. Tell you what, she's tasty, ain't she?'

I grinned. 'Yes, she's very beautiful. Out of our league though, son.' I somehow couldn't picture Liv kissing Juicy Lucy cards in Notting Hill, or spending her day sorting out my boiler.

The main doors to the station were heavy and wooden, with porthole windows protected by metal grilles. We pushed through and immediately came face to face with Santa, who was ringing his bell and demanding money. We sidestepped him.

The interior looked more like a well-kept museum than a railway station, with clean, stone-paved floors, thick granite supporting pillars and unbelievably high ceilings. Little snowmen hung from chandeliers, and the place echoed with public announcements, people talking, mobile phones going off all over the place and, in one corner, a busker who was having a crack at the

Finnish version of 'Good King Wenceslas' on his accordion. The smell of cigarette smoke and fast food was strong and everywhere.

A group of people with Santa hats on and sets of skis over their shoulders tried to squeeze past stressed-out businessmen in overcoats, furry Cossack hats and mobiles glued to their ears. The strange thing was that you couldn't see or hear a single train – this was a cold-weather station and the platforms were outside.

Tom rubbed his hands together. He liked it in here. 'Christ, I almost feel human again. What now then, Nick?'

Father Christmas carried on doing his stuff as we stood and got our bearings, and I thought 'almost' was as close as Tom was ever going to get.

Liv's DLB was very easy to find and, like the one at the Langham, sited well. We were standing with our backs to the main entrance. In front of us was a wide stairway and escalators that led down into the metro. The three sides of the stairway surrounded an open square of continuous wooden benches. The DLB was by a rubbish bin on the left-hand side.

Tom followed as I walked between the DLB and the large ticketing hall to our left, heading for a news-stand. A teenaged girl was sitting reading a magazine, ears full of Walkman, mouth full of gum. She was wearing navy-blue duvet salopettes under a matching jacket which was open to stop her sweating.

I nodded at Tom just before we got level with her. 'There it is, mate. See the girl in blue?'

He nodded back and we carried on past.

'OK, if you put your hand underneath the bench, exactly where she's sitting, you're going to feel a plastic container attached by Velcro. All you do is make sure no-one's looking and pull it off, go away and write a note telling them where they can find you, and they'll come.'

'Isn't this all a bit James Bond, Nick? I don't like it.'

'It's just belt-and-braces stuff. You need to know what to do if it goes wrong. You know, suppose I break a leg and can't get back here? Then it'll be down to you to hand over the goods and get us our money.'

'So long as there ain't no funny business. You know, fucking her about or anything? I don't want that, mate. I just want the money.'

We stopped by the wall next to the news-stand.

'Tom, it's going to go like clockwork. You just need to know this stuff in case I get injured, that's all. You're my insurance policy, and I'll be yours.'

He liked that. The girl got up and walked towards us, nodding her head in time to the music stuck in her ears.

'Go on, see if there's anything there yet.'

'What, now?' He looked absolutely terrified. 'While everyone's here?'

'It's never going to be empty, Tom. It's a station, for fuck's sake. All you've got to do is take a stroll over there, sit down, put your hand under the bench and have a feel around. While you're doing that I'll go and change some money for you, all right?'

I didn't wait for his answer. I wanted him to go

through the motions. If he had to get here on his own, he'd at least know what to do.

I walked further into the station. Signs in front of me pointed to the platforms and the long-term left luggage. I'd be checking that out soon enough.

As busy-looking people passed through the large wooden doors, I saw snow-covered carriages standing at each platform. To my right were shops and toilets, and, about fifty metres away, the exit to the bus station. To the left were more shops and the short-term left-luggage lockers, then another set of doors the same distance away that led out to the taxi rank. Behind me were the metro stairs and a very nervous Tom.

I went left, to the bureau de change, exchanged $500, then wandered back. As I neared the DLB I could see him sitting on the bench, looking very pleased with himself. I sat next to him, squeezing into the small gap between him and a rather large woman peeling an orange.

'Piece of piss, mate. Found it first time, look.'

He started to bend down.

'No, no, not now, Tom. Leave it where it is and I'll show you how to tell Liv that you've put a message in there for her.'

I stood up and he followed. The woman was delighted and spread herself out more. We went towards the platform doors and turned right, passing the toilets.

'Tom, go in there to write your message, OK?'

He nodded, his eyes fixed on the English edition computer magazines as we passed another news-stand, with yet more people wrestling with their luggage and skis.

I explained where to leave his DLB-loaded marker. 'Just beyond this coffee shop, on the right, is a row of telephones. When the time comes, get yourself a marker pen from one of these shops and draw a line down the booth of the right-hand one, OK?'

It wasn't. 'Why?'

'So Liv doesn't have to sit down and feel under the bench every time to check it. If the loaded sign – the marker-pen line – isn't there, she knows that a message isn't, either. Otherwise she'll look just a bit suspicious on Wednesday, won't she, sitting in the same place every hour on the hour?'

He nodded thoughtfully. 'Tell you what, she could sit next to me every hour on the hour, know what I mean?'

I smiled. If the two women at the airport would have had him for breakfast, Liv would probably chew him up and spit him out without looking up from her newspaper.

We were closing the gap towards the bus-station doors when they all opened at once and a coachload of people surged towards us, dragging their skis and luggage behind them.

Ten metres short of the doors was a bank of four phones fixed to the wall, divided by polished-wood booths. We stood against the nearest one, letting the coach party pass with a rumble of suit-case wheels and excited conversation.

'See here?' I said.

'Yeah, you want me to mark . . .' He started to wave his finger.

'Hey, Tom, in spyland nobody points.' I pushed his hand down and tried not to laugh. 'But yes, that's right, mate, a mark. But a line, a nice thick line. Make sure you pretend to be on the phone and make sure they' – I nodded towards the flower shop opposite – 'don't see you.'

Tom's eyes followed mine. 'I get it, but you'll tell me what to say in the letter, yeah?'

'Of course. Now let's go and get cold.'

We walked out through the bus station, a large square concourse littered with sheltered stops.

Once onto the pavement we cut half right in the direction of Stockmann. I handed Tom 2,000 Finnish marks from the wad I'd got from the money changer. It worked out at about six marks a dollar. He thought he was rich; his eyes shone – or maybe they were starting to be affected by the cold as we walked along cobblestoned streets. The rumble of tyres and metallic rhythm of the tram wheels meant we had to speak louder than normal.

'Tom, I want you to give me your passport and wallet for safe keeping. I've got an idea for a little extra insurance, but listen, this is between you and me. It's not that I don't trust her, but better safe than sorry, eh?'

'Nice one, Nick. Makes me feel better.'

He handed them over without questioning. It made me feel suddenly more responsible for him.

'Besides, we want to travel light tomorrow night.'

You could tell Stockmann was Finland's top people's store by the line of large black or dark-blue cars outside with their engines running, waiting for their VIP passengers to come out and load up their Christmas shopping. When we got closer, it was clear who the cars belonged to. Large men with no necks and square heads were waiting beside them. It looked as though Mr and Mrs Mafia were flapping a bit because of the hit on Val last week.

A group of heavies came out just as we approached the main entrance, surrounding a very young, beautiful blonde, who was wearing more fur than a grizzly. For a moment I thought it was Liv.

A limo door opened for her, and the three-car convoy zoomed off up the street.

Tom and I walked through large double doors straight into the perfume department. A little further on, in the luggage department, I picked up two small weekend bags, one dark green and one black, from a display, and two heavy car blankets.

Tom had his big wad of money clasped firmly in his hand and was looking happy. It was time to say my goodbyes.

'I've got things to do, Tom. Insurance.' I tapped the side of my nose and winked. His big hamster cheeks beamed back. 'I'll see you in the coffee shop in about three quarters of an hour. Just get yourself some good warm kit, the sort of stuff I told you about, all right?'

'Yeah, yeah, no drama. Hey Nick, when the going gets tough, the tough go shopping.' He rubbed his thumb and forefinger together.

I clapped his shoulder. 'Remember, get a decent coat and boots. And by the way, if Liv turns up before I get there, just tell her I'm shopping, too.'

I could see he couldn't be arsed to ask why, he just wanted to get spending.

'No drama. See yer.'

Back in the cold, I took out my new holdalls and bulked them out with the blankets. Then I headed for the bus station again. I went past the telephones into Europe's most expensive toilets. It cost me nearly a pound to sit down in one of the cubicles so I could get out the money from my organizer wallet – what was left of the twenty-five grand in $100 bills which I'd brought with me. I removed four grand and then placed the wallet, plus my own documents and Davidson's, into the dark-green holdall. You never know when even a burned ID can come in useful. Tom's documents and $3,000 went into the black bag, and I slipped the remaining grand into my pocket. I then dumped both at left luggage and looked for a decent hiding place for the two tickets – our own little DLB – somewhere that Tom would find easy enough to remember.

I went into one of the shops and picked up a computer magazine with a plastic sleeve holding a free CD-Rom. I was queuing at the checkout when I saw her.

Liv was standing by the doors to the trains. The man she was with was very smartly dressed in a long camel-hair coat, shirt and tie. She was looking quite dolled up herself, in a black overcoat she hadn't been wearing earlier. It must have been in the back of the Merc 4x4.

I ducked out of the queue as if I'd had second thoughts about the magazine, and went back to browsing the racks, watching Liv and her man out of the corner of my eye. They were in each other's arms, their faces just inches apart and talking away. They were doing their best to look like two lovers saying their goodbyes but it wasn't quite working. There were times when they cuddled, but they weren't talking to each other, they were talking at each other. I'd done this enough times myself to know what was going on.

They held each other and talked for a little while longer, then he pulled slightly away from her. He was in his early thirties, with short brown hair, and looked quite the young trendy businessman.

She turned away, heading for the bus-station exit. There had been no final kiss, no last touch or stroke of the hair.

I let her go past me, then moved quickly to the platform doors, pinging him on platform 6 as he looked at his ticket and checked the coaches. It was now time to hurry back the other way and see what Liv was up to.

Barging through the bus-station doors I looked out onto the square. She was walking away from me, putting her Tibetan hat on, heading across the pedestrian crossing. I could see the 4x4 on the other side, parked in a line of other vehicles on meters.

Turning, I ran back into the station. The destination board said the platform 6 train was leaving for St Petersburg in two minutes.

I walked swiftly back to the news-stand and bought the magazine, together with a reel of

Sellotape. Taking off the plastic sleeve, I ripped it into two strips and wrapped the tickets individually. Now all I had to do was find a place to hide them that Tom would remember. It wasn't hard. The long banks of left-luggage lockers by the taxi exit were on legs, with a four-inch gap between them and the floor. Pretending to clean the slush off my shoes, I taped Tom's under Number 10 and mine under Number 11. If things went wrong, both of us had a ticket out of Finland.

As I made my way back to Stockmann, Liv's meeting with the man in the camel-hair coat mulled round in my head.

I took the lift to the sixth floor. Once I'd passed the cold-weather gear a sign told me that on the floor above was 'cold storage for furs'. I passed a restaurant, a juice bar, and found Tom in Café Avec, overlooking the shoppers below on the fifth floor. His half-cup of herbal whatever looked sad and cold on the table in front of him. The light-wood furniture had come straight out of an Ikea warehouse and the place was packed with people snacking on soup or little fish dishes. The noise was deafening – people talking and mobiles going off with a million and one different tunes.

'Wotcha, mate.' He was all smiles, pointing at his bags, then opening one for me to look inside. I was pleased to see he'd bought himself a decent pair of boots, and the dark-blue, thick, woollen check lumberjack coat was just the sort of thing I'd told him to get.

'Great, Tom. Now listen.'

I explained to him where his ticket was hidden.

217

We'd pick them up on Wednesday, but if the shit hit the fan tomorrow night, he should head straight for the station, grab his bag and catch the first flight home.

He started to look a bit more cheerful. 'I just want to get this job done and get back to London with some dosh. I don't really like it here. Thought I would, but I don't. It must be the cold. That's why I got these for tomorrow.' He bent down and brought out a set of silk leggings and a top.

I tried not to laugh. They were the sort of thing you might buy for your very first ski trip, but never wear.

He looked rather proud of them. 'What do you think? Keep me warm or what? You should get some, Nick. The girl behind the counter said they're great.'

I bet she did; they probably cost three times as much as a set of proper thermals. 'I've got some,' I lied. 'Actually, there's one more thing.'

He packed them proudly back into the bag. 'What's that?'

'I know you said you're nearly there, but can you really break through the firewall by tomorrow?'

He looked at me as if I was mad. 'No problem. But you will look after me, won't you? You know, when we're in there . . .'

I could sense that his bravado was fading slightly as the witching hour approached. I smiled, nodded and then saw him look anxiously over my shoulder.

'Liv's here.'

I turned in my seat and watched her looking out for us both, hat in hand and the black coat still on. She saw my raised hand and came straight over.

She sat down. 'Everything all right at the station?'

I nodded.

'Good. Here are the keys for your car, Nick.' She passed over two keys on a Saab key fob. 'There are maps inside the glove box to get you there, and a detailed one of the area. None of the maps are marked. It will take you more than three hours to get there.'

'There'll probably be a list of things I'll need once I've seen the house.'

'No problem, so long as it's nothing exotic.' Talking of which, she looked at her Cartier watch.

I got the hint and started getting to my feet. 'I think I need to get going. I want to spend as much time as I can on target.'

She stood up. 'I'll show you where the car is, then go back to the house with Tom.'

As we came out of Stockmann, Tom took out his new check coat and put it over the one he was wearing. He looked the perfect tourist.

We walked back towards the station and I could see the Merc 4x4 still parked in the same position, with a shiny new blue Saab next to it.

I said my goodbyes. Tom got in the front with her and they drove off.

18

The journey to the target seemed to be taking longer than she'd told me to expect. Maybe it just felt that way because there'd been nothing to look at but thousands of trees and lumps of granite. I needed to adjust my boredom threshold.

It was just after three o'clock and it was already last light. The reflection from the Saab's headlights twinkled in the snow piled high at the roadside as I stayed obediently in the line of traffic, which all travelled within the speed limit. I hit the seek button on the radio a few times, but there wasn't much to listen to. I hated Europop, and didn't have a clue what was being said on any of the speaking stations.

I used the time to think about Liv's station RV, but didn't come up with any answers. I decided I just had to get on with it. 'It' was simple: I'd do the job, control the exchange with Liv, then get Tom and me back to the UK, leaving Val to do whatever he wanted with the stuff. At least after tomorrow night, once on the ground, I was in control of my own destiny.

After taking the exit for Lappeenranta, signs

for Kuhala began to appear. Pulling into the side of the road, I checked the smaller-scale, more detailed map. I had another twelve Ks to go until turning off the two-lane road and onto what looked like a minor gravel one. Then I'd need to find the private turning to the target building.

I pushed on, driving through dense forest on a tarmac firebreak. Tall trees on either side of me cut down the headlights' capacity as if I was in a tunnel. Then I was suddenly out of it and rumbling across a wooden bridge, my lights blazing across the white ice of the frozen lake beneath me. Twenty seconds later I was back inside the tunnel, with just the occasional postbox to let me know I wasn't the only person around.

Passing a yellow triangle sign showing a silhouetted elk, I knew I'd well and truly hit the countryside. Stopping at the crossroads, I checked the odometer and map. Eight more Ks and the third option right.

I drove on, counting off the Ks, crossing two more bridges and only a handful of postboxes until I found the junction I was looking for. The tyre noise changed as I hit the two-lane gravel road. Like the one leading to Liv's, it was still iced over but had been snowploughed and gritted.

With a few Ks still to go, I wanted to make sure I had the right track to target first time. It wouldn't be a good idea to mince around with headlights on and the engine revving up and down the road. The map showed a scattering of houses in the area, and I was passing a postbox every half kilometre or so. I changed down to first gear. There wasn't a light to be seen as I

221

checked off each track into the woods on the map.

I found the target track, but kept going, looking for somewhere off the road to leave the Saab so it looked parked rather than abandoned. About another 300 metres on I found a small cut in the woodline which seemed to be a firebreak. Once tucked in, I switched off the engine.

It was freezer time again. Putting on the nylon padded gloves and black woollen hat I'd bought myself at Stockmann, I got out and hit the key fob. The four ways flashed as the central locking did its stuff, but I couldn't help that.

Setting off down the gravel road, I made sure the hat didn't cover my ears; I was on a recce, I needed them to be able to work, without fighting to hear through half a lamb's coat.

It was bitterly cold after the snug warmth of the Saab, and there was no noise or light. All I could hear was my own breathing and the snow crunching an inch under my feet before it compressed onto the hard ice beneath. My whole world was trees, snow and a very cold nose and ears.

Once at the top of the track, I stopped, looked and listened. Nothing. It would take another fifteen minutes for my eyes to adapt to the lack of light. Then, with any luck, I'd be able to see a little more of the treeline than just a wall of black.

I turned into the track and started slowly down it. A lot of vehicles had obviously been up and down; there was no snow in the ruts on either side of the small central mound, just compacted ice. The trees were hard up against the edge of the track.

Three feet in front of me was pitch-black, but I

knew it wouldn't be like that for long once my night vision kicked in. I moved like a tightrope walker along the rut, to cut down ground sign. The last thing I wanted was to slip and fall in the snow at the side of the track, leaving evidence that even a five-year-old would pick up.

After about five minutes I began to see weak, intermittent light ahead in the direction of the target. The beams flashed up into the sky or straight at me, disappeared for a while, then bounced towards me again. I knew exactly what they were: vehicle lights, and they were coming my way.

I couldn't even hear the engine yet, so it would be impossible for them to see me. The lights continued to flash against the trees. There was nothing I could do without leaving sign but dive out of the way.

The rumble of the engine reached me and brighter beams of light swept the area around. I faced the drift at the trackside, hopefully aiming between two trees, rocked back to try to get some sort of momentum, then leaped. I managed to clear the first few feet of snow, rolling like a high jumper, and landed like a bag of shit. The snow lay over solid granite and I hit it hard, knocking the wind out of my lungs.

I started to crawl like an animal, trying to burrow under the branches. The vehicle was getting closer.

Still facing away from the road, I dug myself in and waited in the freezing snow, listening as it closed in on me. The transmission was in low ratio, suggesting a 4x4.

It finally drew parallel with me, its wheels crunching into fresh snow on the side of the track as it was steered off line. Without hesitation, it kept on going.

I raised myself slowly onto my knees, keeping my right eye closed: at least that way I would save 50 per cent of what night vision I had. The smell of diesel hung in the air. The track was about five or six metres away from me and it was a 4x4 for sure, but I couldn't make out what type or how many were inside. All I could see was a massive ball of white light in the front, and a red one at the rear, moving slowly along the tree tunnel, followed by a cloud of diesel fumes.

I watched and listened as the light died. They must have reached the top of the track, because I heard revving and the transmission ratios change, then the noise disappeared completely.

Crawling on my hands and knees to avoid the branches, I made my way back to my impact site, stood up, put one foot forward and launched myself over the bank again. My right shin connected painfully with the central mound, and the combination of stones and hard ice did its work on me big time. I lay on my back in one of the ruts, holding my shin, rocking, taking the pain and thinking of the money.

After a minute of feeling sorry for myself, I got up and checked that the snow on the side of the track was still untouched. My dive had been Olympic, but the pain had been worth it. I was covered from head to toe in snow, like a crap skier. Brushing as much of it off me as I could, I readjusted my hat and carried on down the track, walking the tightrope with a bit of a hobble now.

After about a thousand metres, my night vision fully returned. I also started to hear the low, continuous rumble of what sounded like a generator.

What had been concerning me most all along was, How many bayonets? How many were going to fight if I was compromised and couldn't run away? If there were, say, four people in the house, two of them might be Tom-type characters who'd played *Quake* for years but had never held a gun, but the other two could be hoods who had, and who'd go for it. They were the bayonets, male or female. The term went back to the First World War, when it wasn't the whole of an enemy battalion of 1,200 that you had to worry about, it was the 800 fighting men. The remaining 400 cooks and bottle-washers didn't matter. I didn't know how many I'd be up against, and Liv couldn't tell me. It was quite worrying. Getting to the house to discover there was a Hoods Us convention going on in the front room would not make for a good day out.

The track went gently downhill and I got closer to the noise. It began to sound quite substantial; if they were running lots of machinery they would need more juice than the trickle the local substation would give them. To check if they were on the mains I tried to look above me for power lines, but it was too dark to see anything.

The track began to curve. As I rounded a gentle right-hand bend the ground started to open up on either side of me. The treeline here wasn't so close to the track. I could see two dim lights directly ahead, maybe 100 metres away.

Now that I was in line with the house the rumble of the generator was louder still, channelled towards me by the trees. Cupping my hand round my wrist, I pressed the backlight on Baby G. It was just after 4.45.

Edging forwards, still in the rut, I kept looking for places to dive if the vehicle came back or there was some other kind of drama – such as coming across the Maliskia on the same sort of outing. I was a bit pissed off this was the only approach route available to me, but any other would leave sign.

Every five or six paces I stopped, looked and listened.

The trees stopped about five metres from a fence that I could now clearly see in front of me, leaving an empty area running left and right of the track, about two or three feet deep in snow. A large set of double gates was directly ahead. Keeping in the rut, I moved up close. It was made of the same material as the fencing: diamond-shaped lattice work pressed out of ¼-inch steel sheeting; the sort you'd see in the windows of off-licences or the protected kiosks of twenty-four-hour shops.

A large chain fed through both gates and was secured with a heavy steel high-security padlock – a pain in the arse to decode and do up again; it wasn't the type that just snapped into position.

As I lay along the rut, I could feel the hardness of the ice beneath me and knew the cold would start attacking me long before the Maliskia did. I wasn't worried about them at the moment, or the players in the house. Fuck 'em. At such short notice there was no other way to recce this place.

The fence looked about fifteen metres high, and was made up of maybe three sections of lattice work, bolted together and supported by spaced steel poles about a foot in diameter. The house was beyond the fence, about forty metres away. There were no Christmas decorations in this one, just the two lights. One came from a stained-glass panel that I thought was the top half of a door, set back on a veranda. The other was coming from a window further to the left.

I couldn't see that much detail, but the house seemed quite large and old. It had a chateau-style tower on the far right-hand side, with a Russian onion-shaped dome that I could just see silhouetted against the night sky. I remembered Liv on the way to Helsinki saying that the Russians controlled Finland until Lenin gave it independence in 1920.

The old clashed dramatically with the modern: to the left of the house were five satellite dishes, massive things at least three metres across and set into the ground, looking like something an American would have had in his garden in the early Eighties, the sort that picked up 500 channels telling him what the weather was like in Mongolia but still couldn't give him the local news. This was a proper little Microsoft HQ. I could clearly see their dark mesh dishes looking upwards, each in a different direction or elevation, and they all looked as if the snow had been dug away from the base and scraped off the dish.

As I lay there, chin on forearms, taking in as

much information about the target as I could, I saw why the bases were dug out: all of a sudden there was a high-pitched whine that drowned out the noise of the generator, and one of the dishes started to swivel. Maybe they were trying to catch the Japanese repeats of *Friends*. Or maybe they were up and running already?

It seemed a strange location for a set-up like this. Maybe these people were as illegal as Val? I started to wonder, but soon gave myself a good mental slapping. Who cared? I was here for Kelly, to get this job done and paid for before the dollar exchange rate took another tumble.

Getting back to the real world, it seemed that concealment was their biggest weapon. The lattice fence was as high tech as they got on the security front, apart from the sterile area between it and the treeline. That not only stopped anyone climbing a tree to get in, but also meant they could look out of their windows in the morning while cleaning their teeth and see at once if people like me had been lurking about.

I lay in the rut, working out how to get in based on the little information I had. The numbing cold ate through my clothes and the snow that had found its way down my neck when I fell started to attack my back. My toes were beginning to freeze and my nose was running. I couldn't make any noise by clearing it into the snow, so had to be content with wiping it on my icy-cold glove.

There was a sound behind me. I cocked my head so my right ear was pointing back towards the track. The vehicle was returning. No time to think about it, I just got up and ran back to the nearest of my dive points. To clear the bank and the trees, which were slightly off the track, before the headlights rounded the bend, I had to throw myself about three feet up and five feet over, just to get near the treeline's branches. I went for it, not quite making the five feet and hitting rock again. It probably hurt, but I wouldn't feel it until later; adrenalin was doing its job, fighting the pain.

Ploughing through the snow, trying to get under the branches once more, I listened as the wagon got closer. The vehicle noise suddenly increased as it rounded the bend.

I swivelled round on my hands and knees, slowly lifting my head, and tried to get into a position from where I could see the track. I didn't bother to wipe the snow off my face in case the movement was detected.

A moment later the 4x4 passed, its headlights sweeping across the gates, the rear lights turning the snow behind them bright red.

My face was stinging, but now wasn't the time to deal with it. I needed to take in anything from what the occupants of the 4x4 were going to do to what the front and rear lights revealed to me about the surroundings. Fuck the night vision now.

The vehicle stopped just short of the gate and the red glow brightened as the brakes engaged and the engine idled.

Pulling two branches apart with my hands, I saw the right-hand passenger door open and the interior light come on. It was two up – two people aboard – and a very padded body climbed out and started to move towards the gates.

The clatter of the chain was momentarily louder than the engine noise. It was left dangling as both gates were pushed inwards, creaking and rattling, just enough to let the vehicle pass.

The wagon inched forward, its headlights revealing that the snow beyond the gates and inside the target was full of ground sign, feet and tyres. Just as importantly, no alarms or trips appeared to have been turned off before entry.

The headlights splashed across the house, and without the fence in my way I had a clear view. The building was faced with faded red or brown painted wooden slats and closed shutters on all the windows. The dim light on the left that I'd noticed earlier was escaping from a few missing slats in one of the shutters.

The chain rattled again, but I wasn't paying much attention to the gate-closer any longer. It was more important that I saw what was being lit up, looking rather than thinking: my brain would absorb all the information and I'd work out later what I had seen.

I kept my eyes on the 4x4's headlights as they swung to the right. A covered veranda ran along the right half of the house.

The gate-closer came back into view as the 4x4 rolled to a stop parallel with the veranda railings. I could hear the rustling of a nylon jacket and the crunch of snow boots as the brake lights went off and the engine and headlights died. I heard a man's voice as the passenger shouted something I couldn't understand to the driver as he was pushing open his vehicle door.

My nose was stinging and dripping but I

couldn't risk missing a thing as the interior light came on and the driver barked a reply. The gate man carried on past the 4x4 and onto the veranda as the driver leaned into the passenger footwell and lifted out some flat boxes and a small bag. The pair moved together, stamping their feet on the wooden floor of the veranda to clear them of snow.

The driver opened the front door of the house with a key. Light spilled out and I caught a brief glimpse of a hallway that looked invitingly warm and bright before they disappeared into the house.

I stayed still, smearing the contents of my nose slowly into my gloves before wiping them on a tree branch, visualizing my entry – first getting to the house, then into it. After that I'd have to play it by ear. I didn't even know which room the computers were in. So what was new? I seemed to have spent my life breaking into houses, offices and homes, stealing, bugging and planting stuff to incriminate people, all with hardly any information, no back-up if it went wrong and no recognition for a job well done. The best I ever got was a 'What took you so long?'

I had to assume that the five-metre sterile area from treeline to fence ran all round the house; even if I could fight my way through the trees and cover up any tracks, there simply wasn't enough time to check. Fuck it, it was too cold anyway.

Moving forward to my splash point, I dived out again, this time taking the hit on my knees. I recovered on my back in the wheel rut for a while, just long enough for my shoulder to start reminding me that I'd taken a fall on some rocks on the way in. So adrenalin wasn't entirely effective as a means of pain relief. When I'd got my breath back, I rolled over and got up, keeping my eyes on target for that last look about.

There was one more thing to be done. Going back to the gate, I took my glove off and very quickly touched the metal lattice, then leaned over to the left and did the same to the fence. Only then did I turn round and start hobbling back up the track, waiting for my knees to warm up so I could stop walking like an old man.

Once I'd rounded the bend, I pushed my left nostril closed and cleared my right, then changed sides. It felt a lot better.

Twenty minutes later I was scraping ice off the Saab's windscreen. Moments after that I was heading back towards Helsinki, the heater blasting away fit to bust on hot hot hot.

The driveway to the lead house came into sight after just under four and a half hours. I'd stopped at an unmanned petrol station on the way, just two pumps and a pay machine between them. It was in the middle of nowhere and the bright white light burning down from the canopy made it look like a UFO landing site. You just placed your cash or credit card in the slot, selected fuel type and off you went. I wondered how quickly it would have been trashed and robbed if this was the UK. I took the rest of the drive slowly, thinking things through, compiling a mental checklist of all the kit I'd need to make entry.

Pulling up outside the big glass shutters, gagging for a brew and something to eat, I realized I didn't have a key. There was nothing to do but hit the horn. A few seconds later a light came on and Liv appeared at the door. Thunderbird 3's hangar door opened and I drove in. Before I'd even switched the engine off she was making a drinking sign. I nodded and gave her a thumbs up, and she went back upstairs. By the time I joined her she was in the kitchen and I could smell coffee.

'So, Nick,' she called out as I closed the stairway door, 'will you be able to get in?'

'No problem. Where's Tom?'

'He's working.' She came round the kitchen door, indicating the other side of the house with a tilt of her head. 'He's broken through the firewall, as I hoped.' She said it without any excitement, and noticed my surprise. 'You still have to get Tom into the house, Nick. Sit, I'll get the coffee.'

I did, taking off my jacket and checking Baby G. It was just before midnight. I'd see Tom later; there were more important things to be dealt with first. I called out, 'You'll need a pen and some paper.'

She came back in with the coffee tray and writing materials, still dressed in jeans and a pullover. She sat on the settee opposite mine and poured two mugs.

I picked one up. Black would do fine; what I needed was an instant wake-up after hours of car heating. 'I'll run through a list of equipment with you,' I said between sips. 'I'm going to need quite a lot of stuff.'

She picked up the pen and pad and wrote as I dictated. She was surprised by my request for six-inch nails – 150mm once she had converted them – plus a three-foot length of 4x2 wood, which became a one-metre length of 100 x 50mm.

'Why do you need this, Nick? Aren't lock-picks and electronic gadgetry more the sort of thing?'

'Can you get me some?'

She smiled and shook her head.

'That's why I want the electric toothbrush. Don't worry, I'll show you what it's for tomorrow. I'll also need the weather forecast, by the way, for a twenty-four-hour period starting at 9 a.m.'

I liked not telling her what these things were for. At last she was entering my world, things I knew about. There was one last item. 'I'd also like a weapon – a pistol, preferably silenced or suppressed.'

She looked genuinely taken aback. 'Why?'

I thought it was obvious. 'Better to have it and not need it than the other way round.'

'Have you any idea of the weapons laws in this country?'

I reminded her what my Russian friends and I had been doing to her Russian friends only a week earlier at the Intercontinental.

It didn't work. 'I'm sorry, Nick, I wouldn't get you one even if I could. I have nothing to do with that sort of thing. Besides, you were employed precisely because Valentin wanted finesse.'

The last time I'd gone on a job unarmed I'd ended up shot. After that I promised myself I'd always carry, even if I thought I didn't need to. I wanted to tell her it wasn't just finesse that got Val into the boot of the Volvo, but I could see by the look on her face that it was pointless. It was strange, ROC probably had more weapons than the British Army. I thought about asking if her guy from St Petersburg could get me one, but decided against it: it's always best to keep an ace or two up your sleeve.

She stood up. 'I'm going to bed now, Nick. Please, help yourself to food. I should be back by ten thirty tomorrow with your list.'

I was beginning to feel hungry and headed for the kitchen. Digging out tins of tuna and sweetcorn from a cupboard, I emptied them into a bowl and went in search of Tom as I mixed it up with a fork and got it down my neck.

He was sitting at the ThinkPad, his head in his hands.

He didn't look up as I came in.

'All right?'

'Yeah, all right.' There was a blocked-up nasal sound to his reply. All was not well at Camp Tom.

'Seriously, you OK?'

I wanted to sound surprised at finding him so down, but I could guess at the reason. Being so near the witching hour, reality was grabbing him by the throat.

'I'm really worried, Nick. You know, I . . . I . . .' There was a big sigh from him, and I knew he was trying to get out what he really wanted to say. 'I want to get home, Nick. I don't wanna do it, mate. No way am I going back inside . . .'

He didn't want to go back home; he just wanted reassurance that everything would be fine. I'd seen it plenty of times, men on jobs asking for one thing but really needing another, especially when they're scared. It's not a bad thing; fear is natural, and the secret is understanding that it's normal. Only then can you do the abnormal.

'Tom, I told you, this won't get you put away. No way would I be doing anything that would get me within a thousand miles of a prison. I've done some, too, you know.'

He looked up at me with tears in his eyes. 'I don't wanna go back, Nick. There were some hard boys in there, know what I mean?' His mouth quivered. 'I couldn't hack it, mate.'

I knew then exactly what he was crying about. Tom might play at being Jack the Lad, but behind bars he'd been fair game for the boys banged up for a long stretch.

I thought about my time in borstal and how much I'd hated it. If the wing daddies weren't fighting each other, they were keeping a grip on their little empires and just generally fucking up the lives of those who were within reach. The only way I'd survived, being, like Tom, one of the youngest, had been to act mad. That way the older ones, being locked up and confused about their sexuality, thought I was just a weirdo and left me to it. Because, who knew, I might try and kill them if they touched me.

I didn't see Tom being able to act that weird and get away with not being made someone's special friend. I nodded and felt genuinely sorry for him. 'Don't worry, mate. All that's finished with, I guarantee it, Tom.'

He sniffed and wiped his nose, embarrassed at his display of vulnerability.

'Best bet is to go have a wash and get your head down. We have a busy night tomorrow.'

I tapped his shoulder playfully, leaving him to sort himself out. He didn't need me there to embarrass him even more by seeing him like this. Besides, he was coming with me tomorrow night whether he liked it or not. As I headed back to my room I thought that, in addition to nails and lumps of 4x2, Liv had better get Tom a brave or stupid pill, depending on which way you looked at it.

I started to undress and listened as Tom walked past my door, going in the direction of the living area, probably in search of a glass of water to replace all the liquid leaking down his face.

In the shower I checked out the nice knee, shin and back bruises I'd got from my snow jumping and went to bed. I was knackered, but thoughts about the job kept me awake, going over making entry and actions-on if there was a fuck-up.

I must have been lying there for an hour, listening to the hum of the air-conditioning, when Tom shuffled past once more towards the living area. He would probably be like this all night now, but he'd live. If he was still wobbly in the morning I'd remind him again about how much money he'd soon have in his pocket. More than enough to get away from that poxy flat and Janice. I'd already decided that I would give him the full $300,000. Why not? I wouldn't have got this far without him.

Another half-hour hummed by. I was still thinking about tomorrow night, mentally checking that Liv's shopping list was complete, when I realized that Tom hadn't come back.

Yawning, I put on my jeans and shirt and wandered off to have a brew with him, maybe talk him round a bit more.

The lights were still on in the living area, but there was no sign of Tom. I checked the kitchen. He must have gone back and I hadn't heard him. As I turned, I noticed that the door leading to Liv's side of the house was open, and I knew that she'd closed it behind her.

Crossing the living area, I started to mooch down her corridor. The door layout was the same as our side, so she'd be in one of the two bedrooms. It wasn't hard to tell which. There was noise coming from the first door on the left. I didn't know who was doing what to whom, but the grunts and moans were unmistakably theirs.

I turned back up the corridor, leaving them to it, realizing, yet again, that I didn't have a clue when it came to women.

19

Tuesday, 14 December 1999

By the time I got up Tom was showered and dressed, hair still wet, sitting on the sofa drinking milk. He was certainly cheerful enough. 'Morning, Nick. Coffee's in the pot. Liv has gone to get your stuff. Said she'll be back about tenish.'

I went into the kitchen, poured some coffee and checked out the food. I was dying to ask him about last night, but decided to wait and see if he said anything first. I didn't want to sound like a dickhead, and things were getting very weird. First Liv and her friend at the station, and now this. I wondered if she'd been fucking Tom for years, but immediately dismissed the thought. Once you'd had a taste of Liv, you wouldn't decide to settle down with Janice, and why bother to get me to do the job of recruiting him in the first place?

Fixing myself a plate of crispbreads, cheese and cherry jam, I dumped it all on a tray and went and sat opposite him. I put on my concerned face and asked, 'How do you feel this morning, mate? Still want to bin it?' I concentrated hard on spreading my jam.

'I'm sorry about last night, Nick. I was just worried, you know.'

I nodded. 'These things happen to everyone at some time or other. Anyway, you look a lot better this morning.' I gave him a grin. 'There's nothing like a good night's sleep.'

He avoided the subject. 'It is going to be OK, Nick, isn't it?'

'Of course. I had a really good look at the house last night. It's just a big old mansion in the woods, trying to look like Microsoft HQ. Piece of piss. Next stop, the bank that likes to say yes – that's the beauty of it.'

I got back to my crispbread, relieved that I didn't have to deliver another mammoth pep talk.

He grinned back. 'Nice one, mate. Nice one.' His head had gone back into jerky chicken mode.

I took a mouthful of coffee. 'Yep, it's good we both got some sleep. We'll certainly be knackered tomorrow morning.'

He sipped his milk, trying to hide his face in his mug.

I couldn't resist any longer. 'I heard you, you know.'

He turned bright red. 'What? What are you on about?'

'Hey, listen, good luck, mate, but keep the noise down in future, will you? Some of us old fuckers can't take too much excitement.'

He laughed nervously, embarrassed, but at the same time rather proud. I couldn't blame him.

'What's the secret, Tom? I mean, no disrespect to Miss Nordic Myth, but warm and wonderful she isn't. Have you met in a past life?'

He shifted in his seat as embarrassment took over. 'Nah, mate. Never met the girl before. But, you know, I was out here getting a drink when she came out. She saw I was worried, and we got talking and that . . . you know.'

I didn't, that was the problem. One minute he's asking me if I trust her, a minute later he's making the earth move for her. Well, probably the other way round. I gave myself another mental slap. Fuck it, I didn't care what was going on. I realized, with a shock, that I was jealous. I needed to sort my shit out, concentrate on making money and leave anything else that was going on well alone.

I got up, leaned over and tapped him on the shoulder. 'Just make sure you've got those daps of yours for tonight.'

'Daps?'

'Plimsolls, whatever you call them. Make sure they're clean and dry. Don't wear them today, just keep your new boots on, all right?'

With that I picked up my mug and left.

Freshly showered, I lay on my bed and visualized once again making entry on target. I always found it easy to run the film in my head, as if my eyes were the camera lens and my ears the recording equipment. I listened to what the snow sounded like as we walked to the veranda, then the creak of the wooden decking, working out how I would deal with it, attacking the lock on the door and then moving Tom around the house until we found what we were looking for. I replayed the footage three or four times, from leaving the car to returning to it; then I started to edit it with different versions: What if Tom and I were on the veranda and the door opened? What if there were dogs in the compound? What if we were compromised in the house?

I played the different versions and stopped the film at the crisis points, thought about what I should do and then hit Replay, trying to come up with answers. It wouldn't go exactly to script, it never did. On the ground, every situation would be different. But the film was a starting point; it meant I had a plan. From there, if the shit hit the fan, it would be a matter of adapting the plan in the one or two seconds available, so that I could react to whatever the threat was instead of standing there feeling sorry for myself.

I'd been in my room for about two hours when there was a knock on the door.

'Nick?'

Tom poked his head round the corner.

'Liv's back. You won't tell her you know, will you? It's just that . . . well, you know.'

I got off my bed and walked out with him, using my forefinger and thumb to mime zipping up my lips.

She was in the living room, dropping her hat and black leather coat on the settee. There was no exchange of eye contact between them and her whole manner announced there was no time for small talk.

'Good morning,' she said briskly. 'It's been confirmed: they're now online.'

She must have been to meet her St Petersburg friend as well this morning.

'Could you two give me assistance? There are quite a few bags.'

We followed her downstairs, where the first thing she passed me was a sheet of paper with the weather forecast printed out in Finnish. 'It says there is a possibility of snow showers in the early morning. That is good for you, no?'

Tom was busy opening the rear door of the Merc.

'What do they mean by early morning?'

She shrugged her shoulders. 'I asked the same question. I'm afraid no-one could tell me exactly. Anything between two and ten.'

I handed it back to her and walked to the rear of the 4x4, not letting Tom see my concern. This was bad. Snow is good for hiding sign, but bad for making it. We had to get in and out as quickly as possible, otherwise the only footprints left on the ground at first light would be our fresh ones, not mixed in with the others I'd seen in the compound last night. Unless, that was, the shower kept falling for long enough to cover our tracks once we had left. This wasn't good at all; you just don't take that sort of risk if a job has to remain covert. But a deadline is a deadline, and I had no choice but to go in regardless.

I was flapping and hoped that God hadn't really been listening to me in Tom's flat, just waiting to get his own back by stopping the snow the moment we got into the house.

Tom picked up a set of eighteen-inch bolt cutters from the back seat and held them out with a quizzical expression on his face.

I had lifted the tailgate and was holding an

armful of bags and boxes. 'Just a bit of standby kit we might need tonight, mate. Come on, let's give her a hand.'

Tom followed me upstairs, the bolt cutters under his arm and his fists full of carrier-bag handles. He dumped it all next to the stuff I'd carried up on the wooden floor outside the kitchen and was soon sniffing around in the bags like a child on the hunt for sweets. Liv was close behind.

It was time to put the work disk into my hard drive again. 'It's pointless you two hanging around,' I said. 'Give me a couple of hours to sort myself out here, and after that I'll explain why I needed all this stuff. Make sure those daps are clean, Tom. No mud that could flake off, or grit in the soles, OK?'

He nodded.

Liv looked at him, puzzled. 'Daps?'

'The canvas shoes I've been wearing.' He had already put his new boots on.

She nodded, mouthing the new word to herself as she logged it in her memory bank and left in the direction of her room. 'I'll see you both later.'

Tom was looking at me as she disappeared into the corridor and the door closed. I knew what was going on in his head. 'Don't worry, mate, not a word.'

He smiled, relieved. 'Thanks, 'cos, well, you know.' He waved to me as he walked towards our side of the house.

'Tom, is there anything you need me to do for you?'

'No thanks, mate,' he said with a sudden twinkle. 'Liv's already done it.'

He stopped, turned and tapped his forehead with his index finger. 'Nah, seriously, everything I need is up here. Do you want me to run through it?'

'No point. I'll just concentrate on getting us in and out of there. What are you looking for, anyway?'

He grinned. 'I won't know until I see it.'

He disappeared and I emptied the carrier bags and boxes onto the floor. I sorted the clothing first, as it was the easiest to check. Shiny nylon puffer jackets were not what we needed at a time like this; all the stuff I'd asked Liv for was made of wool and thick cotton. We had to have clothes that weren't going to rustle, and they had to be dark and completely non-reflective – no shiny buttons or safety tape. I cut out any Velcro holding pockets or flaps with my Leatherman: Velcro makes quite a noise when pulled apart, and I couldn't afford for that to happen on target. Anything dangling, like drawcords, I also removed. Once in the house, I couldn't afford for something to get caught and be dragged onto the floor. All this might sound over the top, but people have been killed for less. I'd learned by others' mistakes, and I'd never forget seeing a mate of mine hanging from the top of a fence in Angola by the nylon cord in his combat smock. He didn't have anything to cut himself free with and had to watch as guards came, stopped to take aim just metres away, and put at least fifty rounds into him.

Liv had chosen some good woollen outer gloves for us, as well as a pair of thin cotton contact gloves, so I could manipulate the door lock or whatever without my bare hands freezing onto the metal. There was also a pair of trainers for me to wear, from which I cut out the reflective heel piece. I hadn't ordered any for Tom; he had his daps. We would put them on just before entering the house. Heavy-soled boots make noise and drag in snow, leaving sign. The outside world needs to stay out there.

I found the bag of six-inch nails, some lengths of one-inch thick nylon webbing and a handful of metal washers. The length of wood was exactly as specified. I couldn't help laughing to myself at the thought of Liv in a DIY shop. She probably hadn't even known these places existed.

There was a neat little hacksaw in a cardboard and plastic shrinkwrap. I ripped it out of its packaging and used it to cut half a dozen six-inch lengths of wood.

Liv had done her work well; the washers went over the six-inch nails and were stopped by the nail head. I slipped two washers over each, since they would be taking quite a strain.

Fifteen minutes later, I had six fist-sized lumps of wood, each with a nail hammered through. The nail had then been bent into an acute angle about halfway along with pliers, so the whole thing looked a bit like a docker's hook. The exposed metal of the nail, apart from the bit at the bend and about half a centimetre either side of it, had then been covered with rubber bands to eliminate noise when they were used. Tom and I would use one hook in each hand and carry one each as a spare.

The dark-green two-inch webbing was meant for strapping skis to a roof rack. I cut four six-foot lengths of it, knotting together the ends of each so that I ended up with four loops. These I put to one side with the hooks, away from the chaos around me. The climbing kit was ready.

Liv had been right: the old ways sometimes are the best, and this method took a lot of beating. It was a little gem from the files of MI9, created during World War Two when they were asked to think up new ideas and design equipment so that POWs could escape from their camps and travel through occupied Europe to safety. They came up with silk maps, sandwiched between the thin layers of a playing card and sent in Red Cross parcels. They even changed the design of RAF uniforms to make them easily convertible into civilian clothes. This hook-and-loop device, easy to make and easy to use, was just one of the many ideas they'd come up with for scaling POW camp fences. It had worked for them; I hoped it was going to work for us.

Next I unwrapped the Polaroid camera and four packs of film. Once a film was inserted, I took a quick test shot of my foot. The camera was working fine. I stripped the other three films of their wrapping. Each cartridge of film contained its own battery power source, but batteries tend to get sluggish in cold weather, and I couldn't afford for that to happen. To keep them warm I'd make sure I kept them close to my body.

Once we'd put on our trainers and I'd made entry, I would take pictures of wherever we were on target, camera noise and flashlight permitting.

On a covert operation, everything has to be left exactly as you find it. People notice straight away when something is not precisely where it should be. It could be something obvious, like a folded rug that has suddenly been laid flat, but more often it's something almost indefinable that compromises the job; they just feel instinctively that something is wrong. Maybe their pen isn't in the position they always leave it, even by as little as half an inch; or the morning sunlight isn't shining through the blinds exactly how it normally does, lighting up half the desk; or some dust has been disturbed. We might not consciously notice these things, but our subconscious does; it takes in every detail and tries to tell us. We aren't always clever enough to understand, but we *feel* that something isn't right. A switched-on target will know that even an out-of-place paperclip constitutes a drama, and will take whatever action he feels is called for.

The fact that people would be on target gave this job a high chance of compromise, but I couldn't let it affect the way I thought about what I needed to do, just the way I planned it. I'd been successful on similar jobs in the past, so why should this one be any different?

Thinking about making entry reminded me to charge up the electric toothbrush. I went into my bathroom and plugged it into the shaver socket.

Back in the living room, I picked up the set of Allen keys. A large metal ring held about twenty of the things, in order of size. I chose the smallest one and eased it off the ring.

The room was beginning to look like Santa's

workshop, with sawdust, ripped packaging, plastic bags, clothes tags, and me sitting in the middle of it all.

The Allen key had a right-angle bend about half an inch from the end. With the pliers and hammer I straightened it out until the angle was more like forty-five degrees than ninety, being careful not to snap the soft steel. Then, having ripped the metal file from its shrinkwrap, I started to round off the end of the shorter section. It only took about ten minutes. Going downstairs to the main door, I slipped it into the cylinder lock to check. It fitted perfectly.

Back in Santa's workshop I opened the pack of Isopon and mixed equal amounts of resin and hardener from both tubes on a piece of cardboard. I took it and the Allen key back to the bathroom. Not many minutes later the key was fixed firmly to the oscillating steel shaft of the toothbrush, the bit the brush head would normally fit onto. When I'd watched the door of the target house being kicked closed, no keys had been turned, it had just been shut and left, which suggested that the lock was a Yale-type cylinder. This gadget should do the trick.

Bringing back two white hand towels, I sat on the floor and started to file another Allen key the same way. What I had made with the toothbrush and first Allen key was a makeshift Yale gun, a device that simulates a key by manipulating the pins inside a lock. The oscillation of the tooth-brush shaft would move the Allen key tip up and down strongly onto the pins. With any luck it would displace them long enough for the lock to be opened. If not, it would be down to the old way. Still using the Allen key on the toothbrush, but with no oscillation this time, I would have to push up one pin at a time, then hold it there while I attacked the next one in line. For this a second Allen key was needed, and that was what I was busy filing down. Once I had attacked the second pin I would simply move the other Allen key along, so that it held both pins up, then keep on going until, in theory, I could open the door – that was if it wasn't bolted on the inside, of course. Which it probably would be if they had even one brain cell allocated to security.

It took me another hour to finish preparing the kit and packing it into a medium-sized dark-blue daysack. Everything was wrapped in my nice white towels, so as not to make any noise, or get smashed by the bolt cutters, the handles of which were sticking out each side of the top flap like a major league V sign.

Tom wouldn't be needing a daysack. The only kit he'd have with him was the ThinkPad and leads in their carry bag.

Liv emerged from her corridor. By now the jumper was off, and she was in her tight jeans and a white T-shirt – no bra. That would have been interesting a couple of nights ago, but now I was getting on with the job. The circumstances had changed.

She surveyed the mess as coolly as ever. 'Having fun?'

I nodded. 'Want to get Tom in to see what toys I've made for him?'

She walked past me to the lead room and I got

to my feet. I was still brushing off sawdust when they both reappeared.

Tom laughed. 'Tell you what, mate. Lego would have been easier!'

I smiled my yes-very-funny smile. 'Tom, I'm going to show you how to use this stuff.' I pointed at the hooks and straps by the settees.

'OK, but one question.' He was looking quite serious. 'I don't see an egg box or an empty washing-up-liquid bottle anywhere . . .' He looked at both of us to see if we'd got the joke. I didn't have a clue what he was on about, and nor did Liv.

'*Blue Peter*. You know, egg boxes, toilet rolls, sticky-back plastic . . .'

It was too late for a laugh. 'Ah, right, *Blue Peter*.' I'd never watched it as a kid.

Liv still didn't have a clue and clearly wasn't going to wait for an explanation.

Tom watched her disappear into the kitchen. 'I even got a badge once.'

'Right, well, there's your clothes, mate. You're going to need a bit more on than you bought yesterday.'

He picked up the contact gloves and tried them on. 'Hey, Nick, I'll wear my silk stuff underneath and be a bit kinky, eh?'

I smiled. As far as I was concerned silk thermals were about as much use as paper lifejackets. Mr Helly Hansen's stuff was the one for me.

He pointed down at the hooks and straps. 'Go on then, what are they for?'

When I explained, he looked a bit taken aback. 'We'll be like fucking Spiderman, or what?'

His head jutted, but not as confidently as normal.

'You sure you'll be all right doing this, Tom? Have you climbed before?'

'Sure I have.' He thought about that for a second. 'Can I have a practice?'

''Fraid not, mate. There isn't anywhere.'

He picked up one of the hooks and twanged an elastic band. 'Is this the only way, Nick? I mean—'

'Listen, this is the only thing you've got to do for yourself. Everything else I'll do for you.' I broke into a whisper, as if we were in a conspiracy that I didn't want Liv to join. 'Remember, we're in for a lot of money here.'

He seemed to spark up a bit and I felt quite proud of my little speech.

The coffee arrived – well, for Liv and me. The string of one of Tom's newly purchased herbal teabags was hanging over the rim of the third mug. We sat down, Tom at my side.

'OK,' I said, 'what I want to do now is explain exactly how we're going to get into, and out of, this place with your' – I looked at Liv as she pulled her feet up onto the settee – 'box of tricks.'

There was no need to set out the various phases military-style, as if I was briefing an orders group, running through all the actions-on for each phase. It would be counter-productive: I didn't want Tom to have so much stuff floating around in his head that I ended up confusing him. If he got muddled he might get even more scared. He didn't have to know why, just how.

I unfolded the map and pointed at the key locations with a pen. 'This is where we're going to park. Then we're going to walk down here.' I ran my pen down the marked track as he took small, sharp sips of his brew. 'Once we get to the area of the house, we climb the fence using the hooks and straps. Then I'll get us into the house and you can do your stuff. After that, it's out of there the same way. I'll tell you exactly what to do and when to do it. If you see or hear anything different, or there's a drama, stop doing whatever it is you're up to and stay exactly where you are. I'll be there to tell you what to do. OK?'

'OK.'

'I want to leave dead on nine, so you need to be ready fifteen minutes before. If the weather's good, we'll be in Helsinki before first light. Then we'll organize the exchange.'

This time they both nodded.

'OK, now I'm going to get something to eat and then get my head down for a couple of hours, and I suggest you do the same.'

I was going to treat him like an ET (escort to target), telling him only what he needed to know, and if there was a drama, all he had to do was stand still, I would be there to take action and tell him what to do. The less the person you're looking after has to think about, the better.

I stood up and nodded a see-you-later to them both as I went to the kitchen for some of the cheese and cold cuts in the fridge. Tom left for his room.

As well as not telling Tom too much to save confusing him, I also didn't want to scare him by suggesting anything about dramas, let alone the problems we were likely to have with the snow. Once people get negative thoughts into their heads their imaginations go into hyperdrive and they start to flap. Every noise or shadow becomes a major event, which slows down the job and also increases the chance of a compromise. Tom already knew what to do if we got split up, without realizing it: get himself to Helsinki railway station. He had enough money in that bag to charter a private jet home.

I started to pull the fridge to bits, throwing all sorts onto a plate. I'd have loved to have left straight away and be on target before it had a chance to snow, but what was the point, we couldn't get in until people were asleep. I knew better than to worry any more about the job; it only gets you all keyed up, too keen to get on with it, then you hit the target before the time is right and fuck up.

I headed for my bedroom with the food, picking at it as I went. Liv had gone. Once on my bed, I started visualizing again exactly what I was going to do, with some more what-ifs, except that now in my film it had started to snow.

There was a knock on the door. I looked at Baby G. I must have been asleep for three hours.

The door opened and Tom appeared, his long hair dangling over his shoulders. 'Got a minute, mate?'

'Sure, come in.' As if I was going anywhere.

He came and sat on the bed, looking down and chewing his bottom lip. 'I'm worried about this hook thing. Look, to tell you the truth, I ain't never done anything like that before, know what

I mean? What happens if I can't do it? You know . . . if I get it all wrong?'

I sat up. His shoulders were hunched and his hair covered his face. 'Tom, it's a piece of piss. Don't worry about it; it's all in the legs.' I stood up. 'This is how easy it is.' Putting my hands above my head, I bent my knees and slowly lowered myself till my arse was level with the floor, then lifted up again. 'Not exactly difficult, is it? Can you do that?'

He nodded. 'S'pose so.'

'Come on, let's see you, then.'

As he lowered himself towards the floor, knees cracking and creaking, he looked and sounded very uncertain, but he managed to do it.

I gave an encouraging smile. 'That's all you need to do. If your legs can do that later on, we're home and dry. But remember, small movements. No more than a foot at a time, OK?'

'Small movements. Gotcha.' He didn't look convinced.

'Just do what I do. Like I said, a piece of piss.'

'You sure?'

'Positive.'

He bit his lip again. 'I don't want to mess things up . . . you know, get caught or whatever. You know, what we talked about last night.'

'You won't. Fucking hell, kids do this for fun. I used to do it when I was a kid, trying to bunk school.' The school I was talking about was borstal, and I only wished I'd known this little trick at the time. I would have been out of that shithole quickfast. 'Tom, relax. Have a bath, do anything you want. Try your clothes on. Just don't worry about it. The only time to worry is when I look worried, OK?'

He hesitated in the doorway. I waited for him to speak, but he changed his mind and turned to go.

'And hey, Tom?'

His body stayed facing out and he just turned his head. 'Yep?'

'Don't have anything to eat when you get up, mate. I'll explain later.'

He nodded, and left with a nervous laugh as he closed the door behind him.

I stretched out on the bed and went back to visualizing each phase of the job. I wasn't happy about the prospect of snow and I wasn't happy about not having a weapon. The vegetable knife I'd used to cut the cheese with wasn't much of a substitute.

20

I got up groggily just after eight and took a shower. I hadn't slept, but because I'd been trying so hard I now wanted to. Dragging myself to the kitchen for a brew, I found Liv and Tom in dressing gowns, sitting on the settee with mugs in hand. They both looked as tired as I felt, and we exchanged only mumbled greetings. I still had one more thing to do with the kit before I double-checked the lot, so I took my brew with me to my room and got dressed properly.

At just before nine o'clock I took everything down to the car. Tom was on parade, showered and dressed. Liv didn't follow us down; she would be emptying the house tonight and was probably already busy getting it sterile. She'd take our bags with her, handing them back with the money in them.

Tom and I faced each other as I checked him out, first his pockets to make sure the only stuff in them was the equipment he needed: daps, spare hook, nylon loop and money. He didn't need 100 marks in change rattling around in his pockets, just the paper money in a plastic bag tucked into his boot to get food and transport if he was in the shit. Most important was the ThinkPad and leads, jammed into the nylon carry bag hanging over his shoulder but under his coat. I didn't want the battery getting too cold and slow on target. I then had to make sure that none of it fell out, especially his spare hook.

I got him to jump up and down. There were no noises and everything stayed in place in his large, padded blue-check coat. Finally I made sure he had his gloves and hat. 'All right, mate?'

'No drama.' He sounded convincing.

I put the daysack on over my coat. We looked like Tweedledum and Tweedledee. 'OK, you check me now.'

'Why?'

'Because I might have fucked up. Go on.'

He checked me over from the front first, then I turned so he could check the daysack was securely fastened. Everything was fine until I jumped up and down. There was a noise coming from the pocket my spare hook was in. Tom looked almost embarrassed as he reached in and brought out the two nails that had been rattling around.

'These things happen,' I said. 'That's why everyone needs to be checked. Thanks, mate.'

He was very pleased with himself. It's amazing what a couple of well-placed nails can do to boost someone's confidence and make them feel they're contributing to things.

Tom and I got into the car and wheels turned just after nine o'clock. Liv still hadn't made an appearance to say goodbye.

He was pretty quiet for the first twenty minutes or so. As I drove, I talked him through each phase again, from stopping the car when we got there, to entering the house and finding what we were looking for, to me turning the ignition back on once I had the ThinkPad securely in my possession. I concentrated on being relentlessly positive, not even beginning to suggest that things could go wrong.

We got to the drop-off point after three and a half hours, with me flapping every time I'd had to turn the wipers on to clear the windscreen of shit thrown up by cars in front, thinking that the snowfall had started.

Once in the firebreak near the target I killed the lights, but I left the engine running as I looked over at my passenger. 'You all right, Tom?'

When we'd done the drive-past a couple of minutes earlier I'd pointed out the track we were going to go down. He took a deep breath. 'Ready to roll, mate. Ready to rock 'n' roll.' I could sense his apprehension.

'Right then, let's do it.' I got out of the car, closing the door gently onto the first click, just enough for the interior light to go out. Then I unzipped my flies.

Tom was on the other side of the car doing the same, exactly as I'd told him. I could only manage a little dribble as I checked the skies for even the slightest sign of snow. I couldn't see a thing in the darkness, of course, but somehow it made me feel better.

I got the daysack and my coat out of the car and rested them against one of the wheels. It was bitterly cold and the wind was getting up, each gust biting at the flesh of my face. At least we should be out of it as we moved down the track, protected by the forest, and the noise of the swaying treetops would help cover any sound we made. The bad news was that the same wind would be bringing the snow.

I put my coat on and watched Tom do the same as the daysack went on my back. So far so good. He even remembered to close his door slowly to keep the noise down.

After fully closing mine, I pressed the key fob. The lights flashed as I walked round to Tom and made sure he watched me as I placed the key behind the front wheel, covering it with snow. Getting back up, I went to his exposed ear and whispered, 'Remember, no flaps.' I wanted him to keep his ears exposed – two sets were better than one, and I still wanted him to think I needed his help, though I wasn't holding my breath on that one.

He nodded as our vapour clouds billowed together in front of us.

'We're going to have to keep quiet now.' I had to force myself to keep my mouth against his ear. This boy needed to do something about his ear wax. 'Remember, if you want me, don't call, just touch me, then whisper right in my ear. OK on that?'

'Got it.'

'Do you remember what to do if a vehicle comes?'

'Yeah, yeah, make like Superman.' His shoulders heaved up and down as he tried to suppress a nervous laugh.

'OK, mate, ready?'

He nodded and I clapped him on the shoulder. 'Right, let's go then.' I felt like an old sweat in the First World War trying to coax a young bayonet over the top.

I set off slowly, my ears exposed to the night, with Tom two or three paces behind. When we were about five metres down the track I had a check of Baby G. It was just before a quarter to one; hopefully *Friends* was crap tonight and they'd gone to bed.

We were going down the gentle incline, coming towards the bend that would take us into line of sight of the house, when I stopped, and so did Tom, just as he'd been told to. If I stopped, he stopped; if I then lay down, so must he.

Moving back to him, I put my mouth to his ear. 'Can you hear that?' I backed my head away so he could listen.

He nodded.

'Generator. We're nearly there, mate. Need another piss?'

He shook his head and I slapped him on the head in my best what-good-fun-this-is sort of way and started to walk on.

Keeping in the left-hand tyre rut, the compacted snow solid beneath our feet, we slowly rounded the bend. All I could hear was the wind high above us, whipping the tops of the pines; the sound of Tom moving behind, and the generator, its throbbing getting louder as we closed in. I looked up at the sky. Fuck it, it didn't matter if it snowed now or not; I was totally focused on doing the job. Even my nose and ears didn't feel as cold as they had last night. There was nothing I could do about the weather and nothing I could do about the conditions of the contract: it was tonight or nothing, and I was desperate for the money.

Once we were virtually in direct line of sight of the house I stopped again, listened, had a good look around, then moved on another eight or nine steps. My night vision had fully kicked in. I'd explained to Tom how to look at things in the dark – just above or below an object to ensure a good focus – and how to protect his night vision. It was a waste of time explaining why he had to do these things, all he needed to know was how.

From what I could see at this distance there didn't appear to be any lights on in the house, nor anything else to indicate that anybody was up and about. That didn't mean, however, that I was just going to bowl up to the gate. Every few steps I stopped, turned and checked on Tom, giving him a thumbs-up and getting a nod back. It was more for his benefit than mine; I just wanted to make him feel a bit better, knowing that somebody was thinking about him.

We were a few metres short of the gap between the treeline and fence when I stopped again and listened. Tom did the same, one pace after mine. If they had NVG (night viewing goggles) and were keeping watch, we would find out very soon. There was nothing I could do about it; this was our only approach.

Tilting my head so my ear pointed towards the house, I tried to listen just that little bit harder, my hearing trying to overcome the noise of the wind, while at the same time edging my eyes round in their sockets towards the house to check for movement. I must have looked like a mime artist to Tom.

There was a faint glimmer of light coming from the left-hand shutter on the ground floor; it was far weaker than last night. I could only just see it. Did that mean everyone was in bed, or crowded round the TV?

I put my hand up in front of his face and signalled Tom to wait where he was. Then my fingers did a little walking-sign motion.

He nodded as I moved off into the darkness, following the wheel rut towards the gate. I was exposed to the wind once I'd passed the treeline. It was now strong enough to push against my coat, but not enough to affect my walking. Nothing much had changed on the other side of the fence, even the 4x4 was parked in the same position.

On the recce there hadn't been any electrical current running through the fence; I would have known when I'd touched it. If there was some tonight I was just about to find out. Biting off my right outer glove, I pulled the touch glove down and quickly felt the gate, not even taking a breath in anticipation. Fuck it, just get on with it. If it was wired up, the shock wouldn't be any different because I'd hesitated. As I put the gloves back on I checked the padlocks. They hadn't been left undone, not that I'd expected them to be. That would be too much like good luck.

There was no way I could cut the gate chains or fence, because that would compromise the job.

The bolt cutters weighing a ton in my daysack were only to get us out of the compound if we were compromised on target – without them we'd be running around in there like rats in a barrel. Getting out of a place had always been more important to me than getting in.

21

I headed back to Tom and out of the wind. He hadn't moved an inch since I'd left him; head down, arms by his side, a vapour cloud rising above him. Slowly easing the daysack off my shoulders, I knelt down in the wheel rut and tugged on his sleeve.

Tom lowered himself to join me.

You only take out one bit of kit at a time from a daysack, then deal with it, which means packing so the first item you want is the last bit you put in. Getting him to keep the daysack upright by holding the bolt-cutter handles sticking out on either side of the top, I undid the clips and lifted the flap. Then, moving some of the towelling that stopped everything from rattling around, I took out one webbing loop and a hook.

Twisting two turns of the strapping around the nail hook, where it emerged from the wood, I handed the device, now with a three-foot loop hanging from it, to Tom. He gripped the wood in his right hand, exactly as he'd been shown, with the hook angled down and protruding between his index and middle fingers. Attaching another webbing loop in exactly the same way to another hook, I handed it over, and he took that in his left hand. I then assembled the other two devices in the same way, and reclipped and replaced the daysack on my back, then took one in each hand.

Looking around at both the target and the sky, I noticed no discernible change in either. I just hoped it would stay that way.

Taking a step closer to Tom, I whispered into his ear, 'Ready?'

I got a slow nod and a couple of short, sharp breaths in return. I started to move the last few metres towards the gate.

My eyes were fixed on the house, but my brain was already crossing the fence: it was going to be our most vulnerable time. If things went wrong in the house, fine, I could react. Up there on the fence, we'd be fatally exposed, just like my friend hanging from his jacket cord, watching helplessly as they walked up and shot him.

I stopped, my nose six inches from the gate, and turned.

Tom was two paces behind, head bent to the left, trying to keep the wind out of his face.

Turning back to the gate, I raised my right hand to just above shoulder height, the hook facing the diamond-shaped lattice, and gently eased the bent nail into a gap. The elastic bands around the nail were to eliminate noise, but I'd deliberately left the bend itself exposed: when I heard and felt metal on metal, I'd know it was correctly in position. Otherwise, if weight was applied with the hook badly positioned, there was a possibility of the nail straightening under the strain. That was why we both had a spare device. If there was a drama and one of these things started straightening while we climbed, the other loop and hook would have to hold our weight while the knackered one was replaced.

The bend in the nail engaged the fencing with the gentlest of scrapes, the bottom of the strapping loop hanging about a foot above the wheel rut. I inserted the left hook about six inches higher, and a shoulder width apart.

It was pointless at this stage worrying about being so exposed to view from the house. All we could do was just get on with it, hoping they didn't see us. There was no other way. If I'd tried the previous night to find somewhere to cross on the side or rear of the building, I would have left tracks everywhere for someone to spot this morning, and my boot prints sure didn't look like reindeer hooves. Even if I'd been able to recce all the way around, I would still face the problem of sign inside the compound. At least the front of the house was criss-crossed by footprints and tyre tracks.

Gripping both chunks of wood so the hooks took my body weight, I placed my right foot in the right loop and, using my right leg muscles to push my body upwards and pulling up with my hands and arms, I slowly rose above the ground. As the loop began to take the strain I could hear the nylon creaking, stretching just a few milli-metres as the fibres sorted themselves out.

The gate and chains rattled as the structure moved under my weight; I'd expected this to happen, but not so loudly. I froze for a few seconds and watched the house.

Satisfied that the right loop was supporting me, I lifted my left into the bottom of the one about six inches higher. I was now a foot off the ground, only about another forty-four to go.

I didn't bother looking at Tom again. From now on I was going to concentrate on what I was doing, knowing that he would be watching me closely and that he knew what was required of him.

I shifted my body weight again until all the pressure was on my left foot and hand; now it was this loop's turn to protest as it stretched that few millimetres for the first time. Lifting out the right hook, but keeping my foot in the loop, I reached up and put it back into the fence six inches above the level of the left one, again a shoulder width apart. Tom was right, it was like Spiderman climbing a wall, only instead of suction pads my hands had hooks, and my feet had loops of nylon strapping.

I repeated the process twice more, trying to control my breathing through my nose as my body demanded more oxygen to feed the muscles. I checked below me. Tom was looking up, his head angled against the wind.

I wanted first to gain height and clear the snow drifts in the gap, then traverse left over them and continue climbing near a support post. I didn't want us to climb directly above the wheel rut, not only because a vehicle or people might appear at the gate, but also because the higher we climbed, the more noise the fence would make as our weight moved it about. I was aiming for the first of the steel poles that the lattice sections were fixed to. If we climbed with our hooks each side of it, it would stop the fence from buckling and lessen the noise.

I now moved vertically to the left six inches at a time. After three more moves I was off the gate and onto the fence proper, and halfway up the first of the three sections that gave the fence its height. The smooth, unmarked snow was a couple of metres below me. There was still a few feet to go before I reached the support, but I didn't want to get too far away from Tom.

Stopping, I looked down at him and nodded. It was his turn to play now and follow my route. He took his time; there was a slight grunt as he took the weight on his right leg, and I hoped he remembered what I'd said, that it was all in the leg muscles, even though that was a lie. He'd need quite a bit of upper-body strength as well, but I wasn't going to tell him that. I didn't want to put him off before he'd even started.

The gate moved and the chains rattled far too loudly for comfort. Thankfully the wind was blowing from left to right, carrying some of our noise away from the building.

Tom hadn't quite got the hang of how to balance himself. As he went to insert his left foot in the loop he started to swivel to the right, forcing himself round to the left so he was flat against the fence once again. I could hear clown music playing in my head already. As I looked down at him under my right armpit, I thought of all the other times I'd had to climb over obstacles or move along roofs with people like Tom, experts in their field but simply unused to anything that demanded more physical co-ordination than boarding a bus or getting up from a chair. It nearly always ended up in a gangfuck.

He looked so ridiculous that I couldn't help smiling, even though his incompetence was the last thing I needed right now. For a moment I thought I'd have to go back down to him, but he eventually got his left foot into the loop and made his first ascent. Unfortunately he was so jittery that he started to swing over to the left as he released the right hook from the fence.

Tom worked hard at it, huffing and grunting as he struggled to sort himself out, then, strangely, he found the traverse a bit easier. He still looked a bag of shit, but he was making progress. I kept my eyes on target while he made his way towards me.

Moving up and across a few more times, my hooks were soon each side of the first support. The massive steel pole was maybe a foot in diameter. I waited again for Tom, who was generating less noise now that he'd traversed onto the more rigid fence. The wind burned my exposed flesh as I forced myself to look around and check. The snot from my runny nose felt as if it was freezing on my top lip.

Ages later, Tom's head was less than a metre below my boots. Beneath us lay a deep drift of snow which extended back five metres to the treeline.

Now that we both had a hook on each side of the support, the going was good and firm. All we had to do from here was climb vertically and get over the top. Pulling one hook away at a time I checked the nails. They were standing up to the strain.

Tom was going at it like this was Everest, great clouds of vapour billowing round him as he panted for breath, his head moving up and down with the effort of sucking in more oxygen. He'd be sweating big time under his clothes, as much from the pressure he was under as from the huge amounts of physical energy he was needlessly exerting.

I moved another six inches, then another, edging my way upwards, wishing we were going a bit quicker. About two thirds of the way up, I looked down again to check on Tom.

He hadn't moved an inch since I'd last done so, his body shape flat against the fence, holding on for dear life. I couldn't tell what had happened and there was no silent way of attracting his attention. I willed him to look up at me.

He'd completely frozen, a common occurrence when people climb or abseil for the first time. It certainly has nothing to do with lack of strength – even a child has enough muscle to climb – but some people's legs just give out on them. It's a mental thing; they have the strength and know the technique, but they lack the confidence.

At last he looked up. I couldn't make out his expression, but his head was shaking from side to side. From this distance there was no way I could reason with him or offer assurance. Fuck it, I'd have to go down to him. Extracting the right hook, I began descending and traversing to the left. This was turning into a Billy Smart circus act.

Getting level with him, I leaned across until my mouth was against his left ear. The wind picked up more and I had to whisper louder than I wanted. 'What's the matter, mate?' I moved my head round to present an ear for his reply, watching the house as I waited.

'I can't do it, Nick. I'm fucked.' It came out somewhere between a sob and a whimper. 'I hate heights. I should have told you. I was going to say, but . . . you know.'

It was pointless showing him how pissed off I was. That's just the way some people are; it's no good shaking them or telling them to get a grip. If he could, he would. I knew he wanted to get over the fence just as much as I did.

'Not a problem.'

Moving his head away from mine, he looked at me, half nodding, half hoping I was going to call it a day.

I got my mouth into his ear again. 'I'll stay alongside you all the time, just like I am now. Just watch what I do and follow, OK?'

As I checked the house I heard him sniffing. I looked back; it wasn't just snot; he was in tears.

No point rushing him; not only did we have to get over, but we had to do it again once we'd done the job. If it started snowing now this really would turn into Billy Smart's evening performance.

My feet were in the wrong position; his right foot was down, but mine was up. Moving to alter that, I put on my best bedside manner. 'We'll just take it nice and easy. Lots of people are scared of

272

heights. Me, I don't like spiders. That's why I like coming this far north, there's none of the fuckers here. Too cold, know what I mean?'

He gave a little nervous laugh.

'Just keep looking at the top of the fence, Tom, and you'll be OK.'

He nodded and took a deep breath.

'All right, I'll go first. One step, then you follow, all right?' I slowly put my weight on the left strap, moved up one and waited for him.

He shakily raised himself up level with me.

We did the same again.

I leaned towards his ear. 'What did I tell you, piece of piss.' While I was close to him I quickly checked his hooks. They were fine.

I decided to let him have a rest, let him bask in his glory and gain some confidence. 'We'll rest here a minute, all right?'

The wind gusted around us, picking up ground snow in flurries. Tom was staring straight ahead at the fence just inches from his face. I was watching the house, both of us sniffing snot.

When his breathing had calmed down I gave him a nod; he nodded back and I started climbing again, and he kept pace, stride for stride.

We reached the top of the second of the three sections. Tom was getting the hang of it; a dozen or so more pulls on each side would take us to the top. I leaned across. 'I'll get up there first and help you over the top, OK?'

I needed to traverse again. I wanted to cross away from the top of the pole so we didn't kick off any of the snow that had collected on its top.

Something like that would be too easy to notice in daylight.

Tom was getting worried again and started to slap my leg. I ignored it at first, then he grasped my trousers. I looked down. He was in a frenzy, his free hand waving towards the track as his body swung from side to side.

I looked down. A white-clad body was fighting its way through snow that was nearly waist deep in the gap on the other side of the track. Behind him were others, and yet more were emerging from the treeline and moving directly onto the track. There must have been at least a dozen.

I could tell by the position and swing of their arms that they were carrying weapons.

Shit, Maliskia.

'Nick! Whatdowedo?'

I'd already told him a few hours ago what to do if we had a drama on the fence: do what I did.

'Jump. Fuck it – jump!'

22

Gripping the wood hard and lifting with my arms so the hooks took my body weight, I kicked my feet from the loops and let go with my hands. I just hoped the snow was deep enough to cushion my ten-metre fall.

I plummeted past Tom, who was still stuck to the fence, and prepared myself for the jump instructors' command when the wind is too strong and the drop zone, which should have been a nice empty field, has suddenly become the M1: accept the landing.

I plunged into the snow feet first and immediately started a parachute roll to my right, but crumpled as my ribs banged hard against a tree stump, immediately followed by one of the handles of the bolt cutters giving me the good news on the back of my head. It was starburst time in my eyes and brain. Pain spread outwards from my chest, the snow that enveloped me muffling my involuntary cry.

I knew I had to get up and run, but I couldn't do a thing about it: my legs wouldn't play. Eyes stinging with snow, I moaned to myself as I fought the pain and tried to work out how deep I was buried.

Tom had found the courage to jump. I heard the wind being knocked out of him as he landed to my left, on his back. I still couldn't see anything from under the snow.

He recovered, panting hard. 'Nick, Nick!'

The next thing I knew, he was towering over me, brushing the snow from my face. 'Nick. Come on, mate, come on!'

My head was still spinning, my co-ordination screwed. I was no good to him and knew it would be only seconds before we were caught. 'Station, Tom! Go, go!'

He made an attempt to pick me up by my arms and drag me, but there was no way that was going to happen. It would have been hard enough for him in normal conditions, let alone in deep snow. 'Tom, the station. Go, just fuck off!'

His breathing laboured a second time as he tried to take me with him. The pain in my chest increased as he pulled my arms, only to be relieved as he let me drop back down. At last he'd got the message.

I opened my eyes to see him pulling the spare hook out of his coat. For a split second I couldn't work out why, and then I heard grunting right behind me. The Maliskia had got to us.

Tom launched himself over me. There was the sound of a thud, and a scream that was too low-pitched to be his.

The next thing I knew, Tom fell beside me, sobbing. There wasn't any time for that shit, he had to go. I pushed him away from me with my hands.

Not checking behind him, he left, stumbling over me on the way.

I wanted to follow but couldn't. Rolling over onto my stomach and pushing myself onto my hands and knees I started to drag myself up out of the hole. As I crested the top I saw Tom's victim, just three metres away and trying to get to his feet. He brought his weapon up, blood oozing from the thigh of his white cold-weather gear and all around the climbing hook that was embedded in it.

Diving back down into the snow, I heard the unmistakable, low level *click-thud, click-thud, click-thud* of an SD, the suppressed version of the Heckler & Koch MP5. The click was the sound of the working parts as they ejected an empty case and moved forward to pick another from the magazine. The thud was the gas escaping as the subsonic round left the barrel.

I heard another *click-thud, click-thud* as two more rounds were fired. I wasn't his target, but I lay there not wanting to move and risk getting hit. I wasn't even too sure if he knew I was there.

The firing stopped and I heard short sharp breaths as the hooked body took the pain.

Then more arrived and I heard a shout.

'OK, buddy, it's OK.'

My pain suddenly disappeared, to be replaced by an enormous feeling of dread. *Shit.They were Americans*. What the fuck was I in here?

The hooked man answered haltingly between anguished gasps. 'Help me to the track, man. Ah, sweet Jesus . . .'

They were swarming all around me, and I knew it wouldn't be long before I got the good news. I turned my head and, as I opened my eyes and looked up, two white-covered figures with black balaclavas under their hoods were nearly on top of me, their breath clouds hanging in the cold night air. Hovering over me, one pointed his weapon soundlessly at my head.

It's OK, mate, I'm not going anywhere.

The other came forward, snow crunching beneath his boots, keeping out of his mate's line of fire. Vapour was the only thing coming from his mouth. There still wasn't any communication between them.

I heard gasps and laboured breathing as Tom's victim was helped back to the track. He was in a bad way, but he'd live. Other bodies passed, pushing hard through the waist-high snow, heading in the same direction as Tom.

Any thought of escape or trying to give them a hard time was laughable. I curled up and waited for the inevitable subduing, closing my eyes and gritting my teeth to protect my tongue and jaw.

The breathing was now directly overhead and I could feel their boots disturbing the snow around me as I waited for the first kick to open me up for a search.

It didn't happen.

Instead, a cold snow-covered glove pulled my hands from my face and I caught a glimpse of a canister. I didn't know if it was CS, CR liquid or pepper, and it didn't really matter. Whichever it was, and even if I closed my eyes, it was going to fuck me over big time.

The moment I felt the ice-cold liquid make contact, my eyes were on fire. My nose filled instantly with even more snot, and I felt as if I was choking.

The flames spread all over my face. I was conscious of what was going on, but was totally incapacitated. There was nothing I could do but let it take its course.

As I choked and retched, a hand forced my face back into the snow. There were no commands to me, or any communication between the bodies.

Snorting and gasping like a suffocating pig, I struggled for oxygen, trying to move my head against the hand that was still holding it down, desperate to clear the snow pressing on my face so I could breathe, but he wasn't letting that happen.

A kick aimed at the side of my stomach got between my arms which were wrapped protectively around it, and I half coughed, half vomited the mucus that had built up in my mouth and nose. As I rolled with the pain, Sprayman pulled me onto my back, arched because of the daysack. My neck stretched as my head fell backwards. I was still choking and snot was running into my eyes.

A gloved fist hit me across the head and my jacket was unzipped. Hands ran over my body and squeezed my coat pockets. They found the spare hook, the vegetable knife, the makeshift Yale gun. Everything was taken from me, even the Polaroid film. One of them pressed his knee into my stomach with all his weight and vomit flew from my mouth. The taste and smell of strong tea from the journey filled the air around me as it spilt onto the snow. I tried lifting my head to cough up the last remaining bits in my throat, only to be slapped down. There was nothing I could do but try to keep breathing.

The character kneeling on my stomach was joined by the weapon-pointer on my right-hand side, and his freezing, fat muzzle raked against my face, pushing into the skin. The two of them just knelt there, waiting. The only sounds were their heavy breathing and me snorting like a pig.

They knew I was fucked and were just maintaining me in that position. From what I could make out through watery, painful eyes, they looked far more concerned with what was going on by the gate.

I knew I had to recover from the impact of the fall and the spray before doing anything about getting out of this shit. I accepted I had no control over myself physically, but I still had control of my mind. I had to watch for opportunities to escape, and the quicker I tried to do it, the better chance I would have of succeeding. There is always confusion in the heat of things; organization only comes later.

I analysed what I had seen. They were all in winter-warfare whites; they even all had the same weapons and were highly organized, and at least two of them spoke English with American accents. This wasn't the Maliskia, and this wasn't about commercial intelligence. I started to feel even worse about my future prospects and was pissed off big time with Liv and Val, who obviously hadn't told me everything. I just hoped I'd be able to get my own back.

I thought about Tom, and hoped that if he was alive he'd make it back to the real world as quickly as he could. He had tried to save me. The bull's-eye with the hook was probably more to do with luck than skill, but at least he'd had the bollocks to do it. Winning a fight isn't important, it's having the bottle to get stuck in that is. I'd been wrong about him.

As I lay passively facing the sky, I felt something wet and cold dissolve on my lips: the first heavy flakes of a snowfall.

The few seconds of silence were broken by the crunch of snow coming from the direction of Tom's escape route. It must be the bodies returning from pursuing Tom or collecting his corpse. I tried to look, but my vision was too blurred for me to see anything. I was down in my hole and they didn't walk near enough for me to see if they had him. If so, he must be dead; I couldn't hear him, and I assumed he'd be in pain if shot, or crying if captured, thinking about returning to gaol.

There was the crash of the chain as the gate was forced open, but still no sound from the two with me. Their silence made the situation feel even scarier than it was already.

Tom and I were probably a sideshow they hadn't been expecting. They must have had their hands covering their mouths, trying not to scream with laughter, watching our attempt to climb the fence, just biding their time for when we were at our most vulnerable. Whatever we were trying to get hold of, so were they. That scared me very much. It seemed the race wasn't only against the Maliskia.

Things were happening at the house. The front door was being battered. Then I heard screaming cutting through the wind, men's voices that couldn't be from one of the teams. These were the voices that went with high-pitched, big-time flapping.

My two new friends were still looking around, and whatever they were waiting for, they got it. Muzzleman tapped Sprayman on the shoulder and they both stood up. It was obviously time to go. As soon as the pressure on my stomach was released I was thrown over onto my front, face down in the snow while the left-hand strap on my daysack was cut, accompanied by their laboured breathing. My right arm was dragged behind me as it was pulled away from my body. Gritting my teeth, I took the pain it generated in my chest. Then I was kicked over onto my back again, and I brought my knees up instinctively to protect myself.

I didn't want eye contact, not that much of it could be done in this darkness, but I wouldn't want them to construe any look I might give them as defiance and get them sparked up, or as a sign that I wasn't as injured as I was trying to pretend.

Through semi-closed, angled eyes I could only see one of them, swinging his weapon on its chest sling until it was across his back. Nightmare sounds were still coming from the house as he knelt down, gripping my throat with one wet, cold, gloved hand, putting another round the back of my neck, and started to pull me to my feet. I wasn't going to resist at this stage and jeopardize any chance of escape.

As my body emerged from the snow hole, the wind started hitting the tears and mucus on my face. My snot started to feel like freezing jelly.

I was frogmarched, with hands still in place around my throat, following tracks that had already been made in the snow. Not leaving sign didn't seem to be a high priority for these boys.

We went through the now open gate. I could feel the wind forcing the falling snow against my face and hear the crunching footsteps of my escorts. Looking towards the house, I felt like I'd dived into a swimming pool and was moving up towards the surface, the shimmering shapes and sounds slowly becoming more distinct.

I made out more white shapes through the snow falling in front of me, in the lights that were now blazing on both floors. There were ransacking noises, furniture being thrown about and glass breaking, but the screaming had stopped. Still not a murmur from the team. The only reason the injured guy and his helper had spoken was probably because they hadn't realized where I'd landed.

I was dragged past the 4x4 and bounced onto the wooden veranda, my shins banging painfully against the steps, no doubt adding to the bruises I'd got last night. They carried on along the veranda with me, the sound of their footsteps echoing along the boards.

A battering ram had been abandoned on the threshold, a long steel pole with two rectangular handles on either side. The top hinge of the door had been pushed in and the bottom one was holding the door at a 45-degree angle inwards, the glass from its windows in shards on the floor. These guys hadn't bothered with electric toothbrushes.

We crunched over the broken glass and entered the house. The warmth enveloped me, but there wasn't time to enjoy it. A few paces inside I was forced face down onto the wooden floor of the hallway. To my right were three other people, tied up and face to the floor, two of them in just boxer shorts and T-shirts. Maybe this was the reason there was no voice contact. They didn't want these three to know who they were. The three captives looked about Tom's age, with long blond hair. One of them had his done up in a ponytail, another was crying and his hair was sticking to his wet cheeks. Shit, and I'd been worrying how many bayonets would be on target. They looked at me with the same question in their eyes as I had in my head: Who the fuck are you?

I looked away. They weren't important to me. Working out how to separate myself from these Americans was.

As I turned my head a boot tapped me on the side of the face and motioned for me to look down. I rested my chin on the floor and my hands were forced in front of me, where they could be seen. They'd taken prisoners before.

I counted a few seconds, then lifted my eyes and tried to look around, trying to gather as much information as possible to help me escape. I saw no scenes of frenzy; everybody seemed to know what they were doing. There was a lot of efficient movement by bodies in white, some with their hoods down, exposing their black balaclavas. There are many different reasons for wearing uniform, but mainly, in situations like this, it's for identification purposes.

The atmosphere seemed to be that of an efficient open-plan office. They were all armed, everybody had the same type of weapon, all suppressed. The pistol that each of them carried was very unusual. It had been a long time since I'd seen a P7, but if I remembered correctly, it fired 7.62mm rounds. There were seven barrels, each about six inches long, and contained within a disposable, Bakelite-type plastic unit. The unit was sealed and watertight and clipped into a pistol grip. The rounds were fired conventionally by pulling the trigger, but instead of a firing pin, an electrical current was sent to one of the barrels each time the trigger was pulled, via terminals, which married up when the barrels and grip were clipped together. The power source was a battery in the pistol grip. Once all seven rounds had been fired, you simply removed the barrel unit, threw it away and put on another one.

The P7 was originally designed to be fired at divers at close range and underwater, to penetrate their diving sets and, of course, their bodies. I didn't know if they were any good at longer range; all I knew was that they were silent and extremely powerful. Because of their size, they were being carried by these guys in shoulder holsters over their whites, along with thick black nylon beltkit that held their HK mags. I couldn't remember who made P7s, or if it was the weapon's real name. Not that it really mattered to me at the moment. What did matter was that these people were uniformed and efficient, and they hadn't been sent here because the computers on site weren't Y2K compliant.

They had to be from a security organization – CIA, maybe, or NSA – it didn't matter which. It was highly unusual for them to be carrying out such an operation within a friendly nation's territory. That sort of thing was normally left to dickheads like me, so that everything could be denied if it went wrong. The reason they were on the ground must be that they desperately wanted something that belonged to them, and whatever it was, it must be so sensitive that they didn't want, or trust, anyone else to go and get it. Had I been trying to nick American secrets? I hoped not. That was spying, and with no help from HMG I'd be lucky if I got out of prison in time to see Kelly's grandchildren.

I realized what had been causing the dull glow from the left-hand side of the house. Through an open door I could see it hadn't been room light escaping from the broken shutter but the glare from banks of TV screens. I made out CNN, CNBC, Bloomberg and some Japanese pro-gramme, all with anchor men and women talking business. Running captions displayed financial information across the bottom of the screen. So it wasn't *Friends* after all. I felt even more depressed. This was just like the weather, getting worse every minute.

In amongst the TVs were banks of computer monitors, most of them turned off, but some with streams of numbers running vertically down the screen, just like I'd seen Tom messing about with. The computers and VDUs were being unplugged, while more white-clad figures fiddled with other machines and keyboards in the room. I saw one hand sticking out from its whites and working some keys. It was immaculately manicured, feminine and wore a wedding ring.

The rest of the horizontal surfaces were in shit state, covered with sweet wrappings, pizza boxes, cans and large, half-empty plastic bottles of Coke. It looked like a student's flat, but with a couple of truckloads of cutting-edge technology thrown in. I realized what they'd been carrying in last night from the 4x4: it must have been pizza time.

My little recce was cut short when I saw pairs of black boots coming towards me, snow still in the stitching and laces. They were Danner boots, an American brand. I knew the make well, as I had a pair – high leg, with leather outer and GoreTex inner. The US military wore them, too.

The Tom lookalikes on the floor behind me were moving about or being moved. The one who'd been crying suddenly sounded muffled, as if he was resisting something. I risked turning my head to see what was happening, but I was too late. A hood got pulled over my head, smearing the snot even more over my top lip, mouth and chin. It was pointless resisting; I just let him do it as quickly as possible. I'd learned that the best thing to do was concentrate on breathing through these things and let your ears do the work.

The drawstrings were pulled at the bottom and

I was in a world of total darkness. Not even the faintest glimmer of light could penetrate. My face started to sweat up rapidly as the hood moved against my mouth and then out again as I breathed and tried to recover completely from the spray.

I heard boots on both sides of my head, followed by heavy breathing as my hands were forced together in front of me and a plasticuff was applied. The short, sharp sound of ratcheting was accompanied by the pain of the plastic tightening around my wrists.

There was more movement next to me and the rustling of clothes. The pizza boys were getting dressed. That was a good sign; they wanted them alive, and I hoped me, too. Between the sounds of muffled sobs and zips being done up I could hear, '*Danke* ... *kiitos* ... *spasseeba* ... thank you.' Obviously these boys didn't know the nationality of the men in white and were hedging their bets wildly, sounding off like Brussels translators.

The floorboards flexed under the pressure of bodies walking past, heading towards the door. Trailing wires and plugs dragged and clattered across the floor just past my head. Some plugs hit the steel ram in the doorway and sent out a dull ring. I presumed the computers were being lugged out. By the sounds of it, everything was being piled up outside on the veranda.

The roar of engines filled my hood as vehicles drove into the compound. The temperature inside the house had started to drop as the wind whistled through the main door. To my left, I could just make out the low mumble of voices exchanging short sentences on the veranda as the vehicles approached.

They stopped and handbrakes were pulled up on lock. Engines were left running, just like a heli on an operational sortie – it never shuts down in case it doesn't start up again. Doors opened and closed and there was a flurry of bootsteps around the veranda. I could hear the creak and echo of what sounded like the door of an empty van; it was confirmed when I heard a sliding door lock into the open position. This area was beginning to sound like a superstore's loading bay.

I tried moving my arms, as if to get comfortable, but in fact to see if we were being guarded. My answer came very quickly when a boot made contact with my ribs, the same side as my fall. I stopped moving and concentrated on the inside of my snot-lined hood as I took the pain.

I lay there waiting for the agony to subside. The sobbing and snuffling next to me got louder. The culprit was given the same sort of booted persuader to shut him up, but it just made him worse. The boy was flapping big time, and he made me think of Tom. I was still hoping that he wasn't dead and had got away, or was he, like this boy, hyperventilating in a hood, stuck in one of those vehicles?

The floorboards still gave and plugs clattered and rattled out towards the veranda. Others loaded the stuff into the wagons; I could hear their boots on the vans' metal floors.

The floorboards bent even more as the three lying next to me were hauled to their feet, amidst muffled groans and cries. The sobbing one was dragged past me and taken outside; the others followed. As the last of the three bodies passed, I heard a scream from the first one echo inside a van. I tried to convince myself they wouldn't go to all this trouble if they didn't want us alive.

As I listened to the second being manhandled after his mate, boots came for me, the creaking leather stopping just millimetres from my ear. Two pairs of large aggressive hands grabbed each side of me, under my armpits and on the arms, dragging me upright. I let my boots trail on the floor. I wanted to appear weak and slow, I wanted them to think I wasn't any sort of threat, somebody not worth worrying about, just a grey man in a bad way.

The two guys were grunting under the strain as we crossed the threshold onto the veranda, my toecaps banged over the door ram and back down onto the wooden floor. At the same time my hands and neck were blitzed by the freezing cold, then it moved onto my face as the hood, made wet with my condensed breath, started to get cold inside.

Stumbling between my escorts down the steps from the veranda, I was dragged straight ahead, then all of a sudden they stopped at the command of a gloved clap and turned right, jerking me round with them. Perhaps they were going to separate me from the others? Would that be good or bad?

Within five seconds of being dragged in a new direction I knew I was indeed going into a different wagon. It wasn't a cold metal box; it felt like the back-seat area of a 4x4. There was a climb up to get into it and it was carpeted and very warm. I was short-term pleased.

The door opposite was opened and hands reached over, gripping my coat and pulling me in, with grunts to match the effort. My shins scraped painfully over the door sill, and I was finally pushed down into the footwell. I could feel one of the rear heating vents against my neck, blowing out hot air from under the seat; it was wonderful. Even through the hood I could smell the newness of the interior, and for some reason it made me feel a bit happier about my predicament.

The vehicle rocked as somebody jumped into the rear seat above me, their heels digging into me one by one, followed by a muzzle jabbed into the side of my face, smearing mucus back towards my ear. Nothing was said, but I got the idea: keep still. I was powerless to act anyway, so the best thing to do was just lie there and take advantage of the heat.

Our rear doors were kept open and the loading-bay activity was still audible. A few feet away I heard the tell-tale creak of a van door's retaining arm pushed back under pressure and then slammed shut. There was a double tap on the side of the vehicle to let the driver know it was secure, but no-one moved yet. We must be waiting to go in convoy. A few seconds later another sliding door was shut and there was silence.

There was still no talking from these people. Either they were working by hand signals or they knew exactly what to do.

The vehicle's suspension went into overtime as

more bodies piled in. All the doors closed, and it felt as if there were at least three people on the back seat. Boots were all over the place, a couple of pairs digging in their heels to keep me down. Another kicked my legs out of the way so he could rest his feet properly on the floor. I wasn't going to argue.

We seemed to be the first vehicle to move out of the compound, in low ratio to handle the wheel ruts and ice, with the windscreen wipers slapping side to side to counter the snow.

One of the people in the front was pressing switches on the dashboard. There was a burst of music, some terrible Europop. It was turned off, and I heard them laugh quietly. No matter who they were and what side they were working for, at the end of the day they'd just done a job and so far it had been successful. They were releasing a little bit of tension.

I couldn't tell whether we'd reached the bend, because it was a long sweeping curve and I wouldn't feel it at this slow speed. But I soon sensed we were driving uphill; it wouldn't be far to go now before we hit the road. I was in deep, frozen shit and there wasn't a thing I could do about it.

23

We moved on for a few more minutes and stopped. There was a clunk as the driver disengaged low ratio and shifted into high, then set off again with a sharp left turn. We had to be on the gravel road, and the left turn meant that at least we wouldn't be driving past the Saab: that was further up on the right, towards the dead end. Did they already know where it was? Had they been here the night before, watching me carry out the recce, then followed me back to it? It made me worry about Tom again. Maybe they hadn't bothered to chase him too hard because they knew where he was heading. It wasn't whether he was dead or alive that worried me, it was just not knowing.

We began to accelerate gently. The front passenger seat back moved and creaked under what must have been a very large body pushing against my face. He was probably trying to get into a comfortable position with beltkit on.

The snow was now melting off the clothing of the three in the back and dripping down my neck. It wasn't the worst thing that had happened to me tonight, but it pretty much fitted in with the way my luck was going. There wasn't a lot I could do about it at the moment, apart from prepare for the ride by not tensing my body up and trying to relax as much as the three pairs of Danner boots would allow.

The front passenger suddenly bounced around in his seat with a shout of 'What the fuck?'

The accent was unmistakably American. 'Jesus! Russians!'

A split second later the driver hit the brakes. There was a crash of metal and glass behind us and the heavy-calibre sound of automatic fire.

The clear-cut, no-messing New England accent and the sound of rapid fire got me flapping big time. It got worse as our wagon came to a quick, sliding stop, turning sideways on the snow. The doors burst open.

'Cover them, cover them!'

The suspension bounced as everyone leaped down from the wagon, using me as a springboard. I suddenly felt very vulnerable, hooded and plasticuffed here in the footwell – a vehicle is the natural focus of fire. But I didn't care what was going on and who wanted what from whom. It was time to disappear.

Wind whistled through the open doors and the engine was still running. The heavy automatic fire was only about fifty metres away. A series of long, uncontrolled bursts echoed off the trees. This was my opportunity.

Pulling up my plasticuffed hands, I tried to tug the mask off my face, but the drawstring got stuck on my chin. My fingers were grappling with it when I heard hysterical shouting further down the road. The one advantage of working with Sergei and his gang was that I had learned to recognize some Russian. I might not know what it meant, but I knew where it came from. This had to be the Maliskia.

If I could get the hood off, my plan was to crawl into the driver's seat, then just go for it. As I was struggling with the string I got a little reminder to keep my head down. Safety glass cracked as a round came through the rear wind-screen and hit the headrest above me. At almost the same instant two rounds from the same burst ricocheted off a slab of granite at the roadside and shrieked up into the air. There were more shouts, this time from American voices.

'Move!'

'Come on, let's do it! Let's do it!'

My 4x4 wasn't going anywhere, but other engines revved, doors slammed and tyres spun uselessly in the snow.

At last I got the mask off. Pulling myself up, I couldn't feel any of my pain, and had just begun to move towards the gap between the seats when I realized it wasn't an option. About five metres away, at the side of the track behind a mound of granite, a white-clad figure was pointing an SD at my centre mass. I knew, because I could see the red splash of his laser sight on my jacket. The black-covered head screamed at me above the nightmare that was happening down the road: 'Freeze! Freeze! Down, down, down!'

Change of plan. With the laser on me, the only problem he had was not missing. There were more screams and shouts mixed with the heavy Russian fire. I got down as flat as possible in the rear footwell; if I could have crawled under the carpet I would have done.

I was feeling even more exposed now I'd seen what was happening behind me. Headlights shone in all directions, illuminating the snowfall as the Americans tried to make their escape around the van that was directly behind our 4x4. It was off to the side of the track, its left wing wrapped around a tree; the driver must still have been in his seat as I could hear and see the wheels spinning in a frenzied attempt to get back on the gravel.

The shadows thrown by the headlights caused even more confusion as bodies moved within the treeline. I saw the muzzle flash of the Russian fire, but coming from way behind the convoy now. They were moving back.

My cover must have seen movement in the treeline nearer us. He brought his weapon up and started to fire, putting down a series of rapid, well-aimed, three-round bursts. It sounded pathetic compared with the heavier-calibre opposing fire; these weapons were not designed to be used at long range. Even twenty metres was a long way for an SD.

'Stoppage!'

The boy needed to change mags. I watched as he gripped his outer glove in his teeth, keeping his eyes on me. The moment the glove was off I saw a white silk touch glove in the headlights. The empty magazine went down the front of his white smock and, producing a new mag from his beltkit, he slapped it into place. He then hit the release catch, which told me these guys were the newer version of the SD – even more indication that these were official. It was all very slick; I wasn't going to escape just yet. He had a holstered P7 and his weapons drills were so good that even with him under fire there was no way I'd have time to do anything. I kept my head down and lay still.

Wagons screamed past me with skidding wheels, the tree-loving one in the lead, glass smashed and holes in the bodywork, revving far too fast, trying to gain speed. Our vehicle group must have been giving covering fire while they moved out of the danger area.

The New England voice was back in earshot. 'Move on, move on. Come on, let's go, let's go, let's go!'

The guy covering me got up, still pointing his weapon at me as he moved forward. He jumped into the wagon, ramming his heels down into my back and the weapon into my neck. The barrel was very hot and I could smell cordite and the oily odour of WD40. He'd probably smothered it in the stuff to protect it from the weather and it was now burning off the weapon.

The last thing I had a chance to see was him getting hold of the hood then pulling it back down over my head.

All the others were now jumping back in, making the vehicle rock with their weight. I felt the gearshift being engaged and we started to move off faster than we should, the tyres slithering and sliding as we turned back on line to move up the track.

The doors were slammed shut and I was hit by a rush of air from above. The electric sunroof was opening; a moment later I heard *click-thud, click-thud, click-thud* and a yell of, 'Get some, get some, get some!' as New England fired through the open aperture. I couldn't hear any reply from the Russians.

One of the others turned and opened fire through the rear window, adding more holes to the safety glass.

Click-thud, click-thud, click-thud.

Empty cases hit the side window with a metallic *ping-ping-ping*, then fell and bounced off my head.

Freezing cold air blasted through the roof, then the motor whined and the rush of air stopped.

'Anybody down?'

'I didn't see anyone.' That came from the rear. 'If there is, they'll be in the wagons. No-one was left.'

I got a heavy slap around the head. 'Fuckin' Russians! Who do you think you are, man?'

The front passenger was, without doubt, the commander. His accent sounded as if he should have been standing on an orange box fighting an election for the Democrats in New Hampshire, not trying to sort out a gangfuck in Finland, but thankfully he seemed to be sorting it out rather well. I was still alive.

There was a short pause, maybe while he marshalled his thoughts, then, 'Bravo Alpha.' He had to be on the net, listening to his earpiece. 'Situation?'

There was silence from the others. Well-trained

operators know better than to talk when some-body's on the net.

The Democrat let out a cry. 'Shit! They have Bravo's vehicle.' He got back on the net, 'Roger that, did you total the kit?'

There was five seconds of silence before he replied in a low, depressed voice. 'Roger that, Bravo.' He addressed the vehicle crew. 'The sonsofbitches have some of the hardware. Shit!'

There was no reply from the crew as the Democrat composed himself before getting back on the net.

'Charlie, Alpha – situation?'

He checked through all his call signs. There seemed to be four of them: Bravo, Charlie, Delta and Echo. How many people at each call sign I didn't know, but there had seemed to be loads of them at the house. It seemed the whole thing had been a gangfuck for everyone. Me getting caught, Tom; well, I didn't know; the Americans and Maliskia each only getting part of the hardware they wanted; as for the three Tom lookalikes from the house, they must be more pissed off than all of us put together.

The radio traffic had been in clear speech, which indicated they were using secure and probably satellite comms, not like my Motorolas at the Intercontinental. As they transmit, these radios skip up and down through dozens of different frequencies in a sequence that only radios with the same encryption fill, fluctuating at the same rate and frequency, can hear. Everybody else just gets an earful of mush.

He must have got a message from Echo. 'OK,

roger that, Echo. Roger that.' He turned towards the bodies in the back. 'Bobby has gotten hit in the leg. But everything's fine; it's cool.' There was a sigh of relief from the back.

I felt the fabric press against my face as he turned. 'Is that asshole still breathing?'

My cover answered, 'Oh yeah.' He gave me another dig with his heel and a muttered insult in Texan drawl.

I moaned in deep Russian acknowledgement. The commander's arse swivelled again and my head moved with it. He got back on the net. 'All stations, this is Alpha. We're still going as planned. My group will take the extra paxes. Acknowledge.'

I imagined him listening in to the other call signs on his earpiece.

'Bravo.'

'Charlie, roger that.'

'Delta, roger.'

'Echo, roger dee.'

It seemed that I was the extra 'paxes'. Whatever happened to me now, it would be down to the Democrat.

We drove in silence for another twenty minutes, still on the tarmac road. By my estimation we hadn't gone far; we couldn't have been travelling that fast because of the heavy snow.

The Democrat got back on the net. 'Papa One, Alpha.'

There was a pause while he listened.

'Any news yet on Super Six?' More silence, then, 'Roger that, I'll wait.'

'Papa One and Super Six' didn't sound like

300

ground call signs. Where possible these are always short and sharp. It stops confusion when the shit hits the fan or comms are bad, factors which normally go hand in hand.

Ten minutes later the Democrat was back on the net. 'Alpha.' He was obviously acknowledging somebody.

There was silence, then, 'Roger that, Super Six call signs are no go. A no go.'

After a pause of two seconds, he announced, 'All stations, all stations. OK, here's the deal. Go to the road plan; the extra paxes still goes with me. Acknowledge.'

Nothing more came from him as he got the acknowledgement from the other call signs. At least these guys were having a shit day too. The Super Six call signs must have been helicopters or fixed wing aircraft that couldn't fly in these conditions. In better weather we would have been flown out of here by people who worked for their Firm. Nine out of ten times these are civilian pilots with background jobs as commercial fliers, so they have solid cover stories. They'd fly in on NVGs, maybe pick us all up, or at least the kit, injured and prisoners, and scream back out of the country to a US base. Or maybe, if they were helis, they'd land on an American warship in the Baltic, where the computer equipment and its operators would be sorted out and moved on to whoever was so keen to have them. If I didn't sort my shit out soon and escape I'd land up with them in one of the Americans' 'reception centres'. I'd been shown them in the past; the rooms ranged from cold and wet 3x9 foot cells to virtually self-contained suites, depending on what was judged the best way to get information out of 'paxes' like me. No matter how you looked at it, they were interrogation centres, and it was up to the interrogators – CIA, NSA, whoever they were – whether you got processed the easy way or the hard way.

Fuck the pizza boys; I didn't care what happened to them. But now being one of the Maliskia, I'd be checking straight into my personal 3x9 with corner en suite. There was nothing I could do about that for the time being. I could only hope I'd have a chance to escape before they found out who I really was.

24

We drove quite slowly for about another twenty minutes. It was physically painful lying crammed in the footwell, but that was nothing compared with how depressed I felt about what the future held.

'Papa One, Alpha – at blue one.'

The Democrat was back on the net. Papa One must be the operating base. The Democrat was counting down to it, sending a report line so that Papa One knew the group's location.

A minute or so later we turned a sharp right.

'Papa One, Alpha – blue two.'

I could hear the material on the driver's arms rustling as he worked at the wheel, and the tyre noise told me we were still on tarmac and snow.

There was a sharp right turn and my head was squeezed against the door. Then we were bumping over what felt like a sleeping policeman, and drove another thirty metres or so before the vehicle came to a halt.

The Democrat got out, leaving his door open. As the rear doors opened, other vehicles passed and stopped all around me. The screech of tyres on a dry surface told me we were under cover, and judging by the echoes made by the vehicles we were somewhere large and cavernous.

The three on top of me started to exit. Elsewhere, engines were still running as other doors were pushed or slid open. People clambered out and walked around, but there was no voice noise, only movement. Then came the echoing clatter of steel roller shutters being pulled down manually with chains.

Whatever kind of building we were inside, they didn't waste money on heating. Maybe it was an aircraft hangar, which would make sense if we were going to have a pick-up with a fixed wing or heli. Then again, maybe it was just an old warehouse. I couldn't see a single glint of light through my mask.

The air was becoming heavy with vehicle fumes. As soon as the three pairs of feet had used me as a platform to get out of the wagon, a pair of hands gripped my ankles and started to pull me out, feet first. I was dragged over the door sill and had to put my arms out to protect myself as I dropped the two feet or so onto the ground. The dry surface was concrete.

There was lots of movement around me, and the same sort of sound as there had been in the house, the shuffling and dragging of electric plugs. The equipment was being moved out of the vans.

I heard the tell-tale clunk of metal on metal as working parts were brought back and weapons unloaded, along with the clicking of the ejected rounds being pressed back into magazines.

I was turned over onto my back and my feet

were released and left to drop to the floor. I gave a very Russian moan. Two pairs of boots walked round to my head. They pulled me up by the armpits and started frogmarching me. My feet dragged along the concrete, toes catching on bumps and potholes and now and again colliding with a lump of brick or other hard debris.

It might have seemed to the two either side of me that I was doing nothing, but at brain-cell level I was really quite busy, trying to take in all the sensory information around me. They dragged me past a wagon and even through the hood I caught the aroma of coffee, probably them opening the flasks they'd had waiting for them at the end of the job.

We passed some subdued sounds of pain and short, sharp breathing. It sounded like a woman. There were men around her.

'OK, let's get another line up.'

It seemed that Bobby in call sign Echo was a woman. They were getting fluids into her and treating her GSW (gunshot wound).

We kept moving, my feet dragging through bits of wood, cans and newspapers, theirs occasionally crunching down on plastic drinks cups. I heard the rip of Velcro, then was dragged sideways through a heavy door. They steered me round to the right as the door swung back.

The pizza boys were already here: the sound of crying, moans and groans filled what felt like a smaller area than before. The echoes made it sound like we were in a medieval torture chamber, and even in the sanitizing cold this place stank of decay and neglect.

A couple more paces and we stopped, and I realized the others were being kicked; that was why they were screaming. I heard boots making contact with bodies and the grunts of the kickers.

I was pushed down to the ground and given a good kicking as well. The moans and sobs seemed to come from my right, and were now somehow muffled one by one. We weren't all in one big room; I guessed we were being put into cupboards or storage spaces.

The moment my head banged against the toilet bowl, I knew where I was. A toilet cubicle.

Another scream and a grunt echoed as the boys were subdued and persuaded into their new accommodation. I didn't know what was worse, their noise or the fact that the kickers were doing all this without a word, making best use of the echoes to put the shits up everyone.

Guided by their kicks I crawled into the far-right corner of the cubicle, coming to rest on what felt like years of debris. The paper I felt was crispy and brittle, like very thin poppadoms. Still getting kicked, I felt a hard brick wall against my back and the base of the toilet pan against my stomach. I kept my head down and knees up in protection, gritting my teeth and waiting for the worst. Instead my hands were gripped and pulled up into the air, the plastic now tighter against my wrists because they were swelling up. I felt a knife go into the plasticuffs and they were cut. Pinioning my left arm over the waste pipe at the rear of the toilet bowl, they grabbed hold of the other arm and shoved it underneath so I had a hand on either side. It was pointless resisting; they had total control over me. There was nothing I could do yet, apart from save my energy.

They gripped my wrists together. I tensed up my forearm muscles, trying to bulk them out as much as possible. The plasticuffs came on and I heard the ratcheting and felt the pressure as they were tightened. I moaned as soon as it seemed the right thing to do. I wanted to appear as petrified and broken as the pizza boys. They left, slamming the door behind them.

I tried resting my head against the pipe, but it was unbearably cold. If there was any water inside it must be frozen solid.

I lay there amongst the rubble and trash, trying to get comfortable, but feeling very aware of the cold floor through my clothing.

There was a loud, prolonged creak as the heavy main door into the hangar area swung closed. Then there was silence, even from the pizza boys. Certainly no sounds of dripping plumbing; it was too cold for that. I couldn't hear any of the vehicles, either. Nothing but pitch-black silence.

A couple of seconds later, as if the pizza boys had all been holding their breath waiting for the bogeymen to go away, the moaning and hooded sobs began once more; after a few moments of that, the boys muttered a few words to each other in Finnish, trying to give each other a boost. They sounded severely scared.

I shifted my position in an attempt to get some pressure off my wrists, trying to find out if that extra millimetre or two of muscle flexing had given me any chance of moving my wrists in the plasticuffs.

As I stretched my legs, I connected with what sounded like an empty can. The noise as it rattled and scraped over the concrete gave spark to an idea.

I waggled my head past the waste pipe, so that it was resting on top of my hands. Then, feeling with my teeth through the hood, I got hold of my right outer glove. That came off easily enough and I let it drop to the ground, leaving the touch glove still on my hand.

I reached forward with my head, positioning the bottom of the hood over my fingers, and got to work. I now knew the hoods were done up with a drawstring and ties round the bottom, and it wasn't long before it lay on the ground.

It seemed a total waste of effort. The cubicle was in complete darkness, and now that I had the hood off, my head was getting cold. My nose started to run almost immediately.

Leaning as far forwards as I could to free up my hands, I started to feel around on the ground. My fingers sifted through old paper cups and all sorts of garbage until I found what I wanted.

I readjusted my body around the pan to make myself comfortable while I pulled off my other outer glove with my teeth. Then, with both touch gloves still on, I squeezed the thin metal of the drinks can between my thumbs and forefingers until the sides touched in the middle. I then started to bend the two parts backwards and forwards. After only six or seven goes the thin metal cracked, and soon the two halves were apart. I felt for the ring-pull end and dropped the other one next to my gloves and hood.

Feeling gently around the broken edge, I looked for a place where I could start to peel the side down like an orange. The sensation had virtually gone in my swollen hands, but the touch glove caught on the aluminium and I found what I wanted and started to pick and tear. My fingers slipped a couple of times, cutting me on the razor-sharp metal, but there wasn't time to worry about that; besides, I couldn't feel the pain and it was nothing to what would be inflicted on me if I didn't get away from here.

Once I'd pared the metal down to under an inch from the ring-pull end, I tried moving my wrists apart as much as possible. It didn't work that well because plasticuffs are designed not to stretch, but there was just enough play to do what I wanted. Cupping the can in my right hand with the sharp edge upwards, I bent it towards my wrist, trying to reach the plastic. If I'd left more tin sticking out it would have gone further, but the edge would have buckled under the pressure. That was also why I used the ring-pull end: the thicker rim gave the cutting edge more strength.

I knew that establishing a cut into the cuffs was going to take the most time, but once I'd got into that nice smooth plastic I could go for it. It must have taken just a minute or two for the jagged tin to finally bite; then, when I was about three-quarters of the way through, I heard the loud, echoing creak of the swing door opening. Light and engine noise spilled through a gap of about two inches under the cubicle door.

There was the sound of boots on rubbish heading in my direction. The light got stronger and I started to flap big time, dropping the can and scrabbling for the hood, and, once it was on, trying to find my gloves. I didn't manage it, but just as I was gritting my teeth for the inevitable confrontation the footsteps went past.

There was a flurry of muffled pleas in English from the boys as their doors were kicked open and they got dragged out and subdued. They must have heard the Americans during the contact, too, as there was no multilingual begging now.

Doors banged and soon I could hear their feet dragging past me. Within moments, the door swung shut and silence was restored.

I felt around for the can end, not bothering to take the hood off. I couldn't have seen anything anyway. I started to work with more of a frenzy; I had to assume that they'd be coming for me next, and soon.

After two or three minutes of frantic sawing, the plastic finally gave.

Pulling the hood off, I felt around for the gloves and put them in my pocket, keeping just the touch gloves on.

Next I located the other can end. Getting slowly to my feet and enjoying being vertical, I felt around the cubicle. I found the door handle, opened it and walked very slowly and carefully out into what I could feel was a narrow corridor with painted brick walls. A faint glimmer of light under the swing door trickled into the corridor about ten feet up on my left. Picking my feet up

310

and putting them down with infinite care, my left hand supporting me on the wall, I made my way towards the light.

As I got closer I began to hear a vehicle engine revving, then starting to move off.

Once at the door I couldn't find a keyhole to look through, so, clearing the debris on the ground, I got down on my knees. Chains rattled as the roller shutter was pulled open. I wondered if the pizza boys were leaving town.

Lying flat on the floor on my right side, I managed to get my eyeball close to the bottom of the door. Reaching into my pocket, I pulled out the bottom half of the can, the one I hadn't worked on. Using the light to find a place in the metal where I could start peeling this time, I got to work and put my eye back against the gap.

I'd been right, it was some sort of hangar or factory space. It was mostly in darkness, but lit in places by 12-inch-long fluorescent lighting units, the sort that campers use. These had either been perched on the bonnets of wagons or were being carried around. The pools of almost blue light and shadow made the place look like the set of the *Twilight Zone*.

Several vehicles were parked up in a row on the far left, about forty metres away, saloons, estates, MPVs and SUVs, some of which had roof racks piled with skis.

My thumb slipped and ran along the ripped can. I still couldn't feel it, but at least some sensation was returning to my hands. Pins and needles had started to work their way around my fingers while I carried on peeling the metal back.

I looked straight ahead to the exit, my only way out, then at the people who would try and stop me. They were mostly by the two remaining vans, parked haphazardly in the middle of the hangar.

A group of maybe five or six bodies were hurriedly unloading their weapons and taking off their white uniforms and bundling them into what looked like Lacon boxes – aluminium air-freight containers. They were in a hurry, but not flapping. No-one was talking; everyone seemed to know what was required.

When one of the bodies did a half turn so that it was in profile, I realized that Bobby wasn't the only woman on this job.

As they continued to throw off their kit, I could now see where the sound of Velcro had come from: she was ripping apart the side straps from sets of body armour before stacking them in the boxes.

Another group of maybe eight were out of their whites and unpacking civilian clothes from holdalls. Others were combing their hair in the wing mirrors, trying to make themselves look like normal citizens.

I caught a glimpse of the 4x4 I'd been transported in; its back-window safety glass was pock-marked with holes where the rounds had passed through. Beyond it were the shapes of the other vehicles used on the job, which were now probably going to be abandoned. Strike marks from automatic weapons were not the best kind of modification to be sporting at traffic lights.

I couldn't see any evidence of the computer kit. I assumed they'd moved it straight on, along with the pizza boys and probably Bobby and the guy with the hook hanging from his thigh. They'd be in need of proper trauma care. Since the weather had put a stop to a quick exfiltration, the next destination would be a secure area like the US embassy. From there, the equipment would probably be moved by diplomatic bag back to the US. Dip bags are basically mailsacks or containers that by mutual agreement, other governments cannot have access to, which means they can contain anything from sensitive documents to weapons, ammunition and dead bodies. I'd even heard a story of the intelligence service bringing back the turret of a new Russian armoured personnel carrier in what must have been a party-sized one.

The pizza boys would be stuck in the embassy or a safe house until a heli could get in sometime tomorrow and airlift them out of the country, unless there was a US warship in dock. If I didn't get a grip of this situation, I knew I'd soon be following them.

Everyone was now out of their whites and in jeans, duvet jackets and hats. The woman was still organizing the loading of the Lacons. Loud metallic echoes filled the hangar as the boxes were moved into the vans.

One man seemed to be running the whole show. I couldn't see his face from this distance, but he was the tallest of the group, maybe six foot two or three, and a head above everyone else. He gathered everyone around him and seemed to be giving them a brief. They were certainly doing a lot of nodding, but his voice wasn't loud enough for me to understand what he was saying.

While he finished the briefing, the doors of the two vans slammed, both engines revved and they started to leave. Their headlights swept across the group as they turned towards the shutter.

I felt around the rim of the half can in my hands as the chains went into action. I wasn't doing particularly well with it because I hadn't really been concentrating.

I watched the Democrat's team disperse as they moved off towards the line of vehicles like aircrew to their fighters, lights swinging in their hands. They were probably going to split up and do their own thing, probably in exactly the same way as they'd come into the country in the first place.

They would now be sterile of anything implicating them in the job. They would have cover documents and a perfect cover story and would certainly no longer be armed. All they had to do was wander back to their chalets and hotels as if they'd had a good night out, which I supposed they had. None of them was dead.

More engines revved, doors slammed and headlights came on. I could see the fumes rising from exhausts. It looked a bit like the starting grid before a Grand Prix.

The people from the embassy would probably take care of the abandoned vehicles. Their priority was to get away from here now that the equipment and pizza boys were safely on their way. Their only problem was that they had a little bonus – me.

314

It looked like the Democrat and another woman were taking on that responsibility. The vehicles were now leaving, but they were still on their feet, the woman with a set of jump leads dragging along the floor as she moved out of the way of the holidaymakers. They were leaving nothing to chance.

Red brake lights lined up as they took it in turn to exit and hang left. Snow was still falling. I could see it clearly now as full beams shone out into the darkness.

Soon there was just one car left stationary, its engine running and its lights blazing. The Democrat was sitting sideways in the driver's seat with his feet on the concrete, the glow of a cigarette intensifying as he sucked on it. The interior light was on and I could make out thick curly hair on a very large head.

The jump leads were thrown into the rear seat and the woman disappeared into the darkness.

At last I'd finished the other half of the can. The blood from my fingers felt cold as it was soaked up by my touch gloves. It was a good sign. Feeling had returned to my hands.

It was quiet for a few moments, with just the engine ticking over, and then chains started rattling and the shutter closed. The woman emerged from the shadows once again and bent towards the glowing cigarette. I couldn't make out any of her features because her hair covered her face.

They talked for a moment, then he turned back into the car to stub his cigarette in the ashtray. He was clearly too professional even to leave DNA

315

evidence on the floor. By then she was round the back, pulling open the boot.

The Democrat started walking in my direction, his long legs silhouetted by the vehicle's head lamps. There was a flicker of bright white light, then the fluorescent unit in his left hand burst into life. I could see that he'd just finished pulling his balaclava back on. I watched his right hand go under his coat and come out again holding a multi-barrelled P7, which went into his coat pocket.

My body banged into shock. He was coming to kill me. I made myself calm down. Of course he wasn't coming to kill me. Why would they have gone to the trouble of bringing me here? And why the hood to hide his identity? He was taking precautions in case I'd pulled my hood off.

The car edged forward with the boot open as he got within about ten metres of the door, the light still swaying in his left hand. It was time to get in gear, otherwise I'd soon be given a dose of the medicine I'd forced Val to take last week.

I got to my feet and moved to the right of the door, away from the toilets, flapping at the prospect of taking on a guy of his size. All that stuff about the bigger they are, the harder they fall, it's a myth. The bigger they are, the harder they hit you back.

I wasn't sure how long the corridor was, but I soon found out. I'd only taken four steps when I banged into the end wall. Turning back, I faced the door, fumbling in my pocket for the other half can, breathing deeply to oxygenate myself in preparation.

The door swung open with a metallic screech of its hinges, momentarily flooding the area with bright white light. I could hear the car whining in reverse. He had turned right, his massive back to me now as he took the first few steps towards my toilet cubicle.

I moved quickly as the door closed; not exactly running, because I didn't want to trip over, but taking long, fast steps to get some speed and momentum, with my right arm raised. With the main door closed and car engine running, there was no way she was going to hear this.

He did, though, and when I was still a couple of metres away he started to turn.

I focused on the shape of his head as I leaped up and at him. Landing with my left foot forward, I swung my whole body to the left, my right arm crooked and the palm held open. Sometimes a really firm, heavy slap to the face can be more effective than a punch, and that's absolutely guaranteed if you're wielding a sawn-off drinks can with razor-sharp edges.

It hit his head hard. I didn't care where the can connected, just so long as it did. There was a loud groan. I didn't feel the can digging in, just the pressure of my arm being stopped mid-swing as the rest of my body carried on swivelling.

The light danced as the fluorescent unit in his hand clattered to the concrete, and he started to follow it. I swung to the right with my left arm slightly bent, still focusing on his head. I hit the mark; I could feel the softness of his cheek under the left half of the can, then felt it scrape around the contour of his jaw as he fell. He

317

moaned again, this time louder and with more anguish. By now he was on his knees.

As I brought my right hand down hard onto the top of his head, the metal edges dug deep, then hit bone, stripping back the skin as he fell. I gouged a thick furrow from his scalp; the can held for a couple more inches and then broke free.

He slumped to the ground, hands scrabbling to protect his head. For a few more frenzied seconds I continued to slash at his hands and head, then his hands fell away and he lay very still. He wasn't feigning unconsciousness: he wouldn't have risked dropping his hands and exposing himself to further attack. He had gone into shock, but he was still breathing; he wasn't dead. He was never going to get a job modelling for Gillette, but he'd live. There had been no other way out. If you're going to stop somebody, you have to do it as quickly and violently as you can.

The fluorescent unit threw a pool of light across the floor and onto his balaclava. The wool still looked remarkably intact, as it does when a sweater rips and the tear seems to knit itself together, unless you look at it close up. Blood was seeping through the material.

Dropping the cans, I rolled him over onto his back and, putting my knee into his face just to make things worse, I pulled out the P7 and a mobile that was also in there. That went into my pocket.

My breathing was now very fast and shallow and just slightly louder than the engine ticking over immediately beyond the swing door. I could see the red glow from the tail lights under the door gap, and my nose was filling with exhaust fumes.

Getting to my feet, I got hold of the top of his balaclava and pulled it off. At last I saw the extent of the damage. He had some severe gouges where the can had gone right through his cheeks and flaps of skin hung across his mouth. In places I could see bone through the blood-soaked, hairy mess of his skull.

I pulled the mask over my head, trying to cut down on the chances of being recognized later. It was wet and warm. I checked his body for a radio as he whined weakly to himself. There was nothing; he'd have been planning to be sterile like the rest of them. He'd had to hang onto the P7 to sort me out.

I turned towards the door. It was the woman's turn next.

Pushing through, I moved into a cloud of red fumes and brake lights. The vehicle was no more than three feet away, engine idling, boot still open and waiting for me. I moved straight to the left-hand side as the swing door banged shut behind me. Bringing the pistol up into the aim, I pointed it at the woman's face, the muzzle a foot from the glass. If she opened the door, she couldn't knock the pistol out of line quickly enough to do any-thing about it; if she tried to drive forward, she would die first round.

She stared wide-eyed at the barrel from under her multi-coloured ski hat. In the glow from the instrument panel I could see her trying to make sense of what her eyes were telling her. It wouldn't take her long; my blood-soaked touch gloves and the Democrat's mask would soon give her a clue.

With my left hand I motioned for her to get out. I was supposed to be Russian; I wasn't going to open my mouth unless I had to.

She kept staring, transfixed. She was bluffing; she'd drop me at the first opportunity.

Moving further back as the door inched open, I decided to put on a heavy Slavic accent. Well, what I thought sounded like one. 'Gun, gun!'

She stared up at me with frightened eyes and said in a little-girl voice, 'Please don't hurt me. Please don't hurt me.'

Then she opened her legs to show me a P7 nestled between her jeaned thighs. They were definitely travelling sterile, otherwise they would have had conventional weapons for this phase.

I motioned for her to drop it in the footwell. She moved her hand very slowly downwards to comply.

The moment she'd dropped it I moved in, grabbing her by her shoulder-length, dark-brown hair and heaving her out of the car and onto all fours. With the P7 jammed into her neck I felt for a mobile. It seemed I had the only one. Moving back three paces, I pointed at the far wall, where the car had originally been parked, and she got up and started walking. I didn't care what she did now that she was disarmed. All their radios would have been stashed, I had the mobile and there was no-one left that she could turn to for help.

I got into the warm car, a Ford, threw it into first gear and screamed towards the closed shutter. She was probably in the corridor by now to find out what had happened to her friend the Democrat.

Stopping alongside the four vans and the shot-out 4x4, I got out with a P7 in hand and splashed through the small puddles made by melting snow from the vehicles, ready to shoot out some tyres. You don't just go up and fire straight at rubber: there's too high a chance of the round ricocheting back. You use the engine block to protect you, lean round the wing and then do it.

The P7's signature *thud* was nothing to the high-pitched *dingggg* that echoed round the hangar as the round hit metal. Then there was a hiss as air escaped under pressure.

I took a look behind me; there was nothing happening from the corridor yet.

Once all vehicles were taken care of, I jumped back into the driver's seat and aimed for the shutters, though this time in reverse, so the head-lights were pointed at the swing door. If she came for me, I wanted to see.

I braked, threw the gearbox into neutral and leaped out. The ice-cold metal chains burned my hands even through the touch gloves as I pulled down in a frenzy to open the shutters. Raising them just enough to get the car out, I clambered back in and reversed out into the snowfall, point-ing the vehicle in the direction everyone else had gone.

I left the hangar behind, not knowing whether to feel sorry for the Democrat, relieved at still being alive, or angry with Val and Liv. I checked the fuel tank; it was nearly full, as I would have expected. The mobile went out the window and buried itself in the snow. No way was such a fantastic tracking device going to stay with me.

The snow was falling heavily. I didn't have a clue where I was, but that didn't really matter as long as I got away. Pulling at the mask, I felt the Democrat's blood smear across my face. It finally came off, and I threw it into the footwell along with the other P7.

Hitting the interior light, I took a look in the mirror. There was so much red stuff on me I looked like a beetroot. There was no way I could drive after first light or in a built-up area looking like this.

The steering wheel, too, was smeared with blood from the touch gloves. I'd have to sort myself out. After maybe an hour I pulled off the road, and had a quick wash in the freezing snow. Then, with a cleaned-up body and car, and the blood-soaked gear buried in a snow drift, I drove through the night, looking for signs that would steer me to Helsinki.

The more I thought about it, the more severely pissed off I became. Whether Liv and Val knew about the Americans wanting to join in the fun, I wasn't sure, but I intended to find out.

25

Wednesday, 15 December 1999

I sat on the floor next to a radiator in the corner of the station, facing the row of telephone booths that displayed the DLB loaded sign. The black marker strike down the side of the right-hand booth was clearly visible from the bus-station doors immediately to my right. I had a copy of the *International Telegraph*, an empty coffee cup and, in my right pocket, a P7 with a full seven-round unit. Detached from its pistol grip in my left-hand pocket was the other unit, containing three remaining rounds.

As soon as the shops opened that morning I'd bought a complete set of clothes to replace the cold, wet ones I was wearing. I was now in a dark-beige ski jacket, gloves and a blue fleece pointed hat. I didn't care if I looked a numpty; it covered up my head and most of my face. My pulled-up jacket collar did the rest.

Pain lanced across my left shoulder as I adjusted my position. The bruising probably looked horrendous. There was nothing I could do about it but moan to myself and be thankful I hadn't fallen on anything sharp.

I'd dumped the car off at a suburban railway station just after eight o'clock that morning and trained into the city. The snow was still falling, so the vehicle would be covered by now and the plates would be uncheckable. On arrival at Helsinki I'd pulled off the left-luggage ticket from under locker number eleven and collected my bag, cash, passports and credit cards. I also checked for Tom's ticket under number ten. It was still wrapped in its plastic and taped under the locker.

I'd been thinking about him a lot. If the Americans or the Maliskia hadn't killed him last night, the weather would have. Tom had skills, but playing at Grizzly Adams wasn't one of them.

I felt pissed off, but not too sure if that was for him or me. It was then that I wrote him off. There has to be a stage when that happens, so your mind can be free to concentrate on more important things, and I wasn't short of those.

I left his bag ticket where it was. It would be an emergency supply of money and a new passport, once I'd tampered with it, in case what I was about to do went to rat shit.

Despite my best efforts, I found I couldn't help feeling sorry for Tom as I sat and watched a constant flow of travellers moving through the doors. It was my lies and promises that had got him where he was now, face down in the snow or bundled up somewhere in an American body bag. The thing that made me feel even guiltier was that I knew I was just as pissed off about not making any money as I was about his death.

Cutting away from that, I buried my hands deeper into my pockets, wrapping them round the P7 barrels. I was getting even more annoyed because I'd dumped the bag and blanket that could now be keeping my arse warm and comfortable, and because I knew that Tom's death would become yet another of those niggling little glitches that would surface in the hours before first light while I tried to sleep.

The station was packed. Father Christmas had already done two circuits, collecting money for neglected reindeer or whatever. People had been dragging in the snowfall on their footwear and, thanks to the large Victorian-style radiators, puddles had formed around the door area and gradually spread further into the station.

I looked at Baby G. It was 14.17 and I'd been here over four hours already. I was gagging for another brew, but needed to keep a trigger on the doors; besides, once I drank I would inevitably need the toilet at some stage, and I couldn't afford to miss Liv when and if she arrived.

It was going to be a long food- and coffee-free day, and maybe night. From the point of view of third-party awareness, it's not too bad hanging around a railway station; you can get away with it for quite a long time.

I adjusted my numb, cold arse again, deciding not to waste time speculating about what the fuck had happened at the Microsoft house. The facts were, I had made no money, Tom was dead and I could be in a world of shit with the Americans and a universe of shit with the Firm. If my involvement was discovered, I'd end up helping to prop up a flyover in a concrete pillar some-where along the new Eurotunnel high-speed link. I'd never been too worried about dying, but to be killed by my own people would be a bit depressing.

The longer I'd thought about what had happened on the drive last night, the more I'd boiled over with hostility towards Liv and Val. I had to come up with a plan that still got me what I needed and not waste time and energy trying to work out how to get even. Apart from anything else, that wouldn't pay any clinic bills. Plan B was taking shape in my head. The Maliskia's money would pay for Kelly when I lifted Val and offered him to them for cash. My life had been up for grabs for years, and for a lot less money.

I had no idea how I was going to do it yet; I'd have to hit the ground running. But the first phase would be to let Liv think I had the ThinkPad with the downloaded information on it, and, because of last night's fuck-up, I'd only deal with Val now, and only in Finland. Who knows? If Val turned up with the money, I could just take that and save myself the hassle.

But that wasn't the message I'd left in the plastic box I'd placed in the DLB. It was empty, just there so that when she came to get it there was something to unload, so as not to arouse suspicion. Everything needed to be as it should be. As she left the station I would grab her and tell her in person, so she made no mistake about what I wanted.

I'd been sitting there for another twenty minutes when a large group of school kids on an excursion tried to get through the bus-station doors all at once, juggling bags, skis and Big Macs as they tried to walk, talk and listen to Walkmans at the same time.

Less than thirty seconds later I saw Liv come through and walk straight past the loaded sign without even turning her head. But I knew she would have seen it. Her long black coat, Tibetan hat and light-brown boots were easy to spot among the crowd as she moved through the hall, brushing snow from a shoulder with one hand and carrying two large paper Stockmann bags in the other.

She carried on past the kiosks and toilets, manoeuvring through the schoolkids, who were now waiting for one of their teachers to sort his shit out with the tickets. I kept my eye on the peak of Liv's hat.

I had a good check to make sure she hadn't been followed in, just in case she'd brought any protection with her, or worse, in case the Democrat had a few of the party faithful on her tail.

The hat disappeared as she turned left into the ticketing and metro hallway. There was no rush, I knew where she was heading.

Once on my feet and past the school trip I pinged her again, just about to sit on top of the DLB, next to some more kids. The busker was in his normal spot, knocking out some old Finn favourite on his accordion. The noise mixed nicely with the rumpus from a group of drunks on the other side of the benches. They were having an argument with Father Christmas, much to the amusement of those passing.

Liv sat down as Santa poked the chest of one of the drunks. Staff began to step in to separate them. I watched Liv bend down and pretend to mess around with her bags. Her hand moved to pick up the DLB. The empty container was pulled from the Velcro and dropped into one of the bags; it wouldn't get read here.

I waited for her to leave, positioning myself in a corner so that whatever door she decided to head for I wouldn't be in her line of sight. A few minutes passed before she stood up, looking towards the ticketing area and smiling broadly. Her arms went out as the man from St Petersburg emerged, smiling, from the crowd. They embraced and kissed, then sat down together, talking in that smiley, hand-in-hand, nice-to-see-you way, their noses only inches apart. He was dressed in the same long camel-hair coat, this time with a dark maroon polo neck sticking out of the top. Today he also carried a light-brown leather briefcase.

Making sure I wasn't in line of sight of the platform doors, I checked the departures and arrivals board high on the wall. The St Petersburg train, going on to Moscow, was leaving from platform 8 at 15.34 – just over half an hour's time.

They talked for another ten minutes and then both stood up. Liv's contact picked up her bags in one hand, his briefcase in another, and they walked towards the platform doors.

Alarm bells started to ring in my head. Why had he picked up her bags? My heart started to pound even harder when they both went through the doors and out onto the snow-covered platform. Shit, was she going with him? Maybe the courier had just given her the news about what had happened at Microsoft HQ and Liv was bailing out while she could.

I counted to ten and pushed my way out into the cold. Platform 8 was to the right of me as I headed towards the left-luggage area. The snow was falling gently and there wasn't a breath of wind. I walked with my head down, hands in pockets. Glancing sideways across the tracks, I saw they were heading for the carriages about midway along the train. I walked slowly towards the left-luggage room, watching until they got on board. Then, checking my watch as if I'd just remembered something, I turned on my heels. There were about seventeen minutes to go before they left for St Petersburg, and it looked like I'd have to go with them.

I went past two of the Russian train staff, standing in the guard's van at the rear of the train, their high-peaked, Nazi-officer-style caps pushed onto the backs of their heads as they glumly took a swig of whatever was in their bottle.

I climbed aboard and entered a clean, though very old carriage, with a corridor facing the platform and compartments all the way along to my right. I moved along the warm walkway and sat down on one of the hard, fabric-covered seats in the first empty compartment. The strong, almost-scented cigarette smell probably never left these trains.

What now? I had money but no visa. How was I going to cross into Russia? Hiding in the toilets only works in Agatha Christie movies. Maybe a bribe could get me in. I'd play the dickhead tourist who hadn't got a clue about needing a passport, let alone a visa, and offer to be very generous with my dollars if they would just be so kind as to stamp me in or whatever they could do for me. After all, only a lunatic would want to get *into* Russia illegally.

I sat and watched snow-covered Nazi hats strolling along the platforms below the windows. My carotid pulse was throbbing on both sides of my neck and there was a pain running up the centre of my chest as I heard whistles being blown and the heavy carriage doors slamming closed.

I checked Baby G – three minutes to go. It wasn't dealing with the guards and immigration people that was getting me flapping; it was the possibility of losing Liv, my only quick and certain link to Val.

My compartment door was pulled open and an old woman in a long fur came in, carrying a small overnight bag. She muttered something and I gave a grunt in reply. Looking up, I caught a glimpse of black leather moving on the platform. Now what was happening? Liv carried on past with her bags, head down against the snow.

I felt huge relief as I jumped up and moved along the corridor, but I couldn't get out yet in case the courier was watching her and wondered why someone else had decided to jump train.

She disappeared into the station and I leaped onto the platform, not checking to see if he was looking, and headed for the doors she had just passed through. I pinged her hat above the crowd, heading for the bus-station exit. She must know by now that there was no message in the box. I fell in behind, waiting for my chance to grip her.

I was about twenty paces behind as she pushed her way through the bus-station doors. Once through them myself, I looked out into the snowfall. All I could see were buses and lines of people trying to get on them; Liv must have turned off as soon as she hit the pavement.

I was moving down the steps when there was a shout behind me. 'Nick! Nick!'

I stopped, spun round and looked back up towards the doors.

'Liv! How lovely to see you.'

She was standing by one of the pillars, left of the doors, smiling, arms outstretched, getting ready to greet another of her long-lost friends. I switched on and played the game, walking into her arms, letting her kiss me on both cheeks. She smelled great, but what I could see of her hair under her hat wasn't as well groomed as usual and was knotted at the ends.

'I thought I would wait for you. I knew you would be around somewhere, otherwise why leave an empty container?'

Still embracing, I looked at her with my wonderful-to-see-you smile. 'Tom is dead,' I said.

The look on her face told me she knew how I felt. She pulled back and smiled. 'Come, walk with me. You have a right to be angry, but all is not lost, Nick.' She invited me with her gloved

331

hand to carry her bags. As I bent down I saw the boyfriend's light-brown briefcase.

Still smiling at her, I gripped her arm and more or less pulled her down the stairs. Once on the pavement I turned right, towards the front of the station and the town centre. 'What the fuck's going on? We got hit by an American team last night. I was lifted. Then the fucking Russians hit them!'

She nodded as I ranted away at her, doing her normal trick of knowing everything but giving very little away.

I said, 'You already know that, don't you?'

'Of course. Valentin always finds out everything.'

'You and Val have been fucking me over big time. Enough. I want him here tomorrow, with the money. Then I'll give him what he wants. I have the ThinkPad, and it's downloaded with what you want.' I wished I'd taken Tom up on his offer back at the lead house to let him tell me exactly what he was doing.

She hadn't even been listening. 'Are you sure Tom is dead?'

'If he's out in this shit . . .' I held my hand out.

She looked exactly the same as she had done in the hotel, calm and in control, almost as if she was in another place and I wasn't talking to her.

I increased my grip on her arm and guided her down the road, not caring what passers-by might think.

'Listen, I have the download. But I'll only deal with Val now, not you. There will be no more fuck-ups.'

332

'Yes, Nick, I heard you the first time. Now tell me, this is very important. Valentin will not do a thing unless he has all the details. Did the Americans take all of the hardware with them from the house?'

'Yes.'

'Did the Americans capture any of the occupants from the house?'

'Yes. I saw three.'

'Did the Maliskia then manage to take any of the hardware or occupants from the Americans?'

She was like a doctor working through a list of symptoms with a patient.

'Not the occupants. They got one of the wagons that contained some hardware, for sure.'

She nodded slowly. We joined a small crowd at a crossing, waiting for the green man to illuminate, even though there was no traffic to stop us all crossing.

I whispered into her ear. 'This is bollocks, Liv. I want Val here, with the money, then I'll hand everything over and fuck off and leave you lot to it.'

My rhetoric was having no effect on her whatsoever. We crossed the main drag to the sound of the warbling signal, heading for the cobblestoned pedestrian shopping area.

'That, Nick, will not happen. He will not come, for the simple reason that you haven't anything to trade, have you?' She spoke very evenly. 'Now, please answer my questions. This is very important. For everyone, including you.'

Fuck her, I wasn't waiting for any more questions. Besides, she was right again. 'Why did the Americans hit the house? Whatever we were going in for belongs to them, doesn't it? It's not commercial, it's state.'

She treated me to her best Mr Spock look as I dragged her along. 'Turn right here.'

I turned the corner. We were on one of the shopping streets. Trams, cars and trucks splashed through the slush.

'The Americans were NSA, Nick.'

Oh fuck. My heart sank to hear my suspicion confirmed and the pain returned to my chest. I wanted money, but not that badly. This was a big boy fuck-up. Those people were the real government of America. 'Are you sure?'

She nodded. 'They also hit my house last night about two hours after you left.'

'How did you get away?'

She flicked at the ends of her hair. 'By having a very cold and long night out on the lake.'

'How did they know to hit you?'

'They must have been guided to the house, but I don't know how. Now please, you are just wasting time and we don't have a lot of it.'

I didn't even notice a van passing and giving my jeans and her coat the good news with some slush. I was busy feeling more depressed than pissed off now. The NSA. I really was in the shit.

She gave me more directions. 'Cross here.'

We waited like sheep again until a little green man told us to cross. Jaywalking must carry the death penalty in this country. Moving on green, it was safe to talk again.

'Tell me, did you or Tom use email, telephone,

334

fax or anything like that while you were at the house?'

'Of course not, no.'

And then I remembered what had happened at the airport. 'Wait. Tom did. Tom—'

She turned her head sharply. 'What? What did Tom do?'

'He used email. He sent an email to someone in the UK.'

The calm, controlled look drained from her face. She stood still, pushing me away as people skipped around what looked like a domestic row just about to erupt.

'I told you both not to do that!'

I pulled her back towards me, as if I was in command, leading her down the street. She composed herself, and finally, very calmly, she said, 'So, it was Tom who brought the Americans here.' She pointed to the right, down another cobble-stoned street. 'Valentin wants me to show you something, then I am to make you an offer that your pocket and conscience will not let you refuse. Come. This way.'

As we turned I decided to keep quiet about the fact that it wasn't necessarily Tom's fault. E4 might have followed me from the moment I left her flat in London, or kept tabs on us via Tom's credit card. But fuck it; I couldn't do anything about that now.

We'd ended up by the harbour. A fish and vegetable market had been set up on the quay-side, steam billowing from under plastic awnings that protected the traders and their merchandise from the snow.

'Over there, Nick.'

My eyes followed hers, hitting on what looked like the world's largest Victorian conservatory a couple of hundred metres away from the market.

'Let's go and get out of the cold, Nick. I think it's time you knew what's really going on.'

26

The teahouse was hot and filled with the aroma of coffee and cigarettes. We bought food and drink from the counter and headed for a vacant table in a corner.

With our coats over a spare seat and her hat now removed, it was even more obvious that Liv had had a bad night. We must both have looked pretty rough compared with the American tourists who were beginning to fill the place, fresh off the cruise liner I could see down in the harbour. The sharp hiss of the cappuccino machine punctuated their conversations, which for some reason were louder than everybody else's. The Finns seemed to speak very quietly.

Our table was by a grand piano and partly screened by potted palms. The less conspicuous the better. Liv leaned forward and took a sip of tea from her glass while I shoved a salmon sandwich down my neck. She watched me for a while, then asked, 'Nick, what do you know of the UK/USA agreement?'

A camera flash bounced around as the tourists posed with their tea glasses and big wedges of chocolate cake. I took a swig of tea. I knew the bones of it. Set up by Britain and America in the late 1940s, since when Canada, Australia and New Zealand had also become part of the club, the agreement basically covered the pooling of intelligence on mutual enemies. Beyond that, however, the member countries also used their resources to spy on each other: in particular, the UK spied on American citizens in the USA, and the Americans spied on British citizens in the UK, and then they traded. Technically it wasn't illegal, just a very neat way of getting round strict civil liberties legislation.

Liv's eyes followed three elderly Americans in multi-coloured duvet jackets as they squeezed past our table, loaded down with tea trays and elegant paper carrier bags full of Finnish crafts. They didn't seem able to make a decision about where to sit.

Liv looked back at me. 'Nick, the three men in the house last night were Finns. They were engaged in accessing a technology called Echelon, which is at the very heart of the agreement.'

'You mean you were trying to get Tom and me to access state secrets for the Russian mafia?'

She looked calmly around the other tables and took another sip of tea. She shook her head. 'It's not like that at all, Nick. I didn't explain every-thing to you before, for reasons that I'm sure you will understand, but Valentin wants commercial information, that's all. Believe me, Nick, you were not stealing secrets, state or military. Quite the contrary: you were helping to stop others from doing precisely that.'

'So how come the NSA were involved?'

'They simply wanted their toy back. I promise you, Valentin has no interest in the West's military secrets. He can get those whenever he wants; it's not exactly difficult, as I'll demonstrate to you shortly.' She glanced at the Americans to make sure they weren't listening, then back at me. 'What do you know of Echelon?'

I knew it was some kind of electronic eaves-dropping system run by GCHQ, intercepting transmissions and then sifting them for information, a bit like an Internet search engine. However, I shrugged as if I knew nothing at all, I was more interested in hearing what she knew.

Liv sounded as if she was reading from the Echelon sales brochure. 'It's a global network of computers, run by all five nations of the UK/USA agreement. Every second of every day, Echelon automatically sifts through millions of inter-cepted faxes, emails and mobile phone calls, searching for pre-programmed key words or numbers.

'As a security precaution in our organization, we used to spell out certain words over the phone, but now even that has been overtaken by voice recognition. The fact is, Nick, any message sent electronically, anywhere in the world, is routinely intercepted and analysed by Echelon.

'The processors in the network are known as the Echelon dictionaries. An Echelon station, and there are at least a dozen of them around the world, contains not only its parent nation's specific dictionary, but also lists for each of the other four countries in the UK/USA system.

What Echelon does is to connect all these dictionaries together and allow all the individual listening stations to function as one integrated system.

'For years Echelon has helped the West shape international treaties and negotiations in their favour, to know anything from the health status of Boris Yeltsin to the bottom-line position of trading partners. That's serious information to get hold of, Nick. Why do you think we are careful not to use any form of electronic communication? We know that we are tagged by Echelon. Who isn't? Princess Diana's calls were monitored because of her work against landmines. Charities like Amnesty International and Christian Aid are listened to because they have access to details about controversial regimes. From the moment Tom started working at Menwith Hill, every fax and email he sent, as well as phone calls, would have been intercepted and checked.

'Those Finns had designed a system to hack into Echelon and piggyback off it. The firewall that Tom breached was their protection around that system, to stop them being detected and traced. They were online last night for the very first time.'

'Trying to do what? Hack into NSA headquarters or something?'

She shook her head slowly, as if in disbelief at their naivety. 'We knew from our sources that their sole objective was to pick up sensitive market information that they could then profit from. All they wanted was to make a few million dollars here and there; they didn't understand the true potential of what they had created.'

'But what has all this got to do with me?' I asked. 'What is Val's offer?'

She leaned even closer, as if we were exchanging words of love. We might as well have been, the way she spoke with such passion.

'Nick, it's very important to me that you understand Valentin's motives. Of course he wants to make money out of this, but more than that, he wants the East eventually to be an equal trading partner with the West, and that is never going to happen as long as ambitious men like him do not have access to commercial information that only Echelon can provide.'

'Ambitious?' I laughed. 'I can think of plenty of other words I'd use before that one to describe ROC.'

She shook her head. 'Think of America a hundred and fifty years ago and you have Russia now. Men like Vanderbilt didn't always stay within the law to achieve their aims. But they created wealth, a powerful middle class, and that, in time, creates political stability. That is how you must see Valentin; he's not a Dillinger, he's a Rockefeller.'

'OK, Val is businessman of the year. Why didn't he just strike a deal with the Finns?'

'It doesn't work like that. It would have alerted them to what they had, and then they'd have sold it to the highest bidder. Valentin didn't want to take that chance. He was happy for them to make access and try to play the markets while he found out where they were, and got to them before the Maliskia.'

'And the Americans?'

'If you had been successful last night in down-loading the program, Valentin would have told the Americans where the house was. They would then have gone in and closed it down without knowing that he also had access to Echelon. Remember what I said in London, that nobody must know . . .'

Very clever, I thought. Val would have carried on logging on to Echelon, and the West would have slept soundly in its bed.

'But the Americans did know.'

'Yes, but our security was watertight. The only way they could have found out was through Tom.'

Before we got sidetracked into conjecture about who was to blame, there were plenty of other questions I wanted the answers to. 'Liv, why Finland?'

She answered with evident pride. 'We are one of the most technologically minded nations on earth. This country probably won't even have currency by the next generation, everything will be electronic. The government is even thinking of doing away with passports and having our IDs embedded on the SIM cards in our mobile phones. We are at the cutting edge of what is possible, as these young men demonstrated. They had the skills to hack into Echelon, even if they lacked the street sense to know what they could really do with it.' She waited as I took a sip of tea. The sandwiches had long gone. 'Any more questions?'

I shook my head. There were many, but they

could wait. If she was ready to explain the new proposal to me, I was ready to listen.

'Nick, I have been authorized by Valentin to tell you that the offer of money still stands, but your task has changed.'

'Of course it has. Tom is dead and the NSA have Echelon back.'

Her eyes locked on to mine as she shook her head. 'Wrong, Nick. I didn't want to tell you this until the information was confirmed, but our sources believe the Maliskia have Tom. Unfortunately, we believe they also have the ThinkPad. This is very disturbing as it still has the firewall access sequence that—'

I fought to keep my composure. 'Tom's alive? Fucking hell, Liv. I've been sitting here thinking the man was dead.'

Her daughter-of-Spock face never changed. 'The Maliskia think he's with the Finns. They naturally assumed . . .' She waved her hands across the table. 'Remember, they also want access to Echelon.'

'So you want me to get Tom back.'

'Before I tell you the objective, Nick, I must explain a complication.'

A complication? This wasn't complicated enough?

She bent down and lifted her boyfriend's brief-case onto the table. It was dark outside now and Christmas lights twinkled in the market place.

Liv opened the case. Inside was a laptop, which she fired up.

I watched as she reached into her coat and brought out a dark-blue floppy disk in a clear

343

plastic case. As she inserted the disk I heard the Microsoft sound.

'Here, read this. You need to appreciate the situation completely so you can understand the gravity of the task. I could just tell you all this, but I think you might want confirmation.'

She handed the briefcase over to me, the floppy still spinning as the laptop did its stuff before displaying it on the screen.

The disk icon came up on the desktop and I double-clicked it. Adjusting the screen and ensuring that only I could see its contents, I started to read as the group from outside came in and greeted their mates, and lost no time in showing them their purchases of Russian-style fur hats and reindeer-meat salamis.

There were two files on the disk. One was untitled, the other said, 'Read Me First'. I opened it.

I was presented with a web page from the London *Sunday Times*, dated 25 July and displaying an article entitled, RUSSIAN HACKERS STEAL US WEAPONS SECRETS.

Liv stood up. 'More tea? Food?'

I nodded and got back to the screen as she went to the counter. By now the tourists were a group of six and making enough talk for twelve.

'American officials believe Russia may have stolen some of the nation's most sensitive military secrets,' the article began, 'including weapons guidance systems and naval intelligence codes, in a concerted espionage offensive that investigators have called operation Moonlight Maze.'

The theft was so sophisticated and well

co-ordinated that security experts believed America might be losing the world's first 'cyber war'. The hits against American military computer systems were even defeating the firewalls that were supposed to defend the Pentagon from cyber attack. During one illegal infiltration, a technician tracking a computer intruder watched a secret document be hijacked and sent to an Internet server in Moscow.

Experts were talking of a 'digital Pearl Harbor', where an enemy exploited the West's reliance on computer technology to steal secrets or spread chaos as effectively as any attack using missiles and bombs. With just a few taps on a computer laptop it seemed anyone could totally fuck up any advanced nation. Gas, water and electricity utilities could be shut down by infiltrating their control computers. Civil and military tele-communications systems could be jammed. The police could be paralysed and civil chaos would take over. Fuck it, these days, who needed armies?

Even top-secret military installations whose expertise was intelligence security had been breached. At the Space and Naval Warfare Systems Command (Spawar), a unit in San Diego, California, which specialized in safeguarding naval intelligence codes, an engineer was alerted to the problem when a computer print job took an unusually long time. Monitoring tools showed that the file had been removed from the printing queue and transmitted to an Internet server in Moscow before being sent back to San Diego. It was not clear precisely what information was contained in the stolen document, but beyond its role in naval intelligence, Spawar was also responsible for providing electronic security systems for the Marine Corps and federal agencies. It was suspected that several other intrusions had gone undetected.

The piece went on to say that President Clinton had called for an extra $600 million dollars to combat the problem of Moonlight Maze, but that still might not be enough, as China, Libya and Iraq were developing information warfare capabilities, and, according to one White House official, so were certain well-funded terrorist groups. It didn't take much imagination to think of the damage Osama Bin Laden and his mates could do if they got their hands on it. As for the massive Russian probing, that could very well be the Maliskia.

I double-clicked the next file. What came up on screen confirmed the story of the hit against Spawar in San Diego could very well be true. The *Sunday Times* might not know what was in the file, but I did now. The Naval Intelligence crest in front of me headed a list of maybe fifty code words that corresponded to radio frequencies.

Liv sat down with more tea and sandwiches.

'Have you read both?'

I nodded, and as I closed the files down and ejected the disk, Liv leaned over and held out her hand. 'Nick, you can help stop this from happening if you want to.'

I passed the disk over and started to close down the laptop as she continued. 'The Russian government aren't the only people who buy this information from the Maliskia. So can anyone with a big enough chequebook.'

Obviously Val's was big enough, otherwise I wouldn't have been reading the code lists.

'As I said before, Nick, if they get Echelon capability and start to exploit it, even without selling the information to others, just think of the consequences. They are already on the way to achieving the capability to close down the UK or US with their Moonlight Maze operations; with Echelon they will have complete and unrestricted access to any information worldwide – state, military, commercial . . . You can stop it, Nick, if you want.' She paused and looked me straight in the eye.

I handed the briefcase back to her across the table. She was right. If this was the truth, it was an offer my conscience couldn't let me refuse. The idea of these machines listening to everything we did and said was very Big Brother, but shit, I'd rather have just the agreement countries access-ing it than every man and his dog with enough cash. As for the leak of military information, that had to be stopped. I didn't give a shit about people finding out about the latest surface-to-air-missile technical details or whatever. It was people's lives, including my own, that mattered. I had been part of enough fuck-ups where friends had died because of insecure information. If I could stop it and come away with a suitcase full of money, it seemed to touch every base.

'So what exactly do you want me to do?'

She heard the acceptance in my voice. 'You must destroy the Maliskia's Moonlight Maze capabilities and any advance they've made with Echelon. That means, destroy the complete installation – computers, software, the lot.

'This time, however, you'll be completely on your own. Valentin cannot be seen to be attacking the Maliskia. Any conflict would cause disharmony and distract him from his aim. So if you encounter a problem, I'm afraid he or I will not be able to help you.'

I might be the most cynical man in the UK about the UK, but I was not a traitor. And if all she was saying was true, I was sure that Val would be happy to open his chequebook a little wider, especially if I was having to go in single-handed. I sat back and held up three fingers.

There wasn't a flicker in her face. 'Dollars?'

Since she'd even asked the question, the answer was obvious. 'Sterling. The same arrangements as for the exchange.'

She nodded. 'Three million. You will be paid.'

It worried me slightly that she'd agreed so easily.

'What guarantees do I have?'

'You don't. And there's no money upfront. But Valentin is well aware of the lengths you went to to track him down before, and that no doubt you'd do the same again.'

'Correct.' I didn't need to explain about never making a threat you cannot keep. She knew.

'As I've said a number of times, Nick, he likes you. You will get your money.'

'So tell me, where is the installation?'

She pointed behind me, out towards the harbour and the sea. 'It's that way. Estonia.'

348

I frowned. The only thing I knew about Estonia was that it had been part of the old USSR, and now wanted to be part of Nato, the EU, Tesco's loyalty scheme, you name it – anything to detach it from Russia for good.

'The population is still thirty per cent Russian. The Maliskia find it easier to operate from there.'

She lifted the cup to her lips and screwed up her face. The tea was cold.

There was one rather important point she seemed to have overlooked. 'If the Maliskia have Tom,' I said, 'I take it he'll be at this installation. Do you want me to bring him back here after I've lifted him or just take him back to London?'

She stared at me as if I was an idiot. 'Nick, I thought you understood, Tom must be considered part of their capability.'

She kept her gaze fixed on me for several moments while waiting for the penny to drop. It finally did. She saw it in my face. 'I don't wish to state the obvious, Nick, but why else do you think Valentin would pay you three million? Tom must die.'

I was almost lost for words. 'But why? I mean, why don't I just get him out at the same time?'

'That's not an option, Nick. Tom will very quickly be coerced into helping them with Echelon. As we both know, he can breach the fire-wall. We know they have at least some of the software. We know they have Tom, and probably also the ThinkPad. As soon as it all links up, what's in his head, what's in his pocket, what's in the van . . .' She shuddered. 'If the Maliskia get access to Echelon and add it to their Moonlight

349

Maze capabilities, they will have all the ingredients for catastrophe. It will affect not only Valentin's vision for the East, but bring the West to its knees.

'Look, Tom has the ThinkPad. He has the ability to use it. The risk is too great. What if you are killed or taken before finishing the task? Even if you did rescue him he would still be in the country, and the possibility of capture by them is a risk Valentin is not willing to take. It is simply better that Valentin sacrifices Tom and the opportunity to access Echelon himself than risk the Maliskia having it. No-one, Nick, can afford for the Maliskia to have Echelon.'

I was still finding this hard to accept. 'But why not just tell the Americans? Val was going to tell them about the Finns' house.'

'Unthinkable. What if they take Tom and he explains exactly what has been going on? Nick, I don't think even you would want that, would you? Tom would go back to prison for life and you'd be in the adjoining cell.'

Bending down and placing the briefcase in her bag once again, she seemed to be rounding up. 'I'm sorry, Nick, but I have many things to do now, as you can appreciate. We'll meet tomorrow at Stockmann, eleven a.m. in the café. That is the soonest that I'll be able to get more information. One thing is certain, after that you must leave as soon as you can. If the Maliskia have got Tom to co-operate, every hour counts.'

I looked at her and nodded. 'This new information, is it coming in on the 6.30 a.m. train from St Petersburg?'

She didn't bat an eyelid. 'Yes, of course. Nick, I want to apologize once more for what has happened. It was just that if you'd known exactly what was going on—'

'I wouldn't have done the job in the first place?'

'Precisely. I must go now.' She busied herself in standing up and fastening her coat. 'I think I need about fifteen minutes.'

I nodded. I'd get another brew while she got clear of the area, then I'd go and find out exactly where Estonia was and how the fuck to get there.

27

Thursday, 16 December 1999

Ten minutes before she was due to arrive, I settled into a corner seat at the Café Avec in Stockmann. On my way over I'd stopped at an Internet cafe and checked out the Moonlight Maze story on the *Sunday Times* website. It was genuine.

The 'Avec' seemed to refer to the fact that you could have your coffee with a shot of anything from the bar, from Jack Daniels to local cloud-berry liqueurs. The locals were knocking them back like there was no tomorrow.

Placing two coffees and two Danishes on the table, I put a saucer over the top of Liv's cup to keep it hot.

The café was just as packed as when I'd been there with Tom. I'd spent a lot of time thinking about him last night, lying in my cheap and, more importantly, anonymous hotel room. The sad fact was that stopping the Maliskia from combining Echelon with their Moonlight Maze operations, and getting the money for doing it, was more important than Tom's life. Then I pictured him leaping to my defence after we'd come off the fence. Killing him was not going to be easy.

I had even considered going to the consulate and calling Lynn on a secure line, but then I realized I was losing sight of the aim, which was money. If Lynn knew, that would be the end of it. All I would get was a pat on the head if I was lucky. This way I got to pocket £3 million, plus I did democracy a good turn. It was bollocks, of course. The trouble was, it even sounded like bollocks.

After my tea stop with Liv yesterday I'd gone straight down to the harbour to check out the ferries to Estonia. Its capital, Tallinn, seemed to be the destination for an array of roll-on, roll-off ferries, high-speed catamarans and hydrofoils. The faster craft made the 80K journey in only an hour and a half, but the girl at the ticket office told me there was too much ice floating in the Baltic and too much wind for them to make the crossing in the next few days. The only ones that could handle the conditions were the old-fashioned ferries, and they usually took over four hours, and because of the heavy seas they would now take even longer. Story of my life.

I took a sip of coffee as I sat looking at the long words in a Finnish newspaper, and scanning the escalator. I was going to use the Davidson passport to go into Estonia, but had booked the ferry ticket in the name of Davies. Giving the name slightly corrupted always adds nicely to the confusion. If stopped for it, I'd just say it was the mistake of the people who did the ticketing. After all, English was their second language, and my cockney accent could be quite hard to understand when I tore the arse out of it. The method wasn't foolproof, but it might just muddy the waters a bit. I was sure the Firm would still be looking for Davidson now that he was connected with Liv and Tom. I didn't care how much they might have worked out, as long as there wasn't a picture of me to go with it, and thankfully the one in Davidson's passport wasn't much of a likeness. The moustache and rectangular glasses, plus make-up to change the size of my nose and chin slightly, worked quite well. If put on the spot, I'd say that I used contacts to read now and liked my new clean-shaven look.

I'd learned make-up from the BBC. Plastic noses and eyebrow sets are not what it's all about. As I dunked a corner of the Danish into my coffee, I couldn't help a smile as I remembered spending four hours making myself up as a woman for the final session of the two-week course; I'd thought the shade of lip gloss I'd chosen particularly suited me. It had been a laugh spending the day shopping with my teacher 'girl-friend' Peter, who was dressed up in quite a fetching blue number, especially when it came to going into women's toilets. I didn't like having to shave and wax my legs and hands, though. They itched for weeks afterwards.

An insistent electronic burst of the *William Tell* Overture came from somewhere behind my left shoulder, followed by a brief moment of silence, then a burst of Finnish from an elderly lady. Everybody in this country had a mobile phone – I'd even seen small kids wandering around holding their parents' hands and talking into a dangling mike – but no-one settled for the standard ring. You couldn't go five minutes in Helsinki without hearing *The Flight of the Bumble Bee*, snatches of Sibelius or the James Bond theme.

I sat, dunked and waited. I had the passports tucked uncomfortably under my foot inside my right boot, and I had $1,500 in hundreds, twenties and tens in my left.

As for Mr Stone, he was well and truly stuffed away in the bag at the railway station. The P7 and extra barrel were still with me and would only go into the railway bag at the very last minute. There was no way I could take the weapon with me to Estonia. I had no idea how heavy the security was on the ferry journeys.

Liv's head appeared first as the escalator brought her up towards me. She was looking around casually, not specifically looking for me. The rest of her body came into view, wearing the black, belted three-quarter-length leather coat over her normal jeans and Timberland-type boots. She had a large black leather bag over her shoulder and a magazine in her right hand.

She spotted me and headed for the table, kissing me on both cheeks. Her hair was back on top form and she smelled of citrus. An English-language copy of *Vogue* landed on the table between us, and we bluffed away with the how-are-you? smiles as she settled into her seat.

I put her cup in front of her and removed the saucer. She lifted it to her lips. Either it was cold or tasted past its best, because it went straight back down on the table.

'The Maliskia are located near Narva.'

I returned her smile as if enjoying the story.

355

'Narva?' It could have been on the moon for all I knew.

'You'll need a Regio one-in-two-hundred-thousand map.'

'Of which country?'

She smiled. 'Estonia, north-east.' She put her hand on the *Vogue*. 'You'll also need what is inside here.'

I nodded.

Her hand was still on the magazine. 'It's from this location that they have been running Moonlight Maze; and now that they have Tom and the ThinkPad, it's where they will also be attempting to access Echelon. They move location every few weeks to avoid detection, and after what's happened here they will be moving again very soon. You'll need to act quickly.'

I nodded again and her hands came together on the table as she leaned forward. 'Also inside is an address. You'll meet people there who should help you get explosives and whatever else you need. The best way to Narva is by train. Hiring a car is more trouble than it's worth. And Nick' – she fixed her eyes on mine – 'these people in Narva, do not trust them. They're totally un-reliable, the way they conduct their drugs trade is disrupting business for all of us. But they're the closest Valentin can offer you to support on the ground.'

I gave her a smile that let her know she was telling Granny how to suck eggs.

'Also remember, do not mention Valentin at all when dealing with them. There must be no connection between him and any of this. None whatsoever. If they make a connection, the deal will be off, because they will simply kill you.'

Her hands went back together. 'Also in there is a' – she hesitated, trying to find the right word, but didn't come up with one that satisfied her. In the end she shrugged – 'letter from a friend, the same one that has the contacts in Narva. It will ensure you get what you need from these people, but only use it if you need to, Nick. It was obtained at great personal expense to Valentin and shouldn't be abused.'

I asked the obvious. 'What's in it?'

'Well, it's a bit like an insurance policy.' She smiled rather bleakly. 'A Chechen insurance policy. I told you before, he likes you.'

I didn't need to ask any more about it. I'd see it for myself soon. For now there were more important matters. I needed the answer to the bayonet question again. 'How many people are there on site?'

She shook her head. 'We don't have that information, but it will be more than last time. This is their most important asset, which is why it's in Estonia – the geography is the best defence system there is.'

Something else needed answering. 'How will you know I've been successful?'

'You're worried that Valentin will not pay without proof? Don't. He will know within hours – how is no concern of yours. You will get your money, Nick.'

I leaned closer. 'How do you know Tom?'

'I don't, Valentin does. When Tom was caught at Menwith Hill it was Valentin he was working for. You British never discovered that, however, because your threats to him could never compare with the one Valentin was capable of delivering.'

'Which was?'

Her expression invited me to use my imagination.

In my mind's eye I saw Tom, curled up in the back of the car after he'd had the facts of life explained to him by the interrogation team.

'Was Tom trying to access Echelon for Valentin at Menwith Hill?'

She nodded. 'When he was caught, he told British Intelligence only what they thought they needed to know, then told the courts what they told him to say. It was all very simple, really. Well, for everyone except Tom.'

'And how did you know of my connection with Tom?'

'Valentin has access to many secrets. After your encounter in Helsinki, he wanted to know a little more about you. It was easy enough to order that information from the Maliskia, thanks to Moonlight Maze. Even more incentive to get in there and destroy that capability, don't you think?'

Fucking right. I didn't like the sound of any of it.

Liv patted the magazine with her hand. 'Read it. Then all we know, you will know. I must go now. There are so many other things to do.'

I bet one of them was to report back to Val's go-between and tell him that I was on my way to Narva.

Liv and I smiled at each other like parting

friends, kissed on the cheek and did the farewell routine as she replaced her bag on her shoulder. 'I'll check the station every day, Nick, starting Sunday.'

I touched her sleeve. 'One last question.'

She turned to face me.

'You don't seem too concerned about Tom. I mean, I thought you two were, you know, close.'

She sat down again slowly. For a second or two she toyed with her coffee cup, and then she looked up. 'Meaning I had sex with him?' She smiled. 'Tom is not someone I'd seek a relationship with. I had sex with him because he was weakening and very unsure about what was expected of him. Sleeping with him was . . . was' – she searched for a good expression, then shrugged – 'insurance. I had to keep him committed to the task. He's the only one who could do this sort of thing. He is a genius with this technology. He had to go with you. That is also why you must carry out your new task as quickly as you can. His capabilities must not be available to the Maliskia.'

She stood and turned with a small wave of the hand, and I slouched down in my chair, wishing I'd had that information a few days ago. My eyes followed her as she headed for the escalator and slowly disappeared.

I took a small white envelope from inside the magazine Liv had left behind. It looked as if it was made for a small greeting card; it certainly didn't look as if there was much inside.

I stayed put for a while, not bothering to touch it, and drank her lukewarm coffee. After about ten minutes I piled the cups, saucers and plates onto the tray.

Walking away from the escalators, I made my way through the warm clothing department and into the toilets. Safely in a cubicle, I opened the envelope. Inside were three scraps of paper of various sizes and quality. The first was a Post-it, on which was an address in Narva – by the look of it I was after a bloke called Konstantin – plus a long and lat fix. The Post-it was stuck to half a ripped sheet of cheap and very thin A4, with about ten lines of Cyrillic script written in biro. This had to be the Chechen insurance policy, because the third item was a sheet of greaseproof paper on which was a pencilled cross and, towards the bottom left-hand corner of the sheet, a little circle. All I had to do was line up the longs and the lats on the right map and bingo, the circle would be around the location where Tom and the Maliskia were supposed to be.

I listened to the shuffle of feet outside, water splashing into basins, hand-driers humming, and the odd grunt or fart, and started to laugh to myself as I folded up the bits and pieces of paper and tucked them into my socks, out of the way. I felt like Harry Palmer in one of those Michael Caine films from the Sixties. It was ridiculous. I had more stuff around my feet than in my pockets.

I flushed the toilet and opened the door. An overweight Japanese tourist was waiting patiently, his sides bulging with video and camera bags. Leaving him to fight his way into the cubicle, I headed to the condom machine by the urinals. It was decision time. Dropping in some coins, I considered the banana- or strawberry-flavoured ones and those shaped like medieval maces, but in the end went for the bog-standard clear ones. All very missionary. Then, with the packet of three in my pocket, I was out of Stockmann – with any luck for ever.

Checking for surveillance by doing a complete circuit of the store and taking a few turns that meant I'd doubled back on myself, I felt confident I wasn't being followed and headed for the same bookshop where I'd bought my guidebook to Estonia. I soon found the map that Liv had specified.

Back at the hotel, it was time to study it in detail. Tallinn, the capital, was in the west, on the Baltic coast. It faced Finland, which was 80Ks across the sea. Narva was miles away, in the north-eastern corner, right next to Russia and just 15Ks inland. There was one main drag that went from Tallinn to Narva, linking together other, smaller towns on the 210Ks between the two. I could also see the black line of the railway that Liv had told me to take, roughly paralleling the main drag, sometimes near the road but mostly a few Ks south of it.

Narva was bisected by a river, and the border with Russia was an imaginary line running down the middle of it. There were two crossing points, a rail bridge and a road bridge. On the Russian side, the main drag and train line kept going east, with a sign on the edge of the map saying, 'Peterburi 138km'. In other words, Narva was closer to St Petersburg than it was to Tallinn.

I took out the sheet of greaseproof paper and placed the cross over the corresponding longs and lats, then looked at the circle. It ringed a small cluster of buildings a couple of Ks south of a small town called Tudu, which was about 35Ks south-westish of Narva. Basically, the target was in the middle of nowhere, the perfect place for the Maliskia to run their operations. That was where those Finns should have gone to do the job; maybe they didn't because there weren't any takeaway pizzas to be had.

There were still a few hours before the five-thirty ferry, so I fetched out the guidebook and had a read about this north-eastern corner of Estonia. It sounded a nightmare. During Iron Curtain days Narva had been one of the most polluted towns in Europe. Two massive power stations produced enough kilowatts to keep the massive wheels of the USSR industrial base turning, whilst pumping out uncountable tons of sulphur dioxide, magnesium this and aluminium that into the atmosphere. There was a huge lake near by, and I made a mental note not to eat any fish when I got there.

According to the guidebook, 90 per cent of the population in the area were Russian speaking, and, in the eyes of the Estonian government, Russian citizens. They took the line that if you couldn't speak Estonian, you couldn't get Estonian citizenship. The upshot was a big gang of Russians right on the border with Russia, holding old Russian passports, who had to stay in Estonia, a country that didn't acknowledge them.

Five trains a day left Tallinn heading east. Some

went straight on to St Petersburg and Moscow, and some just stopped at Narva, about a five-hour journey. No problem at all; I'd get the ferry tonight, check into a hotel, sort my shit out and get the train in the morning. That would be the easy bit.

I had the Narva contact name and address in my head; an hour of repeating it while reading had sorted that out. I ripped the cross off the greaseproof paper, rolled it in the Post-it and ate it. Everything else on this job was like some spy film, so why not go the whole hog? I kept the guidebook and map because I was going to be a tourist. If asked, I was exploring the region's immensely rich culture. Well, that was what it said in the guidebook. I couldn't wait.

As the final preparation for the journey, I went into the bathroom and ran a basin of warm water. Then, unwrapping the complimentary sliver of soap, I proceeded with a little task I never looked forward to.

28

I followed the herd out of the terminal waiting room and up the embarkation ramp onto a massive roll-on, roll-off ferry that wouldn't have looked out of place at Dover docks. When I saw that we all had to pass through a metal detector I felt relieved I'd left the P7 with my other stuff in the station's left luggage. I was using Nick Davidson's passport. The woman who swiped it at passport control was one of the few immigration officers who'd ever looked at the picture.

Few of my fellow foot passengers appeared anything like as prosperous as the Finns I was used to seeing. I guessed they were Estonians. They all seemed to be wearing fake-fur Cossack-style hats and a lot of leather-effect PVC. Several were in those full-length quilted coats that football managers wear, but they were really old and shabby. They were toting enormous plastic shopping bags, the kind that market traders pack their stock in, all stuffed to the brim with everything from blankets to catering packs of rice. In each case, the whole extended family seemed to have come along for the ride, kids, wives, grannies, everybody going hubba-hubba to each other in Estonian.

My plan had been to keep out of the way and curl up somewhere quiet and get my head down, but once on board I realized there was no chance of that. The air was filled with the binging and whirring of video games and fruit machines, over-laid with kids screaming up and down the corridors, their parents in hot pursuit.

Sometimes, walking sideways to get out of the way of kids and people with their big bundles of whatever coming from the other direction, I saw where the main crowd was headed – towards the bars and buffet. If I couldn't sleep I might as well eat.

The crowd thinned as the corridor opened up into a large bar area. Like the corridors, all the walls were covered with mahogany-effect veneer, giving it a dark, depressing, old-British-Rail feel. This area seemed to be full of well-dressed Finns, who had driven their cars aboard before us. They were laughing and joking noisily amongst them-selves, throwing drink down their necks like condemned men. I guessed they were booze cruisers, going over to Tallinn to stock up on duty free.

These guys didn't have shopping bags and reeked of disposable income. Their ski jackets were top-of-the-range labels, and their thick overcoats were wool, probably cashmere. Under-neath, they all sported big chunky sweaters with crew or polo necks. The only thing they had in common with the Estonians was a love of tobacco. There was already a layer of smoke covering the ceiling, waiting its turn to be sucked out by the overworked air-conditioning system.

The currency desk was just the other end of the bar. I lined up and changed $100 US into whatever the local money was called. I didn't even bother looking at exchange rates to see if I was being ripped off. What was I going to do, take my business elsewhere?

Eventually, fighting my way to the buffet, I picked up a tray and joined the queue. I wasn't particularly fussed about the wait; it was going to be a long journey, and it wasn't as if I was itching to get back and join the lushes in the bar.

Twenty minutes later I was sitting with a family at a bolted-down plastic table. The father, who looked over fifty-five but was probably under forty, still had his woollen hat on. His wife looked about ten years older than him. There were four kids, each attacking a large plate of pale, undercooked chips. Mine looked the same, plus I had a couple of scary-looking red sausages.

The sound of laughter echoed from the bar, along with piped muzak – badly performed cover versions of Michael Jackson and George Michael. Thankfully the ship's safety briefing, which started then carried on for ever in about five languages, cut wannabe George off in his prime.

As I tucked into my chips and surprise bags, the husband pulled out a pack of cigarettes and he and his wife lit up. They smoked contentedly in my face, flicking the ash onto their empty plates, finally stubbing out their dog-ends so they sizzled in the ketchup. I decided it was time for a walk. Their kids could finish off my food.

We were now in open sea and the boat rocked from side to side and plunged up and down. Children were having great fun in the corridors being thrown from wall to wall, and their parents were telling them off much more quietly. In fact, many of them looked paler than the chips I'd left on my plate.

I passed the news-stand. The only thing they had in English was another guidebook to Estonia; I decided to go back to the bar and read my own.

The Finns, undeterred by the heavy seas, were swigging back Koff beer, or at least trying to. The swell meant there was as much liquid on the floor as there was going down their necks.

The only seat was at the end of a semi-circular booth, where six Finns in their late thirties – three men and three women – all expensively dressed, were smoking Camels and downing vodka. I gave them a fuck-off smile as I settled down on the red, leather-look plastic and opened the guidebook.

Estonia, I was told, sandwiched between Latvia and Russia, was about the size of Switzerland and only two or three hours' drive from St Petersburg. It had a population of 1.5 million, the size of Geneva, and if that was the best they could find to say about it, it must be a pretty mind-numbing place.

Estonians seemed to have suffered all the rigours of life as a former Soviet republic. They'd had food coupons, bread queues, fuel shortages and inflation higher than the NatWest Tower. All in all it sounded a pretty grim place, a bit like a giant Slavic version of a South London housing estate.

The pictures of the old city centre of Tallinn showed medieval walls, turrets and needle-pointed towers. I couldn't wait to see the 'gabled roots' which the guide extolled. When I read on I discovered that most of the country's investment had been in this one tiny area, and that almost everywhere else they hadn't had gas or water since the Russians left in the early Nineties. But then again, tourists wouldn't go that far out of town, would they?

I sat there with my eyes closed, deeply bored. There was no way I was going to socialize with the Finns. I had work to do on the other side, and besides, from what I saw I doubted I could keep up with their drinking, especially the women.

I sank as low as I could in the seat to avoid the rising cigarette smoke, which was now a solid fog above me. The ferry was slewing about big time, and now and again the propellers roared as if they'd come right out of the water, accompanied by a collective funfair cry of 'Whooooa!' from the crowd in the bar. There was nothing but darkness to be seen from the window, but I knew there was plenty of ice out there somewhere.

I crossed my arms over my chest, let my chin drop and tried to sleep. Not that it was going to happen, but whenever there's a lull, it pays to recharge the batteries.

An announcement over the PA system sort of woke me up, though I wasn't too sure if I'd been sleeping. I guessed it was telling us what fantastic bargains were to be had in the ferry's duty-free shops, but then I heard the word Tallinn. The system carried on with its multilingual address, eventually coming to English. It seemed we had about thirty minutes before docking.

I packed the book in the daysack, along with my new woollen hat and washing kit, and wandered down the corridor. People were walking like drunks due to the swell, and now and again I had to put my hand up on the wall to stop myself falling. Following signs to the toilets, I slid aside a dark wood veneered door and walked down a flight of stairs.

A couple of blokes were chatting in the gents, zipping up and lighting cigarettes as they left. There was as much alcohol on the floor as there was on the ground in the bar; the only difference was it had been through people's kidneys first. The room was boiling hot, making the smell even worse.

I trod carefully towards the urinals. Each one had a pool of dark-yellow fluid slowly seeping past the piled-up cigarette ends blocking its path. I found one that wasn't so full it would splash back on me, got my left hand up against the bulkhead to steady myself and unzipped, listening to the relentless throb of the engines.

The toilet door was pushed open and another couple of guys came in. By the look of their GoreTex jackets they were Finns. I was sorting myself out, trying to zip up with one hand while using the other to stop me falling over. The boy in black headed for the vacant toilet cubicles behind me, and the other dossed around by the row of sinks to my left. His green jacket reflected on the stainless-steel pipes that ran from the water

369

dispenser for the urinals above my head. I couldn't see what he was actually doing because the pipe's shape distorted him like a fairground mirror, but whatever it was, it just looked wrong. At the same time I heard the rustle of GoreTex and saw black in the reflection, too.

I turned just in time to see an arm raised, ready to do my back some serious damage with some kind of knife.

Never let them come to you.

I screamed, hoping to disorient him, while charging the two or three steps towards him, focusing on his arm. I didn't care about the other guy yet. This one was the main threat.

Grabbing his raised wrist with my right hand, I kept moving. That turned his body to his left, his natural momentum helping me. My left hand then helped to spin him so he had his back to me, at the same time pushing him towards the cubicles. We stumbled into one of the stalls, the thin chipboard walls rattling as we grappled in the confined space. He went down on his knees by the pan. There was no seat; it had probably been ripped off years ago and taken home.

Still gripping his right wrist, I leaped over his back and forced both my knees straight down onto the back of his head. There was no time to fuck about: there were two of these guys to deal with. Bone crunched on ceramic. I heard teeth cracking and his jaw grind under my weight, mixed with an almost childlike, muffled screaming.

I saw him drop the knife. My right hand scrabbled around on the floor in search, and closed around it. Only it wasn't a knife, but an autojet, an American one. I recognized the make and I knew what it did.

Gripping the automatic syringe in my right hand, I had four fingers clasped around the cylinder, which was about the size of a thick marker pen, and my thumb on the injection button, ready to attack the splashing feet and green rustling GoreTex behind.

Too late; the boy was right on top of me. He also had an autojet. I could feel the needle penetrate and then its contents emptying into my buttock; it was like a golf ball was growing under my skin.

I threw myself backwards, crashing as hard as I could into his body, pushing him towards the urinals. The swell made us both stagger as the ferry tilted.

Once we'd banged against the white ceramic, his fists started to hit the side of my face from behind me as I kept him pinned in position. He was even biting into my skull, but I couldn't really feel the outcome. The autojet was having its own effect on me: rapid heartbeat, dry mouth, vision beginning to go hazy. I was sure it was mainly scopolamine, mixed with morphine. When it's injected into a body, the effect produced is a tranquillized state known as twilight sleep; this combination of drugs was formerly used in obstetrics, but was now considered far too dangerous, except when, like the British and American intelligence services, you're not too concerned about the Patient's Charter. I'd done a few targets with this stuff, making it easier to drag them off to a 3x9. I'd never thought I would get the good news myself, but at least now I could personally endorse the product.

Everything was going into slow motion. Even his shouting against my ear was blurred as he bucked and twisted, trying to free himself from between me and a urinal.

Ramming the autojet against the leg that was kicking out on my right, I depressed the button with my thumb. Automatically the needle sprang forward, punctured his jeans and skin, dispensing its juice. Now we were equal; it was just a case of who dropped first.

'Fuck you!' Unmistakably American.

I couldn't get up enough strength to do anything but pin him there, using my legs to push my back against him. He dropped the autojet, but I kept pushing him back against the urinal, my feet slipping on the wet floor as the ship bounced around, hoping that he would be the first to lose total control so I could get away. His arse was in the urinal now, and its contents were getting slopped over both of us as I fought to hold him there.

He was still trying to punch sideways at my face, and might have been doing serious damage for all I knew. The drugs had kicked in good style, depressing my central nervous system.

I bent my head down to avoid his punches as he jerked about as if he was having a fit. In front of me, in the cubicle, a blurred, black figure was slumped on the floor.

The toilet door must have opened. Not that I heard it – just the incomprehensible shouting as my legs started to lose the ability to hold me up in the swell.

I took a deep breath and must have sounded like a drunk as I looked round at the newcomers. 'Fuck off, fuck off, fuck off!'

Even the American joined in: 'Fuck yooou!'

Their hazy, shadowy figures disappeared.

The American's legs were wobbling as much as mine now. My head was still trying to bury itself into my chest as he made wild grabs at my face, hoping to get at my eyes. He wasn't shouting any more but giving off loud moans, as if he'd lost the ability to form words correctly, and pulling on my ears and hair with whatever strength he had left.

I could hear his breathing above me. I threw my hands in the direction of the sound. He released his grip on my head and slapped them down. My legs couldn't hold him in position any more, and I fell, first to my knees, then face down into the liquid swirling around the floor. Feeling it slurp into my mouth, I knew I was on the way out. But as the American fell to his knees to my right, splashing more liquid over my face and snorting like a warthog, I knew I wasn't the only one. He sat back on his heels, resting against the urinal, fumbling to get his jacket zip undone. I couldn't let that happen – he could have had a weapon – so taking a deep breath that took in more swill off the floor, I started to crawl up him.

His hands tried pushing me off as he growled down at me. At least his hands weren't going for his pockets any more, just my face.

I managed to get my hands around his throat, shaking his head from side to side. He made a whining noise, like a two-year-old refusing food. If only I could press one of my thumbs into the base of his throat, at the point just above where the two collarbones met and just below his Adam's apple, I could drop him – as long as his body was still capable of registering what was going on.

I got my hand down the top of his jacket, probing inside with my thumb until I found the bone and then the soft spot, then I pushed in with all my strength.

At once he began to come down with me as I sank slowly to the floor. He didn't like it at all. A quick, hard jab with two straight fingers or a key into this soft point can drop someone to the ground as quickly as if he's been given an electric shock.

He hit the floor, his legs still under him, bucking to free them like some frantic insect as I lay on top of him. He was choking now. Wheezing, gurgling noises issued from his nose and mouth.

Trying to keep focus, and some sort of co-ordination, I ran a hand over his jacket pockets. Nothing. I tried to unzip the jacket, but my fingers couldn't grip the tab. As I pulled down they just fell away.

Still on top of him, watching his hair soak up the spilled contents of the urinal, I started feeling around his waist, wanting to find a weapon. My hands couldn't register if he was carrying or not; they refused to send any type of message to my brain.

I lay there knowing that I must get up, sure that he was thinking the same.

The other boy behind me in the cubicle started moaning and coughing, his boots scuffing the floor as he tried to move. With any luck he was more worried about his dental plan for the next few years than anything else.

Dragging myself to my feet, I staggered on the spot above the American, then my knees buckled and I collapsed on his head. Blood spurted from his nose as I pulled myself up on a urinal. He curled up on the soaking floor, still trying to reach out and grab my leg.

I had to get out of there and hide up for the next twenty minutes or so until I could get off the ferry. I wasn't going to black out: they wouldn't have wanted to carry a deadweight. The drugs would just make me like the Finns in the bar and make it easier to drag me to their car.

Stumbling up the stairs, I seemed to trip on almost every one. After about six attempts at pulling the door open I was back in a corridor. The smell of smoke, the shouts of children and the jingle of gaming machines were all magnified in my spinning, dazed head. I was zigging while the rest of the world zagged.

I had to find myself a little spot where I could sit down and be no problem to anybody. That wasn't easy; I'd been fighting and rolling around in piss, and must have looked in a terrible state. Maybe I'd feign seasickness.

Staggering into a seating area, I made my way into the corner, slumping against the back of a seat before falling into it. The Estonian whose big bag had had to be whipped away before I fell on it shook his head knowingly, as if this sort of thing happened to him every day. Flicking his cigarette ash onto the floor, he carried on chatting to his neighbour before they both inched away. I must have stunk of piss.

Trying to hum a tune, anything to look like a seasick drunk, I decided to take my daysack off. I must have looked stupid sitting with it on my back. Slumped forwards and with the co-ordination of a jelly, I made a complete mess of it. After fighting with the straps for a while I just binned it and collapsed.

Announcements were being made on the PA. My head was swimming. Were they talking about me? Were they appealing for witnesses?

The man next to me stood up and so did his friend. They started gathering together their bits and pieces. We must have arrived.

There was a sudden migration of people, all going in one direction. I just had to try and keep aware of what was going on. I moved off behind them, stumbling amongst the crowd. Everybody seemed to be giving me a wide berth. I didn't know where I was going, and I didn't care, as long as I got off the ferry.

My mind was in control but my body wasn't obeying orders. I bumped into a Finn and apologized in slurred English. He looked down at my wet clothes and glared aggressively. All I was focused on was staying with the herd and keeping the daysack on my back. I just wanted to get off the ferry and find somewhere to hide while all the shit in my body did what it had to do and then left me alone.

Following people with prams and plastic bags,

I lurched down a covered gateway and joined the line for immigration. The woman said nothing as she checked my passport. I swayed and smiled as she eyed me, probably in disgust, and stamped one of the pages. Picking it up at the second attempt I staggered on through to the arrivals hall, focusing really hard on making sure it went back into my inside jacket pocket.

Outside, the cold wind buffeted my jacket as I staggered across a snow-covered car park. The whole area was brightly lit; most of the cars had a layer of snow, and a few were having ice scraped off them as bulging plastic bags were forced inside and exhaust fumes filled the air.

I could see the top half of the ferry behind me, beyond the terminal, and could hear the metallic rumbling of cars and trucks leaving the ship. In front of me was darkness, then, in what seemed the far distance, some very blurred lighting. That was where I needed to go. I needed to find a hotel.

Reeling against a line of vehicles, I got to the end of the car park and hit dark, snow-covered waste ground.

There were a number of well-worn tracks heading in the direction of the lights in the distance. Way over to my right, a convoy of headlamps trailing back to the ferry were heading the same way. I started following a track and immediately fell down, not really feeling anything.

Carrying on as best I could, I was soon in darkness and walking through trees. To my left was a large derelict warehouse. Stopping to rest against a tree, I fixed my eyes on the lights ahead and

377

could hear the faint noises of cars and music in the distance. Things were looking up. I pushed myself off the tree trunk and staggered on.

I didn't even see where the boys came from.

All I felt was two lots of arms grabbing me and dragging me towards the decaying building. I couldn't see their faces in the darkness, just the glow from a cigarette stuck in one of their mouths. My feet were dragging along the ground as my attackers crunched their way through the lumpy snow. I tried to resist but put up the fight of a five-year-old.

Fuck, next stop a 3x9.

They threw me against a doorway which had been filled in with breeze-blocks. I managed to turn so I hit it with my back, but it knocked the wind out of me as I slid down onto my arse.

The kicks started to rain in. All I could do was curl up and take it. At least I was aware enough to know that I'd be too slow to escape or retaliate. I'd have to wait until they'd finished the softening-up process, then see what I could do. No way was I going to let these fuckers take me away if I could help it.

My hands were up around my head to protect it, knees up by my chest. Each time a boot connected my whole body jerked. The drugging was an advantage as I couldn't feel the pain, at least for now. Tomorrow I'd be suffering.

Maybe I could get hold of one of their weapons? At this range, even in my condition, I couldn't miss, so long as I could manipulate the thing once I'd got it. You never know until you try, and I'd rather go down trying than not try at all.

The attack stopped as suddenly as it had started.

The next thing I felt was the daysack being pulled off my back, and even if I'd wanted them to, my arms couldn't have resisted being pulled back as the straps dragged down them.

I was pulled over, exposing my front, and one of them leaned over me and started to unzip my jacket. His own was open; now was the time to react.

Lunging forward, I pushed my hands deep inside his coat. But there was no weapon; he didn't even have one in his hand.

Hands, elbows, I didn't know what they were, hammered into me, pushing me back against the wall, and there was nothing I could do to help myself. I was back at square one.

They both started laughing. Then it was a few more kicks and some cursing in Russian or Estonian. That quickly stopped as they pulled my arms out of the way and finished undoing my jacket.

I was lying in slush and could feel the freezing wetness soaking through my jeans, as if the piss wasn't enough. The jacket was pulled open and I felt their hands going in, pulling up my sweatshirt and jumper, feeling around my stomach, going into the pockets. These were strange places to be searching for a weapon, and it took a while for it to dawn on me. I wasn't being weapons cleared, I was being mugged.

From that moment on I relaxed. Fuck it, let them get on with it. I'd be as passive as I could. There was no need to mess with these people. I had more important things to do than fight muggers. Besides, in my condition I would lose.

They were pretty slick for street thieves, checking around my stomach for a tourist's money belt, with fast whispers between them in whatever language as they did their work. The cigarette still burned in front of my face as they hovered over me. Finally, ripping Baby G from my wrist, they were off, their footsteps crunching in the snow.

I lay there for several minutes, feeling relieved they hadn't been American.

A truck stopped on the other side of the building, its engine idling. There was a loud hiss of air brakes and the engine revved as it drove on. In the silence I heard more music. Then I just lay there, totally out of it, wishing I was in that bar or wherever it was coming from.

The most important thing now was to not let myself fall asleep. If I succumbed I might go down with hypothermia, just like drunks or junkies when they collapse in the streets.

I tried to get to my feet, but couldn't move. Then I felt myself drifting away. The urge to sleep was just too strong.

29

Friday, 17 December 1999

I came round very slowly. I became aware of the wind blowing past the doorway and felt some of it push its way into my face. My vision was still blurred and I was feeling groggy. It was like being hung-over, only several times worse. My head still didn't feel completely linked with my body.

Curled up amongst the beer cans and rubble I was numb with cold and shivering, but that was a good sign. At least I was aware of it; I was starting to switch on.

Coughing and spluttering, I attempted to sort myself out, trying to zip up my jacket with shaking hands to trap some warmth. I could hear a high-revving vehicle moving in the distance – I wasn't too sure how far away, but it didn't seem far. I listened for the music; that had gone now. Once the vehicle moved on there was no more noise apart from the wind and me coughing up shit from the back of my throat. The zip only got halfway as my numbed fingers kept losing their grip on the small tab. I gave up and just held the top half together.

Attempting to get my head into real-life mode,

I checked inside my jacket. I knew it was pointless; they'd had everything away, both the Davidson passport and the money I'd changed. It wasn't worth worrying about the loss; it wouldn't bring them back. Knowing if the contents of my socks were still intact was more important; feeling around with numb fingers I pressed down inside my boots and made contact with the dollars. Even more surprisingly, I still had my Leatherman on my belt. Maybe they weren't as slick as I'd thought, or maybe it had no resale value unless it came with its case.

Once onto my hands and knees, I slowly hauled myself to my feet, using the breeze-blocked doorway for support. I wanted to get moving, find a hotel and get warm; I could still get that train in the morning. But then, it could already be morning, I didn't have a clue.

I had a shivering spasm. Slivers of ice had formed on my jeans as the piss on them had frozen. Feeling in my jacket pockets for my gloves was a stupid idea: they'd taken those too. I needed to get moving and generate some heat.

Freezing air blasted my face as I walked out. The wind was blowing big time, straight off the Baltic. Jumping up and down on the spot, my hands in my pockets, I tried to wake myself up in the darkness but lost my balance. As I breathed in sharply the sub-zero air clawed at the back of my throat and nose. I resumed my aerobics, but it was more of a shuffle than a jump.

The loss of my hat and gloves made me bury my head into the collar of my jacket and my hands firmly in the pockets. I started to pick

382

my way through small piles of snow, which I soon found had gathered round lumps of concrete and twisted steel. I took my time; the last thing I wanted now was to twist an ankle, and the way my luck was going that was quite likely.

Eventually my hands got warm enough to manipulate the zip, and with my jacket done up completely I began to feel the benefit. A car slowly trundled along the road about sixty to seventy metres to my left. Ahead of me, maybe 300 metres away, was the cloudy blue-and-white glow of a petrol station. I bent down, taking my time so as not to lose my balance again, and undid my boot to extract a $20 bill.

After checking that the rest of the money was secure, I staggered and slid towards the blue glow beyond the trees. My condition was improving a little, but I knew I must still look pissed; it was certainly how I felt – like the bloke who believes he's in control when in fact he's slurring his words and failing to notice that matchstick he just tripped up on. Not that I really gave a shit what the people in the petrol station would think of me; all I hoped was that they served hot drinks and food, and that somebody could give me directions to a hotel.

I stumbled on, slipping and sliding on the ice, all the time keeping an eye open for my new mates, or others who might be following the pissed-up foreigner for a few more dollars.

Putting my hand out to rest against a tree for a while, it dawned on me that it was going to be very difficult, maybe impossible, to check into a hotel. In a country like this they'd insist on passport details and possibly even visas. The Russians might have gone, but their bureaucracy would have stayed behind. I could hardly say I'd left my passport in the car. What car? There was also something else; I wouldn't know until it was too late whether the police made spot checks or the hotels had to report anything suspicious, such as a man covered in piss, with no passport, trying to pay in US dollars. It depressed me, but I couldn't take that chance.

Lurching off again towards the petrol station, I was getting nearer to the road. There was virtually no traffic or noise from anywhere, just the odd set of headlights and the rumble of tyres over what sounded like cobblestones and slush in the distance. Intermittent street lights illuminated snow swirling from the ground, making it look as if it was just hanging there.

There were about thirty metres of snow and ice left to cover before I hit the road beside the petrol station; I didn't know what to expect when I got inside, but it looked very much the same as a run-of-the-mill Western European one. In fact, it looked almost too new and shiny to be in the middle of such a rundown area.

I stumbled across to the road; it was indeed made of cobblestones, but not like the ones in Finland. These were old, crumbling or missing, with potholes filled with ice every few metres.

Standing under the bright blue-lit canopy, I banged my boots to clear the snow and tried to make myself look respectable, miming as if I'd lost my glasses when I checked that it was in fact a $20 bill. I wasn't going to risk a $50 or $100; I could get fucked over again if seen with that amount of money round here.

The wind hit the pumps with a high-pitched wail as I went through the door. I entered a new world, warm and clean, with plenty of goods laid out in exactly the way they would be in a convenience store anywhere else in Europe. I wondered if I was hallucinating. They seemed to be selling everything from motor oil to biscuits and bread, but especially rows and rows of beer and a pile of crates with more litre bottles of the stuff next to the spirits. The only thing missing, and which I'd been hoping for, was the smell of coffee. There was no sign of hot drinks at all.

Two guys in their late teens looked up from behind the counter, then went back to studying their magazines, probably feeling ridiculous in their red-and-white striped waistcoats and caps. They didn't look too bright this morning as they smoked and picked their noses, but then, I wasn't exactly looking like Tom Cruise.

I wobbled around the shelves, picking up a handful of chocolate bars, then some shrink-wrapped cold cuts from the chilled compartment. I might not have been at my most alert, but I still knew it was important to get some food down me.

They both stared at me as I dumped my goods on the counter, and it took me a while to realize that I was swaying on my feet. Resting two fingers on the counter to steady myself, I gave them a big smile. 'Speak English?'

The one with the zits saw my $20. 'American?'

'No, no. Australian.' I always said I was from Australia, New Zealand or Ireland; they're neutral, easy-going and well-known as travellers. Tell people you're a Brit or an American and somebody somewhere is bound to be pissed off with you about whatever country you've bombed recently.

He looked at me, trying to work that one out.

'*Crocodile Dundee?*' I mimed strangling a croc. 'G'day mate!'

He smiled and nodded.

Handing him the bill, I pointed at my stuff. 'Can I pay you with this?'

He studied a folder – probably the exchange rates. Behind him, Camel cigarette cartons were neatly arranged around a special-offer Camel clock. I tried to focus my eyes on the hands and managed to make out that it was just after three thirty. No wonder I was freezing; I must have spent hours in that doorway. At least my nose was starting to warm up a bit in here; I could feel it starting to tingle, a good sign that the autojet's effects were wearing off.

He exchanged the bill without a second thought. Everybody likes hard currency. My cold fingers fumbled with the large amount of paper and coins he gave me as change; in the end, I just cupped one hand and scooped the money into it with the other. As he handed me my carrier bag I asked, 'Where is the train station?'

'Huh?'

It was time to play Thomas the Tank Engine. I pulled the steam whistle. 'Oooo! Ooooo! Chug chug chug!'

They liked that and started gobbing off in what I guessed was Estonian. My mate with zits pointed to the right of the forecourt, where the road bent to the left before disappearing.

I put my hand up in a big Australian thank-you gesture, walked out and turned right as they had directed. Straight away the cold wind hit me; my nose and lungs felt as if I was inhaling tiny fragments of broken glass.

The pavement taking me towards the bend was covered with ice the colour of mud. This was so different from Finland, where public paths were kept scrupulously clear. Here the stuff had just been trodden down, turned to slush, then frozen. Empty cans and other lumps of litter sticking out at crazy angles made me lift my feet high to make sure I didn't trip over.

As I followed the road, looking for signs to the station, I threw chunks of very hard chocolate down my neck. I must have looked like someone walking home with a kebab after a good night out.

After fifteen minutes of swaying down a dark deserted street, I came across railway tracks and followed them. Just a quarter of an hour later I was going through heavy glass doors into the dimly lit station. It smelled of fried food and vomit, and like any other railway station in the world it offered a full range of drunks, addicts and homeless people.

The interior was concrete with stone slab floors. It must have looked great on the drawing board in the Seventies, which was when it was probably built, but now it was badly lit, neglected and falling apart, complete with fading posters and peeling paint.

At least the place was warm. I made my way along the main concourse, looking for a place to curl up and hide. I felt as if that was all I'd been trying to do since getting on the ferry. All the good sites were already booked, but I eventually found an alcove and dropped down onto my arse.

The smell of urine and decaying cabbage was overpowering. No wonder the space was vacant; somebody obviously ran a stall there specializing in rancid vegetables, then had a piss against the wall every evening before he went home.

I pulled the food from my pocket. I really didn't want any more, but made myself eat the remaining two chocolate bars and the meat, then rolled over onto my right-hand side, bringing my knees up into a foetal position, with my face resting on my hands amongst the unswept dirt and dog-ends. I was past caring; I just wanted to sleep.

A couple of winos immediately started putting the world to rights with loud, slurred voices. I opened one eye to check on them, just as a bag lady wandered over to join their debate. They all had grimy old faces, cut and bruised where they'd been either beaten up or had got so drunk they'd fallen over and damaged themselves. All three were now lying on the floor, surrounded by a rampart of bulging plastic carrier bags tied together with string. Each had a can in their hand that no doubt contained the local equivalent of Special Brew.

Another drunk shuffled over to my alcove, maybe attracted by my earlier foodfest. He started jumping up and down on the spot, grunting and waving his arms. The best way to deal with these situations is to appear just as mad and drunk as them – and more. I sat up and hollered, 'Hubba-hubba hubba-hubba!' not bothering to try to make my eyes look scary; they probably already did. Picking up a can, I yelled at it for a few seconds, then threw it at him, growling like a wounded animal. He shuffled away, muttering and moaning. That was the only productive lesson I learned in borstal, apart from the fact that I never wanted to go back.

I lay down again and fell into a semi-daze, with what seemed like ten minutes' sleep here and five minutes' there, waking every time there was a noise or movement. I didn't fancy being mugged a second time.

I was jolted awake by a hard kick in the ribs. My head was still aching badly, but at least my eyes were focusing a lot better. I saw a frenzy of men in black, looking just like an American police SWAT team, with black combat trousers tucked into their boots, black baseball caps and nylon bomber jackets festooned with badges and logos. In their beltkit they carried canisters, which were almost certainly full of mace. They were shouting and screaming, hitting vagrants indiscriminately with black metre-long night sticks. For the homeless population of Tallinn, this was obviously reveille. It was certainly similar to some morning calls I'd had in basic training.

Taking the hint, I started to pull myself up onto my feet. My whole body hurt. I must have looked like a ninety-year-old as I shambled out of the station with the rest of them, hoping it wouldn't take too long before my muscles warmed up and relieved some of the pain.

The cold early morning air gripped my face and lungs. It was still pitch-black, but I could hear a lot more movement than when I'd arrived. To my right I could see the main drag, with intermittent traffic. A solitary street light was glimmering, but so weakly it needn't have bothered. Parked up in a row were five black, very clean and large 4x4s, possibly Land Cruisers. Each vehicle carried a white triangular logo, the same as the largest one on the back of the team's bomber jackets. There was still plenty of screaming and arguing going on, and I saw my three debating-society mates being thrown bodily into one of the wagons. Maybe that was where the cut faces came from.

I moved out of the way, round to the other side of the station. There was life of sorts going on here. I hadn't noticed it on the way in, but the building obviously doubled as a bus station. There was a large open area with queue shelters and fleets of dilapidated buses, covered in mud. Plumes of early morning exhaust fumes rose from the rear of some of them. People at the back of the queues were shouting at the ones in front, probably telling them to board before they froze to death. Bags were being placed into the luggage holds, along with wooden crates and cardboard boxes tied up with string. Most of the passengers seemed to be old women in heavy overcoats, with knitted hats and huge felt boots with zips up the front.

The only proper light came from the railway station and the bus headlights reflecting off the icy ground. A tram appeared from nowhere and moved across the foreground.

The station had windows missing in the offices above platform level, and it was covered by decades of grime. It wasn't just this building, the whole place looked in deep decay. The main drag was badly potholed and entire areas of tarmac had broken up like ice floes to create different levels for vehicles to negotiate.

The men in black had finished their task. Some of the street people wandered across the road in a group, maybe heading for the next refuge point, others started to beg by the buses. When they stood next to the passengers it was hard to tell who looked worse off. Everybody seemed to be holding carrier bags, not just the homeless, but the people boarding the buses as well. Not a single one was laughing or smiling. I felt sorry for them – freed from Communism, but not from poverty.

I waited while the black teams climbed into their wagons and moved off, then I wandered back into the station. The place didn't smell any better now it was cleared, but at least it was warm. I thought I'd better clean myself up. I eventually found some toilets, though I didn't know if they were for men or women. It was just a set of cubicles and a couple of sinks. A solitary bulb flickered in the ceiling and the place absolutely stank of piss, shit and vomit. Once at the sinks I found out where all these smells seemed to come from.

Deciding to give the wash a miss, I inspected myself in the mirror. My face wasn't cut or bruised, but my hair was sticking out at all angles. I wet my hands under the tap and ran my fingers through it, then got out of there quickly before I was sick myself.

Wandering around the station, I tried to find out train times. There was plenty of information, all in Estonian or Russian. The ticket office was closed, but a handwritten notice on a piece of cardboard taped to the inside of the glass screen explained that there was something happening at 0700, which I took to be the opening time. I couldn't see if there was a clock in the office as it was cut from view by a faded yellow curtain.

Sheets of paper stuck to the glass also carried various destination names, in lettering I recognized, as well as Cyrillic. I saw Narva and the numbers 707. It seemed there was just seven minutes between the office opening and my train leaving.

My next priority was to get a brew and find out the time. Nothing was open in the station, but with any luck there was some kind of facility outside for the bus passengers. Where there are people, there will be traders.

I found a row of aluminium kiosks, with no unity or theme to what any of them sold; each of them just sold stuff, everything from coffee to hair bands, but mostly cigarettes and alcohol.

I couldn't remember what the currency was –

things were still blurry – but I managed to get a paper cup of coffee for a small coin that was probably worth two pence. From the same kiosk I also treated myself to a new watch, a bright orange thing with the Lion King grinning out at me from a face that lit up at the press of a button. His paws rested on a digital display, which the old woman running the kiosk corrected to 0615.

I stood in between two kiosks with my brew and watched the trams deliver and pick up passengers. Apart from those yelling at each other in queues, there was very little talk from anybody. These were depressed people, and the whole ambience of the place reflected their state of mind. Even the coffee was horrible.

I started to notice people huddled here and there in small groups, passing bottles amongst themselves. One group of young men in a bus shelter, wearing old coats over shiny shell-suit trousers, were drinking from half-litre bottles of beer and smoking.

In a strange way the place reminded me of Africa; everything, even the plastic toys and combs in the kiosk window displays, was faded and warped. It looked as if the West had dumped its trash and it had washed up with these people. As in Africa, they had stuff – buses, trains, TVs, even cans of Coke – but nothing really worked together. Basically it felt as if the whole country was Made in Chad. When I was operating there, the republic used to be the byword for things that looked OK but fell apart in ten minutes.

I thought some more about the ferry attack. The blokes in the toilets must have been NSA, but the only way I could have been pinged was by them checking the ticketing, then taking and checking out this guy called Davies. Once my passport had been swiped they'd cracked it: Davidson was on board. The two who'd attacked me would be out of commission, but would others soon be on my trail?

I bought another brew to get more heat inside me, as well as another bar of chocolate and a loose-foil sheet of twenty-four aspirin to clear my head and help with the body pain, then I wandered around the kiosks looking for maps as I washed down the first four tabs with crap coffee. I found a Narva town map, but not one for the north-east of the country. Glancing at Lion King as I paid for it, I realized I had to get a move on.

On the way to the ticket office I brushed the worst of the dirt from my jeans. My body heat was drying them out slowly, so I hoped I didn't smell too much. For all I knew they might have a rule about not selling tickets to dossers.

I was first in a line of three when the grubby bit of curtain got moved away from the little window to reveal an iron grille behind thick glass, with a small wooden scoop at the bottom where money and tickets were exchanged. A woman in her mid-fifties glowered at me from behind the fortifications. She was wearing a cardigan and, of course, a woollen hat. She was also probably resting her feet on a bulging carrier bag.

I smiled. 'Narva, Narva?'

'Narva.'

'Yes. How much?' I rubbed my fingers together.

She got out a little receipt book and wrote 'Narva' and '707'. It appeared the cost was 707 hertigrats, or whatever the money was called, not that it left at 7.07.

I handed her a 1000 note. $20 US was going a long way here. She moved away from the glass, rummaged around, came back and dropped my change through the scoop. With it was a slip of paper as thin as tissue. I picked it up, guessing it must be some kind of receipt. 'Narva – ticket?'

She gobbed off at me gloomily. It was pointless, I didn't have a clue what she was on about. I didn't ask about the platform. I'd find it.

Tallinn station seemed to be the terminus for all lines. This wasn't St Pancras or Victoria, though; the platforms outside the hall were lumpy, broken tarmac, with ice where the water had puddled and frozen. In places, exposed concrete had crumbled and rusting reinforcement rods protruded. The trains were old Russian monsters with a big Cyclops light; they all seemed to be blue, but it was hard to be sure under all the dirt and grime. Hanging on the front of each loco-motive was a wooden destination board, and that was all the help you got.

I walked up and down looking for the word Narva, brushing past other passengers. I found the train, but needed to confirm it with one of my carrier-bag friends.

'Narva, Narva?'

The old man looked at me as if I was an alien, muttering something without taking the fag out of his mouth, so the light from the tip bounced up and down. He then just walked away. At least I got a nod as he pointed at the train.

I carried on along the platform, looking for an empty carriage, to the sound everywhere of the early morning coughing up of phlegm – people holding one nostril and snotting out on the ground, then putting the fags back into their mouths.

There didn't seem to be any completely empty carriages, so I boarded anyway, taking the first free row of seats I could find. The carriage floor was nothing more than welded steel plates, and the seats were also made of steel, with two small, thinly padded vinyl sections, one for your back and one for your arse. There were a couple of forty-watt lightbulbs in the ceiling and that was our lot. All very basic, all very functional, yet surprisingly clean compared to the mayhem in the station outside. And at least it was warm.

30

The wheels rattled rhythmically over the rails as I gazed out at the darkness. I couldn't see any of the landscape, just lights from what I supposed were factories and from windows of row upon row of prison-like apartment blocks.

I was sitting by the sliding door at the front end, next to a window, with, thankfully, a heater outlet directly under my seat. According to the travel guide I'd be here for at least the next five hours, which was good news for my jeans. There were a dozen other passengers spread about the carriage, all of them male, most with carrier bags, and either deep in thought or doing the nodding dog.

The door slid back with a crash and a woman in her mid-forties came in, wearing a man's grey overcoat that was far too big for her. Draped over her arm were a dozen copies of a tabloid. She started gobbing off and was clearly asking me something. I waved my hand politely to say no thanks but she became very animated. When I waved my hand again and shook my head with a nice Australian smile, she reached into her coat

397

and out came the same sort of book of receipts that Mrs Glum had used in the ticket office. I realized she was the ticket collector, who was obviously running a newspaper concession on the side. Like me, she was taking the money where she could find it.

I fished out my slip of paper. She inspected it, grunted, gave it back and swayed with the momentum of the train on to the next passenger, no doubt telling him that the village idiot was on board. Given what I was about to try, she wasn't far wrong.

We began to slow, and finally stopped. Through the darkness I could just see a factory, complete with a series of enormous chimneys. The station didn't have a platform; the factory workers had to disembark directly onto the tracks. Outside, people seemed to wander all over the place, even between carriages.

The train set off again, stopping every ten minutes or so to disgorge another group of workers. After each halt the old diesel engine would strain to get up speed again, belching smoke which quickly merged with the junk the factory chimneys were pumping out. The railway system made Britain's look positively space age by comparison, but at least these ran on time, were warm, clean and affordable. I thought of inviting a few Estonian train managers to the UK to show our guys how it should be done.

The train snaked, shuddered and shook its way through the industrial wasteland. After half an hour the lights started to die out and I was looking into darkness again. I decided to follow the lead of the one other passenger left in the carriage and get some sleep.

It was shortly after nine thirty and first light had just passed. The sky, in keeping with everything else, was a gloomy grey. Through the grime on the window I saw snow-heavy trees lining the track on each side, a barrier against snow drifts. Beyond them lay either vast stretches of absolutely flat open ground, covered in virgin white snow, or thick forest that stretched on for ever. The electricity and telephone lines following the track were just like the trees, sagging with the weight of the snow and huge ice stalactites that hung from them.

The train was still moving very slowly between stations, maybe because of the weather, maybe because the track was in need of repair.

An hour later, after another couple of stops, the chocolate and meat started to take effect. I hadn't seen any signs for toilets and I wasn't even sure there were any. If not, I'd just have to have a quick dump in the corridor and explain it was an old Australian custom.

I walked the length of two carriages, bouncing from side to side, until I eventually found one. It was just like the rest of the train, very basic but clean, warm and it worked.

Ripping hard sheets from the roll I threw them into the pan until it was more or less blocked. As I pulled down my now dry jeans and sat on the bare ceramic bowl, I had a quick sniff of the denim. Not that bad, considering; I could always blame it on a tom cat. Bruises had developed on both thighs now; they'd soon turn black, complementing the ones I already had.

As the chocolate and meat mix started to force its way out I fought to keep control, wanting to catch the insurance policy, wrapped in two condoms and inserted up my arse with the aid of some Helsinki hotel soap.

This was something else I'd learned in borstal. It was the best way to make sure my fifteen pence weekly allowance wasn't stolen. Clingfilm hadn't been as good as these condoms, though.

It was a bit of a smelly affair retrieving it, but once I'd untied the knot in the first condom, pulled out the one inside and washed my hands – there was even soap and water in these toilets – everything was clean and fragrant again. I was still enthusing about Estonian railways when it was suddenly like being back on the Kings Lynn to London line: the flush didn't work.

I stayed a while and treated myself to a wash. Back in the carriage, it was time to study my Narva town map, working out exactly where I'd find Konstantin. According to Lion King there was about an hour to go before we arrived. I sat there feeling rather pleased the chocolate had worked and that I wouldn't have to waste time in Narva waiting for nature to call.

I dry-swallowed another four aspirin and looked out of the window. No wonder people had been getting off before entering this part of the country. This must be the start of the great industrial north-east the Soviets had created during their reign. Gone were the trees and open spaces of the wilderness; instead the view consisted entirely of slag heaps, with massive conveyor belts, and factories that churned out smoke from every corner.

We trundled past forbidding blocks of flats, with TV aerials hung from every window and sometimes enormous, outdated satellite dishes. There were no gardens or play areas, just two or three cars up on concrete blocks. Even the snow was grey.

The scenery didn't change much as the stops became more frequent, except that every spare inch of ground along the track was covered with little vegetable allotments. Even the spaces under electricity pylons were turned into makeshift greenhouses using a patchwork of plastic sheeting. Just when I thought it couldn't get any more depressing, the train shunted past three cars parked at the side of the road, nose to tail. They were riddled with bullet holes and burned out. There was no snow or ice on them and shattered glass lay all over the place. It looked as if they'd only just been hosed down and torched. For all I knew there might still be bodies inside. A couple of kids walked past and didn't give them a second look.

The train stopped with a judder and a loud squeal of brakes. We seemed to be in a rail yard. Fuel bowsers and freight cars appeared on either side, all covered with Russian script and caked in oil and ice. I was back in a scene from a Harry Palmer film again, only Michael Caine would have had a suit and trenchcoat on instead of piss-stained jeans. The train just seemed to have driven into the yard and stopped, and that was it.

Going by the number of doors opening, it was time to get off. Welcome to Narva.

I looked out of the window and saw people jumping down onto the tracks with their carrier bags. The only other remaining passenger in my carriage was leaving. I did the same, traipsing through the snow across a massive shunting yard, following the others towards an old stone house. I guessed that it hadn't been built until after 1944, because I'd read that when the Russians 'liberated' Estonia from the Germans they flattened the whole town, then rebuilt it from scratch.

I went through grey-painted, metal double doors into the ticket office. The room was only about twenty by thirty feet, with a few old plastic, classroom-style chairs around the sides. The walls were covered with the same thick shiny grey paint as the doors, onto which graffiti had been scratched. I thought the floor was plain pitted concrete until I noticed the two remaining tiles refusing to leave home.

The ticket office was closed. A large wooden board was fixed to the wall near the sales window, with plastic sliders upon which, in Cyrillic, were the names of various destinations. I looked for anything that resembled the word Tallinn. It seemed that the first train back was at 08:22 each morning, but even if they'd spoken English, there was no-one around to confirm it.

I stepped round the obligatory puddle of vomit and came out of the main entrance. Over to my left was what I took to be a bus station. The buses were of 1960s or 1970s vintage, all battered and some even hand-painted. People were fighting to get aboard, exactly as they'd done in the capital; the driver was shouting at them and they shouted at each other. Even the snow was exactly the same as in Tallinn; dirty, downtrodden and viciously icy.

Digging my hands deep into my pockets I cut directly across the potholed road, following the map in my head along Puskini, which seemed to be the main street. It wouldn't be far to Konstantin's address.

Puskini was lined on either side by high buildings. On the left, what looked like a power station loomed behind them and, bizarrely, electricity pylons were set into the street and pavements, so pedestrians had to pick their way round them. Russians seemed to have sited all their industrial units as near as possible to the stations that powered them; then, if they had any space left, they'd squeezed in accommodation for the workers, and fuck the people who had to live there. I'd seen enough to tell me this was a miserable, run-down place. The newest buildings looked as if they dated from the 1970s, and even they were falling apart.

I headed up the street, keeping to the right. It was quiet apart from the occasional tractor and one or two Russian-plated articulated lorries surging past. The roads and pavements were jet black with grease and grime, with a good coating of slush from passing vehicles.

Christmas hadn't arrived in Narva yet. I wondered if it ever would. There were no street decorations, lights or anything remotely festive, even in the windows. I walked past drab shop fronts which advertised everything from second-hand washing machines to Arnold Schwarzenegger videos.

Further along, I came to a small mini-market. It was an old building, but had the brightest lighting I'd yet seen spilling out onto the iced pavement. I couldn't resist it, especially as I hadn't had anything to eat since my chocolate and meat combo, from which I'd long since parted company.

An old man was lying on top of a cardboard box to one side of the main entrance, sheltered by the shop's canopy. His head was wrapped in rags, his hands covered with strips of canvas. The skin on his face was dark with ingrained dirt and he could have grown vegetables in his beard. Beside him was a wooden tomato box turned upside down, displaying a rusty old screwdriver and a pair of pliers that were clearly up for sale. He didn't bother looking up at me as I passed. I must have looked as though I was all right for rusty tools.

The store was laid out to exactly the same template as a small-town Spar in the UK. It even had some of the same brands – Colgate toothpaste, KP nuts and Gillette shaving foam – but not much else apart from crates of beer and a large chiller cabinet that had nothing in it except rows of different sausages, including the dodgy red ones I hadn't eaten on the ferry, strung out in lines to make the display look more generous.

I picked up a family-sized bag of crisps, two packs of sliced, processed cheese and four cake-type rolls. I didn't bother with a drink as I hoped I'd soon be getting a hot one at Konstantin's. Besides, there wasn't much choice apart from beer and half-bottles of vodka. I couldn't be arsed to get washing kit or a tooth-brush to replace the stuff that had been stolen. All that sort of thing I'd grab if I needed it, but I didn't plan to be in-country that long; and in any case, no-one I'd seen so far seemed to give much of a shit about personal hygiene.

As I paid for my goods I helped myself to two carrier bags, putting one pack of cheese and a couple of rolls into one, the rest into the other. Passing the old guy on the way out, I put the smaller bag down beside him. I hadn't bought him any crisps because I didn't think his gums could tackle them. I knew what it felt like to spend hours outside in the cold.

With hands back in my jacket pockets, the bag dangling from my right wrist and banging rhyth-mically against my thigh, I moved on. I skirted a pylon that was half in the street and half over the wall of a small factory, and more rows of miser-able flats came into view, identical to the ones I'd seen from the train. There were no names on the blocks, just stencilled numbers. At last I'd found one thing that my old council estate had over this place: at least every building there had been named after locations in Chaucer's *Canterbury Tales*. The rest of it, though, was much the same – rotting wooden window frames and cracks in the panes taped over with parcel tape. I remembered why I'd promised myself at the age of nine that I'd get out of shitholes like this as soon as I could.

It was only about one thirty in the afternoon, but already the town could have done with some street lights on. Unfortunately, there just weren't that many around to help out.

Things started to liven up after another hundred metres or so. I came to a giant car park, full of buses and cars. People who seemed to be carrying everything from carrier bags to suitcases were shouting at each other, trying to be heard over the noise of air brakes and engines. It looked like news footage of refugees moving through a checkpoint. The closer I got, the more it started to look like somewhere Han Solo might go to get a spare part for his spacecraft. There were some strange looking people around.

I realized I was at the border crossing point, the road bridge into, or out of, Russia. Harry Palmer would have been a regular here.

The car park was clogged with new Audis, old BMWs and Ladas of all sorts, shapes and ages. It was the Ford Sierras that looked strangely out of place. There were fleets of the things. I now knew where all the second-hand ones went when they weren't snapped up by minicab drivers.

Money-changers plied their trade along the edges of the car park, and kiosks sold all other types of kit as fast as Chad could manufacture it. I walked over to a green-painted garden shed with a small sliding window, dodging the artic trucks that thundered past as they cleared border control. If you didn't get out of the way, tough.

Camel, Marlboro and a million different Russian brands were taped to the glass, together with as many different styles of lighter. An old guy who looked like a gypsy, dark-skinned with thick, grey curly hair, showed me his list of exchange rates. It seemed I could get about 12 EEK, whatever they were, to the US dollar. I didn't know if that was good or not, just that Duracell batteries were taped up at just a couple of EEKs each, so either it was the bargain of the century or they were duds. I didn't want to show that I had money, so I went and sat on a dustbin behind the kiosk, got a warm $100 dollar bill out of my sock and replaced the boot pretty sharpish.

Once he'd carried out about five different checks to make sure it wasn't counterfeit, including smelling it, the old guy was very happy indeed with his hard currency, and so was I with my new EEK wedge. I left the refugee camp behind and headed further up Puskini, towards a roundabout which, according to the map in my head, led to the road I wanted.

The only buildings that looked at all inviting were near the roundabout. Flashing neon signs told me these were 'komfort baars'. Music blared from loudspeakers rigged up outside. Originally, I supposed, they'd been ordinary bars or shops, but their windows were painted out now. It didn't need much imagination to work out what was on offer the other side of the emulsion, but for the benefit of anyone in doubt, there were pictures of women and Cyrillic stencilling, no doubt defining exactly what was meant by 'komfort'. The best picture of all was on a blue window, showing the Statue of Liberty with Marilyn Monroe's face, pulling up her robe to reveal an ace of spades between her legs.

Underneath, in English, it read, 'America. Fuck it here.' I wasn't too sure what it all meant, but the Russians who had parked up all the trucks along the road obviously didn't have any trouble reading the menu.

I'd just stopped by the roundabout to check which road I wanted next when two white Suzuki Vitaras with flashing red-and-blue light bars screeched to a halt outside Marilyn's.

Three guys piled out of each, dressed exactly the same as the SWAT team at Tallinn station, but with a different logo. Theirs was also sewn on the back of their bomber jackets. I couldn't make out the wording from this distance, just that it was all in red and in the sort of typeface used on surfwear. Pulling out smaller truncheons than the lot at the station, they piled into the bar.

I stepped into a doorway to watch, taking one of the rolls from my carrier bag. Pulling the bread apart, I threw in a few slices of cheese and a handful of crisps and watched as a very tired-looking green Lada police car turned up and parked near the Vitaras. Two fur-hatted figures inside didn't get out. I stamped my feet to keep them warm.

The Vitaras were showroom clean and had a phone number and logo emblazoned on the side and what looked like the letters 'DTTS'. The police car was falling to pieces and looked as if the insignia on the side had been hand-painted.

For the next few minutes nothing much happened. A stream of vehicles negotiated the roundabout and I ate my roll, along with a few more crisps. A few of the passing cars were quite new – Audis, VWs and even a Merc – but not many. The popularity battle was really between clapped-out Sierras and Ladas.

I was still putting the finishing touches to my second cheese roll when the black teams emerged from the bar, dragging out three punters between the six of them. All three were in suits, with blood pouring down their faces onto their white shirts, while their smart shoes got scraped along the ice. They were thrown into the back of the Vitaras and then given the good news with truncheons. The doors were closed and one of the team, noticing the police car, just waved them away. None of the passers-by even bothered to glance at what was going on; it was hard to tell whether they were too scared or just couldn't be arsed.

The police headlights came back on and off they drove, exhaust pipe rattling, towards the border-crossing car park.

The Vitaras and their crews also left, and I finished the roll as I crossed the roundabout and turned right, towards the river. The address that Liv had given me was on this road, which was known simply as Viru. Still wondering what the three guys had done to cause Marilyn such offence, I started attacking the last roll and the remaining cheese and crisps. Like I didn't have my own stuff to worry about.

31

Viru wasn't any more uplifting than the rest of town, just grey, miserable blocks of housing, more black snow and more uncared-for roads. Then, bizarrely, just up ahead was a burned-out dodgem car, its metal frame and long conducting rod charred and twisted. God only knows how it had got there.

The only thing moving was a posse of five or six dogs, creating a haze of steam above their bodies as they skulked around, sniffing at stuff on the ground then pissing on it. I didn't even feel bad as I dropped my plastic bag, along with the crisp and cheese packets. When in Rome . . .

Now and again a patched-up Sierra clattered past on the cobblestones, its occupants looking at me as if I was mad to be walking in this neighbourhood. They were probably right, if the sulphur fumes I was inhaling were anything to go by. There was obviously another environmentally friendly factory near by.

Slipping my hands deeper into my pockets and my head deeper inside my collar, I tried to adopt the same miserable body language as everyone else. Thinking about what I'd seen at the komfort baar, I decided not to tangle with private-enterprise security if I could help it. The State police looked a softer option.

Viru started to bend to the right, and straight ahead I could see the icy riverbank, five or six hundred metres away. That was Russia.

As I neared the bend I could see into the gorge, with the river Narva about 200 metres below. Following it round, the road bridge was about 400 metres away. Lines of cars were queuing to leave Estonia, with foot traffic moving in both directions, carrying suitcases, carrier bags and all sorts. The checkpoint on the Russian side had barriers across the road and guards checking papers.

If the numbering on the map was correct, number 87 Viru would soon be on my right, a little past the bend and facing the river.

It wasn't an apartment block as I'd been expecting, but a large old house that was now a baar. At least, that was what the sign said, in white but unlit neon lettering above a rotten wooden door. Big patches of rendering were missing from the front of the building, exposing the red clay brick underneath. It was three storeys high, and looked really out of place amongst the uniform concrete blocks surrounding it on three sides. Most of the upper windows were covered by internal wooden shutters; there were no curtains to be seen. There was another neon sign, also not illuminated, of a man leaning over a pool table with a cigarette in his mouth and a glass of beer on the side.

411

According to the sign next to it saying '8–22', it should have been open. Trying the door handle, I found that it wasn't.

Four cars were parked up outside. There was a brand-new, shiny red Audi, and two Cherokee Jeeps that had seen better days, both dark blue and with Russian plates. The fourth vehicle, however, was in the worst state of any I'd seen in Estonia, apart from the dodgem. It was a red Lada that had been hand-painted and had to belong to a teenager. There were domestic music speakers clamped on the back shelf, from which wires hung like spaghetti. Very cool, especially the pile of old newspapers on the back seat.

I looked through the grime-covered ground-floor windows. There were no lights on and no sounds. Walking round to the other side, facing the river, I could see a light shining on the third floor, just a single bulb. It was like finding life on Mars.

Back at the wooden door I hit the intercom button near the baar sign. The building might be in as shit state as Tom's, but the intercom was in better condition. There was no way of telling if it was working, though, so I tried again, this time for longer. There was static and crackling, and a gruff male voice, half aggressive, half bored, quizzed me. I didn't know what the fuck he was on about. I said, 'Konstantin. I want to see Konstantin.'

I heard the Russian or Estonian equivalent of, 'Eh, what?' then there was more gobbing off from him and voices shouting in the background. When he came back to me it was with something that obviously translated as, 'Fuck off, big nose.' The static ceased; I'd been given the brush off.

I buzzed again, working on the theory that if he got pissed off enough he might come down to the door to fill me in. At least then I had a chance of making some progress. There was more shouting, which I didn't understand; I got the gist but carried on regardless.

'Konstantin? Konstantin?'

The machine went dead once again. I wasn't sure whether there was going to be some action now or not, so I stayed where I was.

After about two minutes there was the sound of bolts being thrown on the other side of the door. I moved out of the way as it was pushed open. Behind it was an iron grille door, still closed, and behind that was a guy of maybe seventeen or eighteen, who looked like the style fairy had crept up on him and waved her LA-street-gang wand. I bet he owned the Lada.

'Do you speak English?'

'Yo! You want Konstantin?'

'Yeah, Konstantin. Is he here?'

He gave a big smile. 'Yes, he sure is, for that's me, man. You are the England guy, right?'

I nodded and smiled, holding back laughter as he tried to match his speech with his dress sense. It just didn't work, especially with a Russian accent.

He beamed as he looked me up and down. 'OK, smart guy, come on in.' He was right, I didn't look as if I'd come straight from the dry-cleaners. Or maybe he'd been expecting a man in a bowler hat.

The grille was secured from the inside with two lever locks. As soon as I'd walked in, both the door and the grille were locked behind me and the keys taken out.

He held up his hands. 'Hey, call me Vorsim.' He wiggled his fingers, or rather, the ones that hadn't gone missing, in the air. 'Everyone does. It's Russian for eight.'

He gave me another quick once-over as we both smiled at the joke he'd probably cracked a thousand times. 'Hey, follow me, England guy.'

I followed Eight up a narrow wooden staircase to the first floor. The banisters and handrails were bare wood, and the exposed steps sagged with age. There was no light apart from the dull glow coming through the ground-floor windows. I could only just see where my feet were going.

It was an old, once-grand house. I couldn't see any evidence of a bar, but at least it was warm and dry – almost too dry. It had that dusty smell places get when the windows are never opened and the heating is on all the time.

Our footsteps echoed round the stairwell. Eight was about three steps above me, wearing a pair of the most blindingly yellow and purple Nike trainers I'd ever seen, beneath a pair of baggy, blue hip-hop-style jeans that were stonewashed – the kind with big horrible streaks of white – and a black PVC leather-look bomber jacket with the LA Raiders pirate logo stitched on the back.

We hit a landing and turned for the next flight which would take us up to the second floor. Weak light filtered through the slatted shutters. All the doors leading off it were panelled, with faded flowers painted on ceramic door knobs; it must have been a splendid place when it was first built.

We passed the second and carried on up to the third floor, then walked along a larger landing. He opened one of the doors towards the river. 'Your name is Nick, right?'

'Yeah, that's right.' I didn't return the eye contact as I walked past him into the room. I was too busy checking what I was walking into.

There was just one bulb in the centre of the room, producing the dingy, yellowy light I'd seen from outside. The very large room was in semi-darkness and was boiling hot. The only job the lighting did was expose a layer of cigarette smoke that clung to the high ceiling. There was a glow from the TV to my left, its volume set at low, with a body in front of it. Directly in front of me, about fifteen metres away, was a single sash window, its shutters open in the hope of letting in a little natural light. The shutters on each side were still firmly closed. There were no carpets or wall hangings, just empty space.

To my right, near a large marble fireplace, three men were seated on fancy chairs around what looked like an antique table with ornate legs. They were playing cards and smoking. Beside them, and to the right of the fireplace, was another door.

The three heads at the table turned and stared as they sucked on their cigarettes. I nodded without any reaction from them at all, then one of the guys said something and the other two guffawed and went back to their game.

The door closed behind me. I looked at Eight,

who was bobbing up and down with excitement. 'Well, man' – arms moving around like a rapper – 'you hang here, Vorsim won't be long. Things to do.' And with that he placed the grille keys on the table and disappeared through the door near the fireplace.

I looked over at the guy by the TV. The colour picture was a bit snowy, perhaps because it was perched on a chair with a coat hanger for an aerial. He was sat on a chair opposite, his nose nearly touching the screen, too engrossed to bother looking round at me. His area was giving out more light than the bulb in the ceiling; it was a mystery how the other guys could see their cards.

No-one offered me anywhere to sit, so I went over to the window to have a look outside. The floorboards creaked with every step I took. The card school, now behind me, just got back to mumbling to each other as they played.

It was easy to see what went on here. Two sets of electronic display pharmaceutical scales sat under the table at this end of the room. Next to them were stacked maybe ten to twelve large Tupperware boxes, some containing white stuff that definitely wasn't flour, others holding dark-coloured pills that similarly weren't Smarties.

Directly beneath the window was Viru, dirty snow and ice covering overflowing dustbins. At the corner of the building three scabby cats lay perfectly still in the snow, gathered around a drain, waiting for their black furry dinner to serve itself up.

Over the lip of the gorge the river on both

banks was iced up, but the centre third was carrying big chunks of ice and garbage sluggishly from right to left, towards the Baltic about 12Ks downstream. Further upstream the bridge was still jammed with cars and people.

I turned back to the room. It might be sweltering in here, but I was desperate for a hot brew. The only drink I could see was a bottle of Johnny Walker on the table, which was being emptied by the card players. They all had black leather jackets draped over the backs of their chairs. They'd obviously watched too many gangster movies, because they were all dressed in black trousers and black crew-neck jumpers, with enough gold dripping off their wrists and fingers to clear Estonia's national debt. It looked like a scene from *GoodFellas*. Packs of Camel and Marlboro lay on the table in front of them, gold lighters placed neatly on top. I made sure they couldn't see my Lion King watch. I didn't want them to start by taking the piss, as there might be a time when they had to take me seriously. A smiling Disney character on my wrist wouldn't help.

I turned to the TV-watcher as he clicked at his lighter and lit up, holding the cigarette between his thumb and index finger, then leaning forward, elbows on knees, to get his nose back into some low-budget American soap. What was really strange was that the dialogue was still in English; only after the actors had delivered their lines did the Russian dubbing take place. There was absolutely no emotion in the translation; a woman with more make-up than Eddie Izzard gushed, 'But Fortman, I love you,' then a Russian voice translated it as if she was buying a kilo of cabbage. I suddenly knew where Eight got his English and dress code from.

The door opened and in he came. 'Yo, Nikolai!' The bomber jacket was now off to reveal a red sweatshirt with Bart Simpson karate kicking another kid with fistfuls of dollars. Printed underneath was 'Just take it'. Dangling from Eight's neck was a thick gold chain that any rapper would be proud of.

He came and stood by the window with me. 'Nick, I've been told to help you. Because, hey, guess what, crazy guy, I'm the only one here who speaks English.' He shuffled from trainer to trainer as he clapped his hands. The GoodFellas looked at him as if he was a basket case, and got back to their game.

'Vorsim, I need a car.'

'Car? Whoa, could be a problem, my man.'

I half expected to hear his response followed by some bad Russian dubbing. He turned to the GoodFellas, spoke some very fast stuff and did some mock begging. The oldest one, maybe in his early fifties, didn't look up from his hand but replied really aggressively. He must have been drinking liquid nasty instead of Johnny Walker. I caught his drift, though: 'Tell the Brit to fuck offski.' I wondered if I should produce the insurance policy but decided not to. Better to save it until it really mattered.

Another one of the three sparked up with an idea, pointing first at Eight, then at me, and made out he was hitting something with a hammer. The other two really liked that one. Even the TV addict joined in as they all had a good laugh. It was Merlin's laugh: King Arthur used to get frustrated when he made a kingly decision and his wizard just laughed, because Merlin knew the future and the king didn't. I felt the same sort of thing was happening here. Liv was right: don't trust them an inch.

Eight's shoulders slumped. He walked back over to me. 'I'll have to give you my car.'

'Is it one of the ones outside?' I'd already guessed, but was hoping I was wrong.

'Yes. But hey, man, I need it for bitches. Will I get it back soon? How long do you need it for? A couple of hours?'

I shrugged. 'Maybe a couple of days.' Before he could react I added, 'I also want to see you later tonight. Will you be here?'

'Cool, I'm always here. I live here, my man.'

He pointed up at the loft. Rather him than me.

'OK, I'll be back later. Will your friends be here?'

'Oh sure, Nikolai, they'll hang for a while. Business to do, people to see.'

I put my forefinger and thumb together and shook my hand. 'Keys?'

'Keys? Oh sure, sure. I'll have to come with you, my man. Show you something cool.' He ran through to the other room. The GoodFellas ignored me completely as I waited, concentrating instead on throwing more liquid nasty down their necks.

Eight reappeared, pulling on his bomber jacket and zipping it up as he took the keys off the table. We went downstairs and out into the cold.

After locking the door and grille behind us, it turned out that the cool thing he wanted to show me was that I'd have to hit the starter motor with a hammer before it would turn over. He said he liked it busted like this because no-one could steal it.

While he was busying himself showing me what to do, it was pointless talking about licences or whatever if I got stopped. I just wanted to get away from here and do my job. I didn't have time to fuck about. The Maliskia knew the NSA were out and about and would be moving location any day now.

But Eight wanted to remove his speakers and music first. I looked at the cassettes as he piled them on the passenger seat. There was an array of American rap bands I'd never heard of, all following Eight's lead in the gold-chain department, plus some really hip Russian artistes who looked as though they were on the way to a reunion of the Jason King fan club. It was the white tuxedos that really gave them class.

I was waiting for him to disconnect the speakers when a 5 Series BMW, with a hint of silver beneath the dirt, cruised down the road from the direction I had walked. I noticed the plates first because they were British – P reg – and it was right-hand drive, then I looked at the driver.

The subconscious never forgets, especially when it comes to trouble.

Carpenter. I couldn't believe it. As if he hadn't fucked up my life enough these past couple of weeks.

He was slowing down as a van approached

from the opposite direction, but it wasn't to let him past; he was heading over to where we were, and if he saw me I bet I wouldn't be getting the Russian for, 'Hail good fellow, well met.'

I jumped into the back of the car with Eight and made as if to help him pull out the speakers, my knees badly creasing up his newspapers.

The BMW pulled into the car park, its tyres crunching louder and louder on the ice the closer it got. I suddenly found the speakers very interesting indeed, and made sure my arse faced very definitely towards the BMW. I was feeling extremely vulnerable, but not as much as I would if he saw me.

The engine shut down and the driver's door opened.

Eight was the other side of me and glanced over my shoulder as Carpenter's door slammed, then turned back to his beloved speakers.

After hearing the wooden door close, I was still pulling out some very dodgy wiring as I asked, 'Who's the English guy?'

'He's not England, you crazy guy!' He tutted into the air.

'So why has he got an England car?'

I'd obviously said something very funny. 'Because he can, my man! Some England guy isn't going to St Petersburg just to get his car back; that would be crazy, man.'

'Oh, I see.'

In this part of the world it obviously didn't matter if you drove around with a hot car's plates on show. After all, if you had the money to have a BMW stolen to order, why not flaunt it? I could see the dealer's sticker in the rear window; it was a firm in Hanover, Germany, which probably meant that some British squaddie had been saving up for ages to buy his tax-free bargain, only to get it lifted so it could rumble around Narva in the snow.

The first speaker came free. I had no idea how he was going to wire it up again; it looked like a telephone junction box in there. The chain around his neck made a curiously tinny noise as he moved around. The rap bands probably had the real thing, but I was sure his bitches never knew the difference.

'Who is he, then?'

'Oh, just one of the guys. Business, you know.'

He must do a lot of business here to have his own set of house keys.

'Don't say anything about me to anyone, Vorsim,' I said. 'Especially guys like him. I don't want people to know I'm here, OK?'

'Oh sure, my man.' The way he said it was too blasé for my liking, but I didn't want to push the point.

Once the speakers were out I virtually threw the cassettes at him, wanting to get away before Carpenter reappeared. The bonnet was still open and I gave the starter motor a seeing-to with the hammer.

Eight stood by the door holding an armful of cassettes, with the speakers on the doorstep. 'Be careful with the bitch machine, Nikolai.'

Before he'd even turned to unlock the door I had the bonnet down, the engine in gear and was away, heading back the way I'd come.

My head was churning over about Carpenter. What if he was still there when I came back to see Eight after I'd done the recce? Or if he arrived while I was in the house? I had fucked up in my attempt to get out of the way so quickly. I should have told Eight I wanted to meet elsewhere.

I had to control a rage that was brewing inside me as I thought about Carpenter's drugged-up, fucked-up work that night. It had not only cost me money, but nearly got me killed.

Should I even go back and see Eight again? I had no choice: I was going to need help obtaining explosives or whatever else I needed. I drove past the komfort baars thinking of my professional options and what I would unprofessionally really like to do about him. Fuck it; I pulled into the border crossing car park. It took about a minute to work out how to secure the Lada, as the driver's door lock was knackered.

With the starter motor persuader in my pocket I turned and began to walk back to the house. As the saying so rightly goes, there's not much you can't sort out with a two-pound ball hammer.

32

I would have to luck it out and wait for him to leave the house, setting myself a cut-off of two o'clock the following morning. I still needed time to get on with the recce; lifting Carpenter and keeping him tied up somewhere until the job was finished wasn't an option. There was no time for that.

Now I'd got my bearings in this part of town I cut between apartment blocks and saw some of the worst conditions yet, sheds burned out to match the cars and buildings that should have fallen down years ago. There was still an hour and a half to go before last light at about three thirty, but the overcast sky was making everything darker than it should have been.

Following the ice tracks in the snow, I turned corners and walked around car wrecks and rusty prams until the house came into view. Carpenter's BMW was no more than thirty metres away. The other three vehicles were also still there, all with a thin layer of ice forming on the windows and top surfaces. One or two people were walking around, but just from block to block, some accompanied by little dogs with knitted coats on.

It was dark and cold enough for me not to be noticed as I stood inside what was left of one of the sheds, leaning against the wall with my head down, my hands in my jacket pockets, the right one grasping the hammer. I felt no apprehension, no emotion at all about what was coming. Some kill because they have a good reason. Others, like Carpenter, because they just like it. For me it wasn't that deep. I did it only when I had to.

Flexing my toes in my boots to keep the circulation going, I tried to think of other options, but still couldn't come up with any. There were more important things at stake than this maniac's life; I thought back to the sobs from the man in the lift in Helsinki as he held his dying wife. Carpenter could fuck everything up if he discovered I was here. I was still pissed off with myself for not switching on with Eight and asking for a change of meeting place; because of that fuck-up I'd got myself into a position where I could land up dead myself if I messed this up.

One or two more dull yellow lights came on in the apartments. The noise of a TV hung in the air as a car rattled along the road, then I heard a baby screaming. I continued with my trigger on the door, listening to the occasional bang of pots and pans from behind steamed-up kitchen windows and their sagging, dirty net curtains. Somewhere in the neighbourhood, dogs barked at each other, probably just out of boredom.

No sign of movement or light came from the house. Lion King said it was 3.12.

Still I watched and waited, feeling the cold attacking my ears and nose, wishing I'd made the effort and bought a replacement hat and gloves. I got another four aspirin down me as my body started reminding me that it had taken a good kicking the night before. I spent long minutes trying to get enough saliva in my mouth to swallow them.

Another check of Lion King – 3.58. I hadn't even been here an hour yet, but it felt like six. I always hated the waiting. Another thirty minutes crawled by, then there was movement at the door, a dull, yellowish glow at the grille.

Slowly I took my hands from my pockets. Taking a firm hold of the hammer head in my right hand, I laid the handle along my forearm, on the outside of my jacket.

Two men were standing there smoking, waiting to come out once they'd opened the grille. In the glow from the cigarettes and the hall light, their breath vapour was indistinguishable from the smoke as it rose above them. I couldn't make out if either of them was Carpenter. I hoped not. Taking on two with a hammer would not make for a good night out, and Carpenter was bound to be armed.

They continued to talk as the grille squeaked open and one of them came out onto the ice. The grille was then closed, leaving one of them on each side. Maybe it was going to be OK. Whoever was leaving had a quick laugh with his mate, who now looked like a prisoner behind bars. Then, as he walked away, he pushed the wooden door closed, rubbing his hands together against the cold. From this distance I couldn't hear the bolts being thrown.

He looked like a Yorkshire vet; I could make out the shape of a flat cap as he moved to the vehicles. I still couldn't tell if it was Carpenter.

The man moved towards the 5 Series that was parked side-on to me, facing the house, then there was a jangle of keys.

I still couldn't identify him. I would have to get closer. He'd be there a while, scraping the ice from the windscreen.

My legs were feeling rubbery after so long standing still. Stretching, I moved out of the darkness, trying to pump a bit of blood around.

There were only about twenty metres separating us, but as he neared the BM I still couldn't be sure it was him.

The car door opened and the interior light shone across his back as he leaned in and started up the engine. Exhaust fumes filled the air as he shoved one leg inside and hit the gas. Then he turned the headlights on. They shone brightly away from both of us, but silhouetted his profile. I recognized Carpenter at once.

I took one last look around me to make sure the area was clear. From this moment on I'd be concentrating solely on the target, who was now ten metres away, hopefully with the engine noise hiding my movement.

He was focusing on the windscreen, his back to me still as he leaned over to clear the ice.

My eyes never left his head as it moved back and forth in a cloud of breath.

He must have heard me, and started to turn. I was no more than five metres away but too far to react quickly. I just had to keep walking, but now veering slightly left, as if I was heading for the road. I got my head down, not wanting to look at him as I approached the rear of the car, my hands under my armpits, concealing my weapon. I had to assume that he was checking out the dickhead who thought he could ponce around in this weather without a hat and gloves.

The focus of my whole world was on this man, waiting to hear the noise of the scraper again. I was nearly past him, just approaching the BM's boot, when it finally began again.

Scrape scrape scrape.

It was time to look up and find his head once again as it bobbed up and down in time with the noise.

Scrape, scrape, scrape.

Supporting the hammer head in my left hand I ran my hand down the handle and gripped it hard.

At that moment he looked up again, towards the road.

I, too, saw the four white DTTS Vitaras screech to a halt outside an apartment block on the other side of the road. I had no choice but to keep walking past him as black-clad bodies jumped out of the vehicles and ran into the building, leaving the drivers standing outside, nightsticks in hand.

I got to the road and turned left towards the roundabout, not once looking behind me. I could hear screams and the sound of smashing glass as the DTTS team did whatever they did in apartment blocks of an afternoon.

I was cursing to myself, but at the same time feeling lucky they hadn't turned up a few seconds later. What concerned me now was that he could be there when I returned to the house for any kit I might need.

I took the first opportunity to turn left again, off the road and back into the blocks as the BM drove past me, heading for the roundabout.

I drove out of town, heading west and following signs along the Tallinn road to a place called Kohtla Jarve, about thirty-five kilometres away. The road didn't hold any surprises for me. The car bumped all over the place, slithering over the different levels of tarmac under the ice and slush. I couldn't complain; I was just happy to have got the thing started again.

I went through a couple of small towns, trying to avoid the bus and truck drivers who wanted me to join their death race. This was supposed to be dual carriageway, but it didn't work out like that; everyone took the centre of the road because that was where there was less ice and more tarmac. Seeing signs for Voka, I made a mental note of the time since leaving Narva. I'd be wanting that road later.

The wipers were slapping away ineffectually against the shit that was being sprayed up by trucks and dumped on us smaller vehicles. I had to keep stopping, using the newspaper from the back seat to wipe the windows. At one stage, I even had to piss over the windscreen to clear the icy grime, trying to avoid the splash as the wipers did their stuff before it froze once again.

Kohtla Jarve, it appeared, was the home of the giant, brooding slag heaps and long conveyor belts I'd seen from the train. Bright white light spilled from factories on either side of the road as I duelled with my trucker friends. They eventually dwindled with the industry, and soon there was complete darkness, apart from kamikaze trucks and bus lights on full beam, mixed with cars with only one light trying to overtake the lot of us.

I followed the road west for about another twenty kilometres, then turned left, heading south for a place called Pussi. I was in no mood for gags, otherwise I might have passed the time wondering where it might be twinned with.

In the Lada's headlights I could see that the road was single track and hadn't been used or cleared for quite a while. There were just two tyre ruts worn into the snow. It was going be like riding on rails.

It was another 20Ks further south to the target. There had to be a quicker way of doing it than driving a right-angled box, west and then south, but I didn't know how accurate the maps were. Besides, I wanted to stay on the mains as long as possible, and then I could at least be sure of getting there. I was feeling quite pleased with myself, considering I had no map; one of the muggers in Tallinn was probably wiping his arse with it right now.

The headlights reached about five to ten metres either side of me, exposing banks of snow and the occasional ice-laden tree waiting to spark up in the spring.

I drove through Pussi, which looked like a small farming community. The buildings were rundown shacks made of bare, unpainted wood, and surrounded by wrecked cars. The roofs were bowed in with age or bad construction. Most had two lengths of wood, with strips going across to form a ladder, permanently attached as a means of getting the snow off. By the look of it the timbers would have collapsed without them.

I reckoned this was the place for Eight, without a doubt. A hand-painted Lada would be the ultimate passion wagon in this neck of the woods.

They had electricity, because there was the occasional glint of light coming through the curtains of very small windows, and a dull bulb shone in the back of a barn. But there obviously wasn't running water because I kept seeing the sort of communal handpump that Clint Eastwood used to strike a match on to light his panatella. These ones, however, were wrapped up in tarpaulin and bits of rag to stop them freezing. The chimney stacks were going for it big time. They must have been chopping logs all summer.

There were no warning signs that I was about to bump over the railway track from Tallinn, and after that I didn't see a single sign of human activity. The road got steadily worse. The Lada slid all over the place and didn't enjoy the potholes one bit now that my own personal snow railway had come to an end. I checked the odometer, counting down to the only T-junction, which, if I remembered rightly, was a couple of Ks away.

Once there, I at last got help: a small sign told me it was right to Tudu. I turned left, now knowing that the target would be the first building on the left after two more kilometres.

Just after two Ks a high concrete wall appeared in my headlights, about ten metres in on the left-hand side. I drove slowly for another forty metres or so, encountering a pair of large metal gates the same height as the wall. I drove past them, and the wall continued for about another forty metres before it turned at a right angle into the darkness.

The second building, just a bit further on and maybe thirty metres in length, resembled a large hangar. It was slightly closer to the road and wasn't fenced or walled in.

I waited until I'd rounded a bend and was physically out of line of sight of the target, then I threw the Lada into a little driveway on my left, stopping after a three-foot slide. It was probably an entrance to a field or something, but it wasn't as if people were going to be working on the land for a few more months.

I closed the door quietly onto its first click, then the second, and used the wipers to secure a sheet of newspaper over the windscreen. I started to walk back down the road, trying to keep warm by moving as fast as I could, and sticking to the ice that had formed on the road to keep footprints to a minimum.

I didn't have a clue what I was going to do yet.

33

After two hours of straining my eyes to see the road through a dirty, smeared windscreen, it was taking a while for my night vision to kick in.

A bird screeched in the distance, but there were no other sounds apart from my own breathing and the crunch of my boots on the ice. I found I had to step quite gingerly. So much for warming up.

By the time I'd reached the target the rods in my eyes had realized there was no ambient light and they had to get to work. Not that I could miss the first building, just off the road to my right. The gap of five metres or so in between them was knee-deep with snow, covering the fallen brickwork that had spilled out across the verge. It was, or had been, quite a substantial building, though most of the masonry had collapsed, exposing what I supposed was the steel frame; I could see right through it to the field beyond. It was one storey, lower than the concrete wall further along, but very wide and with a low-angled pitched roof covered with a thick layer of snow. A very tall chimney stack, resembling a ship's funnel, soared out of the roof on the right-hand side and disappeared into the darkness.

Continuing towards the concrete wall, I crossed the ten metres or so between the hangar and the target compound. As I approached, I began to make out the dark shape of a normal-sized door set in the concrete wall. I'd have loved to have gone and tried it, but I couldn't risk leaving tracks in the deep snow.

As I walked on towards the gates the front wall towered above me. There was no light pushing skywards from the compound, and no noise. I tried looking for CCTV cameras or intruder devices, but it was too dark and the wall was too high and far away. If there were any, I'd soon find out. A depressing thought hit me: I hoped they hadn't changed location already. I moved the forty metres or so it took to reach the point where the compound driveway joined the road.

Turning right, I started to walk to the gates. It was pointless skulking about, I just had to get on with it. The depression didn't lift when I failed to see light spilling out from under the gates as I got closer.

As I slowly closed in on them, keeping within the right-hand tyre rut, I began to see that the wall was constructed of enormous concrete blocks, maybe twenty-five metres long and at least three to five metres high. There must have been a fair thickness for them to rest on top of each other like that; they looked as if they should be laid flat, end to end, to construct a runway. I still couldn't see anything that even resembled CCTV or alarms.

The two large gates were as high as the wall itself. I was right up against them now and still couldn't hear anything on the other side. The gates were made of steel plate with a thick coating of dark, anti-oxide paint which was smooth to the touch, without a trace of blistering or flaking. I could also see white chalk markings, the sort scored on to guide the welder. I gently pushed against them both, but they didn't move, and there were no locks or chains I could see holding them in position. They were newly made, but judging by the exposed reinforcement rods jutting out of the crumbling concrete, the wall wasn't.

Set into the right gate was a smaller, pedestrian door. It had two locks, one a third of the way up from the bottom and another a third of the way down from the top. I gently pulled the door handle, which of course was also locked.

The gap between gate and ground was four to six inches. Lying down slowly on my side, and using the length of the tyre rut to avoid making prints in the snow either side of me, I pressed my eye against the gap. I could feel the frozen ground under my body as it made contact, but that no longer mattered; there was light on the other side.

I became aware, too, of the gentle hum of machinery. I couldn't be sure, but it was probably a generator.

I made out the shapes of two buildings about sixty metres away. The smaller one on the left had two lights shining from ground-floor windows; their patterned curtains were drawn, but light still spilled onto the snow in front of the building. The noise must be a genny; there wasn't enough wattage in this country to penetrate curtains. The building was too far away for me to notice anything else about it; it was just a dark shape on a dark background.

I studied the larger building to the right. There was a dark area in the middle front of the building, its rectangular shape, with a semi-circular top, suggesting a large access. Maybe this was where they kept their vehicles. But where were the satellite dishes? Were they around the back? Or was I doing a recce on the local beetroot-boiling factory? And where would they have banged up Tom?

What now? I had the same problem as at Microsoft HQ: too much virgin snow and not enough time. It would have been great to have been able to do a full 360 of this place, but tough, I couldn't. I even wondered about trying to climb up the outside of the hangar funnel to get a better look around, but even if there was a climbing rail attached to it, I was likely to leave sign on the roof or on the rungs, and anyway, what would I see at that distance?

I lay there and reminded myself that when you are short of the two most important commodities, time and knowledge, sometimes the only answer on target is P for Plenty – of explosives.

I stayed where I was, visualizing how to defeat the wall and get in on target, going through a mental checklist of the kit I'd be needing. Some of the stuff would have to come from Eight, because it would be impossible for me to access it on my own in the time available. If Eight couldn't get it, plan B would have to be to tie a suicide bandanna round my head and bang on the gates making really rude threats. I might as well; anything else but P for Plenty of explosives would be futile, given the time scale. The rest of the kit I would get myself to make sure it was exactly right: I hated depending on other people, but when in Chad . . .

The cold was getting to me and I was starting to freeze. I had seen all I was going to see tonight. Being careful not to disturb the snow on either side of the tyre ruts, I got up, checking with my hands that I hadn't dropped anything. It was just habit, but a good one. Then I slowly checked the snow on either side of the rut as I moved back to the road, getting ready to play repair man. If any sign did need covering up I would have to collect snow from the area around the car and carry it over. Detail counts: there would be no point in picking up snow from near the repair and just creating more sign.

I had warmed up quite a bit by the time I got back to the Lada. Unfortunately, the first thing I had to do after lifting the bonnet was take off my jacket and ram it down onto the starter motor. I didn't want Tom's new friends to hear me when I battered it with the hammer.

Ripping the newspaper from behind the wind-screen wipers I got into the driving seat quicker than last time, now knowing how to play the door lock. The engine fired third time. Keeping the revs low I drove away, not going past the target this time, but taking a few lefts instead to try and box round and get back on the main drag to Narva. I got lost a couple of times, but eventually found it and rejoined the death race.

34

I parked up once more in the border crossing car park. It was 9.24, according to Lion King. There was no way I was going to drive straight to Eight's place; I wanted to check out the area first, just in case Carpenter had returned. If so, I would have to spend the night hanging around, waiting for him to leave again.

I locked up the car and headed back to the baar, hands in pockets, head down. Approaching from the direction of the burned-out shed, I could see the BM hadn't returned, and only two of the other vehicles were still there, both now covered in thick ice.

It was one of the Cherokee jeeps that was missing. What did that mean? Fuck it, I had no time to mess about. When would be the right time to enter the house? I'd just take my chances and go for it. All I wanted was to get the kit together and make some money as soon as possible.

I pressed the intercom button and waited, but got no answer. I pressed it again. A crackling male voice answered, not the same one as before, but just as rough. I knew the routine now and even a little Russian. 'Vorsim. Vorsim.'

The static stopped, but I knew to wait, even moving out of the way after a minute or two for the main door to open. Soon bolts were being pulled on the inside.

The door swung open and there stood Eight, still in his red sweatshirt. As he unlocked the grille, he peered anxiously out into the car park.

'My wheels?'

I walked in and waited as he locked up behind, still frantically scanning the car park.

'The car's fine. Is the guy with the BMW coming back?'

He shrugged his shoulders as I started to climb the stairs behind him.

'You'll need a pen and paper, Vorsim.'

'But what about my wheels?'

I still hadn't answered when we entered the third-floor room. With no natural light the TV room was much darker, but it still smelled the same, heavy with cigarette smoke. No-one was here. Nothing had changed apart from the fact that next to the plastic-coated playing cards on the table, there was now a lamp, dimly glinting on the Johnny Walker bottle, which was three-quarters empty. Three ashtrays were full and spilling dog-ends on the once highly polished table. The TV was still on, throwing bursts of light around the other side of the room. Through a snow lens I could see Kirk Douglas playing a cowboy with the volume down low; I could just hear the dialogue.

'Yo, Nick. The table.'

He pointed at several cheap biros and sheets of lined A4 paper scattered amongst the crap. Some had tally marks on.

I sat down and started to write a list, wondering if the marks were card-game scores or a record of today's deals.

Eight pulled up a chair opposite me. 'Come on, you play. Where's the car, man?'

'Down the road.'

He searched my face. 'It's OK?'

'Yeah, yeah. Just let me finish this.' I wanted this kit organized and to get the fuck out of there as quickly as I could. 'Where is everybody?'

He moved his arms around like a breakdancer on fast forward. 'Business. You know, my man, business.'

I finished writing and pushed the sheet of paper over to him. He looked at it and didn't appear fazed. I was expecting lots of sucking through teeth, but the only question I got was, 'Eight kilos?'

'Yeah, eight kilos.' They certainly weren't the sort of kilos he normally dealt with.

'Eight kilos of what, Nikolai?' His shoulders went up and his face went down. It was obvious he didn't understand anything I'd written apart from 8kg. He'd learned to speak English from the TV, but he couldn't read it. Maybe he should have spent more time watching *Sesame Street* and a bit less watching *NYPD Blue*.

'Shall I just say what I need and you write it down?' I didn't want to embarrass him, and besides, anything to speed this up.

He smiled now there was a way out. 'Telling me would be cool, yeah.'

Halfway through dictating the list I had to explain what a detonator was. A few minutes later, when he'd stopped holding the pen in his fist like a child and his tongue was back in his mouth, he looked very pleased with himself.

'OK. Cool.' He jumped out of his seat, studying his handiwork and feeling very important. 'Wait here, Nikolai, my man.' He disappeared through the door near the fireplace.

A few seconds later I heard a much older voice roaring with laughter. I wasn't sure if that was good or bad. I didn't try to see who it was; if it was the older voice who decided whether I could have it, then spying on him while he made that decision wasn't going to change anything, apart from pissing him off and making my life more difficult than it already was.

The sound of footsteps echoed from the stairwell, accompanied by volleys of quick, aggressive talking, slowly getting louder as people came up the stairs. I told myself not to worry, even though my heartbeat quickened as I listened for Carpenter.

As the voices got louder I still couldn't work out whether they were pissed off or that was just the way they talked.

The door burst open and I watched as the GoodFellas came in one by one, ready to grip Johnny Walker and use him over someone's head.

There was no Carpenter. It was the same four card players, taking off their leather jackets and hats. The old one, carrier bag in hand, kept on his silver-grey fur Cossack-style number.

I stayed put, my heart beating even quicker

with relief as I screwed up the first list and put it in my pocket.

They crossed the room towards me without any acknowledgement, except from the fur-hatted older one, who shouted and waved the back of his hand at me to get the fuck out of his chair and away from the table. I got up and moved; no skin off my nose, I was there for other things, not to get macho.

From the window I watched the traffic queuing at the checkpoint. It looked even more like a movie scene now that floodlights were soaking the area in a brilliant white glow. The same couldn't be said for the lighting this side of the river.

All four were now sat at the table, pouring the last of the whisky and lighting up. There was a lot of talk from them, which drowned out the low-volume gunfight Kirk was winning on the opposite side of the room. The old guy pulled packets of sausage and dark rye bread from the carrier bag and threw them onto the table, while the others tore open the plastic protection around the sliced meat and ripped off lumps of bread.

I watched, feeling a bit hungry myself, but I didn't imagine I'd be on the guest list.

It became obvious, as heads nodded in my direction, mixed with quick glances, that I was the subject of conversation. One of the boys said something and they all looked over. There was a little joke said and a few sniggers. Then it all got serious again as they got back to eating.

I kept pretending to look out of the window

and be unaware of what was going on behind me.

A chair scraped on the bare wooden floor and shoes echoed on the boards as one of them came towards me. I turned and smiled at the old guy in his hat, watching as the TV shone on him in the gloom when he passed the screen. He was facing me, but talking back to the others, looking very serious. This wasn't another piss-take. An index finger started pointing at me as he got closer, as if to reinforce whatever he was gobbing off about. I looked down in submission and slightly turned back towards the window.

From less than a foot away he began to poke me in the back, shouting very close to my head. I turned and looked at him, confused and frightened, then looked down, just like Tom would have. I smelled garlic and alcohol, and as he continued to rant and poke, flecks of sausage hit my face. His face, creased and leathered and showing a day's stubble, was now no more than a few inches away as the fur from his hat brushed against my forehead. He bellowed at me again.

I wasn't going to react by moving or wiping away his shit from my face; it might antagonize him even more. I just stood and let him get on with it, just like I'd done at school when teachers went ballistic. I was never scared; I knew they would finish or get bored with it quickly, so fuck 'em, let them get on with their fun so I could bunk school straight afterwards. It was one of the attitudes that had fucked up my life.

I moved my left hand to the window and supported myself, as I was getting the four-finger poke now, my body jerking back with each jab.

Glancing across, I could see the other three at the table, their cigarettes glowing in the semi-darkness, enjoying the cabaret.

The shouting and bad breath continued.

Sounding as frightened as I could I stammered, 'I am here for Eight . . . er . . . V–v–v–orsim.'

He mocked me. 'V–v–v–orsim.' Turning towards the table, he mimed injecting his arm, laughing along with the other three.

He turned back and gave me one last shove against the window. I took it and then steadied myself as he headed back for more garlic sausage. He was obviously talking about me as he pretended to take a line from his index finger, to the accompaniment of further laughter. Let them think it; the drama was over. Now where the fuck was Eight?

I looked out of the window again, slowly wiping all the shit off my face as the floorboards echoed towards me once more. He was coming back for seconds.

He got right up on me again and gave me a push with both hands. He was fucking with me; he was having some fun, maybe taking out some frustration. The others laughed as I rode the pushes and tried to lean against the window frame, still showing no resistance, looking for-lornly at the floor to appear even less of a threat.

He got more serious with each push and I began to get pissed off. After one particularly hard one I stumbled backwards towards the television. He followed me, the pushes now punctuated with the odd slap round the head. I kept my face down, not wanting him to see in my eyes what I was really thinking. He kept repeating the same word over and over, then he started gesturing, rubbing fingers and pointing at my boots. Did he want my money and Timberlands? Money I could understand, but boots?

This was getting out of control. If I was right he would be getting a lot more than he bargained for if my boots came off. I couldn't let that happen.

I held my hands up in submission. 'Stop! Stop! Stop!'

He did, and waited for his cash.

I slowly reached into the inside pocket of the jacket and pulled out the insurance policy, still inside its protection. He looked at the condom and then at me, his eyes narrowing.

Untying the knot at the end, I probed inside with two fingers.

He barked a question at me, then, shouting something at the others, he grabbed the condom and roughly fished inside. Opening the thin paper and partly tearing it in the process, he turned to the table and waved it at them, as if sharing the joke in a Christmas cracker.

Bending down into the light given off by Kirk on his horse, he pushed the note in front of the screen. His laughter subsided as he started to read. Then it stopped completely. Whatever the bit of paper said, it was doing the business.

He walked over to the others, looking extremely pissed off as he muttered, 'Ignaty. Ignaty.'

I hadn't a clue what that meant and I didn't really care. They all had a read, and it had the same effect on everyone. They slowly turned their heads and stared at me across the room. I brought my hands together in front of me, not wanting to appear a threat. It was good the policy had worked, but it meant I might have to put up with their loss of face. Some people have the fuck-it factor when this sort of thing happens, and regardless of the possible fallout they'll still retaliate because their pride has been hurt. I couldn't afford to fuel that by appearing at all cocky; I still wasn't out of the woods. Walking over to the table, my face full of respect, I put out my left hand, making sure that Lion King wasn't exposed. It wouldn't exactly help me maintain my new standing. I nodded at the sheet of paper. 'Please.'

He may not have understood the word, but he knew what it meant. He handed it back, hating every second of it, and I folded it carefully and put it in my pocket. Now wasn't the time to start putting it back into a condom. 'Thank you.' I gave a little bow of the head and, with my heart pumping as hard as if it was forcing crude oil through my arteries, I turned my back to them and walked to the TV.

Sitting as casually as I could in the chair facing the screen, I watched Kirk still taming the Wild West, leaning forward to hear what was happening out there in the desert. My pulse was louder than the TV.

I could tell that once I was out of earshot there was going to be some very loud shouting, but for now there was just low, disgruntled murmuring behind me. Where the fuck was Eight? Not wanting to turn or look in any other direction than the screen, I sat like a child who thinks he can't be seen at bedtime if he just concentrates hard and doesn't move.

They carried on mumbling as glasses were banged with the neck of the whisky bottle to drown their anger. My eyes were on the screen and my ears were on them.

Five minutes later, just as Kirk was about to save the girl, Eight came back into the room. I didn't understand what he was saying as he fought with the zip on his leatherette jacket, but by the look of it, we were leaving. Muttering a silent prayer of thanks, I got to my feet and tried not to show my relief.

As Eight went to the door and I passed the table, they got a respectful bow from me before I followed him downstairs at the speed of sound.

35

Eight was a happy teddy the moment he caught sight of his beloved Lada in the noisy car park.

'Where do we go now, Vorsim?'

'A block.' He already had the Lada's bonnet open.

'A block?'

'You know, an apartment.'

I heard two metallic bangs as the starter motor got a reminder as to what it did for a living.

The Lada eventually fired up and he drove us both out of the car park and turned right, towards the roundabout. The komfort baars all had enormous doormen standing under their flashing neon to control the evening's trade. Turning left this time at the roundabout, away from the river, we drove past even more establishments and parked trucks.

The baars' lights slowly disappeared and the darkness took over again. Now apartment blocks and industrial buildings lined the road, in between pylons and shells of crumbling masonry.

Fighting with two trucks that were trying to overtake each other, both throwing up waves of ice and snow, we turned left without indicating, then left again down a narrow street, with apartments to the left and a tall wall to the right.

Eight threw the Lada into the side of the road and jumped out. 'Wait here, my man.'

Skirting the inevitable pylon leg, he headed for the main door of one of the blocks. He stopped and checked the stencilling, gave me the thumbs up, then turned back towards the Lada to lock up. I got out and waited.

The loud, constant noise of machinery came from behind the wall as I entered a very cold, dimly lit hallway, so narrow I could easily have put my arms out and touched both walls. It stank of boiled cabbage. Tiles were missing from the floor and the walls were painted blue, apart from the places where big chunks of plaster had fallen to the ground. Nobody had bothered to sweep them up. The apartment doors, which were one-piece sheet metal with three locks and a spy hole, looked so low that you'd have to stoop when entering.

We waited for the lift by rows of wooden letter boxes. Most of the doors had been ripped from their hinges and the others were just left open. I'd have felt more comfortable walking into a South American gaol.

The wall by the lift was covered with a mass of hand painted instructions, all in Russian. It gave me something to look at while we listened to the motor groaning inside the shaft.

The machinery stopped with a loud shudder and the doors opened. We entered an aluminium box, its panelling dented everywhere it was possible for boots to have connected. It reeked of urine. Eight hit the button for the fourth floor and we lurched upwards, the lift stopping suddenly every few feet, then starting again, as if it had forgotten where to go. Eventually we reached the fourth floor and the doors opened into semi-darkness. I let him step out ahead of me. Turning left, Eight stumbled, and as I followed I found out why: a young kid was curled up on the floor.

As the doors slammed shut again, cutting out even more of the dim light, I bent down to examine his small body, bulked out by two or three badly knitted jumpers. By his head lay two empty crisp packets, and thick, dried snot hung from his nostrils to his mouth. He was breathing and he wasn't bleeding, but even in the feeble light from the ceiling bulb it was obvious that he was in shit state. Zits covered the area around his mouth and saliva dribbled from his lips. He was about the same age as Kelly; I suddenly thought of her and felt a surge of emotion. As long as I was around she would never be exposed to this kind of shit. As long as I was around . . . I could see the expression on Dr Hughes' face.

Eight looked down at the boy with total disinterest. He kicked the bags, turned away and carried on walking. I dragged the local gluehead out of the way of the lift and followed.

We turned left along a corridor, Eight singing some Russian rap song and pulling a string of keys from his jacket. Reaching the door right at the end, he messed about, trying to work out which key went where until finally it opened, then groping for the light switch.

The room we entered definitely wasn't the source of the boiled-cabbage stench. I could smell the heavy odour of wooden crates and gun oil; I would have known that smell anywhere. Proust's mate's childhood might have rushed back to him when he caught a whiff of Madeleine cakes; this one took me straight back to the age of sixteen and the very first day I joined the Army as a boy soldier in '76. Cakes would have been better.

The inevitable single bulb lit up a very small hall, no more than a couple of metres square. There were two doors leading off; Eight went through the one on the left and I followed, closing the front door behind me and throwing all the locks.

Only one of the four bulbs worked in the ceiling cluster that any 1960s family would have been proud of. The small room was stacked with wooden crates, waxed cardboard boxes and loose explosive ordnance, all stencilled with Cyrillic script. The whole lot looked very Chad – Chad that was dangerously past its use-by date.

Nearest to me was a stack of brown wooden boxes with rope handles. Lifting the lid off the top one, I recognized the dull green bedpan shapes at once. Eight, grinning from ear to ear, made the noise of an explosion, his hands flying everywhere. He seemed to know they were land-mines, too. 'See, my man, I get what you want. Guarantee of satisfaction, yes?'

I just nodded as I looked around some more. Piles of other kit lay wrapped in brown military greaseproof paper. Elsewhere, damp cardboard boxes stacked on top of each other had collapsed, spilling their contents onto the floorboards. Lying in a corner were half a dozen electric detonators, aluminium tubes about the size of a quarter-smoked cigarette with two eighteen-inch silver wire leads coming out of one end. The silver leads were loose, not twisted together, which was frightening stuff: it meant they were ready to act as antennae for any stray extraneous electricity – a radio wave, say, or energy from a mobile phone – to set them off and probably all the rest of the shit in there, too. This place was a nightmare. It seemed the Russians hadn't been too fussed about where this kind of stuff ended up in the early Nineties.

Picking up the detonators one by one, I twisted the leads together to close the circuit, then mooched around the rest of the kit, ripping open cardboard boxes. Eight did the same, either to make me think he knew what he was doing or just out of curiosity. I gripped his arm and shook my head, not wanting him to play with anything. It would be nice to get out of here with all my bits and without him losing any more fingers.

He looked hurt, so once I'd finished sorting the dets out and had stored them in an empty ammo box, I pulled out the policy to give him something to do. 'What does this say, Vorsim?' I presumed he could read his own language.

As he moved under the light, I spotted some dark-green det cord. It wasn't in its handy 200-metre reel as I would have liked; there seemed to be two metres here, another ten metres there, but then I saw a partly used reel with maybe eighty or ninety metres left, which would certainly do the trick.

I put the reel of det cord to one side and went to check the other rooms. That was easy enough because each was about the size of a broom cupboard; there was a tiny kitchen-cum-bathroom-cum-toilet arrangement and a bedroom that was even smaller. What I was looking for was plastic explosive, but there wasn't any. The only PE around here was in the anti-tank mines, and there were certainly enough of those to give me P for Plenty.

I returned to the main room and lifted one of them from the open box. These were either TM 40s or 46s, I could never remember which was which; all I knew was that one was made of metal and the other of plastic. These ones were metal, about a foot in diameter and weighed around twenty pounds, of which over twelve pounds was PE. They were shaped like old-fashioned brass bed-warmers, the sort that hang on stone fireplaces, alongside the horse brasses, in country pubs. Instead of the long broomstick, these things had a swivelling carry handle, like on the side of a mess tin.

It was going to be a pain in the arse to get the PE out of these things, but what was I expecting?

Placing the mine on the bare floorboards, I tried to unscrew the cap, which was in the centre of the top. Before laying it, all you had to do was replace the cap with a detonation device – normally a fuse and detonator combination – then stand well back and wait for a tank.

When it eventually started to move, shifting the years of grime that had formed a seal, I knew at once that it was really old ordnance. The smell

of marzipan hit my nostrils. The greenish explosive had become obsolete in recent years. It
still worked, it did the job, but the nitroglycerine
fucked up not only armour, but also the head and
skin of anyone preparing it. You were guaranteed
a fearsome headache if you worked with it in a
confined space and extreme pain if you got it on
a cut. I was taking enough aspirin already without having to deal with that.

Eight sparked up. 'Hey, Nikolai, this paper is
really cool.'

'What does it say?'

'First of all, his name is Ignaty. Then it says, you
are his man. Whatever you need must be yours.
He protects you, my man.' He looked at me. 'It
gets heavy. It says, "If you do not help my friend,
I will kill your wife; and then, after you have been
crying for two weeks, I will kill your children.
Two weeks after that, I will kill you." That's
heavy shit, my man.'

'Who is Ignaty?'

He gave a shrug. 'He's your guy, am I right?'

No he wasn't, he was Val's. The card players
had certainly recognized the name, that was for
sure. I took the policy from Eight's hands and put
it back in my jacket pocket. Now I knew what Liv
meant about Tom receiving the kind of threat that
made the Brits look a bit weak by comparison. No
wonder he'd kept his mouth shut and just done
his time.

Between us we carried several boxes down to
the car, passing the kid still lying where I'd left
him. On the last trip down, Eight locked up the
flat and we stood by the Lada with the hum and

groan of the factory in the background. He was going to walk from there as he wanted to go and see a friend.

I said goodbye, feeling more than a bit sorry for him. Like everything else in this place, he, too, was just fucked over.

'Thanks a lot, mate, and I'll bring the car back in about two days.'

I shook his cold hand and then grabbed the door handle as he walked away.

He called after me. 'Yo, Nikolai. Hey . . .' There was suddenly a less-confident tone in his voice. 'Can I . . . can I come to England with you?'

I didn't look back, just wanting to get on my way. 'Why?'

'I can work for you. My English is cool.'

I could hear him getting closer. 'Let me go with you, man. Everything will be cool. I want to go to England and then I will go to America.'

'Tell you what, I'll be back soon and we'll talk about it, OK?'

'When?'

'Like I said, two days.'

He shook my hand again with all the fingers he had left. 'Cool. I'll see you soon, Nikolai. It'll be cool. I will sell my car, and . . . and get new clothes.'

He virtually skipped back up the road, waving at me, thinking about his new life as I gave the starter motor a bit of hammer, fired it up and did a three-point turn to back out onto the main, passing Eight on the way.

I'd only driven a hundred metres when I stopped and put the car in reverse. Fuck it, I couldn't do this.

As I drew alongside and wound down the window he greeted me with a big smile. 'What's up, my man?'

'I'm sorry, Vorsim, I can't take you' – I corrected myself – *'will* not take you to England.'

His shoulders and face slumped. 'Why not, man. Why not? You just said, man . . .'

I felt an arsehole. 'They won't let you in. You're Russian. You need visas and all that stuff. And even if they do, you won't be able to stay with me. I don't have a house and I haven't got any work I can give you. I'm really sorry, but I can't and I won't do it. That's it, mate. I'll drop the car off in two days.'

And that was it. I wound the window up and headed back into the centre of town, so I knew where I was and could pick up the main Narva–Tallinn drag again.

I could have lied to him, but I remembered as a kid all the trips that my parents were going to take me on, all the presents I was going to be given, all the promises of nice holidays and all the rest of the shit that had never happened. It was just said to keep me quiet. I couldn't have let Eight get all sparked up, burning bridges, and all for nothing. Liv was right: sometimes it's better to fuck people off with the truth.

I found my bearings in town and headed west. My destination was a hotel room where I could prepare all the shit I had in the boot.

I was still feeling quite sorry for Eight; not for dumping him, because I knew it was the right thing to do, but because of what the future held for him. Absolute jack shit.

A filling station appeared, exactly the same as the one in Tallinn, very blue, and as clean, bright and out of place as an alien spacecraft. I pulled in and filled up. Parking off to one side of the building, I went to pay just as the two staff had started to think they had their first runner of the night.

I was the only customer they had. There was a small section in their shop that actually sold bits and pieces for cars; the rest of the space was given over to beer, chocolate and sausages. I picked up five blue nylon tow ropes – their entire stock – and all eight rolls of black insulation tape on display, together with a cheap multi-tool set that would probably break the second time it was used. Finally, I picked up a torch and two sets of batteries, and two of the small rectangular ones with terminals on top. I couldn't think of anything else I needed just now, apart from some chocolate and meat and a couple of cans of fizzy orange.

The guy who took my money had more zits on his head than brain cells in it. He was trying to work out the change, even though the register had told him. Eventually he handed me my carrier bags; I wanted some more and pointed. 'More? More?' It took a few seconds of miming and a couple of small coins, but I came out with half a dozen spares.

It was sausage and chocolate time. I sat in the car with the engine running, filling my face as I looked out at the main drag. Beyond it was a massive poster site, covering the whole side of a building. Mr Bean was grinning at me like a Mormon, showing me the wonders of Fuji film as the trucks screamed past. I didn't blame them; I was in a hurry to get out of town, too.

Feeling sick after eating everything I'd bought, I rejoined the mayhem on the road. My destination was Voka, a coastal town to the north, between Narva and Kohtla Jarve, where I was going to prepare for the attack tomorrow afternoon. I had chosen Voka for no other reason than that I liked the name, and that, since it was on the coast, there was probably a better chance of finding a room.

36

Voka turned out to be just what I was expecting, a small seaside resort with one main drag. Maybe it had been a bit of a hotspot during the Soviet era, but from what I could see of it in my head-lights and the occasional functioning street light, it was now very tired and flaky, the Estonian equivalent of those Victorian seaside places in Britain that reached their sell-by date in the Seventies when everyone started getting on planes to Benidorm. When the Russians had packed their bags a few years earlier, this place, too, must have rolled over and died. There was no-one about; everyone was probably at home watching the end of another Kirk Douglas movie.

I drove slowly along the coast road with the Baltic on my left and the car rocking with the wind off the sea. There weren't many lights on in the apartments to my right, just the glow now and then of a TV.

Eventually I found a *hotelli* with a sea view. At first glance it had looked more like a four-storey apartment block, until I saw the small, flickering neon sign to the left of its double glass doors. As

I locked the Lada, waves crashed onto whatever sort of beach was behind me, and the wind buffeted my jacket and hair.

The fluorescent lights in the hallway nearly blinded me. It was like walking into a television studio, and almost as hot. A TV blared away somewhere in Russian. I was starting to catch the intonation quite well.

The sound came from in front of me. I walked along the corridor until I found its source. At the bottom of a flight of stairs, a sliding window was set chest high into the wall. Behind it sat an old woman, glued to the screen of an old black-and-white TV.

There was plenty of time to study her while trying to attract her attention. She wore thick woollen tights and slippers, a chunky black cardigan, a gaudy flowery dress and crocheted woollen hat. While she watched the TV, she spooned lumpy soup out of what looked like a large salad bowl. The TV had a coat hanger for an aerial – that seemed to be the law round here. It reminded me of the times I had to dance around the room with an indoor aerial in my hand so my stepdad could follow the horse racing. No wonder I never got to watch *Blue Peter*.

She finally noticed me, but didn't bother with a greeting or asking what I wanted. Nodding politely and smiling, I pointed at a sheet of paper taped to the window, which I presumed was the tariff.

'Can I have a room, please?' I asked in my favourite Australian accent. I was getting rather fond of my Crocodile Dundee impression. It was wasted on her.

There was a clatter of footsteps from the wooden staircase and a couple appeared, both dressed in long overcoats. He was a small, skinny guy in his late forties, slightly balding on top, but with the rest of his hair greased back in the style that Eastern Europeans, for some reason, think looks marvellous, and a big droopy moustache. They walked past without giving me or the old woman a second glance. The woman, I noticed, was at least twenty years younger than Baldy, and considerably less smelly. He had a body odour that no deodorant could tame.

The old woman handed me a towel the size of a teacloth and a set of what had once been white sheets. Muttering something, she held one finger in the air, then two. I guessed she meant number of nights. I showed her one.

She nodded, writing down some numbers which I took to be the price. EEK 150 for the night – about $10. A bargain. I couldn't wait to see the room. I gave her the money and she put the key, attached to a six-inch length of 4x2, on top of the sheets and got back to her soup and TV. I didn't get to learn the Estonian for 'have a nice day.'

I walked up the stairs and found room 4. It was bigger than I'd expected, but every bit as drab. There was a dark veneered chipboard wardrobe, three brown furry nylon blankets on the stained, multicoloured mattress, and a pair of old, saliva-stained pillows. I was surprised to find a small fridge in the corner. When I checked I found it wasn't plugged in, but it was still probably worth an extra star from the Estonian Tourist Board.

Next to it, sitting on a brown veneered table, was a Seventies style TV, also unplugged. The carpet was made up of two different colours of hard-wearing office-type stuff, in dark brown and what might once have been cream. The wallpaper was bubbling in places, with brown damp stains rounding off the decor. But the *pièce de résistance* was a cushioned corner unit and coffee table, set off by a large, triangular thick glass ashtray that any pub would be proud of. The beige nylon seating was heavily soiled and the coffee table had cigarette burns all around the edge. The room was cold and it was obviously up to the guest to put the heaters on.

To the right of the main door was the bathroom. I'd check that out later. First, I bent over one of the two electric fires. It was a small, square three-bar thing on the door side of the bed. Plugging it in, I threw the switch and the elements started to heat up, filling the air with the acrid smell of burning dust.

The second heater, nearer the window, was a more elaborate, decorative model, with two long bars and, above that, a black plastic log effect with a red background. I hadn't seen one since I was at my auntie's house, aged about seven. I plugged it in, too, and watched as its red bulb lit up beneath the plastic and a disc started to spin above it to provide a flame effect. It was almost better than the TV.

I went into the bathroom. Its walls and floor were tiled, mostly brown, but others, blues and reds, had replaced some of the broken ones in the days when broken ones were replaced. The management's policy had evidently changed in recent years.

There was another two-bar electric fire on the wall above the bath, as well as an ancient, oval-shaped gas geyser with a visible pilot light and a long steel tap which swivelled so you could fill either the bath or the sink. I was expecting the worst, but when I turned the tap on the pilot light became a raging flame, with sound effects to match. I was jealous. I wanted one in my house. The water was instantly hot, which was good news; I'd be needing a lot of that soon. Turning it off, I went back into the bedroom, where the fires were starting to do their stuff. Pulling the netting aside, I had a look out to sea. I couldn't see a thing, except snow swirling in the light spilling from the window.

I closed the curtains and went down to unload the car, starting with two mines in a box and the bits and pieces from the gas station. The old woman never looked up once as I came and went, either because she knew better than to enquire into a punter's business, or because she was genuinely gripped by the dubbed version of the Sixties Batman TV series.

Once back in the room I started running the bath, slowing the flow to a steamy trickle. I used a screwdriver from the multi-tool set to help remove the two mine caps, and could smell the green PE the moment the first came off.

Holding each mine in turn under the tap until it filled with hot water, I then lowered them into the bath, still letting the water run so that it would eventually cover them. Then I went down to the car and collected another two. They were heavy and I didn't want the drama of dropping one. It took three trips in all to get everything upstairs. On the final trip I took another newspaper from the back seat and covered the windscreen.

I kept unscrewing mine caps until all six were in the bath in two layers, representing a total of over seventy pounds of PE. Molten explosive would have been injected into the dull green casings at the factory and left to set to an almost plastic state; I'd have to wait for the hot water to soften it again before I could scrape it out.

Back in the bedroom I turned on the television in time to see Batman and Robin tied together in a giant coffee cup, an animated American voice-over telling me I'd have to wait until next week for the next exciting instalment, followed by the Russian translation which said they really couldn't give a fuck what happened.

I got hold of the reel of det cord, which looked just like a green washing line, except that instead of string inside the plastic covering, there was high explosive. This stuff would have the job of initiating the two charges I was going to construct with the PE once I'd got it out of the mines. I cut off about the first foot of cord with my Leatherman; it was probable that the explosive core had been affected by the climatic conditions and/or age, but if so, the contamination normally wouldn't have penetrated further than six inches. The reel then went the window side of the bed; only prepared kit would go this side from now on. That way things wouldn't get confusing as I became more tired.

465

Without any announcement, *Charlie's Angels* suddenly burst onto the screen. I hoped it was the series with Cheryl Ladd. Farrah Fawcett never did it for me when I was a kid. As the monotone Russian translation started up I went back into the bathroom. The water level still had a way to go as the steaming water trickled out of the geyser.

Time to check the batteries. They were normal rectangular nine-volt ones with press-stud tops for the positive and negative terminals, the sort that are used in portable radios or toys. One of them would be the initiation device, providing the electrical charge that would run along the firing cable, which I still had to obtain. It would then initiate the detonator, which would fire up the det cord, and, in turn, the charges. All this could only happen if the power from the battery was strong enough to overcome the resistance from the firing cable and det. You attach the firing cable to a torch bulb; if it lights up when you transmit power along the length of firing cable, you've got enough juice to make the thing go bang.

It was getting warm enough to take my jacket off now. I took the insurance policy out of the inside pocket; it was looking a bit the worse for wear, so I folded it neatly, fished around for the condom, and stuck it into the small key pocket on the front right-hand side of my jeans.

Next, I pulled the plug off the bedside lamp and ripped the other end of the flex out of the lamp base, ending up with about five feet of firing cable – not enough. I needed to be close to the explosion, but five feet was suicidally close. The fridge flex gave me another five.

The bath ought to have been almost full by now. I went and checked just as Charlie's Angels, dressed up as old women but still looking very glamorous and without a hair out of place, were about to infiltrate an old people's home on some secret mission.

All the mines were covered with hot water, so I turned off the tap on the geyser. I couldn't see a toilet brush anywhere, but there was a rubber plunger. Using its handle to prod the PE in one of the mines, I found it was still too hard.

Footsteps in the corridor signalled that the hotel had some new guests. There was a female giggle and lusty Russian male talk as they passed, then I heard the door next to mine bang shut. Stretched out on the bed watching *Charlie's Angels* free the world of evil, I connected the two lengths of flex and taped them up.

Ten feet of firing cable was still not enough. The trouble was, I wouldn't know how much I needed until I was on target, and I'd have to err on the side of safety. I wished I had about a hundred metres of the stuff, but where would I find some at this time of night? Tomorrow would be too late; I wouldn't have enough time to fart about looking for a B&Q. I had to make more of my own, so it was bye-bye, Cheryl. Due to the positioning of the wall sockets, the power line for the TV was quite long; in total I ended up with about eighteen feet of cable.

With the TV now off I could hear the romance developing next door. There were plenty of oohs and aahs, a bit of giggling and a few slaps on bare flesh. I didn't need the dubbing.

I joined the last section of wire together using the Western Union pigtail method. Chinese labourers used it to repair downed telegraph lines in the Wild West; it's basically a reef knot with the tail ends twisted together. It not only guarantees conductivity, but makes it unlikely the connection will get pulled apart.

The three lengths were all of different thicknesses and metals, but as long as they conducted electricity that was all I was worried about. I wrapped the copper wires at one end around the torch bulb and taped it in place. Now all I had to do was complete the circuit with the two steel wires at the other end of the cable on the battery terminals – and bang, perfect, the bulb glowed.

I repeated the process with the other battery, and both worked – for now. If they both failed on target and I didn't get detonation, I'd have to switch to plan B and put on the bandanna.

Untaping the wire from the bulb, I twisted the two copper wires together, then the two steel wires at the other end, and earthed it against the back of the fridge. That would take away any electricity still in the cable; the last thing I wanted was to connect the wires to a detonator and have the thing explode immediately. That wouldn't be a good day out.

The coil of firing cable joined the det cord on the window side of the bed and I placed the two batteries on top of the TV. You never keep the initiation device with the detonators or the rest of the equipment; the fuck-up factor is never far away, and I wasn't taking any chances. The only time all the equipment should come together is when you are going to detonate the charges, a lesson one or two PIRA boys learned the hard way back in the Eighties.

The foreplay was over next door and they were getting down to the heavy stuff. Either she was really enjoying it or she was going for an Oscar as the bed tried to bang itself through the wall and into my bathroom.

When I checked the mines, the water in the bath was rippling with the vibrations coming through the wall. There was still a while to go before I could start digging out the PE; to use the time productively, I took a sheet of toilet paper with me, put my jacket back on and walked out into the corridor. The shagfest reached a rousing crescendo as I placed a small strip of the toilet paper by the bottom hinge and closed the door on it, checking there was just enough paper to be seen. Silence fell next door as I left my neighbours to their cigarettes and *Charlie's Angels* and headed for the stairs.

The old woman was still glued to her TV. Frozen air clawed at my lungs as I peeled the newspaper off the Lada's windscreen. The engine turned over sluggishly after I'd zapped the starter motor, but eventually it sparked up. I knew how it felt.

37

I cruised slowly around town looking for the materials I needed to construct the explosive charges, attacking another four aspirin to sort out the headache that I'd developed after playing with the mines.

Spotting a row of skips behind a small parade of shops, I pulled in and sifted through the old bits of cardboard packaging, tins and rags. There was nothing that would do for me, apart from a partly broken wooden pallet resting against the wall. Three sections, each about a metre long, were soon in the back of the car while a dog, cooped up in one of the shops, barked its head off in frustration at not being able to get at me. One section was going to help me get over the wall, the other two were going to prop the charges in place on target.

Lights were off and curtains were drawn as I left the area in search of more stuff, driving through the heavy mist that rolled in from the sea. After ten minutes of patrolling the ghost town I saw a building that was worth a closer look. Rubbish was piled up outside it, but it was the structure itself that made me curious.

It turned out to be an air-raid shelter, built in the days when they were expecting Uncle Sam's hairy-arsed B52 bombers to come and dump on them big time. There was a concrete stairwell down to below ground level and a thick metal door, which was padlocked. The stairwell was full of wind-blown litter and heavier stuff that had been fly-tipped, and it was in amongst all this that I found some expanded polystyrene packaging. I selected two pieces, each just under a metre square. The corners were higher than the middle, which was contoured to fit the shape of whatever it had been made to protect; here and there holes had been punched to save material and give the structure a bit more strength. I now had the frames for the charges. It reminded me of having to make claymore anti-personnel mines out of ice-cream cartons before going into Iraq during the Gulf war.

The last item I needed was a brick, and in a place like this I didn't have to look far for one.

Back at the hotel, the old woman had deserted her post and the TV was running what looked like a Russian talk show, with the host and his guests talking at each other very glumly. It looked as though they were trying to decide which one of them should commit suicide first.

I walked up the stairs with my finds in my arms, feeling pleased that I had everything I needed for the attack and could now sit tight.

The old woman had just come out of the door next to mine and was heading along the corridor away from me with rumpled sheets in her arms. The room was probably rented by the hour, and she was mucking out after the latest event.

With the faint sound of the talk show in the distance, I checked the tell-tale. It hadn't moved. I opened the door and waited for the heat to hit me.

As I took the first step inside, I knew straight away that something wasn't right. The plastic log-effect fire wasn't dancing round the walls, but it had been when I left.

I dropped the stuff I was carrying. The brick hit the carpet as I started to step back into the corridor. And that was the last thing I did for a while, apart from trying to get off the bedroom floor, only to get a blow to the kidneys that put me back down. It was grit-the-teeth-and-curl-up time. There was no time to draw breath. I was roughly turned over and a weapon muzzle was pushed hard into my face. I felt my jacket being pulled up as a hand frisked me.

Once I had curled up again and played nearly dead, I risked opening my eyes. The oldest of the GoodFellas towered above me, wearing his silver fur hat and black leather coat.

I could also see another pair of legs belonging to someone else, also in black. The two men stood on either side of me now, whispering aggressively to each other with lots of arm movement and pointing at the dickhead on the floor.

I made the most of this time while they waffled, trying to take long deep breaths but finding I couldn't. It was too painful. I had to get by with short, sharp gasps, trying to minimize the pain in my stomach.

Then I looked up and saw Carpenter. Our eyes locked and he spat at me. I wasn't scared, I was just depressed that this should be happening to me, so much so that I couldn't even be bothered to wipe the mucus from my face. I just lay there not really caring. How had Carpenter even known I was here? Fuck it, who cared? I'd been dropped by two very pissed-off people and I didn't know if I was ever going to leave the room alive.

They pulled me up by my armpits, one man on each side, and propped me up on the end of the bed. Pushing my hands into my armpits, I tried to bend forwards and get my head down onto my thighs to protect myself, to be the damaged grey man that was no threat to anybody.

It wasn't going to happen. I took a blow on the right side of my face, which took me straight down onto the bed. I didn't need to pretend; it had done me some damage.

Expecting more, I curled up on my side. Starbursts did their best to black me out as pain scorched through my body. I could feel myself starting to lose it, and I really couldn't let that happen. I worked hard to keep my eyes open. I was a bag of shit, but I knew that I had to pull myself together or I'd be dead.

The two of them were still talking, arguing – I couldn't tell which – in the background some-where. I just lay there taking short, sharp breaths, keeping my eyes open and coughing blood onto the furry blanket.

My jaw joint was grinding on itself. I probed with my tongue and discovered one of my side teeth moving as a numb, swollen feeling developed on the right side of my face. I felt as if I'd just had a session with a psychopathic dentist.

With my head on the bed, I was level and in a direct line with the coffee table. My fuzzy vision locked on to the large glass ashtray.

I switched my attention to Carpenter and the old guy. They didn't even stop their waffle as a couple of people passed our door, heading towards the end of the corridor. The older guy had a pistol in his hand; Carpenter had his weapon in a shoulder holster, which I could see as he put his hands on his hips and pulled back on his unzipped jacket. They were both pointing at me. Carpenter seemed to be explaining who I was, or at least what I had done.

I could also see now what the older guy had hit me with. His hands could have done the job just as well, judging by the size of them, but he'd opted for a leather strop that looked like a big dildo, and which was probably filled with ball bearings.

The two of them were a couple of metres to one side of me, and the ashtray was one metre to the other. Both men were still more interested in their argument than in me, but would no doubt come to a decision very soon as to how to kill me – probably slowly if Carpenter had anything to do with it.

I had to act, but I also knew that first I had to take a few seconds to sort myself out. I was still fazed; I'd have to break my actions down into stages in my head or I was going to fuck up and get killed.

474

I squinted at the heavy lump of glass on the table that might save my life and, taking a deep breath, I sprang off the bed. Keeping my head down, I charged at the two black shapes in front of me. All I needed was to get them off balance to give me just a few seconds. Holding out my arms, I bulldozed into the two lots of black leather and, not waiting to see what happened to them, I swung my head round and looked for the ashtray. A wheezy gasp came from behind me as they made contact with the wall.

Eyes still fixed on the glass shape on the table, my body pivoted as my legs started to move towards it. Muffled shouts came from behind. That didn't matter, the ashtray did. If they were fast enough to recover, or I was too slow to react, I would never know about it.

Slapping down my palm, as if swatting a fly, I gripped the ashtray. My body was still facing the table with the two guys behind me. Swinging my head round, I focused on the old guy's now hatless head. My body turned as I took the three paces towards him, brandishing the fistful of glass in the air like a knife.

I closed in, ignoring Carpenter as he came towards me from the right. The one I wanted was the old guy, the one with the pistol in his hand.

His face didn't register surprise or fear, just anger, as he pushed himself off the wall and raised his weapon.

My eyes were fixed on his face as I swung the ashtray downwards, making contact above his cheekbone. His skin folded over just below his eye, then split open. He fell with a scream, his body banging against my legs on the way down. Stage three was complete.

I heard, rather than saw, the black shape from the right, almost on top of me.

I didn't have a stage four. It was open house now. Not even bothering to turn and look at Carpenter, I just lashed out wildly. The thick glass hammered against his skull twice on his way down, both times with such force that my arm jarred to a halt as I made contact.

I jumped onto his chest and continued to rain blows onto the top of his head. Somewhere in the back of my mind I knew I'd lost it, but I didn't care. I was just remembering the way this fucker had kept firing rounds into the woman in the lift, and the bastards who'd ruined Kelly's life by hosing down her family in Washington.

Three times there was a crunching, cracking sound as his skull gave way.

I raised my hand, ready to hit again, but stopped myself. I'd done enough. Thick, almost brown blood oozed from his head wounds. He had lost function in his eyes and had a vacant stare, wide open and dull, pupils fully dilated. The blood spread onto the carpet, which soaked it up like blotting paper.

Still sitting astride him I rested both hands on his chest, not enjoying the fact that I'd lost control. To survive, you sometimes have to get really revved up, but losing it completely, I didn't like that.

I turned to check the old guy. The strop and the handgun were on the floor, and so was he, curled

476

up, holding his hat against his face like a dressing and moaning to himself. His legs flailed weakly on the carpet.

Slowly hauling myself to my feet, I kicked away both weapons. The gun looked like a .38 special revolver, the short-barrelled sort used by 1930s American gangsters.

Pulling his jacket off his shoulders and midway down his arms, I dragged him over the top of Carpenter and into the bathroom, leaving his bloodstained fur hat behind. It was obvious now why he always wore it: only a few wisps of hair covered his head.

He was still moaning and probably feeling quite sorry for himself, but he was alive and that meant he was a threat. My jaw was aching as I jolted up and down with the effort of dragging him, but at least my heart rate was starting to calm. There was no other option, he had to die. I wasn't happy about it, but I couldn't leave him here alive when I set off for the Maliskia compound tomorrow. He could compromise everything I was here for.

I let go of him and he slumped onto the tiled bathroom floor. I turned on the hot water and the geyser surged into action.

The extent of the injury to his face was now clear to me. A two-centimetre furrow was gouged in his cheek, wide enough to put a couple of fingers in. Beneath the mess of torn flesh gleamed an area of exposed white cheekbone.

A check of his wallet as he lay and groaned to himself revealed all the normal stuff. Only the money was of interest, both Russian and

Estonian; once that was tucked into my jeans I went back into the bedroom.

Stepping back over Carpenter, I picked up the .38 special from the floor and one of the furry blankets.

I pulled back the hammer so the weapon was cocked. When I came to squeeze the trigger I didn't want the hammer moving all the way back before coming forward to fire the round; it might get caught in the blanket.

I walked back into the bathroom and, not even looking at his face in case his eyes were on me, I unceremoniously jammed the muzzle into the blanket and onto his head, quickly wrapped the furry nylon around the weapon and fired.

There was a dull thud and then a crack as the round exited his head and shattered the tile beneath it. I let the blanket fall and cover his face, and listened. There was no apparent reaction to the round from outside the room; this was the sort of place where you didn't ask too many questions, even if there was a gangfuck going on next door. The only things my senses picked up were the noise of the geyser and the smell of burned nylon.

I turned the water off and the geyser died as I moved into the bedroom. I dug out Carpenter's wallet and tucked his money into my jeans, too. His weapon was still in its shoulder holster, but only just. I realized how lucky I had been. Another fraction of a second and it could have been a totally different story. The pistol was a Makharov, a Russian copy of James Bond's Walther PPK, and only good as a close-up, personal protection weapon, perfect for when someone got the hump with you in a komfort baar. At longer range it would be more lethal to throw the thing at them. No wonder its nickname in certain quarters was 'the disco gun'. I decided to keep this one. The pistol grip on these Russian versions was bulky, making it awkward to get a firm hold first time when drawing down with small hands like mine, but it was more use than the .38 special.

Carpenter's blood was thickening on the carpet, which couldn't absorb the amount leaking out of him. Pulling another blanket off the bed, I trod it down around his head to try and stop it seeping through the floorboards. I ended up grabbing his head and wrapping it in the blanket.

I opened the main door into the corridor, checked left and right, then had a look at the intact tell-tale. Why had it failed me, why was it still in place? I could see the answer at once: it was stuck to the door frame. The sponge-strip draught excluder must have been put there soon after the stuff was invented; it was now brown and gooey with age. Lesson learned. Don't mix tell-tales with old draught excluders.

Switching the fire back on, I rolled up my sleeves and got to work.

38

I used the toilet-plunger handle again to prevent burning my hands, wedging it into a mine cap and fishing it out, then turning it upside down to drain.

I carried it like that into the bedroom, treading on the old man's hat on the way. The blood hadn't soaked in as much as it had into the carpet or blanket, which probably meant the fur was real and was resisting penetration.

Laying the mine on the coffee table, I crossed the room to open the window, letting in the cold sea air big time. Waves were breaking on the other side of the road.

The explosive, which had been more or less rigid plastic, was now soft enough to extract and manipulate. I began to scoop, having first put a carrier bag over each hand to prevent the nitro from entering my blood stream via cuts on my hands or straightforward absorption. It wouldn't kill – hospitals use nitroglycerine on heart-attack victims – but it would give me a massive fuck-off headache.

By the time I'd finished the room stank of

marzipan, and in front of me on the table was ten pounds of what looked like green, lumpy plasticine. It had hardened a little as it cooled, but I knew that once I played with it in my hands a bit it would become quite pliable again. The remaining two pounds or so of PE were stubbornly sticking to the sides of the mine and were too difficult to get out, so I just left it.

With the bags rustling on my hands I worked away at it as if kneading dough, trying to keep my head turned so the fumes didn't get to me so quickly. Even so, it made me feel dizzy and nauseous, though that might also have something to do with the way Carpenter and the old guy had greeted me at the door.

Once I'd got it all nice and malleable in three equal-sized balls, I pulled off the rubber part of the plunger and used the handle as a rolling pin to flatten them out. The smell of marzipan reminded me of being a kid at Christmas, binning the icing sugar and going straight for the yellow stuff underneath.

As I played mum, the room adjacent to my bedroom was about to become a love nest. There was the rattle of a key, the door opened and closed and then I heard voices, but this wasn't fun sex talk, this was heavy, serious stuff.

I kept rolling as the hooker ran through her repertoire of moans and sighs, though not giggly ones, like before; this sounded more like grand opera. The sounds of male grunting and rhythmic humping started almost straight away; poor girl, she probably hadn't even had time to put down her bag of chips.

When the dough was about a quarter of an inch thick and the diameter of a medium takeaway pizza, I used the ice scraper to cut strips about two inches wide, getting six per base. That done, I stepped over the head in the blood-soaked blanket, went into the bathroom and pulled the plug to refill the bath with more hot water.

The old man's eyes were fixed open in an astonished stare. I ignored him as I turned on the tap and tested the water, as if for a baby's bath, wishing I could stay in here because the geyser noise drowned out the duet next door, but there were five more mines to be dealt with. Leaving the bath still running, I went back to the bedroom with another piece of dripping Soviet war machinery hanging off the plunger.

It was now so cold in the room that my nose was beginning to drip. Wiping it carefully on my jacket sleeve to make sure I got none of the marzipan on my exposed skin, I sat back down with more PE-in-a-can and set about digging out the contents.

Plastic explosive is nothing more than a substance which, when detonated, undergoes almost instantaneous decomposition. Until that moment, most forms of the compound are harmless and waterproof. You can even burn some types of PE and it won't explode; it'll just help you make a brew very quickly. When detonated, however, it delivers a shattering blow known as brisance, and that is why it can be used to cut through materials as strong as steel.

I still had another four mines to empty and was gagging for that brew, but I didn't think they did room service here; not the kind I wanted, anyway. I just got on with it, gouging out the PE, rolling and cutting two-inch-wide strips, serenaded by the bear next door, who sounded as though he was heading for his final grunt. I hoped he might follow it with a spell of hibernation.

An hour or so later, with all of the PE now in strips, I opened the knife blade of the Leatherman and rested it over the hot bar of the fire. I then laid the first piece of foam on the bed, base down. Carpenter was pissing me off, as I had to keep stepping over him, so I pulled at his feet, his head making a dull thud as it hit the thin carpet as it moved out of the blanket, and dragged him closer to the door. Once there, I rearranged the sodden blanket once more around his head and wiped my hands on his black crew neck.

Using the towel as an oven glove, I lifted the hot Leatherman from the fire and quickly sliced off all the little lumps, bumps and moulded corners from the upper side of the foam. What I was left with was a metre square, one side naturally flat, the other cut more or less level. Next I used the hot blade to mark out a two-inch-wide channel all the way round, following the line of the square and about three inches in from the edge. The smell of burning polystyrene was even more overpowering than the marzipan.

Holding the blade at an angle, I started cutting an inverted V in the channel, ending up with what looked like a trench all around the foam square, with four very long bars of Toblerone lying in the bottom of it, peaks upwards. The strips of explosive would be laid along the sides of the Toblerone, and when the frame charge was complete, it would be the flat side that would ultimately be placed against the target.

You can't drop a bridge by just dangling big sticks of dynamite against it. To cut through whatever you're trying to destroy – concrete, brick or steel – with the least amount of PE and maximum effect, you have to channel the brisance by using the Munroe Effect. Because of the thirty-degree angle made by the peak of the Toblerone facing the target, the majority of the detonation force would surge towards the imaginary chocolate bar's base and beyond. Had the Toblerone been made of copper, the brisance would be able to penetrate many inches of steel, because the detonation would melt the copper and take most of the molten flow forward with it, cutting through the target. I didn't have copper, just styrofoam, but there was enough force in the PE alone to do the job required of it.

My nitro headache was really pounding now. I downed another four aspirin; only four more left.

As I went back to my cutting, the sound of an argument between two men filtered through from the corridor. They were soon joined by a woman, who seemed to be charming them down.

The door opposite mine opened and closed and there was silence. I waited for the customary sound effects to start in the room opposite, but all I got was more argument, the woman now chipping in her two EEKs' worth.

When I'd finished cutting the Toblerone shape all the way round the polystyrene, the base of the triangle was just over an inch and a half from the base of the foam. This was the 'stand-off', which would give the Munroe Effect space to gather enough force to cut through the target's brickwork.

Now all I had to do was lay the explosive along each side of the Toblerone and over its peak, making sure the strips were moulded together seamlessly to make one big charge. Protecting my hands with the plastic bags once more, I started placing, pressing and pinching, as if shaping and joining pastry. The three-way argument was still going on opposite; I didn't mind, it was nice to have neighbours who were talking instead of grunting and throwing the bed around.

Once the Toblerone was covered by two layers of PE, I got some det cord and cut off two lengths, one about three feet long, the other about five. Putting two knots into one end of each length, I pressed these into the PE that lay over the Toblerone, on two opposite sides of the square. To keep the knots in place, two offcuts of PE were pressed down on top so the knots were well and truly moulded into the charge.

The reason for having two sites for the det cord was that I needed the detonation to come from two directions simultaneously so the charge was more efficient. To make sure that happened, I tightly taped together, over a distance of about six inches, the two different lengths of det cord so that, from the binding to the charge, they were both of equal length. Trailing from the site of the binding was the two-foot surplus from the longer piece; that bit was called the det tail. As the shock wave travelled along the det tail and reached the binding, it would also detonate the second, shorter length of det cord. The two shock waves would then travel down towards the charge at the same speed and distance, therefore reaching the Toblerones on two opposing sides simultaneously. The Munroe Effect would direct the force of the detonation towards the base of the Toblerone, gathering energy as it travelled the inch and a bit through the foam before impacting the target. All being well, I should be left with a gaping hole about a metre square in the wall of the target house.

I was still in the process of taping over the Toblerone to keep it in the foam when two male voices, drunk and laughing, came up the stairs and passed my door, going into the room on the other side of the bathroom.

I still had another charge to make, so I put the knife back on the fire as my two new neighbours laughed, joked and turned the TV on loudly. At least it drowned out the three still entertaining themselves opposite.

It took me thirty minutes to complete the second charge, done to the accompaniment of an American comedy, dubbed, of course. I preferred the jokes in Russian.

To make them easier to carry, I sandwiched both sets of charges together so the Toblerone peaks were facing each other, storing the attached det cord in between. I wrapped one of the tow ropes around to keep it all together, then slid two of the pallet sections, taken from behind the shops, under the rope. I'd also secured the reel of unused det cord to the pack by running the rope through its centre while wrapping it round. Everything I'd be needing on target was now together, and the whole thing looked like a badly packed Boy Scout's rucksack.

There were one or two other little jobs to do before I could get out of here. Gathering together the remaining blue nylon tow ropes, I tied them together until there was one rope about thirty metres long, adding extra knots so that there was one every metre. One end was then tied onto the rope, which had been wrapped around the charges.

Next I picked up the third length of pallet wood. It was MI9 time again as I cut a groove all round one end, about three inches in from the top, around which I secured the free end of the rope attached to the charges. Holding the brick against the unroped end of the wood, so that its longest edge was parallel to the plank's, I wrapped the towel around both and secured it with yards of insulating tape. All the equipment was now prepared.

The Lion King told me it was 3.28, in theory too early to leave, but I didn't know who else knew that Carpenter and the old man had come to visit. The threesome started arguing yet again, this time probably about payment, as I took the charges, draped in a blanket, down to the car.

39

Saturday, 18 December 1999

In the pitch-dark of the afternoon I drove west towards Tallinn on the main drag, turned left to Pussi and headed once again over the railway track and towards the target, passing the sad shacks where people were holed up for the winter.

In the twelve hours since leaving the hotel I'd been cruising around, stopping only a couple of times to fill up with petrol. Anything to keep the heater going.

On my way out I'd paid the old woman for another two nights, so with any luck there should be no need for her to come and check the room.

Tented stalls were dotted along the roads like miniature service stations, the steam that poured from their vents making them look like refugee-camp field kitchens. When I stopped to buy coffee and pastries, it actually helped to have a swollen mouth with visible bruising, because I could get away with just mumbling and pointing. The problem came when I tried to eat and drink; my tooth was killing me and these places didn't sell Nurofen. My last four aspirins had gone hours ago.

I'd kept Carpenter's weapon on me, and the .38 special was in the glove compartment. Neither of them had spare rounds.

Now, sliding slowly along the single-track road, my headlights picked up the concrete wall of the target on my left. Nothing appeared to have changed; there were still no lights or movement and the gates were still closed. Parking in the same driveway as before, I turned off the engine and sat for a while in the rapidly cooling car, running through the plan one last time. It didn't take long, because there wasn't really much of a plan.

Forcing myself out into the cold, now wearing the old guy's gloves and bloodstained fur hat, I covered the driver's side of the windscreen with newspaper before taking the charges out of the boot. The tow rope wrapped around them made a handy shoulder strap. Finally I hid the key under the rear right wheel. If I got caught by the Maliskia, then at least they wouldn't have my keys if I managed to escape. What was more, I could tell Tom if I linked up with him, and he would also have a means of escape if I didn't make it to the car.

I wasn't going to kill him. I owed him that much after what he'd done by the fence at the Finns' house. What was more, I didn't want his death on my conscience, as well as Kelly's illness. At first I'd put my change of heart down to the fact that I wasn't thinking of saving Tom's skin as much as my own. He would be the only one who could back up my story to Lynn if this whole thing went completely to rat shit. And why shouldn't it?

Everything else had so far. But then, much as I hated the idea, I had to admit to myself that I'd come to like the chubby-cheeked fucker. He might not be the sort of bloke I was used to associating with, and we certainly wouldn't be seeing each other for coffee mornings, but he was all right and he needed a break as much as I did. I'd been toying with the idea since I lay in my cheap hotel room in Helsinki. That was why I'd brought his passport with me, just in case I decided.

It was as cold as ever, but as I walked along the road I tied up my new fur-hat ear flaps so I could listen. Drawing level with the hangar and its funnel, I still couldn't hear any noise from inside the compound. I reached the driveway leading to the large steel-plate gates, turned and took a few paces towards them. Then I stopped and listened. Now that I knew it was there, I could just make out the generator churning away in the distance. Apart from that I could hear nothing.

I tested the gates, but they weren't open. I tried the small door set into the larger right-hand one, but again they were still locked. I wasn't expecting it to be that easy, but I'd have felt like a real dickhead if I'd gone to all the trouble of climbing over the wall when all I had to do was stroll in through the front gate.

Lying down in the right-hand tyre rut, with the charges behind me, I pressed my eye to the gap beneath. Nothing that side of the gate had changed; there were still two lights on the ground floor and the larger building to the right was just as dark. I wasn't sure if what I was looking at was good or bad; not that it mattered that much, I was still going to get amongst it and destroy the place, and hopefully find Tom.

Once on my feet again, with the Boy Scout rucksack reshouldered, I started back in the direction of the car, but about seventy or eighty metres past the hangar I stepped left off the road and into the high snow. My aim was to walk out into the fields, turn left and approach the hangar from the rear. I couldn't prevent leaving a trail in the snow, but at least I could try to keep most of it out of sight of the road.

The snow had a thin layer of ice on top and varied in depth from calf to thigh height. As I pressed my foot down on the not-so-deep stuff, there was initial resistance, then my weight pushed through it. In the deeper drifts I felt like an ice breaker in the Baltic.

I laboured on, my jeans soaking and my legs starting to freeze. At least there wasn't much cloud and my night vision was adjusting to the starlight.

The rear of the hangar loomed in front of me and I climbed inside. The floor was concrete and the steel structure supported what looked like corrugated asbestos. Moving slowly and carefully towards the wall of the compound, after about twenty paces I began to make out the dark shape of the doorway. When I reached the edge of the hangar, I stood still and listened. Not a sound, just the gentle moan of the wind.

Wading across the five or six metres of snow between the two buildings, I realized as soon as I reached the door that I was going to be disappointed. The metal was a lot older than the front gates and was flaking with rust. The door itself was solid, with no hinges or locks this side of it. I pushed, but there wasn't a hint of movement.

Turning right, I followed the wall and waded fifteen metres further away from the road. Hopefully I was now facing the gable end of the larger building on the other side of the concrete.

Placing the charges on the snow, I unravelled the rope attached to the plank with the brick at the end. With just two or three feet of slack, I started swinging it around me like a hammer thrower, finally letting go with upwards momentum to make the plank clear the wall.

I'd never make the Highland Games. The whole lot fell back down in front of me. I was just sorting out the rope for another try when vehicle lights raked the wall of the compound.

I dropped to my knees, ready to bury myself in the snow. Then I realized that on my knees I *was* buried in it.

The lights got stronger, disappearing for half a second as the vehicle dipped in the road, only to light up the sky before settling down again. As it got closer the inside of the hangar was lit up and moving shadows were cast by the steel supports.

The ponderous chug of a big diesel told me that a tractor was heading in my direction. I felt good about that: if the Maliskia were coming for me, I doubted they'd be riding a Massey Ferguson.

The noise got louder and the light even stronger until the tractor burst into view in the gap between the compound wall and the hangar. It looked like some old relic from a Soviet collective, with far more silhouettes in the cab than the thing was designed for. Maybe the local pub-quiz team was heading down to the Hammer and Sickle for a few pints of vodka.

The lights and noise gradually faded and I got on with my task. It took me two more tries, but I eventually got the plank to sail over the wall, the charge end firmly anchored in my hands. The rope jerked as the plank finished its flight, probably ending up dangling about three or four feet over the target side. Gently, I started pulling it back, waiting for the bit of resistance that would tell me that the point where the rope was wrapped around the plank had connected with the far top edge of the wall. The way this thing worked was that the counterweight of the brick made the top of the plank anchor itself against an angled wall. It's one of the reasons why prisons have a large oval shape made of smooth metal on top of their walls, so that contraptions like this don't have anything to bite into. MI9 had done it again.

Maintaining the tension in the rope, and half expecting the plank to come plummeting back down onto my head at any second, I slowly let it take my whole body weight. The cheap nylon rope stretched and protested but held secure. With my feet against the wall, and using the pitted sections as toeholds and knots I'd placed along the rope, I started to climb.

It didn't take long to reach the top, and I scrambled up and rested along its three-foot width. The large building blocked most of my view of the target beyond; all I could see was the light from the windows, where it hit the snow. The generator now provided a constant rumble in the foreground.

Snow and ice cascaded from the wall as I swivelled round on my stomach, turning to face the way I'd come. With my legs now dangling down the target side, I began to pull the charges carefully up the wall. It wasn't the noise I was worried about, I didn't want to damage them.

When I'd finally got the charges up on top with me, I swivelled round again and lowered them gently down the target side. It was now simply a question of moving the plank to the other edge in order to reverse the climbing process.

Keeping the tension in the rope, I slowly lowered myself over, twisting my right foot round the rope as my hips got to the edge of the wall. Then I let the rope take my weight and climbed down as quickly as I could.

I piled snow on top of the charges so the weight of the plank didn't pull it down the other side, taking everything with it. It was important to keep the rope in place while I went off and did a quick recce; for now, it was my only escape route.

The hum of the generator was louder at ground level, more than enough to drown the crunch of my feet on virgin snow and ice as I moved towards the rusty side door. I took the torch from my pocket and switched it on. Just a tiny pinprick of light emerged; I'd taped over most of the reflector, leaving just a small hole.

There was work to be done on the door. It's all well and good getting on to a target, but it's just as important getting away. If I didn't have a better escape route organized than just climbing up a rope, I'd be in deep shit if I was compromised. Working with the torch in my mouth, I could see that the door was secured by a large bolt, maybe two feet long, set in the middle, covered in rust and looking as if it hadn't been opened for years. I began to work on the lever with both hands, gently lifting it up and down as I pulled it back and forth, making a little progress with each movement until the thing finally gave. Pulling the door towards me about three or four inches to confirm that it would open, I then pushed it back into position. Job done, I stopped and listened: no noise but the generator.

There was no point in risking the rope being spotted now that I had an alternative escape route, so I untied it and let it go.

Shouldering the charges, I crunched along the front of the larger building, trying to keep as close to it as possible to minimize sign. Now I could see that it was built of chalk-coloured bricks that were way past their prime. If the target house was built of the same stuff, it wasn't going to be difficult to make entry.

The generator noise increased as I reached the large opening. A mass of tyre tracks led in the same direction. Going inside, I moved off to the right so I wasn't silhouetted in the entrance, and stood still in the darkness, listening to the genny noise to my far left. It felt warmer in here, but I knew it wasn't really, it was just more sheltered.

Taking the torch out of my pocket, I pulled off the tape but kept two fingers over the lens to control its brightness. A quick shine around the cavernous interior revealed three vehicles: a Mercedes box van, with its nose pointing out, and two saloons haphazardly parked at different angles, pointing in. The floor was concrete, covered in several years' supply of frozen mud, lumps of wood and old crates.

The torchlight was too weak to reach the generator itself, but thirty paces took me right up to it. The machinery was standing on a new section of concrete floor, about two feet above ground level to keep it well out of the shit. Beyond it was the fuel tank, a large, heavy plastic cylinder supported on breeze-blocks. Seeing it gave me an idea for later on.

Jutting from the front of the generator was a power cable a good three inches thick; it ran through the gable wall, where three or four bricks had been knocked out to accommodate it, and towards the target house.

I dumped my kit at the back of the generator, turned off the torch, and went back to the large opening and out into the compound.

Following the many footprints that had been made between this building and the target about fifteen metres away, I made my way towards the main door. Directly ahead I saw the triangle of darkness that stretched from directly below the ground-floor window sill to about a metre out into the snow, where the light hit the ground.

I checked my weapon was properly placed in my jacket pocket so that, if needed, I could bite off my glove and draw down with ease.

Checking before passing the two-metre gap

between the two buildings to my right, I could see where the generator cable came out of the barn wall and went into the target's. I also saw plenty of footprints from the track I was on, branching off between the two buildings and towards the rear of the target. People must be in and out of here all the time.

Bending down, I edged my way under the first window, as close as possible to the wall. The glass above me was protected by steel bars. A television was on. The voices were English, and it didn't take me long to work out the channel was MTV. This got weirder by the minute.

With my back to the wall, I looked and listened. The light above me was shining through yellow floral curtains, though the material was too thick to see through. I couldn't hear any talking, just Ricky Martin singing. Putting my ear to the wall I listened again. I didn't have to try hard. Bursting in with the chorus was a heavy Eastern European accent trying to give Ricky a hand.

40

The target building seemed to consist of a concrete frame infilled with red clay brickwork with
air holes and serrated sides. Whoever had put it
together had never heard of a plumb line, and too
many bad winters had taken their toll on the
bricks; they looked as crumbly as the one I'd tied
to the plank.

With Ricky Martin reaching the end of his song,
I moved up the two concrete steps to the main
door. It was the same arrangement as the baar in
Narva, except the other way round, with the steel
grille on the outside and the wooden door set
back about six inches further into the frame. I
needed to find out if it was locked. It wasn't my
chosen point of entry, but if the charges didn't
work and the door happened to be open, at least
I'd have options. More to the point, if I fucked up
inside, I had an extra escape route.

The grille wasn't locked. I moved it gently
backwards an inch and it made no noise, so I
pulled it towards me a couple of inches, returned
it an inch and pulled another two, controlling the
quiet squeaks as it gradually opened. Eventually

the grille was open enough to squeeze my arm past and try the door. There were no sounds apart from MTV and the generator as I pushed the door handle down gently and gave a small push. It was locked.

I stood and listened, hoping to hear Tom's voice. Something was being fried, and the smell was wafting under the door. From upstairs came a shout, muffled by the sound of the TV, but it wasn't Tom's voice.

Then I realized the shouting wasn't shouting, it was meant to be singing. My friend the Ricky Martin impressionist was on his way back downstairs.

Moving out of the doorway, I pulled my glove off with my teeth and gripped my weapon. If he came out, I'd be stepping over his dead body and going straight in with so much speed, aggression and surprise that I'd scare even myself.

His voice got louder as he reached the ground floor. A chorus of other voices bellowed from the rear of the building, maybe in Russian, but definitely telling him to shut the fuck up.

He had reached the hallway and was only feet from the door, shouting back, along with at least two other voices from the TV room. It was banter, nothing more.

The singer went back into the room and the MTV show died down to a slightly quieter level as the door was closed.

I moved back to the front door and listened. Nothing now but the sound of more music being played. Replacing my weapon, I slowly closed the grille the same way as I'd opened it.

Moving back down the steps, I followed the tracks towards the far end of the target, ducking under the left-hand window and into its dark triangle. Even with my ear to the wet, cold wall, I could hear no sound from inside. The windows were steamed up behind the steel bars; maybe this was the kitchen?

I reached the corner of the building and cleared it. There were no windows this side, but plenty of footprints in the snow leading to the rear. What could easily be seen, however, even in this light, was a large satellite dish, slightly jutting out to the left of the building and pointing upwards at about forty-five degrees. I felt as if I was having a Microsoft HQ flashback, and hoped the NSA didn't arrive to complete the story. At the same time I was pleased I'd seen it. The dish was my only confirmation that this really was the target.

I counted the paces as I moved towards it, in preparation for laying the charges. Seventeen one-yard steps took me to the rear of the building.

I cleared the corner and the generator gained a decibel or two. Light was shining through curtains from both of the upstairs windows, just enough to cast a dim glow over the satellite dish's two mates. All three were about the same size as those at Microsoft HQ, but made of solid plastic, not mesh. They pointed skywards in different directions. They weren't static, dug-in dishes, but on stands, with ice-covered sandbags over the legs to keep them in position. Like the Finnish ones, they, too, were clear of snow and ice, and the whole area around them was trampled down. Beyond them, maybe forty metres away, was the dark shape of the rear compound wall.

I turned the corner and realized that hidden in the shadow of the top windows' dark triangles were two more windows on the ground floor, without light. All four mirrored the ones on the front of the target.

To get under the first window took five paces, making it twenty-two in total so far. I crouched by three thick, snow-covered satellite feeds which came out of the snow and disappeared into a hole in the brickwork directly beneath the first ground-floor window. The gap around the cabling was roughly refilled with concrete.

The downstairs windows on this side were also barred. I could now see chinks of light around the edges of the frame I was crouching beneath. Lifting my eyes to the sill for a closer look, I saw that the glass was boarded over from the inside.

I heard a humming noise coming from the other side of the boards, high-pitched and electrical, unlike the throbbing diesel further along in the other building. No human voices, but I knew they were there somewhere. I never thought I'd find myself longing to hear Tom asking for a cup of herbal tea – 'My body's a temple, know what I mean, Nick?' – but it didn't happen.

Stepping over the cables, it took me another nine slow and careful paces to the next window to add to the twenty-two. I'd soon know how much det cord I'd need to take off the reel.

This window was also boarded up, but there was a little more light spilling out. Two sheets of quarter-inch ply, which should have been flush against the glass, were not, leaving a half-inch gap on the right-hand side.

Doing a Houdini, I adjusted my head to try and get a good viewing angle, pressing it right up against the iron bars, the hat working as a perfect insulator for my head. I got a glimpse of very bright lighting, under which I could see a bank of about five or six grey plastic PC monitors facing away from me, their rear vents black with burned dust. Judging from what I could see, this rear half of the building was one big room.

As I adjusted my head in an another attempt to see more, everything inside went dark. A body blocked my view. I watched as he leaned forward on his arms, his head moving from side to side as he studied the different screens in front of him, no more than two feet away from me. He must have been about mid-thirties with short dark-blond hair on top of a very square head, and he was wearing a patterned crew-neck jumper that any train-spotter's mother would have been proud of. He started to smile, then nodded to himself as he turned towards the gap. He was no more than a foot away now as he answered a quick aggressive Russian voice behind him. He looked down at something, and whatever it was he was happy about it. Maybe Tom had come up with the goods for them and they had Echelon. If so, it wouldn't be for long.

He picked up a sheet of printed A4 and waved it at whoever was behind him, then he moved out of my line of vision, back into the room. It was probably the Christmas lunch menu from the Space and Naval Warfare Systems Command in

San Diego. They seemed to know everything else that was happening there.

At least I knew where the kit that had to be destroyed was – all I needed to find now was Tom. I waited for further movement for another fifteen minutes with my eye to the gap, but nothing happened. I was getting very cold and my toes were numb. Lion King told me it was only 5.49; it was going to get a whole lot colder yet.

I moved to the next corner of the target, towards the generator. It was another five paces, which made thirty-six in total. I was happy; there was more than enough det cord.

I turned right and walked down the small gap between the two buildings, stepping over the generator cable lying in the snow. Just as with the satellite cables, a hole had been punched through the target's brickwork and the gap refilled with handfuls of concrete.

I made my way back to the generator building and started to prepare the kit. The first thing I checked was that I still had the batteries in my inside pocket: in dems, it's the ultimate sin to lose control of the initiation device, on a par with leaving your weapon more than an arm's length away from you. I'd been keeping them close to my body to stop them getting sluggish in the cold; they needed to work first time.

I didn't need light for unrolling the det cord because I knew what I was doing, but the generator noise would drown out any human movement coming into the building, so I had to keep my eyes on the entrance while I was working. Placing the reel between my feet, I held the loose end in my right hand and stretched out my arm, pushing the det cord into my armpit with my left. I did that thirty-six times, plus an extra five to cover what I needed to do on the wall this side of the target. I added two more for luck, cutting it with my blackened Leatherman. I then laid it on the floor, next to the charges. This was now called the main line, and would be used to send the shock wave to all the charges at once via their det tails.

The next thing I had to sort out was the little brainwave I'd had for the fuel tank. What I had in mind was the most spectacular explosion this side of Hollywood. When the fuel tank blew it wouldn't be the most productive bang in the world, but the effect would be phenomenal.

I climbed the ladder of the tank with the det cord in my hand, slowly unfeeding it from the reel. When I lifted the flap on the tank, the torch beam hit on the surface of shiny liquid that filled about three quarters of the cylinder. After tying a double knot on the end of the cord, I pulled the petrol-station carrier bag from my jacket. In it was the spare four-pound ball of PE that any dems man worth his salt always carries to plug up any holes or damage to a charge. The smell wasn't too bad out in the open as I ripped off about half and played with it to warm it up.

Once it was pliable enough, I squashed it around the double knot, ensuring it had worked its way into the gaps of the ties, and finally I taped the whole thing up to keep the PE in place.

I lowered the ball of PE into the tank by its

string of det cord, stopping when it was dangling about two or three inches from the surface of the fuel. It only takes a split second for fuel to vaporize after an explosion, but when that detonates, the effect is Vesuvian. If I fucked up this job, it would certainly give the appearance that I'd given it my best shot. How could Val doubt my word when the fireball would probably be big enough for him to see it in Moscow?

I taped the det cord onto the side of the fuel tank, then climbed back down the ladder, carefully unreeling the rest of the cord as I moved towards the hole in the wall. I wanted to cut a long enough length so that, once laid out, it would reach the target house. Nine extra arms' lengths seemed to put me on the safe side. I made the cut, then started to push the end of the det cord through the hole in the wall.

Just then, torchlight came bouncing down the gap from the front of the buildings. I couldn't hear anything above the generator. I quickly pulled the det cord back in and froze. The only things moving were my eyes; they flicked from the hole to the entrance, waiting for any movement from either direction.

A shiny wet pair of wellies and a pair of normal outdoor boots were illuminated by the beam of light as it searched for the generator cable. What worried me was the AK Wellie-man had hanging down by his side, its large foresight at the end of the barrel level with his knees.

Once over it, they carried on towards the rear and moved out of sight. There wasn't any talking, or if there was, I couldn't hear it above the generator. I didn't even hear their feet in the snow.

They must have been doing something with the dishes. I waited; there was nothing else I could do. No way was I going out there again until I knew they were safely tucked up back in the house.

I lay on the frozen mud and waited for their return, my eyes still moving between the gaps in the brickwork. The cold soon penetrated my clothing, numbing my skin. The six or seven minutes it took before I saw the torchlight flickering about on the snow again didn't pass quickly enough.

Craning my neck to get a better view, I watched their silhouettes fade as they reached the corner of the building. I waited a few more frozen minutes in case they'd forgotten something or realized they'd fucked up and had to come back to redo it.

While I waited I had another brainwave. When I eventually got to my feet, I went across to the vehicles and let down their tyres. The fireball ought to sort out the vehicles and guarantee they couldn't be used in a follow-up, but it didn't hurt to play safe.

I grinned stupidly to myself as the air hissed out and the tyre rims settled on the frozen mud. Watching the hole in the wall for torchlight, I was eight years old again, crouching by my step-father's car.

Moving back to the kit, I pushed the det cord through the hole in the wall once more, then cut several eight-inch strips of gaffa tape from the roll and stuck them around both forearms. Finally I shouldered the pack of charges, gripped the coiled-up main line in my left hand and moved back out into the cold.

41

I headed for the gap between the two buildings. Ahead of me the dim light from the house still spilt onto the snow.

I cleared the gap and moved towards the rear. Stepping over the genny cable, I checked the det cord was still in the hole, ready for when I came back for it later, then continued down to the corner. The elevations of the dishes had changed dramatically.

I wanted to make one last check for Tom through the gap in the boards. Maybe I'd be in luck; there's a first time for everything.

Angling my head, I peered through, but couldn't see any movement.

Stepping over the satellite-dish cables, I made my way to the far corner, then turned and counted three paces towards the front of the target. I crouched down at that point and placed the charges and reel of det cord onto the snow. The computer room was on the other side of this wall. It was going to be gloves on, gloves off for the next twenty minutes as I positioned the charges.

Undoing the tow rope that kept the charges together, I placed one of the foam squares against the bricks, the base of the Toblerones facing the target, so the det tail dangled in front of me. Then, ramming the end of one of the wooden pallet slats into the snow at an angle, I used it to keep the polystyrene square in position against the wall.

When I checked the charge with the aid of the torch, I discovered a tiny break where a PE joint had come apart. This didn't mean to say the PE wouldn't initiate, since the gap was less than a sixteenth of an inch, but why take that chance?

Manipulating a small lump of PE between my gloved hands until it was pliable, I broke off a piece and plugged the space. After a final check, I killed the torch and moved over to the nearest dish. I lifted one of its ice-hard sandbags and placed it halfway along the wall, using it to weigh down the free end of the main line. I then began the process of laying out its forty-three arm's lengths back towards the charge. The weight of the sandbag enabled me to pull the cord gently to ensure there weren't any kinks or twists, so the shock wave had a free run to the dettails.

Once I reached the propped-up charge it was gloves-off time again. Peeling one of the strips of tape from my forearm, I began to bind the det tail to the main line, taping the two sections together as tightly as possible. I did it strictly by the book, binding the main line one foot down the det tail in case some of the explosive had fallen from the exposed end. The binding was four inches, to guarantee enough contact between the two for the shock wave to transfer across from the main line to the det tail. Then, of course, it would journey on down to the charge.

As I peeled off another strip of tape it dawned on me that whenever I was working on dems, I always used feet and inches rather than metres and kilos. That was the way I'd been taught, one of the main reasons being that it made life a lot easier when working with Americans, who weren't too keen on the metric system.

There was a sudden burst of loud music from an upstairs window around the back, stopping as abruptly as it had started. I instinctively ducked, and through the rear windows I could hear various voices shouting. At least another three different voices could be heard shouting back and laughing.

It brought me back to real life. The act of tactically placing charges always seems to detach you from reality. Maybe it's because there's so much concentration involved, because there are no second chances. That's why you normally make sure that whoever is doing the technical stuff can just get on with it and concentrate. It wasn't a luxury I had tonight.

I nicked another sandbag from the base of the dish and placed it on top of the main line, on the dish side of the det tail. I didn't want to pull on it and disrupt the charge I'd already set up as I picked up the second charge. I began to unreel the main line over the satellite cable towards the gap between the two buildings.

Someone was fucking with the volume as

Aerosmith's theme song 'Armageddon' got louder and then suddenly died above me, prompting more shouts from the computer room. Just as I reached the next corner, the heavy Eastern European voices above bellowed out yet again and the music blared out at full volume.

I knelt between the two buildings and rigged up the second charge on the other side of the target house so that it was exactly facing the first. Once it was propped and checked, I began taping its det tail to the main line. The music hit full blast again for two seconds, then subsided. There were more shouts from downstairs. The boys in the computer room were getting ever so slightly pissed off. I reckoned there was a minimum of five people in the building.

I gave the charge a final check; it was looking good. Demolitions can appear to be a dark art, but actually all you need to understand is how explosives work and then learn the hundreds of rules for using them. I'd broken many of them today, but what the hell, I hadn't had a lot of choice.

I went over to the generator cable hole and gently pulled out the det cord that ran into the fuel tank, taping it to the main line in the same way as I'd done with the other two.

Aerosmith were still doing their best to annoy the computer room. It was a good game, and I hoped it would keep the boys occupied for a moment or two longer. I thought about Tom and hoped he wasn't standing too close to either of the walls.

Gloves back on, I pulled the main line for the

last few arms' lengths towards the front of the building. Now I just had to attach the electric detonator, which was already fixed to the firing cable, then unreel the cable round the corner and get down below the MTV window before the shit, and everything else in the building, hit the fan.

I was a bit worried about the amount of extraneous electricity flying about and its possible effect on the firing cable. Once I'd untwisted the two leads that were to go on the battery, they'd be potential antennae, just like the dets in the Narva flat. The manuals would say I was either supposed to be one kilometre away when the shit went up or very well protected. I didn't think hiding round the corner with a few clay bricks as cover was quite what they had in mind.

The main line stopped about six or seven paces short of the corner of the target. Great, at least the firing cable would be long enough for me to be well under the window.

As I gently pulled at the press studs holding the zip flap of my jacket to extract the firing cable, the volume of the music changed again. It was escaping outside. Then I heard the noise of the grille swinging open and the front door slamming shut.

There was no time to think, just do. Biting off my gloves, I jammed my hand into my jacket pocket for the Makharov, right thumb taking off the safety as I moved towards the corner, taking deep breaths.

I couldn't hear him – them – yet, but whichever it was, I had to take the fight to them.

Three more paces until the corner.

There was torchlight ahead. I stopped, pushing my thumb down on the safety catch to ensure it was off.

One more second and a body appeared, heading towards me. He was looking down at where his torchbeam hit the snow. It glinted off his weapon barrel.

I couldn't give him time to think. I jumped onto him, wrapping my left arm around his neck and pushing the Makharov into his stomach, digging it into him hard. My legs wrapped around his waist, and as we fell together I pulled the trigger, hoping that our two bodies sandwiching the weapon would suppress its report. No chance. The job had just gone noisy.

Jumping to my feet, I sprinted round to the front of the house, focusing solely on the next corner, heading for the other end of the main line, leaving a screaming Russian writhing in the snow.

I racked back the weapon's topslide to eject whatever was in there and feed in another round, just in case we'd been so close that it had been prevented from sliding back correctly when I'd fired and hadn't reloaded.

I had the same feeling in my stomach as I used to have as a kid, running scared. As I neared the main entrance, I scrambled frantically with my left hand for the firing cable and det in my inside pocket.

The door opened, MTV still blasting, and a body, too small to be Tom, emerged. The grille was already open.

'Gory? Gory?'

I raised my weapon and fired on the move. I couldn't miss.

There was a scream and one round hit the grille with a high-pitched metallic ricochet.

I carried straight on past, turned the corner and made a headlong dive towards the sandbag, dropping my weapon and desperately fishing for the main line coming from under the sandbag. I didn't look up to see if anyone was coming for me. I didn't have time.

The wounded man's screams echoed around the compound. I tried to calm myself and slow my frenzied movements. I held the det onto the main line and wrapped a strip of tape around both – not as tightly as I would have liked, but fuck it.

I pulled out the battery and yanked the twisted end leads of the firing cable apart with my teeth. Then, falling to the floor, I squeezed my legs together, opened my jaw and buried my head in the snow as I pushed the two leads onto the terminals.

Less than a single heartbeat later the detonator exploded and initiated the main line. The shock wave of the explosion travelled along it, met the first det tail and then the one leading to the fuel tank. Then the second det tail got the good news.

The two wall charges exploded virtually simul- taneously, and the resultant shock waves met in the middle of the room at a combined speed of 52,000 feet per second.

42

My whole world shuddered, trembled, quaked. It was like being inside a massive bell that had just been given an almighty bang.

The air was sucked from my lungs as hot air blasted over me. Around the compound snow and ice shot upwards a foot or so from the ground. My ears rang. Brick dust, snow and shattered glass cascaded around me. Then the shock wave rebounded off the thick concrete perimeter walls and came back for more.

Crawling forward to the corner of the target, I watched, mesmerized, as an enormous fireball whooshed from the entrance of the generator building and leaped high into the sky. Thick black smoke mixed with bright orange flames that burned like an oil-rig flare. The entire area was bathed in light and I could feel the heat scorching my face.

Chunks of brick, glass and all kinds of other stuff that had been blown sky high started clattering around me. Scrambling to my knees, I threw my arms over my head to protect myself. You're supposed to look up to prepare for the stuff coming towards you, but fuck that, I just kept close to the wall and took my chances. I wouldn't be able to see it anyway. The sandstorm of red brickdust had arrived, blanketing the compound; it was just a matter of hanging in there and waiting for the last of the fallout to rain down. I began coughing like a lifelong smoker.

I cleared each nostril in turn, then tried to equalize the pressure in my ears. A sharp, stinging pain seared across my buttocks. My arse must have taken some of the shock wave as it passed over me. At least it wasn't my face or bollocks. I checked for blood, but my fingers came back just wet with water from the snow-soaked jeans.

It was time to get to my feet and start moving back for my weapon, which was still in the snow somewhere. I felt around on my hands and knees, my arse in agony, as if I'd just been caned. I found the Makharov by the sandbag and, checking chamber with my finger to the heavy rumbling sound of burning fuel, I stumbled towards the main door.

There was a secondary explosion in the generator building, probably a vehicle fuel tank in the path of the firestorm. For the next few moments the flames burned higher and more intensely.

The guy in the gap wasn't screaming any more, but he was still alive, coiled up and holding his stomach. I went over to where he lay trembling in the snow. I picked up his AK and threw it towards the main gate, out of his reach. I certainly wouldn't be needing it myself inside the house.

When the two shock waves from the opposing explosions had met, they would have wiped out everything in the computer room. The force would then have taken the line of least resistance to escape the confines of the building: the windows and doors. Surging along the hallways, it would have destroyed everything in its path. The MTV man wasn't looking good. Some bits of him were draped on the grille like strips of meat hanging in a smokehouse. The rest would have been scattered out in the snow. When humans burn they smell like scorched pork, but when they're blown apart like this, it's as if you've walked into a butcher's shop a week after a power cut.

The torchlight wasn't much good in the hallway; it just reflected off the wall of dust like a car's headlights in dense fog. I blundered around, stumbling over bricks and other debris, trying to find the gap to the right that would lead to the MTV room.

I found the door, or rather the place where it had been. As I moved through, my feet collided with sticks of furniture, then what was left of the television set and a whole lot more bricks. I was still coughing shit out of my lungs, and was the only one doing so. I could hear no other movement, no sounds of distress.

Tripping over a large bundle on the floor, I switched on my torch and knelt down to check it. The body was on its side and smouldering, facing away from me. Rolling him towards me, I shone the light into his dust-covered face. It wasn't Tom. Whoever this man in his early twenties had been, he wasn't any more. The skin was pulled back from his head like a partly peeled orange and the blood he'd lost was mixing with the dust to look like wet, red cement.

I continued across the room, kicking out and feeling like a blind man as I searched for more bodies. There were two, but neither of them was Tom. I wasn't going to call out, in case someone decided to reply with something other than a voice.

I tried to get into the room opposite – the kitchen – but the door was jammed. Leaving it to go upstairs, I decided to check the easy places first. I didn't bother with the computer room: even if there were any bodies there, they wouldn't be recognizable. In other circumstances I might have taken a moment or two to be quietly proud; I was shit at most things, but in A-level Demolitions I'd got a distinction.

I headed up the stairs, my left hand on the wall, having to feel for every step as I made my way to the top. I cleared my nostrils again, gobbing the dust out of my throat as I equalized my nose again to clear the ringing in my ears.

As I reached the top landing I heard a short, faint cry; I couldn't tell where it came from. I went left first, since it was nearer. Feeling my way to the door, I pushed, but it wouldn't budge more than four or five inches. Pushing even harder, I managed to get my foot round and made contact with the body on the other side that was stopping it going further. I squeezed through and checked. It was just another poor fucker in his twenties who wanted his mother.

I stumbled into a chair, moved round it and heard someone else moaning at my feet. Kneeling down, I got in there with the torch and turned the body over.

It was Tom, red brick dust over his face and head, red snot running from his nose, but alive. I'd thought this would be a cause to celebrate, but now I wasn't too sure. He didn't look good.

He was whimpering away in a world of his own, reminding me of the glue-sniffing kid in Narva. I checked him over to make sure he had all his limbs. 'You're OK, mate,' I said. 'You're all right. Come on.' He wouldn't have a clue what I was saying or who was saying it, but it made me feel better.

I brushed the crap from his face so at least he could open his eyes at some stage, then I reached under his armpits and dragged him out onto the landing, stopping twice to snort muck from my nose.

Still gripping him, I went down the stairs backwards. His feet bounced from step to step. He was out of it, still bound up in his own little world of pain and confusion, aware that he was being moved, but not really conscious enough to help.

We got clear of the brickdust and into the fresh air. Dumping him on the ground, I cleared my nose again and gasped clean air into my lungs.

'Tom. Wake up, mate. Tom, Tom . . .'

I grabbed a handful of snow and rubbed it over his face. Beginning to recover, he coughed and spluttered but still couldn't speak.

The flames coming from the generator building were licking hungrily at the barn door and dancing on the snow, illuminating us quite clearly.

Tom was wearing the same sweatshirt as when I last saw him, but he had no shoes or coat.

'Wait here, mate. Don't move, all right?'

As if.

I headed back into the dust-filled MTV room. The cries upstairs were getting louder. I wanted to get away from here before they sorted themselves out and the police or DTTS arrived.

I found the first body again, still smouldering. He hadn't been wearing a coat, but it was his footwear I was after. They weren't exactly walking boots, more like basketball trainers, but they'd do. Kicking and fumbling around, I also came across an AK and a coat amongst the shredded furniture.

Tom was lying spreadeagled on his back, exactly as I'd left him. I shook the dust out of what turned out to be a parka, and put it around him. The white trainers were about two sizes too big, but what the fuck, he only had to make it as far as the car.

As I began to pull them onto his feet he finally made a noise. He lifted a hand to wipe the shit from his face and saw me.

'Tom, it's Nick . . .' I shook his head. He would have been deafened by the explosion and I couldn't tell whether his hearing had come back yet. 'It's me – Nick. Get up, Tom. We have to get going.'

'Nick? Shit. What the fuck are you doing here? What the fuck happened?'

I finished tying his laces and slapped his feet. 'Get up now, come on.'

'What? What?'

I helped him up and into the parka. It was like dressing an exhausted child. 'Tom . . . '

He still couldn't hear.

'Tom . . . Tom . . .'

'Huh . . .?' He was trying to get an arm into a sleeve.

'I'll be back in a minute, OK?'

I didn't wait for a nod. Leaving him to it, I went back to retrieve my gloves. I found them just feet away from the first man I'd shot, who was now clearly dead.

Tom had sat down again in the snow. I got him upright, zipped up his parka, then helped him move slowly to the small gate leading to the derelict hangar.

'We've got to get a move on, Tom. Come on, let's go. There's a car just round the corner.'

Turning left onto the road, I checked for vehicle lights. I lengthened my stride, keeping a tight grip on Tom, holding him as if we were a couple out for the night, arm in arm.

Trying to keep upright on the ice as I urged him on, I looked behind me. The glow from the generator building was still visible, but the sky was no longer filled with flames. In the small amount of ambient light I could see Tom's face. He was in a bad way; his hair was sticking up all over the place, still covered in dust and blood, and he looked like the victim of a cartoon explosion.

'Tom?' I looked into his eyes for signs of acknowledgement but got none. 'We're going to the car. It's not far. Try to keep up with me, OK?'

I wasn't too sure what his answer was. Something between 'maybe' and 'what?'

His hearing had recovered a bit by the time we got to where I'd parked the car, but he still didn't know what day it was. I collapsed on my hands and knees, gulping in cold air. Fuck the teeth, my arse hurt even more now. But what hurt most of all was realizing that the car had gone.

My head spun. Maybe I had the wrong place? No, there were the tyre marks. There, too, were some other tyre marks; and besides my footprints there was a mass of others. The new tyre marks were very wide and deep, probably from a tractor. The fuckers; the pub-quiz team must have had the car away, along with my two spare weapons.

'Shit, the car's been nicked.' I wasn't too sure if I was informing Tom or trying to get my own head around it.

Tom was confused. 'You said—'

'I know what I said, but the car's gone.' I paused. 'Don't worry, it's not a drama.'

It was.

Chances were they hadn't even had to break into it, just hitch it up and slide the locked wheels across the ice. Mr and Mrs Fuck-up had been well and truly at home from the moment I first stepped into the Intercontinental Hotel.

For a second I wished I hadn't let the tyres down on all three vehicles in the genny building, then I remembered that by now they'd all be toast. The best thing I could hope for in this neck of the woods was another tractor, but if I lifted one I'd be making people aware that we were on the ground. In any case, we didn't have the time to search. There was only one option right now, and that was to walk it.

I got up off the ground. 'Tom, change of plan.'

Well, there would be once I'd worked one out. But first we had to get further away from the area, and quickly. At least the stars were now fully out and it was easier to see – and be seen.

Slowly coming to his senses, he stood there, arms crossed and hands tucked under his armpits, coughing up brick dust and waiting for my decision.

'Follow me.'

I started to move down the road, putting distance between us and the target. Tom trailed slowly behind. We'd gone about 400 metres as I sorted out a plan, then stopped and checked for Polaris, the North Star.

Tom was starting to spark up a bit more now that he was generating some warmth. He closed up to me as I gazed skyward. 'It was a fucking nightmare in there,' he muttered, 'but I knew Liv would get you to come—'

I cut in, hoping to shut him up. 'That's right, Tom. Liv's your fairy godmother.'

I didn't tell him what she had planned for midnight.

His hood was down and I could see steam coming off his thick red-bricked hair now that he had worked up a sweat. I pulled his hood up over his head to retain some of the body heat and checked the North Star again.

'Nick, what happened to ... you know ...? Fucking nightmare or what?'

'What?' I had a load of questions for him as well, but now wasn't the time or place.

'You know, the fence, the house. What was all that about?'

It just wasn't important right now. 'Tom.' I kept looking skyward, even though I'd finished up there.

'What?'

I gave him the thousand-yard stare. 'Shut–the–fuck–up.'

'Oh.'

I'd got the reply I wanted.

I confirmed the plan in my head for the last time before I actioned it. We'd head north and cross country until we hit the railway line. If we turned left along it, we'd be facing west, towards Tallinn. Then we would follow the tracks to a station and catch a train, maybe the first one out of Narva. I wasn't sure, but I thought it left there at about eightish in the morning, so we'd need to be at a station about an hour after that. Only once we'd reached Tallinn would I start to worry about how to get us both out of the country.

According to the Lion King, we had the best part of fourteen hours in which to cover what I guessed would be about 20Ks – not a problem so long as we got a move on.

Tom was still facing me, trying to work out why I was gazing at the heavens. I got in there before he had a chance to ask. 'We'll have to get back to Tallinn by train now.'

'Where's that then, mate? Aren't we going to Helsinki?'

I looked down, but I couldn't see his face. He had moved the wire sewn into the rim of his hood so the fur closed off his face, making him look like Liam Gallagher after a big night out.

'We are,' I said, 'but we've got to go to Tallinn first.'

From behind the fur came a muffled, 'Why's that?'

'It's the easiest way. We've got to move up to the railway track, get a train to Tallinn, then catch a ferry to Helsinki.'

I didn't even know if he was aware what country he was in. I got right up close so he could see me smiling, trying to make it sound not too much of a big deal.

His mind was obviously on other things as his voice came out of the darkness. 'Are they all dead? You know, that lot back there?'

'I think so. Most of them, anyway.'

'Shit, you killed them? Won't we get in trouble? You know, the law . . .'

I couldn't be arsed to explain, so I just shrugged. 'It was the only way I could get you out of the shit.'

His shoulders began to heave and I suddenly realized he was laughing. 'How did you know when to set the bomb off? I mean, I could have been killed if I hadn't been upstairs.' It was nervous laughter.

I looked up, searching for the North Star again so he couldn't see my face. 'You've no idea the trouble I went to, mate. Anyway, we'll talk about that later. We have to get a move on now.'

'How far, do you reckon?'

His parka hood was looking skyward, too, but he didn't have a clue what he was looking for. He started to shiver.

'Not far, Tom. Just a couple of hours. If we play our cards right, we'll be in a nice warm train carriage soon.'

Why tell him the truth now? I hadn't bothered to so far. 'You ready then?'

He was coughing up the last of the brick dust like a TB patient.

'Yeah, I s'pose so.'

I started down the road and he followed on behind. After just a couple of hundred metres we hit a treeline, about fifteen metres off the road on our left. I headed for it, leaving ridiculous amounts of tracks in snow which was up to my knees and sometimes waist high. It didn't bother me. Why worry about things you can't change?

I waited for Tom to catch up. The pace wasn't going to be anything to write home about. You have to move at the speed of the slowest; that's just how it is if you want to keep together. I wondered about improvising snow shoes by tying tree branches to our feet, but quickly decided against; these things look good on paper but in the dark it's just a pain in the arse to prepare and wastes time.

I looked up. Wispy clouds were starting to appear and scud across the stars.

Tom caught up and I allowed him a minute's rest before we moved on. I wanted to get out into the open fields before starting cross country, following Polaris. That way we'd give the compound a wide berth as we had to head north, back towards it.

At the end of the treeline, visibility was about fifty to sixty metres in the starlight. The landscape was white, fading to black. In the middle distance to my half left I could see the dim glow of the target area.

I felt the cold bite into my face as I looked up at the sky once more. Tom shuffled up next to me, knees buried in snow, standing so close that his breath merged with mine, losing itself in the wind. His hood was off again as he tried to cool down. I put it back up and slapped him on the head. 'Don't do that, you'll lose all the heat you've just generated.'

He pulled the fur around his face once more.

I tried to find a reference point on the ground north of us, but it was too dark. The next best thing was to pick a star on the horizon below Polaris and go for that – it was easier than constantly checking skywards. I got one, not as bright as some, but good enough.

'Ready?'

The hood moved and the material rustled as a head nodded about in there somewhere.

We headed north. The only positive thing I could think of was that the pain in my arse had now disappeared. Either that or it was even colder than I'd realized.

43

The ground beneath the snow was ploughed, so both of us kept slipping and falling on the angled, frozen furrows. The best way forward seemed to be to keep my feet low and push through the snow. I became the icebreaker and Tom followed in my wake; anything to speed him up.

Clouds drifted across the sky more frequently now, intermittently blotting out my guide on the horizon. Polaris, too, was in and out of cloud cover.

Tom lagged about ten metres behind, hands in pockets, head down. There was nothing to do but keep pushing north as the clouds moved faster and gained in mass.

After about an hour the wind began to pick up, attacking my face and tugging at my coat. It was time to put down the furry ear flaps.

Each time we lost direction, all I could do was keep heading in what I thought was a straight line, only to find that we were way off course when the cloud cleared. I felt like a pilot flying without instruments. Our trail through the snow must have been one long zigzag.

My major concern was that the wind and cloud would bring snow. If that happened, we'd lose our means of navigation, and without protection, catching the train would be the least of my worries.

With a bad feeling that we were going to be in even deeper shit very soon, I stopped when I found a natural dip and used my back to push a groove in the snow to get us out of the wind. I scraped a channel in the lip to act as my north marker before Polaris disappeared again.

Tom reached me as I dug myself in with my gloved hands. I expected him to follow my example, but when I turned he was having a piss, the steam and liquid disappearing almost immediately in the wind. He should have been retaining his warm body fluids at all costs, but I was too late. I went back to preparing our makeshift shelter. Stress hormones are released in cold weather, filling out the bladder more quickly. That's why we always seem to urinate more when it's cold. The problem is that you lose body heat and a serious thirst develops. Unless hot fluids are taken on board it's a vicious circle from there on in, with dehydration helping to bring down the body's core temperature. If your core temperature falls below 28.8 degrees C you will die.

Tom was done, and putting his hands back in his pockets he turned and collapsed arse first into the dip.

The wind hit the lip, sounding like one of the gods blowing across the neck of a bottle, and blasting the snow onto our backs and shoulders.

Tom's fur rim turned to me as I slid into the dip beside him.

I knew what he was going to ask.

'Not long now, mate,' I pre-empted. 'It's a bit further than I thought, but we'll have a rest here. When you start to get cold, tell me and we'll get moving again, OK?'

The hood moved, which I took to be a nod. He brought his knees up to his chest and lowered his head to meet them.

I bit off my gloves and held them between my teeth while I fumbled to tie the ear flaps under my chin, then I unzipped his parka a bit so he could ventilate, yet still retain his body heat. Finally, standing up into the wind, I undid my trousers and tucked everything back in, and pushed the bottoms of my heavy, wet jeans into my boots. It was a cold and uncomfortable process in wet, clingy clothes, but it was worth it. I would have lost heat doing it, but sorting my shit out always made me feel better.

As I was about to lie down again in the dip, I saw Tom tucking his hand into his sleeve and lifting some snow to his mouth. I put out a hand. 'That's off the menu, mate.'

I wasn't going to waste energy explaining why. Not only does it use up crucial body heat through melting it in your mouth, it also cools the body from the inside, chilling the vital organs. Nevertheless, water was going to be a problem. I put my gloves back on and scooped up a handful of snow, but only passed it over when I'd I worked it into a compressed ball. 'Suck on that. Don't eat it, OK?'

I looked at the sky. The cloud cover was now more or less total.

Tom soon lost interest in the ice ball, hunching once more into a foetal position, knees up by his chest, hands deep in his pockets and head down. His body was starting to shake, and I had to agree with him; I'd had better days out.

Now that we'd cleared the danger area and were resting for a while, it seemed the right time to ask him a few questions. I hoped it would help take his mind off the shit we were in. I also needed some answers.

'Why didn't you tell me you knew Valentin? I know you were trying to access Echelon at Menwith Hill for him.'

I couldn't see his reaction, but there was movement in the hood. 'I'm sorry, mate,' he mumbled. 'She's got me by the bollocks. I'm sorry, I really wanted to, it's just that . . . you know . . .'

His hood dropped down as if his neck muscles had lost control.

'You mean threats? Some kind of threat to you or your family?'

His shoulders jerked up and down as he fought to contain the sobs.

'Mum . . . Dad . . . and I've got a sister with kids, know what I mean? I wanted to tell you, Nick, honest I did, but . . . well, you know. Listen, it ain't Valentin doing this shit, mate. It's her; she's freelancing. He don't know a thing about it; she's just using his name, letting you think you're working for him.'

He didn't need to say any more. Things were suddenly making more sense to me than they had in a long time. That was why she'd been able to say yes straight away to the three million. That was why she'd insisted there was to be no contact with anyone apart from her. It even explained why she didn't want me to have a weapon: she probably thought that if I found out what was happening I'd use it against her.

'How did you get sucked back into all this?'

I waited for him to try to compose himself.

'Liv. Well, not her to begin with, but this bloke – Ignaty – he came and saw me in London. The day before you did.'

Where had I heard that name before? Then I realized. He was the underwriter; it had been his name on the piece of paper in Narva. So maybe Liv wasn't the only one of Val's people to be going freelance.

Now Tom had started babbling it was important not to ask the sort of questions that might suddenly make him realize he was saying too much.

I just said gently, 'What happened then, mate?'

'He said Liv had a job for me and that I'd be going to Finland. That someone would come and persuade me and all that stuff. I shat myself when I found out it was Echelon again, but I had no choice, mate. My sister and what have you ... Nick, you gotta help me. Please, she'll kill everyone if I don't sort this shit out. Please help me. Please.'

He wept into his hood.

'Tom ...'

He didn't register. Maybe his sobs were too loud for him to hear me.

531

'Tom. She wanted you dead. She *will* think you're dead if I tell her.'

His hood came up. 'You were going to kill me? Oh fuck, Nick. Don't . . . please don't . . .'

'I'm not going to kill you.'

He wasn't listening. 'I'm so sorry, Nick. She made me ask those questions. You know, in the train station. She wanted to know if you were gonna stitch her up or what. I had to do it. She knows everybody's addresses and everything. The bloke showed me pictures of my sister's kids. Honest, Nick, I wanted to tell you what was happening but . . .' His hood dropped back down as a new spasm took hold of him.

I felt like a priest in a confession box. 'Tom, listen. Really, I'm not going to kill you. It was me who got you out of there, remember?'

There was a small nod from within the hood.

'I'll make sure that you and your family are looked after, Tom, but we have to get back to the UK first. You'll have to talk with some people and tell them exactly what's been happening, at Menwith and here, OK?'

I sensed an opportunity for everything to work out whichever way this went. I wasn't exactly sure how, but there had to be a way that Tom could get a new life and I could get my money. And if the money didn't materialize, at least I could still work for the Firm. I could come up with enough bullshit to make it sound as if I'd known all along what was happening, but couldn't tell anyone because of the security risk of someone printing off the information I'd told them in Russia.

Liv need never know that Tom was alive, and I could still pick up my money and then go to Lynn. I knew it was flimsy as plans go, but it was a start – assuming she didn't stitch me up.

What was more important was getting out of Estonia. After that, I'd sit down with Tom, get the full story and sort my shit out.

'Why didn't she just tell me that it was you coming with me, rather than getting me to try and talk you into it? You were already coming, right?' His babbling before hadn't exactly explained it clearly.

'Fuck knows. You'll have to ask her. That's why I shat myself when I saw you. I thought your lot had heard about it. She's weird, mate. Did she talk as if it was all coming from Valentin?'

'Of course.'

'Well it ain't, she's talking about herself. It's all her own plans, mate, I'm telling yer. If Valentin knew he'd cut her in half, know what I mean?'

Well, not quite in half, but I bet he'd have her watching a few squirming eels before he'd finished with her.

For all that, there was a part of me that admired what she was doing. Maybe the man from St Petersburg was her feed in Val's set up, leaking her information to set this whole thing up? What was in it for her? What was her goal in all this? Maybe Tom was right, it was everything that she had talked about? Question after question leaped into my head, but the snowflakes hitting my face made me remember that there were more pressing matters to attend to.

We had no shelter, no heat and now no

navigation. The cold was getting to me as the sweat on my back began to cool rapidly now that we had been stationary for a while. Tom shivered badly where he sat curled up on the snow beside me. Both of us had inherited a layer of snow. We had to move, but in which direction? The marker would only be good for a hundred metres or so; after that, and without Polaris, we'd get disoriented and spend the rest of the night walking round in circles.

I looked at Tom and felt him shivering in almost uncontrollable bursts. His brain was probably telling him he must start moving, but his body was begging him to stay where he was and rest.

I lifted the cuff of various layers of clothing and had a quick look at the Lion King. Just under twelve hours to go until we should RV with the train. Even if I knew which direction to take, trying to cover that distance in these conditions without navigation aids would be madness. Visibility had worsened; it was down to about five metres. In any other circumstances we should have been digging in for the night and riding out the storm, but we didn't have the luxury of time. Quite apart from making it to a train, I didn't know what sort of follow-up the Maliskia would go for, and I didn't want to find out. Trying to think of a positive, I finally dredged one up; at least the snow would cover our trail.

Tom mumbled under his hood. 'I'm really cold, Nick.'

'We'll get going in a minute, mate.'

I was still racking my brain for some sort of

navigation aid. It had been years since I'd had to use or even remember any survival skills. Scrolling through the pages of crap in my head, I tried hard to call up what I'd learned all those years ago. I'd never been one for all that hundred-and-one-uses-for-a-shoelace stuff; I'd just got on with it and only did the snow-hole and snared-rabbit routine when I had to.

I put my arms around him. He wasn't too sure what was going on and I felt his body stiffen.

'It's a snow thing,' I said. 'We've got to keep warm.'

He leaned in towards me, shivering good style.

'Nick, I'm really really sorry, mate. If I'd told you the truth we wouldn't be in this shit, know what I mean?'

I nodded, feeling slightly uncomfortable. It wasn't all his fault. I'd have tried to drag his granny over that fence if it would have given me half a chance of pocketing 1.7 million.

'I'll tell you the best thing I've found to get over all this cold stuff,' I said, trying to sound as relaxed about it as possible.

From under the hood came a muffled, 'What's that, then?'

'Dream, mate. Just think to yourself that this will all be over soon. This time tomorrow you're going to be in a hot bath with a huge mug of coffee and a fat sticky bun. This time tomorrow you'll be laughing about all this shit.'

He kicked his heels into the snow. 'That's if these poxy trainers stay on.'

'Don't moan,' I said. 'They're better than those fucking stupid daps of yours.'

He started to laugh, but it turned into a cough.

I looked up and saw nothing but blankets of white tumbling down at us out of the blackness. If I'd had access to a genie at that moment, the one thing I'd have wished for was a compass.

Jesus, a compass. A compass can be made from any ferrous metal. It should have been so simple, but it seemed to take me for ever to work it out: Tom had a faceful of the stuff in the rim of his parka hood.

Could I use it? And if so, then what? It was like trying to remember the ingredients of a particularly complicated cake I'd been shown how to bake twenty years ago.

I tried hard to visualize the process, closing my eyes and thinking back to all those times when I'd got so bored making shelters, traps and snares with bits of string and picture wire.

Tom had other ideas. 'Let's go, Nick, I'm cold. Come on, you said . . .' He was clinging to me like a baby monkey on its mother's back. It was good, I needed him to warm me just as much as he needed me for reassurance.

'In a minute, mate. In a minute.'

Something had to be in the memory banks somewhere. We never forget anything; it can all be brought back to the surface if you press the right button.

It happened. The trigger was remembering being given a silk escape map in the Gulf, with a needle pinned in it.

'Tom, are you still wearing those silk thermals?'

He shook his head. My heart sank.

'Nah, just the top. I wish I did have the

bottoms, I'm freezing. Can we go now? You said to tell you, Nick, and I'm telling you.'

'Hang on a minute, mate, I've just had a great idea.'

I unwrapped my arm from him. As I moved, I was forcibly reminded of the awful discomfort of my wet clothing. My jeans clung to my legs and my T-shirt was cold and clammy.

I removed my glove, holding it in my mouth while I pulled out the Leatherman. Opening the pliers, I put the glove back on before the skin of my hand was exposed for too long.

'Look at me for a sec, would you, mate.'

The parka hood came up and the snow that had collected on it fell onto his shoulders.

Feeling around the frozen ring of fur with my gloved hand, I located the wire, then trapped it in the jaws of the pliers and squeezed until I felt it give. Teasing apart the material at the site of the cut, I exposed the metal, gripped one end of the cut with the pliers and pulled, grasping the exposed wire in my hand. I made another cut and put the two-inch strip inside my glove for safe keeping.

I thought Tom might have been interested, but he was concentrating 100 per cent on feeling cold and miserable.

Bending down some more, I peered into the darkness behind his hood. 'I need some of that silk, Tom.'

He shrugged. 'I don't have to take it off, do I?'

'Just unzip your coat a bit more so I can get a hand in. I'll be as quick as I can.'

His hands slowly came out of his pockets and

fumbled for the zip. In the end I shoved both of my gloves between my teeth so I could help him; then, having battled with numb fingers to open the blade of the Leatherman, I felt under his shirt.

He sat there like a tailor's dummy as I pulled at his clothing. I didn't have enough feeling in my hands to be gentle about it, and he flinched as my freezing fingers gripped the silk and came into contact with his skin.

My nose was streaming as I grabbed a handful of the vest and started cutting, pulling so hard that I nearly lifted Tom off the ground. I wanted to make sure the material ripped, so there were loose threads dangling.

The knife jerked as it made its final cut. Tom yelped as the tip of the blade flicked into his chest. He sat there with an exposed finger over his little cut, the snow settling on his hand.

I said, 'For fuck's sake, Tom, keep the heat in.'

He pulled his clothing together, shoving his hands back in his pockets, and dropping his head. 'Sorry.'

'I tell you what,' I zipped him up once more, 'I'm going to be a couple of minutes doing this. Why don't you do some exercises to get some heat going?'

'I'm all right. How much longer do you reckon to the train, Nick?'

I dodged the question. 'Come on, move about, it'll warm you up.'

He started to move as if he was snuggling under a duvet, but the only thing covering him was snow.

'No, Tom, you've got to get up and get your

body moving. Come on, we haven't got that far to go, but we won't make it if you start seizing up.' I shook him. 'Tom, get up.'

He hauled himself to his feet reluctantly as I brushed the snow from his shoulders. His fur rim was now a white ring of snow framing his face.

'Come on, with me.'

Hands in pockets, we started to play aerobics with his back to the wind, squatting down and standing up again, elbows out, flapping like demented chickens.

I kept my head down, protecting it from the wind as I got him to keep in time with me. 'Good stuff, Tom, now keep going, I won't be long.' I got back on my knees and into cover.

It was gloves-off time again as I lay them in the snow. I crouched over to protect myself from the snowstorm; my hands were so numb that I had to pull threads from the silk with my teeth. Once I'd teased out a decent bit – about five inches long – I put it between my lips and fished out the needle-sized length of wire from my glove. Tying the loose end of the silk shakily around the middle of the metal, I finally managed a knot on the fourth attempt.

Mr Motivator next to me grunted and groaned, but was sounding a bit happier. 'It's working, Nick. I'm getting warmer, mate!' He beamed, blowing out the snot from his nose.

I muttered encouragement through gritted teeth as I held the thread and wire, shaking the snow off my gloves and quickly putting them back on. My hands were now so wet they stuck to the inners.

After trying to get some blood circulating by clapping them together for a while, it was gloves-off time yet again. As I bit on the free end of silk thread with my teeth, it seemed to take for ever to grasp the dangling wire in one hand and the square of silk in the other. At last I began stroking the wire along the silk, repeating the motion over and over, always in the same direction. After about twenty strokes I stopped, making sure there were no kinks in the thread that would affect the balance of the metal once I let go.

I fished in my pocket for the torch, switched it on and put it in my mouth. Still crouching over it to make sure the wind wouldn't affect the thread and needle, I let go and watched it spin. The short length of wire eventually steadied, just moving slightly from side to side. I knew the direction of the North Star from my snow marker, which was now quickly disappearing in the storm, so all I had to do was identify which end of the wire, magnetized by the silk, was pointing north. I could tell the difference between the ends from the way the Leatherman had cut them.

The huffing and puffing went on behind me as I shivered and worked out what I was going to do next. Getting through this weather tonight was going to be a nightmare, but we absolutely had to be at that rail track by morning. In theory, moving cross country in these conditions was a huge no-no, but fuck the rules, it was too cold for them now. I didn't care about leaving sign; I needed roads to make distance, and besides, if Tom, or I, for that matter, started going down with hypothermia, we were more likely to find some form of shelter near a road. My new thought was to go west until we hit one, then hang a right and head north for the rail track. One of the few things I knew about this country was that its main highway, and the one and only rail track, ran east to west between Tallinn and St Petersburg. The roads on either side were bound to make their way to it eventually, like streams towards a river.

Nobody was going to see the torchlight in this weather so I turned it on again and looked down as I let the metal drop and had another check to make sure it still worked. As the compass needle oriented itself, I realized that the wind was doing its bit to help. It seemed to be prevailing from the west, so as long as I kept it in my face I would be heading the way I wanted.

I was ready to go, gloves back on, the silk in my pocket, the compass thread and needle wrapped round my finger. I turned to Tom, who was squatting up and down with a vengeance, his arms swinging wildly.

'OK, mate, we're off.'

'Not long now, Nick, eh?'

'No, not long. A couple of hours, tops.'

44

The gale had become a blizzard, bringing close to white-out conditions. I was having to stop every ten or so paces, rubbing the needle again with the silk to reactivate the magnetic effect before getting another navigation fix. In this visibility there was no way I could keep us moving in a straight line. We were vaguely zigzagging west, still hoping to hit a road.

We'd been going for about forty minutes. The wind was still head on and its stinging cold made my eyes stream with tears. I had nothing to protect my face with; all I could do was bury my head into my coat for a few moments' respite. Freezing flakes blasted their way into every gap in my clothes.

I still led the way, breaking the trail, then stopping, though no longer turning, to allow Tom to catch up. When I heard him move up behind me I'd go on a few more steps. This time I did stop, turning my back to the wind, and I could just make him out coming towards me in the storm. I'd been so concerned about navigating that I hadn't noticed how much he was slowing down.

I crouched over on my knees to protect the silk and magnetized the wire while I waited.

He finally got level with me as I was trying to stop the wind affecting the compass, which was dangling from my mouth. His hands were buried into his pockets and his head was down. I grabbed hold of his parka and pulled him down next to me, positioning him so he could give the compass some shelter, too.

I wrapped up the compass but this time didn't get to my feet, instead I just stayed where I was and shivered with Tom, both of us bent over in the snow. The snow that had built up on the outside of his hood had frozen, and my hat probably looked the same, matching the front of our coats.

'You OK, mate?'

It was a bone question, but I couldn't think of anything else to say.

He coughed and shivered. 'Yeah, but my legs are really cold, Nick. I can't feel my feet. We're gonna be OK, aren't we? I mean, you know all about this outdoors stuff, don't ya?'

I nodded. 'It's a fucker, Tom, but just dig deep, mate. It's not going to kill us.' I was lying. 'Remember what I said? Dream, that's all you have to do. Dream, and this time tomorrow – you know the rest, don't you?' His iced-up fur moved in what I took to be agreement as I added, 'We'll be on a road soon and the going will get much easier.'

'Will we get a car when we get to the road?'

I didn't answer. A nice warm vehicle would be heaven, but who would be mad enough to be out here on a night like this?

543

I struck out into the snow and he reluctantly followed.

We had a result about twenty minutes later. I couldn't see any tarmac, but I could make out the shape of tyre ruts under the newly fallen snow, and the fact that the snow suddenly wasn't as deep as it had been everywhere else. It was only a single-track road, but that didn't matter. It could be enough to save our lives.

I started to jump up and down on the spot to make sure I was right. Tom took a long time to catch up, and when he arrived I could see his condition had worsened.

'Time to sort yourself out, Tom. New phase, just jump up and down and get the body going.' I tried to turn it into a bit of a game and he half-heartedly joined in.

It wasn't that long ago that he'd been crying. Now it was sarcasm. 'Not long to go now, I s'pose?'

'No, not long at all.'

We started to make distance, huddling together at junctions to protect the compass. Whether a road ran north-east, north-west or even due west, we took it. Anything to get us in the general direction of Tallinn and the rail track.

After about three hours Tom had slowed down dramatically. I was having to stop more and more and wait for him to close up on me. The fight through the snow and the extreme cold had definitely got to him and he couldn't stop shivering.

He pleaded with me. 'I've had it, Nick. Everything's spinning around me, mate. Please, we have to stop.'

The wind whipped the snow against our faces. 'Tom, we must keep going. You understand that, don't you? We're fucked if we don't.'

The only reaction from him was a moan. I pulled his hood apart so he could see me.

'Tom, look at me!' I pulled his chin up. 'We must go on. You must help me by keeping going, OK?' I moved his chin again, trying to get eye-to-eye. But it was too dark, and every time the wind got into my eyes they started to water.

It was pointless trying to get any sense out of him. We were wasting time and losing what little heat we had by just standing still. There was nothing I could do to help him here and now. Our best bet was to get to the railway track and make the final push to a station. I wasn't too sure how many Ks we still had to cover, but the most important thing was to get there. I'd know when he'd finally had enough, and that would be the time to stop and take some action.

I grasped his arm and pulled him along. 'You've got to dig deep, Tom.'

We moved on, me with my head down and Tom past caring. It wasn't a good sign. When the body starts to go into hypothermia, the central thermostat responds by ordering heat to be drawn from the extremities into the core. This is when your hands and feet start to stiffen. As the core temperature drops, the body also draws heat from the head, circulation slows down and you don't get the oxygen or sugar your brain needs.

The real danger comes from the fact that you don't realize it's happening; one of the first things hypothermia does is take away your will to help yourself. You stop shivering and you stop worrying. In fact, you are dying, and you couldn't care less. Your pulse will get irregular, drowsiness will give way to semi-consciousness, which will eventually become unconsciousness. Your only hope is to add heat from an external source – a fire, a hot drink or another body.

Another hour passed. Soon I had to push Tom from behind. He took a few steps forward, stopped and complained bitterly. I grabbed his arm and dragged him. At least the extra effort warmed me up a bit. The cold was taking its toll on me, too.

We moved on, painfully slowly. When I stopped to check direction, Tom couldn't help me any more; he just stood on the spot, swaying, as I turned my back to the wind, trying to create shelter for the compass.

'You OK, mate?' I shouted behind me. 'Not far now.'

There was no reply, and when I'd finished and turned for him he'd collapsed in the snow. I got him to his feet and dragged him on. He had almost no strength left now, but we had to crack on. Surely there couldn't be that far to go?

He mumbled to himself as I pulled him along. Suddenly he stopped resisting and ran forward with a burst of manic energy.

'Tom, slow down.'

He did, but only to stagger a few metres off to

the side of the road and lie down. I couldn't run to him; my legs couldn't carry me that fast any more.

When I got to him I saw that the trainer on his right foot was missing. His feet were so numb that he hadn't noticed.

Shit, it had been there minutes ago. As I'd dragged him along and protected my face from the wind, his trainers had been the only things I'd seen.

I turned back down the road and retraced his quickly disappearing sign. I found the shoe and trudged back to him, but getting it back onto his foot was not far short of impossible, my numb fingers trying to tie the laces which were frozen with ice. I touched my little finger to my thumb to make the old Indian sign that means 'I'm all right'. If you can't do that, you're in trouble.

'You've got to get up, Tom. Come on, it's not that far.' He didn't have a clue what I was saying.

I helped him to his feet and dragged him on. Now and again he would shout out and summon up another burst of energy – fuck knows from where. It didn't last for long before he slowed down or fell back into the snow with exhaustion and despair. His voice had become a whine as he begged to be left where he was, pleading with me to let him sleep. He was in the latter stages of hypothermia and I should be doing something about it. But what, and where?

I pushed him on. 'Tom, remember mate, DREAM!' I doubted he understood a word I was saying. I felt sorry for him, but we couldn't rest now. If we stopped for even a few minutes we might not restart.

It was about fifteen minutes later that we stumbled onto the railway line, and only by chance did I notice it. We'd reached a level crossing and I had tripped over one of the tracks. Tom wasn't the only one losing his core heat and spiralling down through the spectrum of hypothermia.

I tried to summon some enthusiasm to celebrate, but I couldn't manage any. Instead I shook him. 'We're here, Tom. We're here.'

No reaction whatsoever. It was obvious that what I said would make little difference to him now anyway. Even if he showed any awareness, what was there to get excited about? We were still in the shit – wet, freezing cold, with no shelter, and I didn't know how or where we were going to get on the train, even if it turned up.

He collapsed on the crossing next to me. I bent down and got my hands under his armpits, heaving him up again and nearly collapsing myself in the process.

He couldn't control his mouth or teeth and began to make strange snorting noises.

'We have to keep going just a bit further,' I shouted into his ear. 'We have to find a station.'

I didn't know any more whether it was him or myself I was talking to.

I turned him left, towards Tallinn.

We staggered west, over the snow-covered hardcore at the side of the track. At least the trees on either side gave us some protection from the howling wind. It was thirty minutes? an hour? since we'd got onto the track. I didn't know; I'd given up clock-watching long ago.

Tom started to go crazy, screaming at the trees, crying, apologizing to them, only to fall down again and try to cuddle up in the snow. Each time, I had to pick him up and push on, and each time it got a little bit harder.

We came across a row of small sheds, visible only because of the flatness of the snow on top of their angled roofs. We still couldn't see further than about five metres and I didn't notice them until we were right on top of them.

I fumbled excitedly for the torch, leaving Tom on his knees, shouting at the trees that were coming to get him.

It seemed to take for ever to press the switch. Soon my fingers wouldn't be able to perform even a simple task like that.

I shone the light around and saw that the sheds were made of wood and built in the form of a terrace, the door of each facing onto the track. Most were clamped shut with old rusty padlocks, but one was unlocked. After kicking the snow away, I pulled it open and turned round for Tom.

He was curled up in the snow on the track and pleading to be allowed to sleep. If he did there would be no waking up.

As I gathered him in my arms, he lashed out with his final reserves of strength. He was having a fit. It was pointless struggling with him; I simply didn't have the energy. I let him drop to the ground and, gripping his hood with both hands, pulled him along like a sledge, stumbling backwards and falling over with the effort.

I didn't talk to him any more; I didn't have the strength.

The door was so low that I had to bend down to get in, and the roof wasn't much higher, but the instant I was out of the wind I began to feel warmer. The shed was about eight feet square, and the floor was cluttered with bits of wood and brick, old tools and a rusted shovel with a half-broken shaft, crap from over the years lying on a frozen mud floor.

Tom just lay where I dropped him. As I put the torch down to give me some light I could see him curled up in a ball, his hands exposed, wrists bent as if he had suddenly developed severe arthritis. His short, sharp breaths mixed with mine and looked like steam in the torchlight. Not long now and he would be history unless I got a grip on myself and sorted him out.

If only this was a hunter's cabin, not a rail worker's shed. It's the custom in extremely cold climates to leave kindling in huts so that someone in trouble can rewarm themselves quickly. It's also the custom to leave a box of matches with the ends sticking out so that frozen, numb fingers can grasp them.

I got my gloves off and started to fantasize about warm train carriages and hot mugs of coffee. I dragged over a lump of wood that looked as if it used to be part of the panelling. I then played about with my Leatherman with shaking hands, trying to pull out the blade. Once my soaking gloves were back on I started to scrape at the edge of the wood. I wanted to get to the dry stuff underneath.

Tom filled the room with his screams and cries. It was as if he was speaking in tongues.

I yelled just as loudly, 'Shut the fuck up!' but wherever he was, it was a place where he couldn't hear me.

Once I'd cut away the damp stuff and exposed the dry wood I started to scrape thin shavings onto the shovel face. This was the tinder. My hands hurt as I tried to keep a firm grip.

Tom's body had started jerking around in the corner of the hut. We both needed to get this fire burning soon, but I couldn't rush what I was doing or I'd fuck up completely.

Next task was to cut kindling, a stage up from tinder, so that larger bits of wood could then be placed in the fire and stand a chance of catching. I picked up any sticks of wood I could find, and also pulled off some of the roof lining and tore it into strips. It would burn well because it was partly coated with tar. Then, with the rest of the small bits of wood, I started to make fire sticks, cutting very thinly into the side of the wood and pushing out the shavings until each piece looked as if it had grown feathers.

Tom was no longer thrashing around on the floor. Mumbling incoherently to himself, he was kicking out, as if fending off an imaginary attacker. It was pointless talking to him. I needed to concentrate on building the fire. Survival training might not be my strong suit, but I knew about fire. It had been my job to make up the one in the front room every morning before my stepdad got out of bed, otherwise it was slapping time. Usually it was slapping time anyway.

Once I'd prepared about five fire sticks I stacked them around the tinder like tepee poles. Then I got out my pistol, taking off the magazine and pulling the topslide to eject the round in the chamber.

Using the pliers of the Leatherman, I eventually pulled the heads off the three rounds and poured the dark grain propellant onto the tinder. My hands were shaking as I poured, trying my best to get it over the wood and not the mud. I left the third round half full of propellant.

Tom's frenzied movements had dislodged his hood. Placing the round carefully on the ground so I wouldn't lose its contents, I got up and crawled over to him, my muscles protesting now that they'd had a rest. My cold, wet clothes clung miserably to me as I moved.

I got hold of his hood and tried to pull it back on. He lashed out with his arms, shrieking stuff I couldn't understand, his hands flailing around and knocking my hat off. I collapsed on top of him, trying to control him as I got his hood back up and my iced hat back on.

'It's all right, mate,' I soothed. 'Not long now. Remember to dream. Just dream.' But I was wasting time here. It was heat he needed, not bullshit.

Crawling back to the shovel, I dug inside my glove for the compass silk, held it in my teeth and cut some off with my Leatherman scissors. Then, using the screwdriver, I rammed the cut silk into the half-empty case as wadding on top of the propellant.

552

I loaded the round into the weapon, pointed it at the ground, and fired. The signature was a dull *oomph*.

There was no reaction from Tom as I knelt on the ground to pick up a glowing, smouldering bit of silk. Once it was in my fingers I waved it about gently to fan the glow, then put it into the tinder. The propellant flared, lighting up the whole hut. I must have looked like a witch making spells.

Once the tinder had caught, I started inserting more little bits through the fire sticks into the flame. It wasn't yet giving out much heat; that wouldn't happen until the tinder was hot enough to ignite the fire sticks. I got in close and blew gently.

The fire sticks started to crackle and hiss as they released their moisture and smoke. I could smell burning wood. I fussed around the flames on my hands and knees, carefully placing wood for the best effect as the hut filled with smoke and my eyes started to water.

The flames were now higher and threw dancing shadows on the walls of the hut. I could feel the heat on my face.

I had to get more wood before all my good work was undone. I looked around and gathered up as much as possible from what was to hand. Once I'd established the fire, I'd be able to venture outside into the howling wind for more.

I kicked the door open slightly to get rid of the smoke. It let some of the wind and snow whistle in, but it had to be done. I'd block up most of the gap as soon as I could.

Tom was much quieter. I crawled over to him, coughing smoke from my lungs. I wanted to see if there was any wood under him or in the corner. There was; only a few bits and pieces, but it all helped. I couldn't make a big fire as the hut was too small, and besides, we wouldn't need it; the walls were so close that the heat would bounce straight back on us anyway.

I checked the flames and started to feed on some more wood. 'Not long now, mate. We'll be getting our kit off in a minute because we're so hot.'

My next priority would be a hot drink, to get some heat directly to Tom's core. Placing the rest of the wood near the fire to dry it out, I turned and looked at his face. 'Tom, I'm just going to see if I can find something to heat snow in for a—'

He was lying too still. There was something very odd about the way his legs had now curled up to his chest.

'Tom?'

I crawled back to him, pulling him over and getting the hood off his face. Illuminated by the flames it told me all I needed to know. Tilting his head towards the fire, I pulled open his eyelids. There was no reaction to the light. Both pupils stayed as fully dilated as a dead fish's. It wouldn't be long now before they clouded up.

I could hear the fire sticks now collapsing on each other, with glowing embers as well as flame. It was a wonderful sight, but it was too fucking late.

I tried his carotid pulse. Nothing. But that could be just my numb fingers. I listened for breathing and even tried his heart. Nothing. His mouth was still open from when he had taken, or fought for, his last breath. I gently closed his jaw.

It was time to think about me. Pulling off my wet clothes, I wrung them out one by one before putting them back on.

I sat and fed the flames some more, knowing there were still things that I should do to him. I should try to resuscitate and reheat him until I was so exhausted I couldn't carry on, in the million-to-one chance he could be revived. But for what? I knew he was dead.

Maybe if we'd dug in for the night once the weather had closed in he would still be alive. We would have been in a desperate state in the morning, but maybe he would have survived. Maybe if I hadn't pushed him so hard to get here, or had realized what condition he was in and had stopped earlier. All these questions, and the only thing I was certain of was that I had killed him. I had fucked up.

I looked at his limp body, its mouth reopened, his long hair wet against his cheeks, the ice crystals on his bum fluff now melting down his face. I'd try and remember a gobby but happy Tom, but I knew this image was the one that would stay with me. It was going straight to the top of the list of my sweaty, guilty, wake-up-in-the-early-hours nightmares. When I was put into the counselling programme the Firm sets up for operators now and again, I'd told the shrinks I didn't have them. I was talking bollocks, of course. Maybe it was a good thing I was going to be part of Kelly's treatment now. I started to realize I might need it just as much as her.

Dragging him to the doorway, I sat him up against the gap, leaving a space of a foot or so above him for the smoke to escape. I covered his face with his parka.

Feeling was already starting to come back to my extremities and I knew I was going to be OK. All I had to do was find a station.

I turned back to the flames and watched the steam rise from my drying clothes. There would be no sleep for me tonight. I had to keep the fire going.

45

LONDON, ENGLAND
Wednesday, 5 January 2000

I was nursing a hot frothy Starbucks in the church doorway opposite the Langham Hilton, the only place I could keep a trigger on the hotel and also keep out of the drizzle.

It was breakfast time, and the pavements were packed with overcoated wage slaves throwing Danish pastries and coffee down their necks, and shoppers out early for the sales. Judging by the frenzy, it was clear the Y2K bug hadn't brought the world to its knees after all. It had been the last thing on my mind as I'd seen in the new century aboard an Estonian fishing boat, along with twenty-six cold and seasick illegals from Somalia. Slipping away from a seaside village under cover of darkness, we'd battled across the Baltic in huge seas, heading for a peninsula east of Helsinki. Lion King told me it was midnight as we approached the Finnish coastline, where we were suddenly treated to one of the finest fireworks displays I'd ever seen. The whole place seemed to light up as towns all along the shore celebrated the new millennium. I wondered if it held in store any new beginnings for me. Christ, I hoped so.

It was eighteen days since I'd left the hut and set off again into the blizzard. Tom had stayed behind, parka draped over his face, his body sterile of any item that could ID him. They probably wouldn't find him before the spring. I only hoped they'd give him a decent burial. If things worked out well here in London, maybe I'd go back and see to it all myself. Man down and all that.

At first light, and without Tom, I was able to make distance at my own pace, even in the driving snow, and it was only a couple of hours before I hit a station about six or seven Ks away.

A train arrived heading west, towards Tallinn, but I let it go without me.

The one after that was heading east, towards Russia, and I climbed aboard. Without a passport it could take weeks to get out of Estonia on my own, but with Eight helping me, maybe it would be a different story. That was why I jumped off at Narva, and that was how I'd ended up on the fishing boat with my new Somalian friends. It had cost me all the dollars in my boot and had meant spending several uncomfortable days and nights hiding in the apartment with the land-mines while Eight got things arranged, but it had been worth it.

Eight wasn't too happy about his car becoming history, but he still seemed thrilled to help me, even though he must have been aware of what had happened to Carpenter and the old guy in Voka, and put two and two together. I wondered if he gave a shit.

Eight didn't ask me again about helping him to escape to England, but as I stood on the jetty waiting to board the fishing boat, I turned to him and handed over Tom's passport. From the expression on his face and the tears in his eyes, you'd have thought I'd given him the three million.

I knew I was taking a big risk, but I felt I owed him that much. I just hoped he did a good job of doctoring Tom's picture, or that the day he tried to use it, immigration weren't checking their computer screens too closely. Otherwise poor Eight would find himself being lifted by a team of heavies and whisked off to a 3x9 sooner than he could say 'Crazy boy'.

I'd told myself then that the passport was part of what I owed him for his help, along with a new car. But now, standing in London with a hot coffee in my hands and time to think, I knew it was more to do with trying to get over my guilt about Tom. I had pushed him beyond his limits in outrageous conditions and I'd killed him. Giving Eight the possibility of a new life was an attempt to square my conscience and make things right: the job was done, now cut away.

At first I thought it had worked and that things were all right. But I knew they weren't, not with Tom, not with Kelly. She was much the same; the New Year had passed her by, too. I'd phoned the clinic twice in the two days since I'd got back. I'd lied both times, telling them I was overseas but would be back soon. I was desperate to see her, but I just couldn't face it yet. I knew I wasn't going to be able to look her in the eye. Hughes picked up the phone the second time and told me that her plans for Kelly's therapy sessions, which included me, would have to stay on hold until I got back. I still felt confused about it. I knew it had to be done, and I wanted to do it, but . . .

To add to the confusion, I'd also had a call from Lynn. He wanted to see me this afternoon. There seemed to have been a change of heart since our last meeting. He said he had a month's work for me. I'd been tempted to tell him where he could shove his £290 a day, because if all went well with Liv this morning, I'd never have to depend on the Firm again. But there was no guarantee that she was going to appear, and though a month's pay wasn't much, at least I would be working instead of thinking.

The exchange was going to be simple. I'd opened a bank account in Luxembourg by telephone as soon as I returned to the UK. The message I'd left Liv in the Helsinki DLB was that she'd be required to move the money electronically using a Fed-wire reference, which would guarantee the transfer within hours. When we met in the hotel in a few minutes' time, she would call her bank with the transfer instructions I would give her, and then we'd both just sit and wait until it happened. I would call Luxembourg each hour giving my password and would be told when the money had been deposited. In my own mind I'd set a cut-off time of four p.m. If she hadn't turned up by then, I had to assume she never would. Then it would be decision time about her, and how to go about contacting Val to explain what Mr and Mrs Liv's little girl had been getting up to.

As my parting shot when I was sure the money had gone through, I'd toyed with the idea of revealing that I'd saved Tom's life and that he'd told me the whole story, just for the satisfaction of letting her know she hadn't outsmarted me. After all, I intended having nothing further to do with ROC. All I wanted was the money, and then they could carry on blowing up buildings and ripping people's guts out for all I cared. Deep down, however, I knew that telling her would achieve nothing except to put me in the shit. She hadn't got as far as she had without damaging a few bodies, and I didn't want to be the next one on the list.

Twenty minutes before the RV time, a taxi pulled up at the hotel's main entrance.

As I watched, Gunga Din stepped forward and opened the cab door, and I saw the back of Liv's head as she got out and went inside. We had the taxi between us, but I could see she had decided on the jeans today, together with her long leather coat, collar up against the cold.

I let her go in and watched for any surveillance or another vehicle pulling up shortly afterwards. Neither happened. I waited, elated. She was here. She wouldn't have come all the way to London just to announce that she was stitching me up.

The three million was now so close I could almost smell it. I had earned this money. No, after a lifetime of shovelling shit for peanuts, I *deserved* it. I'd been working hard to control my excitement as I stood in the doorway, but now I reckoned it wouldn't hurt to let myself enjoy the moment. I ran through my game plan one more time. As soon as the transfer was confirmed and Liv and I had said our goodbyes, I'd call the clinic and tell them that Kelly's new treatment could start straight away. It still worried me a bit, but I'd just have to get on with it. Who knows, I might even sort myself out.

Hughes had said there was no telling how long the therapy would go on for, so I'd been thinking it might be a good investment to buy a little flat near by and sell it afterwards. I could also start throwing a few builders at my house in Norfolk and get it sorted for when Kelly was ready to come home.

Less than ten minutes to go now. She still had to unload the DLB under the telephone, which held the keycard for the suite I'd booked. I'd also left instructions to place the 'Do Not Disturb' sign on the door handle once she entered. I waited and watched. There was nothing to see, apart from a woman getting splashed by a passing bus.

I could almost feel the three million between my fingers as I counted it in my mind. For about a millisecond I thought about giving Tom's share to some kind of charity. For a millisecond. Because then I saw Kelly again, sitting like a frozen statue in the clinic and staring into space. Fuck it, she needed all the charity she could get.

With just two minutes to go, I dodged the traffic and approached the hotel. Gunga Din wasn't there to help me as I pushed past the revolving doors and into the warmth of the foyer. The marble reception area was teeming with businessmen and tourists. I walked around them, past the Chukka Bar and the reception desk, then took the stairs.

I climbed to the third floor, opening my leather jacket and checking the position of the USP, tucked centre front of my jeans. I'd gone back to Norfolk last night specifically to pick up a weapon, and had found myself mopping up the worst of the flooding that had come through the hole in the roof. Still, it wouldn't be long now before that useless tarpaulin was replaced by solid Welsh slate.

Outside the door of room 316 I stopped and listened. Nothing.

I pushed my own keycard into the lock and opened the door.

She was at the far end of the living room, her back to me, looking out of the windows that overlooked the main entrance. The door closed behind me with a gentle click.

'Hello, Liv, it's really good to—'

I went to open my coat to draw down, but knew it was useless. The overcoated body that had moved out from behind the cabinet housing the TV and minibar already had his pistol on me. The other body that sprang from the toilet to my left was no more than four feet away, his weapon at my head.

I released my grip on the leather and let my arms drop to my sides instead of raising them. There could still be a chance to draw.

Liv turned towards me, only it wasn't her.

She spoke in a soft accent which I couldn't identify. 'Step forward and keep your hands high in the air, please.'

I did as I was told. The toilet man moved

behind me and started to run his hands over my back and legs. It was pointless trying to bullshit them. As he removed my USP I couldn't exactly claim I was just delivering room service.

She said nothing as I was pushed from behind towards the settee. Cabinet man stayed where he was, to my right. The other one was somewhere behind me.

The woman pushed past and headed for the door to the corridor. Her blond hair was dyed; I could see her brown eyebrows.

As she opened it I could see another overcoated man outside. She left and he came in. He'd been there to block the exit if anything went wrong during the lift. It wouldn't have been hard for him to stop me. He more or less matched the dimensions of the door.

Nothing was said as I sat and waited. But for what? I remembered Sergei's face in the 4x4 as he told me about the Viking's revenge. My heart was starting to pound big time.

Where the fuck was Liv? Had she been lifted too? Were these guys the Maliskia? The three square heads didn't speak or move. A feeling of dread came over me. Were they NSA? Was I really in Big Boy shit?

The pulses in my neck kicked up a gear and, not for the first time on this job, I could feel them pumping against my collar. The human door, who was still standing by the real one, must have seen it and recognized the feeling, because he gave me a knowing smile. I did my best to return it. Fuck 'em. I wasn't going to let them see how much I was flapping inside.

* * *

Long minutes that felt like eternity passed, then there was a knock. The human door looked through the peephole, immediately reached for the handle, then stepped reverentially aside.

'Hello, Nick,' Val said as he entered. With him was Liv's trainstation contact. They both wore dark-grey suits. 'May I introduce Ignaty?'

Ignaty smiled and bowed his head slightly towards me. 'Hello, Nick, I never managed to meet you personally at the station, but knowing so much about you, I feel as if we are old friends.'

I nodded back, not wanting to say a word yet as my mind was too busy working out what the fuck was going on. I was scared, confused and beginning to realize that I was in serious trouble. My best bet was to shut up and play stupid. That wouldn't be hard.

Val sat on the settee opposite, while Ignaty stayed on his feet and fell in behind. The Chechen looked into my eyes for just a bit too long for my liking, and then he placed a large white envelope on the coffee table that lay between us. 'That', he pointed, 'is for you.'

I reached for it, more confused than ever, and pulled open the flap. He settled himself into the settee and adjusted his suit trousers before crossing his legs. Inside was a sheaf of documents in Cyrillic. I stared at them for a long time, not knowing what the fuck they were.

'They are deeds for two apartment blocks in St Petersburg,' he said. 'Their combined worth exceeds three million sterling. I thought you'd prefer an appreciating asset to cash.'

565

My mental calculator was working overtime. I was a few weeks in credit with the clinic, but the bills would soon be racking up again. The three weeks that I'd been away would already have cost me £12,000, and I'd soon be running on empty. One month with the Firm at £290 a day would earn me precisely £8,700. I might as well chance my luck.

'I'd rather have the cash. That was the arrangement.'

He shook his head slowly, as if he was about to tell a child the trip to Disneyland was cancelled. 'But, Nick, there was no arrangement. Liv has been deceiving us both in pursuit of her own greed.' His eyes suddenly went twenty degrees colder, demonstrating with a single glance why he was the top man to be afraid of in his line of work. 'Thankfully some are not as disloyal.' He waved his hand behind him.

Ignaty looked smug.

I stared at them, as if I didn't have a clue what he meant.

'It is quite complicated, Nick, and you really don't need to know the details. Suffice to say, not only did she betray the trust that I had placed in her, she has now made it virtually impossible for me to access the Echelon dictionaries for a very long time. The only reason *you* are still alive is that you thought you were acting on my instructions.'

The smile returned. 'Come, work for me in Russia and you can then take advantage of your new property portfolio. The rents are extremely high in that part of the city. This is a fantastic opportunity for you, Nick. There might even be time for us to get together so that I can explain this whole sorry affair.'

I shook my head. 'I have things that keep me here.' I hesitated. 'I really could do with the money instead.'

He pointed to the envelope still in my hand as if I hadn't even spoken. 'In there are the details of a contact, here in the United Kingdom, when you wish to come to Russia.'

He stood up, and everyone moved with him.

I had to ask. 'How did you know I was here?'

Val stopped just as the human door was about to open the real one. 'Liv told me, of course. She told me everything.' He paused. 'Before Ignaty . . .' He shrugged. His smile hadn't disappeared. He waited to see my reaction.

I bluffed it and looked even more confused, but in my mind's eye I saw her belly slit open and the eels writhing all around her.

'It shocks you?'

I shook my head.

'I didn't think so. You see, I cannot be seen to exhibit such a lack of judgement about the people close to me. I must show strength. You could help me do that when you come to Russia, Nick. Think about it, won't you?'

I nodded, just wanting him to leave.

'She did mention your apology for the deaths of my nephews.'

I nodded. 'Yes, I'm sorry.'

'Don't be. I never really cared for my sister's family. I hope to see you in St Petersburg soon, Nick.'

As he turned to leave, I said, 'Can I ask one more thing?'

He stopped.

'There's a body. My friend. It's still in Estonia and . . .'

'Of course, of course. We are not barbarians.' Val waved a hand at the envelope. 'The contact. Give him the details.'

I lay on the settee for the next fifteen minutes, trying hard not to think about how long it must have taken Liv to die. It certainly took the edge off my enthusiasm for the St Petersburg property market.

I needed the money, but I wasn't too sure about anything now, apart from the fact that the meeting with Lynn wouldn't be the best moment to fuck the Firm off.

I gave Val and his boys another five before walking downstairs and out of the hotel. Then I went into one of the phone boxes under the scaffolding and fed in a fistful of coins as I picked up the receiver.

'Hello, East Anglian Properties. How may I help you?'

'James Main?'

'Speaking.'

'Nick Stone here. Slight change of plan, James. I want you to sell the house as soon as you can, for anything you can get.'

'But all the offers so far have been well below your purchase price. You'd do much better if you got the roof finished and the interior work done, then put it on the market in the spring. It would be a—'

'Straight away, James.'

'But I was driving past the place only a couple of days ago and there's still a tarpaulin over the roof. Really, nobody's going to offer anything like—'

'James?'

'Yes?'

'Which bit of straight away don't you understand, for fuck's sake?'

I only had to put a twenty pence piece in for the second call. It was to a London number.

'Still abroad, I'm afraid,' I said when I was finally put through to Hughes. 'Looks like I'm going to have to stay here for another month. What effect would that have on Kelly?'

'Well, she won't get any worse, let's put it that way. She'll stay more or less exactly as she is until you can start the sessions with her.'

Exactly as she is.

I closed my eyes and tried so hard to see her looking at me and smiling, but the only image that came to me was of her on that chair, her head strangely tilted, and sitting so still it was as if she'd stopped breathing, or had been frozen to death in an invisible blizzard.

I had hours to kill before seeing Lynn and so I ended up walking all the way to Vauxhall Cross. As I walked, I thought about the two other phone calls I might have to make very soon. One was to her grandparents, to break the news that they might have to sell their house as well, though there was more chance of being struck by lightning. They'd nodded and agreed so far that Chelsea was the best place for Kelly, but I bet they'd suddenly discover how wonderful the NHS was when I told them they'd have to start shouldering some of the cost.

The other would be to the friend who'd put me onto the freelance job against Val. I'd ask him if he had more work going, and this time somewhere warm, like the Bahamas.

The same Asian guy ushered me into Lynn's office. Nothing had changed apart from the fact that Lynn had a different shirt on and wasn't writing this time. I stood in front of his desk. Once again, there was no coffee on offer, so I knew I was in for another short meeting.

'It's my last few weeks in post, and quite frankly the last person I wanted to see was you.' He sat and stared at me, with an expression that said I was 100 per cent responsible for his early retirement. I felt sorry for the mushrooms.

I knew to just keep my mouth shut and listen.

'Moonlight Maze,' he said. 'Do you know anything about it?'

'No.' I felt the sharp pain in my chest once again. He knew what I had been doing. He knew and was letting me drop myself in the shit. I had to play along. 'Well, not really. Only what I read in the papers a couple of weeks ago.'

'That's about to change. Your job is to assist an NSA officer and his team while in the UK. They will be here for about a month, trying to stop this dammed ROC infiltration into Menwith.'

I nodded, as if I assumed it would be a boring

BG-cum-escort-cum-tour-guide job, which these things normally are. But I still had the feeling he was playing games with me. 'Why me, Mr Lynn? You said before Christmas that—'

'It has been deemed that the cost of your training and retainer is not being effectively utilized. Now get out.'

I didn't know how he did it, but the door behind me was opened by the Asian guy right on cue. 'Please, sir, follow me.'

I did and we went up two flights in the lift to the briefing area and into a sparsely furnished, unoccupied office. There were no windows and all I could hear was the noise of the forced air ducts.

'If you wait here, sir, the officer will be with you shortly.'

The door was closed behind me. I sat against the desk and flapped. I was being set up.

As it opened again, I stood up and turned to face the person walking in. My chest pain returned with a vengeance. I had fucked up big time.

'Nick Stone, right?'

The Democrat was smiling at me as he held out his hand. His face looked like I'd gone at him with a pastry cutter. The bright-red, scabby scars around his face were held together with black sutures, along with patches of his scalp, where his hair had been shaved before the wounds were treated. His hands were in shit state, too, but they were all healing nicely.

'There isn't much time, Nick. Me and the team are going to need a lot of help here.' He saw me looking at his scars and dropped the smile.

'Hey, I know. Not good. If I ever find the sonofabitch that did this, I'm gonna be pulling the ring back on one big can of kick-ass . . .'

THE END